A Killer for the Queen

Shaun Webb

All the best,

Works by Shaun Webb

A Motion for Innocence...And Justice for All?

Black Jacks

A Killer for the Queen

Behind the Brick

www.shaun-webb.com

This book is a work of fiction. People, places, events and situations are the product of the author's imagination. Any resemblance to actual persons, living or dead, or historical events, is purely coincidental.

Copyright © 2012, by Shaun Webb

No part of this book may be reproduced, stored in a retrieval system or transmitted by any means without the written permission of the author.

Editorial Coordinators: Lynn Gillard and Lisa Czyz

Creative Consultant and Quality Control: Minka Misangyi

Cover Art by Lisa Forbes ©, copyright 2013, All Rights Reserved

Website Design and Quality Control by Lisa Forbes

1st Edition, 2012
2nd Edition, 2013

ISBN-978-1492701101
ISBN-10: 1492701106

This book was produced in the United States of America

Published by In Motion, LLC ©, All Rights Reserved.

Songs from Alice in Wonderland written by: Bob Hilliard, Sammy Fain, Oliver Wallace, Cy Coben, Winston Hibler, Ted Sears, Don Raye, Mac David, Al Hoffman, Jerry Livingston, and all quotes and characters by Lewis Carroll

We ask that you forgive any minor editorial errors. We do our very best. Thank you.

Reviews for Black Jacks

This is a great book if you have time on your hands because you won't want to put it down! Every page is filled with characters that you either love or hate and can't wait to see what their next move is. It takes a hard look at what people with power and authority are capable of doing and what lengths they will go to keep it. You will want to read it over and over and you'll be amazed at the clues you keep finding! This is a wonderful read and the author keeps our attention from cover to cover!-**Mary T.**

Black Jacks is an intense thriller that keeps you in suspense until the very last chapters. The characters are well developed and the plot is new and different. A great read!-**J. Skaife**

This book is so good! I could not put it down. The character development, the plot, the entire story is exciting, and brings out every human emotion possible.-**Mary Masters**

Mr. Webb does an excellent job spinning a suspenseful thriller. You feel as if you know these characters and are disturbed by what many are capable of doing. This book is a real page-turner. I thoroughly enjoyed it and am looking forward to the next installment!-**LAC**

I really enjoyed this book. The characters were well thought out and the story was suspenseful. Although not my typical genre of choice, I was surprised at how much I enjoyed it. -**Lisa**

I really liked this book and couldn't put it down. I am very anxious for the next book. Highly recommend it.-**DD**

I read this book while on vacation! Was hard to put it down and go off and do "vacation things" Mr. Webb You have a WINNER here! Thanks for putting out such a great read! Loved it!
I thought I knew the "who done it" about 1/2 way through but to my surprise... Nice twist! - **Lisa K**

Reviews for A Motion for Innocence...And Justice for All?

The book was read and the review is by my Wife Esther.

I just finished reading the book that I purchased from Amazon Kindle and would recommend it to anyone interested in what could happen to you if someone wanted to "get even" by using the Court system. How fair is the Judge and how good is your attorney?

I feel bad if someone is not guilty but the Court says they are guilty and the family (Mother, Father, Wife and Kids), relatives, neighbors, friends, people at work, etc. must suffer from the results. You may lose your job and not find another one. You may have a record for the rest of your life. The out of pocket cost for you and your family could be a hardship for a long time.

The book is food for thought and you will want to read it to the finish.-**Russ Wheater "Russ"**

What an awesome book! It was definitely a page-turner. It really made me think hard about the "justice" system, or lack there-of in the United States. It is written in such an easy-going style - just like it was a conversation. However, there also is a really cool wit and humor mixed in that will make you laugh out loud. I loved this book.-**J. Totz**

Naiveté should not be a crime, and faith in the American justice system should not destroy one's life, but that is exactly what happens in Shaun Webb's tale of a simple man up against an overzealous, corrupt judicial system. "A Motion for Innocence" is written in a voice filled with incredulity as a young girl, a girl whose vindictive parents had found the perfect way to "punish" Sean for reporting their thievery from the Church in which they worked, unjustly accuses Sean West of unspeakable acts.

From the first accusation to Sean's eventual release, we are brought into a world that an ever-larger percentage of individuals in the United States will experience. Webb takes us on a journey through the degradation of the human soul, when innocence is ignored, and results and votes are the ultimate goal.

"A Motion for Innocence" is a definite must-read by anyone who believes that bad things happen only to bad people, and the fates preserve the dignity of the righteous. I would especially recommend this novel to young adults as the statistics alone have great educational value for anyone on the verge of a life of crime.

One final thought, don't ever think you are infallible--we are after all, human.-**Patty76**

A great read from start to finish. It is scary to see how easily lies, incompetence and people too busy to listen to the truth can destroy someone's life. I highly recommend this book. --**AMB**

I just finished this book and had a hard time putting it down. It re-enforced how corrupt the legal system can be and how a person is guilty until proven innocent. --**RPL**

This is a compelling and emotionally wrenching story of a man wrongfully convicted of sexual abuse of a minor. A doctor for physical proof did not examine the teenage girl who accused Shaun of this crime; all that was required was her verbal testimony. This alone was enough to indict, prosecute and convict an innocent man. His family was thrown into disarray, his job prospects nonexistent, all because of a justice system that took the words of a teenager as the gospel truth, thus ruining the prospects and future of a man who committed no crime. I recommend this book highly to anyone interested in crime, justice and punishment in our world today.-**Jasmine**

The speculation placed on a person's life when put in this situation is nothing anyone would ever know, unless you or a family member has gone through it!

Although I have not went through it, after reading this book I did a lot of research on the web because I was MORTIFIED the way it all took place. And to my surprise... It happens more often than we would like to know! Not all are innocent, but not all are guilty either! GREAT BOOK Mr. Webb.
Thank you for opening my eyes. **-Phyliss J.**

This is a thought-provoking extremely well written exploration of the ramifications of our legal system and how it works; or doesn't. It is the story of a man falsely accused and convicted of a heinous crime he did not commit and how it has shattered his life and family. I highly recommend it to all of us who may pass judgment first and ask questions later.**-L.Gillard**

This book made me cry and laugh aloud. The author is very talented in that aspect. The events are so shocking that I'm still left amazed that a jury could be so stupid. Having a loved one go through the same process, I suggest everyone read this. Whether you want to admit it or not, this CAN happen to you or someone you love. **-Rachel 1917**

The world is run by agenda, constantly. This book proves that. It takes only a mere moment of hearsay or false allegations (accusations) to ruin a person's life forever.
Thank you for writing this book. Wake-up the world to the abuses of the legal system. **-S.L. Rach**

A Killer for the Queen

Shaun Webb

In Motion Publishing

Michigan

To: My mom. You are an inspiration.

"Fear cannot be banished, but it can be calm and without panic; it can be mitigated by reason and evaluation." – Vannevar Bush

"Panic is a sudden desertion of us, and a going over to the enemy of our imagination." – Christian Nevell

Introduction
Mad like A Hatter?

It began with the abduction and murder of his son Jimmy. The Black Jack Killer in Flint, Michigan snatched him off the street while he was in the care of his mother, Kurt's then wife Kathy. In Kurt's mind, Kathy dropped the ball by worrying more about who was watching her than her actually watching their son. Kurt seethed. The drama continued as Kurt was ordered by Kathy to identify the body. This was another in a long line of Kurt being bullied by his then wife. If there was anything hard to do, Kathy wanted no part of it. The only things she worried about were her new fake boobs; which looked unnatural on her; her fake blond hair, and her attention whore attitude. Again, Kurt seethed. The anger building up in him reached a crescendo when she left him for another man. As he destroyed his house and blew into a rage fit for the most violent of individuals, he found Jimmy's collection of Alice in Wonderland Cd's, movies, and stuffed toys. These items seemed to calm the rage, and he was better able to look at his situations from eyes that were more serene.

*

Shaun Webb

  As he watched the trial against his son's alleged killer, John Garrison, he discovered that he didn't think the old man committed the crime. The main culprits in the subsequent judgment were Soo-Chin Xing, Kathy herself and Amy Fraser; the lawyer who passed out in the courtroom and seemed more preoccupied with her surroundings than she did about the old timer. In Kurt's mind, the state prosecutor was only doing his job. The same held true for the jurors that convicted Garrison. How could they not convict? The jury heard nothing from the defense's side, and it only made sense that someone had to take the hit. When Kathy left Kurt, it set off a chain of events that caused him to loathe women, especially the women involved in the trial. Jack Beauregard, the big bad Governor to-be, would have been on Kurt's list too, except that he was already dead. It all came down to the three women: Kathy, Soo-Chin and Amy. In Kurt's eyes and with advice from a special "friend", they were the responsible parties in his vengeance.

  Kyle Beauregard, Jack's son, was the real Black Jack Killer. The boy was misjudged and treated poorly by those around him. Kurt now understood why Kyle acted the way he did. Kyle wanted to draw attention to the corrupt, evil ways of the political and criminal justice systems. He worked his magic almost flawlessly in exposing his father, the Michigan State Police Colonel and would be Governor, as a fraud. Soo-Chin, Jack's ex-girlfriend, walked out the door when Kyle needed her the most, thus she was to be treated harshly. It didn't matter that Jack had beat her to a pulp and threatened to kill her. In Kurt's eyes, Kyle needed help and she fled.

A Killer for the Queen

A top hat adorned Kurt's head. It was black and carried a rose in its band. As he rifled through his late son's collection, he came upon two things that interested him, The Red Queen of Hearts and The Mad Hatter. Both characters constantly swirled around in Kurt's mind. Who? Why, and most notably, Where? He would soon find out the answers to his questions. The magic would appear in Kurt's world in the tradition of evil madness.

The top hat signified Kurt's evil. He was now a hatter, a vengeance taker, a righter of wrongs.

The story continues...

Any remnants of self-worth that remained with Kurt had disappeared when Kathy walked out the door. Since his ex-wife had left him, his hoarded home had dwindled to a few narrow paths cut through the living room, kitchen and basement. The majority of his days and nights were in the basement, the area most comfortable for him. He was surrounded with mounds of debris and other non-distinguishable items.

Among the things he saved and used were the newspaper articles depicting the Black Jack of Spades killer in his leather outfit. He had them posted all over his lower ground floor area. The walls were covered with articles explaining the murders, the trial against old John Garrison, the scapegoat and subsequent death of Kyle at the hands of his own father. He had also painstakingly sewed another outfit by hand. Although his was a bit different, it still carried the feeling and meaning that the original murderer had used to darken Flint, Michigan's streets. Kurt sewed Jack of Spades playing cards into the leather fabric, and made a mask that carried on the dark, murderous tradition. It hung near his work area, but that's where it would stay. Kurt intended to wear the outfit, as it was made in homage of someone he thought to be a hero, but the plans would change. In reality, Kyle was nothing more than a harbinger of death and pain, along with mental illness. Kurt himself had thoughts of torture and killing, but it would only be against those who were directly responsible for Kyle's death.

*

Kurt was taking classes at the local night school to try to improve the stutter that had become so prevalent in his speech. It probably had more to do with his self-esteem, but Kurt was determined to make a mark in the world of speaking impediments.

"Th-th-that c-cat l-l-lives in the alley" quickly became "That C-cat lives in the a-alley."

He practiced night and day to improve his tongue and it was slowly coming together. He was better able to recognize when and what triggered the stuttering and worked on facing some of those situations in speech therapy. Stress was a big factor, so his therapist would put him in a controlled stressful situation and work on the sentence structure. It worked well and pleased Kurt immensely. It felt good to be able to walk down a street and simply say "Hello, h-how are y-you?" without tripping all over himself in a sloppy wad of stuttering blubber. It built his confidence quickly and helped him get what he thought was a better grip on life. No wife? No problem. No friends? Who cared? He *did* care however. He cared that his wife had dumped him like a ton of bricks in a river. When confronted with his thoughts and feelings, the stuttering would disappear.

"Why that bitch. I'll cut her head off her fucking shoulders."

When Kurt would calm himself, the stuttering would return. When angered again, he was able to speak with a clearness that surprised him.

*

Kurt was spending a lot of time watching the Alice in Wonderland movies that he found in his deceased son's room. The story fascinated him like no other, and he took to it like a fish to water as it reminded him of little Jimmy. The score was especially thrilling for him. The White Rabbit reminded him of getting to the point and not wasting time. The Smoking Caterpillar spoke good logic and the Cheshire cat was alarmingly eerie and ultimately unattainable.

Kurt began obsessing over the songs and began whistling, humming, and singing them in the shower. When he shaved, it was the White Rabbit's *"I'm late, I'm late, for a very important date."* The Mad Hatter's *"a very merry unbirthday"* was another of his favorites. Out of all the characters that he had begun enjoying, none was better or more powerful to him than the Red Queen of Hearts. She was evil and vindictive. She was vindictive, but not in his mind. What he liked most was her propensity to lop off your head if you were what she considered to be "in the way." That character who interested him the most because she said everything without saying much at all. She was the highest of all females. All other women were considered want-to-be Queens in Kurt's world, but only one was worthy of his affection: The Red Queen of Hearts.

*

Before Jimmy was kidnapped and murdered, Kurt was dealing with life the best way he knew how; by keeping his stuttering mouth shut and letting Kathy do all the talking, reasoning, figuring and anything else that was necessary for day-to-day living. Following the abduction and murder of his son, Kurt dealt with it well, as he still had Kathy to lean on. He would work on his stuttering, take care of things around the home and care for his wife, who unfortunately, was growing more and more distant every day. It came to a head when she approached him one day and told him she was leaving for another man. That straw broke Kurt's back. For years, Kathy had degraded and taunted him. She wouldn't have sex with him and teased his stutter. There was pressure building inside Kurt that threatened to explode at any given moment. When she announced her intentions, it was quite surprising that Kurt didn't kill her on the spot.

*

After months of struggling with the stress and hoarding, the Queen paid Kurt a visit. She was lovely and stunning in her red suit. She had beautiful long red hair and a crown that gleamed with jewels and gold. Her eyes were a deep green with a look of emerald fire. The suit she wore was tightly clung to her, extenuating the curves of her perfect figure. The Queen carried a golden staff in her hand, and the room lit up with her presence.

The first conversation between the two took place six months after Kathy's departure. Kurt had collected most of Jimmy's Alice in Wonderland collection and watched over it with a careful eye. He listened to the music, read all the books and displayed the action figure dolls carefully in a cleared out spot of the basement. The night she arrived was dark and unnerving, causing Kurt to have trouble sleeping. A few minutes after leaving his bed in exchange for his favorite chair in the basement, he saw her bright red light coming down the stairway with a glow that made him shield his eyes. Trumpets blared and a voice exclaimed loudly, **"All hail the Queen of Wonderland! Bow before her royal highness!"**

Kurt did just that. He jumped from his chair and bowed completely to the floor, all the while looking at the staircase. To his astonishment and awe, she finally showed herself. When she traveled down the staircase, there was no hint of shoulder or knee movement. It was as if she were…*floating*. Kurt watched her approach between boxes and junk; the walking path he had cut out for himself. She *was* in fact levitating. It was mesmerizing to Kurt as he was meeting his child's fairy tale character.

"Bow before me, oh ye of such disrespect and ignorance. I will certainly take thy head with my hatchet and display it for all to see!"

"I'm s-sorry your highness, I w-was in awe of your b-beauty and presence. F-forgive me m-most royal of royals. Highest of the high."

"Are you the subject Kurtis Joseph of whom I am here to convey my orders?"

"Y-yes, Red Queen. I am Kurtis Joseph. W-what may I d-do for you oh high…"

"SILENCE! Listen closely so that you heed my wishes and follow my guide."

"Y-yes, you're Majesty."

"I have Queen of Hearts cards in my hand, Kurtis Joseph. You shall take them and look them over."

The cards fell abruptly at the end of Kurt's nose. He scooped them up quickly and looked. They were in fact Queen of Hearts cards as the mystical one had said. The only difference is that the some had pictures of different people, all of whom he had known at one time. It was Kathy, his ex-wife, Soo-Chin Xing, the former county coroner and Amy Fraser, the defense lawyer defending old John Garrison in the death of his son.

"Do you know those subjects, Kurtis?"

"Y-yes, my Queen. I kn-know them all."

"I have orders for you Mr. Joseph. You will make travel across the countryside, find them and collect their heads for me. You will wear a top hat as the Mad Hatter himself does. You are my hatter here on earth Kurtis."

Kurt was astonished, worried and honored. He wasn't sure if this was a dream or real. He quizzed the Queen, hoping he wouldn't upset her too badly.

"My Queen, m-may I c-call you that?"

"Speak!"

"Oh y-yes, m-my Q-Queen. W-what shall I d-do with the heads after I c-c-collect them?"

The Red Queen; beautiful, mysterious and gothic, floated at least eight inches off the floor. Kurt could not see her feet as they were hidden in a red mist. She mulled over Kurt's question and answered.

"You shall keep the heads in glass jars. I will collect them when the job is finished. What you do with the bodies is your choice. I shall expect you will come up with a plan suitable for my pleasing."

"Oh yes, Red Q-Queen. I shall d-do just that. I shall m-mark them with a r-red circle and a crossed out "Q" indicating th-that they are n-not worthy of your l-lofty status."

"That is a noble honor, Kurtis. You shall be rewarded for your obedience. I shall take you to my kingdom of madness, wonder and eternity when the task is completed."

"Oh R-Red Queen. It would b-be such an honor."

"Take extra jars, Kurtis. If anyone is to get in your way, kill him or her. If anyone who gets in your way is female, collect her head. Do not wear that hideous Red suit you've made with Jacks of Spades. Those Jacks cannot match the intensity with which I compel you."

"Y-yes Queen. I shall not f-fail."

After looking at Kurt in a puzzled manner, she was surrounded in a fog of mist and a puff of smoke, the Queen rose up toward the ceiling. She appeared to evaporate before Kurt's eyes. The next moment, she was gone. The mist, smoke and vapor followed her into the abyss. Kurt was given orders from the highest of the high and he intended to carry them out with enthusiasm and care. He would not fail his Queen.

*

The Visit from this Queen convinced Kurt of a few things. He was the chosen one to carry out the vengeful plan. Jimmy's death at the hands of the Black Jack Killer was necessary for the plan to take place, and the Queen had a thirst for heads, which she passed on to the trusting Kurt.

Kurt often wondered if the visit were true or a figment of his imagination or dreams. The truth of the matter would be found out later, but for the time being he was to carry out her plan and collect the heads that he was assigned. He would carry out the vengeance for himself and Kyle, while bringing vindictiveness courtesy of the Red Queen.

Questioning her would bring sure death, perhaps by beheading. Kurt wasn't going to take the chance. She christened him a Hatter, because she saw in him a combination of madness and logic. The black top hat and red rose in the brim were the perfect touches to complete the transformation from Kurt Joseph to mad...Mad Hatter.

"Well, I went along my merry way and I never stopped to reason, I should have known there'd be a price to pay some day, some day."

Shaun Webb

1
Is our situation not dismal?

"I'M GOING TO DIE RIGHT HERE AND RIGHT NOW!"

Blake Thomas was driving to his mother's house when the Panic Attack hit him. The attacks often started unexpectedly, mild at first, and then increasing in intensity and duration. This particular attack was in full effect, and Blake could not concentrate, as he felt what he thought to be life threatening chest pain and trouble catching his breath. He had to get off the expressway. It was a horrible struggle as he pulled his pickup truck off to the side of the interstate while other motorists zipped by, oblivious to him or his crisis. They had places to go and people to see. If some unfortunate fellow was about to die on the side of the road, they would never notice, let alone care. For Blake, it was a dread of epic proportions.

"I can't breathe, **I CAN'T BREATHE!**" He whimpered as he laid his head on the steering wheel and began sobbing for relief.

"PLEASE, I DON'T WANT TO DIE NOW! I WANT TO SEE MY FAMILY AND FRIENDS AGAIN! PLEASE, LORD IN HEAVEN, SAVE ME FROM THIS HORRIBLE FEELING. OH GOD, PLEASE!"

In a matter of seconds, the symptoms began to decline. His lungs relaxed and his breathing opened up and normalized. He could now take a deep, cleansing breath. The savage beating of his heart calmed. The sweat that had been dripping down his brow was drying up, and the frightening feeling of impending doom was alleviating. He looked up and saw that traffic was still zipping by him at an alarming rate of speed, shaking his vehicle with every pass. The panic wasn't quite as daunting as it had seemed only fifteen seconds ago. The young man uttered a small bark of laughter, as if he had narrowly escaped death and couldn't believe it. He carefully eased his vehicle back into traffic and continued to his destination silently, as if uttering a single word would tempt the buzzing of another attack lurking deep within his subconscious mind.

*

The woman was yapping on her cell phone with the bliss of ignorance. Her speedometer had reached a dangerous eight-five MPH, but she had no idea, nor did she care. Her emphasis remained on telling her friend about what she intended to pick up during her shopping excursion of the day.

"I'm going to get a new coat today, Nettie. I've only spent twenty grand of my credit limit, so I have another five thousand to blow. What did you say? Oh, I'll just declare bankruptcy. Who cares? By the way….Oh wait a minute, **WHOA! Holy Jesus!** Who and what the hell? Nettie? Yeah, I'm still here. Oh, some jerk pulled off to the side of the road and I almost smashed right into his rear end. Who in their right mind would go to the curb in this traffic? Jeez. How stupid and rude can someone get? Anyway, Nettie."

She had almost collided with Blake's pickup truck while he was *off to the side of the highway*, yet she still had the arrogance to blame him for the near miss. The reason she came so close didn't matter in the grand scheme. Had she not lifted her head at the last moment, the results would surely have been disastrous. She continued on her way with the same blasé' attitude that she'd been exhibiting before and after the narrow escape. Up the road two exits, it would be different.

*

The road rager was driving even faster. He was pushing ninety-five, an accident waiting to happen. He reasoned that keeping in the flow of traffic was of the upmost importance. He was an angry man. Every time he passed another vehicle, he flipped the bird, mouthed a nasty two-word phrase or intentionally cut into the lane just beyond any passed car, causing it to veer left or right with the sudden braking. This person was nothing more than a common bully. He felt he owned the traffic and the highway. Yet to him, it was everyone else who were doing wrong and driving bad.

As he continued along, he saw that a pickup had pulled to the side of the road, and some woman in an SUV very nearly rear-ended it. He felt his hair-trigger temper get the best of him. He slowed down to the side of Blake's pickup and yelled an expletive out his window to let Blake know he thought he was in the wrong by pulling aside. The only thing the rager saw was a man slumped over his steering wheel, and he appeared to be terrified. He also gave the impression that he was sobbing.

"Pussy!" yelled the nasty motorist, **"no time for fuckin' crybabies out here!"**

The menace forged on, hoping to catch up with the broad that almost rear-ended the pickup. He had something to say to her too. He'd catch up soon enough.

*

Blake sucked it up and moved forward. He took a spot in the slow lane and cruised at sixty-five MPH. The motorists blew past him in unfathomable flurries, occasionally giving him a one-fingered salute, but he stuck to his guns and kept his stare intently on the road in front of him while concentrating on pleasant thoughts. After a mile, traffic began to slow. After a mile-and-a-half, it crept to a stop. He continued to keep his eyes forward, as the nasty drivers who had belittled him earlier also slowed to a crawl. It amazed him how people changed their attitudes when faced with possible confrontations. They stared forward as he did, not wanting to give away their ugly secret of road rage and bullying when someone could actually get out of the car and slug them; or worse yet, shoot them.

As his pickup moved slowly forward, he caught a distant glimpse of police lights flashing in the dull gray light of the day. He figured it was either an accident, or a pullover that netted drugs or worse. He was right on his first guess. The still tense Blake finally moved close enough to see what the problem encompassed. It happened that the girl in the SUV, who had almost hit him on the curb, had an accident with the man who had given him the verbal assault. The scene was gruesome. The girl had been thrown from her vehicle. She skidded along the road for a good one hundred and fifty feet before coming to a stop in the center lane. The man was still in his vehicle, which had rolled over after losing control. In his roll, he took out another two vehicles. The passengers in those cars appeared to be unhurt, but badly shaken. As Blake moved closer and saw the man hanging half out of the *passenger* side of the truck. It was apparent that he had died, as blood and brain matter oozed down the side of his vehicle. He had a wound on his head that was both wide open and undoubtedly the fatal injury. The scene sickened him. He again felt the tremor of nervousness grip him. He fought it as hard as he could and soldiered forward.

"In through the nose, out through the mouth. In, out. Inhale, exhale. Relax. One, two, three, four in…hold…one, two, three, four out."

He then came upon the girl who had skidded on the pavement. She was sprawled and bloodied, her skin scalped away from her body on her arms and face. The sight was too grisly and graphic for Blake. He once again pulled off to the side, exited his vehicle and began vomiting with a violence reserved for the worst of stomach flus. Each upchuck brought more thoughts of physical problems manifested by his brain. His heart palpitated and his mind flooded with the thought of death. Other drivers went by and advised him to get in the car and puke there, sparing them the discomfort of having to watch despite the grim scene that lay before them. A police officer arrived, and instead of asking Blake if he was okay, ordered him back into his vehicle to move along. He obeyed and continued his spell in the car. He finally passed the brunt of the accident and traffic began speeding up again. Life seemed to have a way of moving on quickly; either ignoring or blocking out disasters as if they were tiny blips on a rather large radar screen. Blake sped along with traffic until he found the exit he wanted, and then left the grim, death filled road for the smaller, less obtrusive, two-lane highway.

By now, Blake had given up all thoughts of visiting his mother. Instead, he turned around at his first opportunity and made a beeline back to his home, where he could find comfort in the familiarity of his own living room, bedroom and bathroom. That was a mistake, as therapists tell you that you should face down your demons and overcome them. Blake turned tail and allowed them to win the battle. It was one of many encounters Blake would face in his uncertain future.

*

Panic attacks and anxiety can lead to depression and agoraphobia. The latter being an unwillingness to leave the *perceived* safety of your own house for fear of open spaces. The relief Blake felt upon getting back home was dangerous. He called his mother and told her he wouldn't make it over because he was feeling nauseous and flush. His mom knew better. She had been dealing with this problem since her son was eighteen, and now it seemed to be getting worse. It was funny how he thought he was fooling her, but deep down he knew better. He didn't want to burden her with his problems. There was a minor sense of divide as he explained his situation before he hung up. He turned on the TV and saw the story about the accident on the news. It was a breaking story that he was present for not an hour earlier. The feeling worming inside his body was much like ice water running through one's veins. He quickly found something else to watch and settled on the couch with a blanket and a cold soda. He didn't want to face life with anxiety, panic and depression. He saw his doctor, who prescribed Effexor and Xanax. It relieved his symptoms, but did nothing to reach into the root of the problem. He would need extensive psychotherapy to believe that. He met with a Therapist who helped him dig down into the root cause of his nervousness. While it didn't "cure" him by any means, it better equipped him to handle the situations as they came along. After a few visits with the wise man, Blake decided he needed a change of scenery. Perhaps, he thought, it was time to move somewhere else and start life over. The therapist agreed, but warned him that the anxiety and panic would still exist. He would need to work hard and practice the techniques he was taught if he were to come out successful in his search to end the problem altogether.

2
Blake's Wonderland

Blake Thomas was born in March of 1990. He was a handsome man who didn't look anywhere near the twenty some odd years he had lived in the world. Strangers talking amongst themselves would guess him early to mid-teens, max. He apparently had been born with good genes, blessed from a combination of both his mother and father. Good skin, a full head of dishwater-brown hair, a dimpled baby face and longevity; all were trends in his family. Blake grew up in Toledo, Ohio, so he was a stone's throw from Cleveland, to the east, and Detroit, just north. This gave him options when thinking about where to have fun, which sports teams to root for, and from where his friends came. He had contacts in Detroit, Cleveland and Toledo. His schooling was in Toledo, so most of his friends were from there.

Blake spent his childhood playing baseball in the summer, but hated winter. The snow, ice and nasty weather never appealed to him, even as a young lad. Where other kids would sled, skate and play hockey, Blake took the winter off. He spent the cold months studying and watching TV. When the weather would break in April, back out he would go for another baseball season. He loved the Detroit Tigers, so when they played in Cleveland or Detroit, he would occasionally go see them with his dad, who was a huge Indians fan. Living in Toledo, you rooted for one or the other, never both. That would be what his dad called 'Sacrilege of the Baseball Gods.'

The childhood of Blake Thomas was good. His parents stayed happily married and treated the boy quite well. He excelled in school; up to eleventh grade, and behaved himself perfectly; give for the occasional minor brush. He was the apple of his mother's eye. She would do anything for her son, as long as he remained well-mannered and polite. If he ever lost his track and became snappy, he heard about it directly. That changed when intoxicants entered the picture.

By eleventh grade, drugs, followed by unrealistic fear entered Blake's life and changed everything about him. Why he would use dope and hang around with the wrong crowd would baffle his parents. They couldn't understand why such a clean cut kid would make the kinds of decisions that destroyed formerly strong people. He quit the baseball team, ran around with thugs and was only a shell of his former friendly and jovial self.

*

The partying had been going on for Blake since his fifteenth birthday, when he was introduced to, and fell in love with, marijuana. His first experience with the ganja left him face down in his friends' lawn for four hours in an inebriated state of uselessness. It was a floating feeling that kept Blake from getting up, although his friend, Tom, wished he would have.

"C'mon dude. You're trippin' me out by lying there. Get up man. You look like death."

"Nah. I'm good," was Blake's stoned response. It was all he had the coherency to utter.

"Okay, at least you're talking" Tom replied, "but you gotta get up before you get us busted dude."

Blake kept floating until it was time to get up and go home. He tripped the light fantastic. He knew eventually he'd have to rise, but it was with a major effort that he did so. Getting up and moving were the last things Blake had any interest in doing. When he did rise, the leaves on the trees stirred to his delight, while it seemed that his hearing and sight were far better and more vivid than they had ever been in his life.

On the walk to his house, which encompassed about two miles, he rejoiced in the spectrum of his newfound friend, THC, which had successfully given him the exact feeling for which he was looking. He longed to feel that same buzz again as soon as possible. It would quickly turn into an obsession that caused his grades to suffer along with having him dabbling in more potent and potentially deadly choices of drugs and alcohol. He remembered a lesson from Biology class when his teacher had mentioned that you'd know if you're an alcoholic from the first time you drank. Well, Blake was definitely a pothead from the very first toke, so there must have been some truth to that theory. Marijuana graduated to cocaine, which led to pill popping, mescaline, acid, speed and downers. You name it; Blake used it. Where pot made him feel mellow and safe, mescaline caused him to laugh uncontrollably. He and some of his classmates would pop a pill before school and buzz the day away without a care in the world. Blake liked acid too, but didn't care much for speed. Black mollies made his heart feel like it was coming out of his chest. Mild downers, on the other hand, left him in the mellowest of moods. He had no worries and no stress. It was only Blake and his vivid imagination.

*

On one forgettable occasion, Blake went to his friend Steve's house and between the two of them, took four high potency *what he thought were downers*. Both boys made a decision they assumed to be fundamentally sound.

"One was enough to put you in a stupor, so two would be twice as good, right?"

The two sat on separate seats in the living room and quickly lost their ability to so much as move. Their fingers, toes, heads and limbs were paralyzed. Blake sat in his chair wide-awake on the inside, but completely immobilized physically. It was much like being trapped in a box, shoulder to shoulder and head to toe. It was his first foray into a panic attack-like situation, but the panic itself never materialized because the drug was so powerful, it kept him decelerated inside. He could hear each heartbeat within him, and see everything around him, but could not budge even a fingertip. The clock on the wall ticked and tocked with a slurred sound, the TV played its programs in an outstretched and mirrored reality and every sensation perceived by Blake was a zip of light or a dull murmur. That was when things went further south, a place Blake thought impossible to go. He thought he had already reached rock bottom on this particular day. He promised himself that if he came out of the paralysis, he was going to clean his friend's clock.

As the two teen-agers sat in their paralyzed funk, the door knocked. Not only could they not answer it, they couldn't even utter the words "come in." After a couple more raps, the door slowly creaked opened, and two very pretty eighteen year-old women let themselves in. A blond and a red head perused the room and saw Blake and Steve sitting helpless before them.

"Which one of you is Steve?" The pretty blond asked. There was no answer. They could see them, hear them, even *smell them*, but couldn't react.

"Are you guys *like*, dead?" Asked the red head in a contrived valley girl accent. *"Like*, what's your deal?"

Blake tried moving his eyes left to right so the girls could see he was, in fact, among the living, but they didn't notice.

"Put your ear to their chest," the blond requested. "Let's see if their hearts are beating."

The red haired beauty heard in Blake's chest the soft murmur of activity. She did the same to Steve and declared them both alive.

"You idiots are *like*, fuckin' with the "new" morphine pills, huh?" The red head stated this with a hand on her hip and her head tilted to the extreme left.

"Don't you guys *like*; know that shit will fuck you right up?"

The two hot women huddled up before the boys and spoke quietly between each other, undoubtedly planning their next maneuver. Every three or four words, their eyes glanced toward the two stoners. The conference ended and the two walked over to the immobile pair. The blond stood by Blake and the red head by Steve. The next thing that happened was disturbing and embarrassing for the boys, but entertaining for the two girls. Everything was rolled up into one twisted wreck of emotion. The teasing came first.

"You like me, dude?" The blond herself seductively asked Blake. "You want a lap dance, hot stuff?"

Blake wanted a lap dance, but couldn't come close to expressing his interest. The red head was doing the same thing to Steve, five feet away.

"Maybe I'll show you my tits, cutie." The blond teased as she rubbed her clothed but less than ample breasts. "Would you like that?"

"Of course I would." Blake thought silently. "I wish I could reach out and grab you."

He felt the pulsing of his heartbeat now enveloping his crotch, but could do absolutely nothing about it.

"Well, I've decided I'm not going show them to you." The blond disappointingly informed him as she ceased her seductive dance pose. "I have a better idea sweetie." She was inches from his face.

The two girls looked at each other, nodded, and then began undressing the two stoners. First the shirts, then the pants. Adding insult to injury, down came the underwear. The two hotties giggled with delight as a pair of tootsie roll sized and completely flaccid penises lay before them. As if they hadn't inflicted enough pain, they took it a step further and did the unthinkable.

They went through the boy's clothes and took out their money and pot, and then the red head pulled out her cell phone and began taking humiliating pictures. Not only were they now broke and naked, but they were to become viral. Blake promised himself again to punch Steve in the mouth when, and if, they came out of this stupor. Blake had two hundred bucks and an ounce of pot. Now he had nothing. He could feel the anger seething through him, but was powerless to react. The two very cute girls gave a little wave and a smile, blew the boys a worthless kiss, and then left. The two idiots lay naked next to each other for another eight hours before they started getting the feelings back in their extremities. Starting with the tingling of the fingers and toes, and eventually working into having feeling back in the hands, arms and legs, the two boys finally came around. Upon fully re-gaining their strength, which they thought may never return, Blake started the questioning.

"What did you give us, asshole?" Blake angrily asked Steve as they redressed.

"Synthetic morphine. I didn't know it'd be so strong, though."

"You owe me two hundred bucks, jackoff. A bag of pot, too." Blake had failed to realize that the two could very well have died. His friend also seemed to miss the point.

"Fuck you. They took my cash too. You're not the only loser here."

"Who were they, Steve? I've never seen them before."

"No clue, I don't know 'em and I've never seen 'em before either."

As the two continued getting the remainder of their bearings back, another of Steve's friends let himself in the unlocked door. It was their friend Chico.

"Ay Steverino!" Chico roared with a rough under growl, "How you like the two babes I send over last night? Did you get some ass, bro?"

"You sent 'em?" Steve asked wide-eyed.

"Yeah, dude. They wanted smoke, and I send 'em your way. I knew you not mind. Why? Is there problem, Stevo?"

Embarrassed, Steve went with the flow, as did Blake. "It was all good." Steve glanced at his friend with a sheepishly straight face. "We both got laid. Gee, uh, thanks man."

After a slightly confused hesitation, Chico smiled again. "Good, good. Ayy, you guys got a joint, or what?"

"No. No smoke today. It's pretty dry right now." Blake replied.

Blake found out later that Steve's friend had sent a couple of hookers over, not knowing they were hookers, because they wanted to get high. Chico was trying to be cool. In the weeks following the encounter, Blake didn't see any naked pictures of himself or Steve on the net or at school, and never heard anything from his other friends, so he figured it was for the personal stash of penis photos the two ladies must've kept somewhere. Perhaps Blake and Steve weren't the first guys they'd ripped off.

The experience wasn't enough to get Blake to straighten out his ways. He would soon be given an even harder lesson.

*

The disaster with his friend was only one example of the debauchery that had engulfed Blake's life. He was in a drugged, alcoholic daze and continued with his abuse. He managed to graduate high school, but he'd never know how he accomplished it. It was also a wonder he wasn't dead with all the chemicals and other strange narcotics he'd ingested through his teen years. His personality went bad and he treated the people that loved him the most with nastiness and cruelty. He loved his mom and dad dearly, but argued every point they made. He shunned their good advice and walked on them like an elephant on a mouse. The drugs caused him to act like a jerk, but there was no way you could ever tell him that. He was bordering on full-fledged junkie.

Mom knew Blake was using, but didn't have a clue as to how to approach the problem. She was so enamored with her boy that she almost refused to believe he was acting with such petulance. She tried talking with him, but it would always end up with her being ridiculed and treated like a stray mutt. It could be over the simplest things.

"Blake, time to get up for school, dear."

"Get out of my fuckin' room and go screw yourself, bitch."

"Now that's uncalled for, son." Mom would chuckle, "I'll have breakfast ready in ten minutes, cutie."

"I SAID FUCK OFF!"

"Okay, honey, see you downstairs."

She always trotted away as if nothing were wrong. She ignored the disrespect, thus enabling him further. She simply didn't have the tools to combat the problem. Normally, she demanded respect, but lately had allowed her son to be completely incorrigible.

Blake's mom was patient. She loved her boy with all her heart and he could do no wrong in her eyes. This made for a spoiled kid with a sassy mouth. His dad tried to instill a bit of discipline and order to Blake's teen-age life. He was always met with the same indignation that was cast on his wife.

It turned tense between Blake and his father. They ran into occasional arguments over his attitude and drug use, but Blake was indifferent to his pleas of sobriety. He talked to him in much the same way as his mom. There was simply no reasoning with the kid while drugs and alcohol influenced him.

"You know, son; I'm trying to help you for your future. I don't need the lip from you. Do you have any idea what you're going to do with your life? Have you made any plans past tonight's party with your friends? C'mon Blake, talk to me."

"You want me to talk, Dad? Okay. Fuck off!"

"That's not what I mean Blake and you know it. I was a kid too. I know what's up."

"You don't know shit, Dad. Your life as a kid was very different from mine. Everything was probably in black and white when you were young. Like on TV. Now leave me **ALONE!**"

Blake found himself chuckling at his defiance, and actually had the nerve to pat himself on the back for it.

"Alright, kid. You keep the attitude and watch what happens. You may not see it now, but it's coming."

With a wave-off, Blake dismissed his dad's diatribe and left the house to go find trouble elsewhere. What, who, when and how were questions Blake would deal with as the day laid itself out before him. A smart aleck kid with a lousy attitude; those teen years were hell on wheels for Blake, and his parents.

Shaun Webb

"Who... are... you?"

"Why, I hardly know, sir. I've changed so much since this morning, you see..."

"No, I do not C, explain yourself."

"I'm afraid I can't explain myself, you see, because I'm not myself, you know."

"I do not know."

"I can't put it any more clearly, sir, because it isn't clear to me."

Shaun Webb

3

Don't Smoke from the Caterpillar's Pipe

The first panic attack happened when Blake was eighteen. He and four of his best friends were on their way to Cleveland to see a baseball game. The night before the two-and-a-half hour trek, they partied like it was a new year. The beer flowed and the pot burned as the group stayed up until 3 a.m. watching reruns of the Twilight Zone and getting stoned to the nines.

"It's going to be fucking awesome going to Cleveland on a party filled road trip." Blake quipped.

The group thought there was nothing better than doing whatever you wanted whenever you liked. Blake had been collecting unemployment for the previous six weeks, so he could blow cash and be as irresponsible as a rich spoiled brat. Blake didn't know that his partying days were coming very close to an abrupt end. He had pushed the envelope over the previous three years and regret was about to rear its ugly head. In what way would he pay the price? Time would answer the question.

*

The day began as normally as any other did. After a night of hardcore partying, the group of Blake and his four friends packed the last of their stuff, *mostly pot and whisky,* and headed out the door for Cleveland, Ohio. Blake, with his friends Greg and Ross, Greg's girlfriend Andrea Jimenez, and her girlfriend Sandy Arnold were going on a road trip. Andrea and Sandy had been busy making up signs to wave at the game the night before as they all, *except for the more conservative Sandy,* partied. Everyone was pumped for the trip.

Sandy liked Blake. She had practically begged him to sleep with her, but Blake had refused up to that point. She had tried every trick in the book, less stripping naked in front of him. Sandy was a very nice looking girl. She had brown hair, green eyes, and wore thin, square lens glasses, which framed her face nicely. There was always a tiny tendril of hair that hung down both sides of her face, soft and more attractive than any man could bear. Blake had urges to sleep with her, but fought them off, as he considered her a friend and nothing more. He thought that evening might be different. She looked so beautiful to him and his libido could only take so much punishment. It wouldn't be as much a lovemaking excursion as it would be a friend with benefits romp, or a secret coupling like the one he used to have with Andrea before she met Greg.

The game was at one, the drive home was two and a half hours, so there would be plenty of time to shoo everyone away and offer to give Sandy a ride home himself; *the next morning*. Everything was perfect at that moment; then it happened. Something went horribly wrong.

"Hey Ross. I feel kind of weird." Blake complained.

"What feels weird, dude? Are you okay?"

"I don't know how to explain it. I feel like I'm having some trouble breathing and I feel kind of....you know....strange."

"I have just the thing for that." Greg reasoned from the back seat. "Let's smoke a fat one."

Greg lit up the joint and passed it around. Andrea and Sandy passed on it, but the three guys puffed with aplomb. After the second pass, Blake leaned forward in his seat. He felt a kind of stirring in his chest and lungs, and his left arm went numb. His heartbeat felt like it was speeding up and his airway, it seemed, was closing on him fast. Blake had his hands on his knees and his head between his legs. On top of everything else, he felt like vomiting.

"Pull over Ross, I'm gonna puke."

"What's the matter, man? Are you okay?" Ross was growing concerned. "You're not okay, are you Blake?"

"No. I'm not. Pull over, will ya?"

Ross did as he was told and Blake stepped out of the car on the side of the I-80-90 Interstate and dryly wretched. He didn't eat much, so his stomach was empty. The only result from his heaving was a thick brownish fluid that hung from his mouth in phlegmy strings. Sandy and Andrea were starting to feel alarm for him, but they stayed quiet to see how things would play out. In the meantime, Greg was trying to convince him that he was fine.

"Come on, Blake. You're good. You just need some food. You haven't eaten anything. Don't be such a pussy dude."

Blake turned back toward the car and had a look of pure white fear on his face. This was the wake-up call for everyone involved. He was not only insipid, but had red blotches forming on his face. Ross ordered him back into the car and turned around at the first exit, heading back home.

"What are you doing Ross?" Greg asked.

"I'm taking Blake home. Something's wrong."

"Oh, so were not going to the game, I take it?" Greg announced while clapping his hands on his thighs.

Andrea, aghast at Greg's indifference, piped in. "Shut the fuck up Greg. He's sick. We need to get him home. You're so fucking selfish."

Greg flipped the bird and sat back hard in his seat, not attempting to hide the scowl on his face. He uttered and stewed as the others looked after Blake.

"What the fuck man? There goes this day." He crowed, now staring out the car's window.

Ross drove especially fast as they made the trip back home. Blake was lying on his side in the front seat with his head against the window. He was tearing up because he thought he was dying. His heart was beating alarmingly fast and he felt it flipping around in his chest. Sandy rubbed her hand on his face and stroked his hair gently. Greg and Andrea argued quietly under their breath. Blake leaned forward and again gained everyone's attention.

"OH MY GOD, I'M DYING! OH NO! I DON'T WANT TO DIE!" He felt a surge of heat rush through his body from his feet to his head and his heart raced even faster than before. He started to fidget and squirm. The feeling was ten-fold; fear, death, the urge to evacuate his bladder and bowels, and severe nausea; all while the car seemed to be closing in on him. Overwhelmed and completely out of sorts, Blake whimpered and moaned. Sandy was weeping quietly so not to further alarm the struggling young man. Andrea shifted her attention to Blake. Ross continued on his path with full concentration and a hand on his friend's shoulder.

"You're not dying, Blake." Sandy softly whispered to the stricken eighteen-year-old. "You'll be fine. We'll get you home and you'll feel better, I promise."

Blake was sobbing. He started asking for his Mom. "I want my mom. I don't feel good. I'm scared. I want my mom."

"Shhh," Sandy softly comforted. "It'll be okay. I won't let anything happen to you."

She was fearful that Blake was in harm's way, but wouldn't dare suggest that. The truth was she had no idea what was happening to him. A few years earlier, her grandfather had a heart attack at her house in her full view. That was different, as there was no whining and no complaining. Her grandfather cringed and went face first to the floor quick and with no warning. Blake wasn't acting that way. He'd seem to calm for a bit, and then continue with the intense sobbing. When she felt his shoulders and neck, the muscles were rock hard and tense. It was as if he were literally "petrified."

The words she whispered in his ear were a relief to Blake. He was glad to know that his friends, especially Sandy, cared so much. All except for Greg, that was, who continued to sulk in the back seat. Little did he know that his display was ruining his relationship with Andrea before everyone's eyes. His selfish attitude made her wonder what would happen if it were her feeling bad right now. His true colors were shining bright and she didn't like them. People don't mean to get ill, they simply do. Right now, Blake needed help and the ballgame meant nothing. Blake also knew that if he lived through this, his relationship with Greg would be wounded, perhaps mortally. The crew finally reached Blake's house, and Sandy walked the sick young man inside.

*

Mrs. Thomas met the pair at the door. Blake walked in and went straight to his room.

"What's the matter," she asked.

"I don't know. We were about an hour into the trip and Blake started feeling strange. I can't tell what's wrong with him."

Blake's mom went into his room to check on him, and knew right away that he was suffering a panic attack. She remembered having episodes of panic here and there while she was going through menopause. She recognized the symptoms almost immediately.

"Sandy? Thank you for bringing him home. I think he's having a panic spell. I'll take it from here."

"A panic spell? What's that?"

"It's when you *think* you're dying, but you aren't. It's a really scary feeling."

"Please, Mrs. Thomas, can I stay and help?"

"No. Thank you dear, but he'll need rest after it subsides. I'm going to run him up to emergency and make sure that's all it is, but I can virtually guarantee you that he'll be fine. Give us a call tomorrow, and maybe you can come over then."

Sandy gave the visibly more relaxed Blake a kiss on the forehead and then went back outside to inform the group of the situation. When she reached the car, it was only Ross and Andrea remaining.

"Where's Greg?" Sandy inquired.

"He's walking home." Andrea answered. "I'll be packing my shit and moving back to my parent's house. Can I stay with you tonight?"

"Yeah sure; of course. Whatever you need."

Sandy wasn't stunned at this turn of events. She always thought Greg was a jerk to Andrea. He was bossy, whiny and degrading. Sandy thought it was about time she stood up and told him to get lost. Andrea had tears coming from her eyes, but they were more for Blake. Sandy informed them that Blake was probably okay, just having a 'panic spell', as Mrs. Thomas put it. Ross and Andrea both knew what panic was and felt relieved. They weren't happy that Blake was going through it, but from what they had read and heard; panic was not a fatal condition. They left for home and trusted Blake to his mother. Sandy thought about the night she thought they might have had and cursed her luck.

*

"Come on Blake. We're going to the emergency room."

This caused the panic in Blake to double. Hearing the E-R word sent more shivers down his spine.

"Am I going to die, Mom?" was Blake's big question.

"Not today, kid. Someday, yes but not now."

Mrs. Thomas was such a loving, understanding soul. As badly as Blake had treated her and her husband through the past few years, she still had a place for him and would do anything imaginable to help the young man. This was her baby, her son, her *blood*.

She gathered him up into a throw blanket and walked him out to the car for the trip to the ER. She had to make sure there were no other complications going on with him besides anxiety and panic.

Blake's Mom called Mr. Thomas and enlightened him as to what had happened. He decided he would stay at work and wait for word about his son's condition. Deep down he felt a satisfaction that he couldn't explain.

"Perhaps," he thought, "this will give the kid a wake-up call that's badly needed."

Mrs. Thomas, along with her son, arrived at the ER and she explained to the desk nurse what was happening. Not taking any chances, they rushed Blake back to the cardiac area where they could begin the job of ruling out any heart related problem. Blake was feeling some relief since the attack happened, but he was still extremely uncomfortable and nervous. Being at the hospital was helping him feel better because he was in the right place should something catastrophic happen. The nurse placed Blake on an IV drip to help with the dehydration he probably suffered from not drinking nearly enough water, and placed an oxygen tube under his nose. In the ten minutes they waited for the doctor, Blake felt worlds better. The cocktail of air and fluid was a lift for the otherwise panicked teen. After a light knock, the doctor entered the room.

"Well son, how are you today?" Dr. Keller asked.

"I don't know, Doc, I'm feeling weird and shaky. I don't feel normal."

"What is normal? Is it good or bad?"

Blake thought about the silly question, laid back in the hospital bed and scowled as if he'd missed the final jeopardy answer, thus losing thousands. Mrs. Thomas stood with her hands clasped in front of her at the waist. Dr. Keller smiled, put up his hands, and began speaking anew.

"Okay, you got me. There is no such a thing as "normal." Everyone's normal is different. Where one person suffers an anxiety or panic attack, another gets angry, while yet another gets depressed. People are different. They simply react according to their situation. Do you get that young man?"

"Yeah, I get it, but it doesn't answer the question of why this happened to me. I thought I was a healthy eighteen-year-old guy. What gives?"

Dr. Keller rubbed the day old scruff of whiskers on his chin and gave both Mom and son a fair answer. "I'm going to give you a few tests today; a stress test, to rule out heart. I don't think it's a heart issue, but we'll make sure for your sanity. I also want to do a drug screen on you. Have you used drugs?"

Blake ducked his head low, not answering right away. Mrs. Thomas piped in for him.

"Yes, Doctor, he has, and he still uses drugs. He thinks I don't know, but I do."

She glanced at her son and winked.

All Blake could do was turn a sheer red in his cheeks and express puzzlement in his own head. He had no idea that she knew, but failed to realize his personality change, along with the reek of pot when he would come home from a night out were both dead giveaways.

With no further stalling, Dr. Keller called in a nurse to get a blood sample, urinalysis and set-up a stress test. She nodded at the Doctor and went to work right away. Before Blake could think, she had a needle stuck in his arm, drawing the oxygenized red answer of all questions from his vein. She gave him a plastic jar and ordered him into the bathroom to pee. The nurse warned against flushing or dipping into the toilet, as the water in the bowl contained a protein that would show up on the test. Blake, still scared, did what he was asked and gave the nurse a true sample of his own urine. After that task was completed, another nurse entered the room with a wheelchair and shuffled him down to the stress test area. Mom followed; as interested in her son's well-being as she was curious about his exploits.

*

Four and half hours, and one stress test later, no results had come back. The IV was still in Blake's arm, and he was feeling as hydrated as ever. The attack that had bent him over in submission earlier was completely gone. Surprisingly to Blake, he could only remember small bits of it, even though it seemingly tore through his soul. He was also getting a bit impatient. He wanted a cigarette and was already beginning to feel antsy with not having smoked marijuana in the last few hours. He had smoked pot every day for the last three years and was feeling what could be described as withdrawal symptoms. He didn't want to smoke any more weed, though, because of the fear instilled in him earlier in the day. He decided that this was a good time to have a frank talk with his mom about his future.

"Mom, It's time for me to stop the drugs and alcohol. I need to clean it up and move forward in my life. I'm a hindrance to you and Dad and a pain in the ass to myself."

Mrs. Thomas tried to speak, but was abruptly cut off. "Wait, Blake. You don't have to be so hard on yourself…"

"Let me speak Mom. I need to get this off my chest without the interruptions.

"Fine. I won't stop you. Continue."

"Mom, I'm going to stop using. When, *If,* I make it home, I'm flushing the dope in the toilet. I can't go on like this and I don't want to die. Let's call today a huge wake-up call. Now say what you need to say."

"I don't want you to do this just because of panic. I want you to do it because you need to. It's easy to make that kind of promise to yourself when you're scared out of your wits. The panic will pass, but the big question is; will you stay off after you feel better?"

Blake was listening to his mom for the first time in years. He was almost nineteen years-old and needed to straighten up his confused life. He decided he'd spoken enough and wanted to relax until the tests came back. He was emotionally exhausted.

*

Mrs. Thomas rousted her son thirty minutes after he nodded off. The Doctor was coming soon with the test results. Blake woke up both excited and leery. He didn't have any interest in hearing that he was dying. He began to hyperventilate and struggle with his emotions. Mom rubbed his forehead while gently urging him to calm down by sharing some breathing techniques she had learned.

"Breathe in through the nose…two…three…four, and out through the mouth…two…three…four." Blake felt relief.

After what seemed like forever, the Doctor finally entered the room, smiled at Blake, and gave him the not so catastrophic news.

"You're fine, kiddo. No heart defects of any kind, no brain trauma or anything like that. You, my friend, are suffering from panic attacks. That mixed in with a bit of anxiety, although they go hand in hand. As hard as it may be for you to believe, there is nothing physically wrong with you."

"How do you figure, doc?" was Blake's skeptical question. "You can't possibly feel the way I did without having a major physical problem going on. I'm really having trouble with this diagnosis."

"Trust me, Blake. These tests would've shown a problem if one were present. What you require is a Psychiatrist, not a medical Doctor. I must also tell you that you need to stop using drugs. Your body is filled with hashish, marijuana, and other harmful chemicals. That's where you need to start. If you stay *on* these drugs, I'll guarantee more panic. Get off the crap and I can't promise you won't feel panic or anxiety, but it will be much less severe."

Doctor Keller nodded and smiled as he gave Blake the caring discipline. Reluctantly, Blake agreed and he left for home with his Mom. He considered himself very lucky and knew a lot of work was ahead. If he were to kick the drug habit, he would need help. He knew what he had to do. The guilt over how he'd treated his parents was nightmarish every time he thought about it. It was time for change.

Shaun Webb

"All the flowers would have very extra special powers. They would sit and talk to me for hours when I'm lonely in a world of my own"

Shaun Webb

4

Amy's Wonderland

Amy Fraser, after her difficult trial in Flint, Michigan unsuccessfully defending the crotchety old John Garrison, had moved to Seattle with her boyfriend Hank. Their relationship, however, was souring. Hank was finding it very difficult dealing with her sarcastic brand of humor mixed with a tough outer shell and wasn't sure if they were right for each other. They were both working at The Williams Architect Agency, making good money while negotiating with the Seattle city council on zoning, building and permit businesses. The job wasn't perfect for Amy, who spoke plainly, when it came to telling it as she saw it. Her attitude-triggered dissention at the agency while at the same time causing Hank to feel alienated. He was as meek as a four-day-old kitten. He didn't have the wherewithal to speak his mind and come out with what bothered him. He'd go to bed angry, wake up angry and go about his day angry. He had no idea how to communicate with his feisty girlfriend. Amy sensed his soft interior and appreciated it. She wasn't going to change her attitude or mode of thinking for anyone. Where Hank had laughed with Amy a year ago, he now cringed.

He called her on a Tuesday at 3:00 p.m., and asked her to meet him at the 5-point Café downtown at six. He said he needed to speak with her. She knew why, as his voice was as squeaky as a frightened mouse. Amy didn't fret over it. She was an independent woman with a drive to move forward. Conquering her ghosts of Post-Traumatic Stress Disorder had a lot to do with it. She was a much more confidant woman than before and took everything at face value.

Six O'clock came and she met Hank at the café. He was seated in the rear of the bar with his back to the door. She walked up, patted him on the shoulder and sat down. Hank couldn't look at her. He moved his eyes toward anything but Amy, the wall photos, the waiters, and the other tables. It didn't matter as long as he wasn't meeting her glare. The cantankerous Amy stood up and forced herself into his line of sight, no matter which way he turned his head.

"Okay, okay." Hank finally whispered. "Sit down. I'll look at you."

Amy had known Hank was feeling strange for some time, but she thought they could work through to the other side. This time it'd be different. She didn't care.

"Amy. I have a very important matter we need to discuss."

"Save your breath Hank. I know what you're going to say. Where exactly did this go wrong? What was so bad that you have to run away like this?"

Hank leaned on his index finger against his cheek and looked at the Rockwell painting on the wall depicting rain at a baseball game; a regular occurrence in Seattle. "It's not you, Amy, It's me."

"Spare me that clichéd, tired drama, Hank. I *will not* allow this relationship to end with a reverse guilt trip. You can do way better than that."

After mulling Amy's words for a moment, Hank prepared to speak. Amy eagerly awaited Hank's response. She tapped her fingers on the table in an impatient manner while staring daggers at the hapless soon-to-be ex. He again couldn't meet her glances.

"I'm moving back to Flint. I can't stay here with you any longer. I need the familiarity of home. This city is too wet, rainy and cold. You can have the apartment. I don't care."

Amy stood up and pointed her finger inches from his face. She told Hank clearly how she felt.

"You know what, Hank? You take that sorry ass back to Flint and cozy up to the boring, dull life you're missing."

Amy shook her head. She had taken offense to Hank.

"I'm staying right here in what I think is a beautiful city, and I'm going to make something of myself. I will in fact take the apartment and I will get over you, *quickly*. There's many fish in the sea buddy. I don't sweat the lame excuses."

Amy wouldn't allow Hank another word. She was a no nonsense gal, and this was nonsense to her. She grabbed her purse and jacket and made a b-line out of the café. She went straight back to the apartment, gathered Hank's clothes and personal items, and stacked them near the door so he could grab them and go without having to come inside. She had tears streaming down her face as she did this; it was more out of anger than hurt. She was angrier about living on her own in the Northwest than being without Hank. She certainly had no interest in spending her days with someone who didn't want to reciprocate. Hank never showed up in the week following the break-up to pick up his stuff. Amy threw everything out of the third floor apartment window, and then went downstairs, scooped it up, and pitched it all in the dumpster. With a simple clap of her hands, she closed the book on this chapter of her life. It wasn't an easy thing for Amy, but indeed a necessity.

*

Blake was feeling better. He threw away all the dope he had in his possession and twice daily took the Xanax pill the Doctor prescribed him. It was a low dose; just enough to take the edge off, but the anxiety lurked within Blake's soul. He knew it was there and tried his best to ignore it. He used breathing techniques that were taught to him by the nurse to help chase the buzzing inside his brain. She taught him how to take a full breath into his diaphragm as opposed to the shallow "chest" breathing technique that most people employed. From time-to-time, he would experience an intense attack, but for the most part, they remained at a minimum. Blake's mom also helped him cope with the strange feelings and offered him any help he needed to stay off the drugs. He wasn't thinking about turning tail; he wanted to be drug free and it seemed that he had finally grown up a bit. His personality was softening and he was more at ease with the anger issue that clouded his judgment when he was under the influence. He was lucky in two big ways. He never had to go to jail or prison for drug possession, and better yet, he was still alive. Not everyone escapes the grip of the dope buzz. Some die, some are arrested, and some simply fade into oblivion, a shell of their former selves.

The day came when Blake decided to get a small apartment in downtown Toledo so he could exercise some independence and get ahold of his emotions through responsibility. He stopped hanging out with the people whom he had shared drugs and alcohol. It was especially tough for Sandy, as she wanted a relationship with Blake. She would have settled for a night or two, but really liked the guy. She decided to try to stay close so that maybe she'd have a shot with Blake. He allowed her to visit from time to time, as she had no interest in drugs or alcohol and wouldn't pose a threat to his sobriety. The visits were strictly platonic and well mannered.

As tough as it may have been to abandon his friends, Blake had to move forward. It was his only opportunity to stay sober. He found work at a small tubing factory for a few bucks an hour, and was able to fend for himself. There were still minor attacks here and there, but nothing like the first one he experienced on that awful car ride to Cleveland. Deep down inside, he felt that a change beyond a piping shop in Toledo was necessary. He wasn't quite sure what that would be, but he thought about it often. Living in Toledo caused him to think far too much about his past. He thought moving away from the small Midwestern town would help him in the long run.

*

The panic attack that caused him to pull off the road while traveling to his mom's house was the last straw for the young man. The sight of two mutilated people from a car accident also contributed to his decision. Blake couldn't take another second in Ohio. Change was needed for his healing. He attributed his latest attacks to being in surroundings that were far too familiar and memory inducing. He wasn't sure how it would help, but he started sending out resumes and applications for jobs in different cities across the USA. If something came along that would help him sustain himself, he would be tempted to take it. It took a month and a half for a result.

A docking company in Seattle, Washington called him and asked if he would be willing to come to the city for an interview. It was a well-paying job on the shipping docks downtown, and would be a good experience for him. He needed to think of his future, and moving out to Seattle *might be* the change that was so desperately needed. It was a huge moment for Blake; one that would affect him in ways unimagined.

*

The rain poured hard outside Amy's bedroom window as she lay snuggled up with her pillow. The fog shrouded any sightlines toward the city, so Amy quietly thought about her life. It had been a tumultuous past year plus, with the trial, her battle and eventual victory over PTSD, and a relationship with Hank having gone sour. She wondered what she was doing wrong to bring these misfortunes on herself. Amy was afraid of further symptoms such as voices and visions that weren't real, but pushed the possibility aside in her mind. She had beaten the dreaded affliction and had her life going in the right direction. Upon added thinking, she thought she'd figured it out.

"Maybe I'm too hard-headed. I know I can be terribly sarcastic, but I don't mean to hurt feelings. Can't some people handle my demeanor? I guess it's for the better that Hank left. If he didn't want to deal with me, he shouldn't have to. I'll be okay."

Her work would fill most of her time. It wasn't the easiest job, dealing with city council and making sure building ordinances were followed. She had first hoped to be involved directly with the construction of skyscrapers and other such buildings, but found out that there were a lot more intricacies to architecture than met the eye. She reluctantly accepted her duties. She had a tenth floor office with a panorama of downtown. She was left alone most days. She had her job to do; she did it, and heard nothing of scolding or company drama besides the few moans and groans that went along with being an outspoken sort. Her bosses liked her effort and did keep in mind possibly, one day, having Amy help with the more important work that her office contracted. She, like everyone else, had to earn her keep before stretching out her talents. Amy was a smart woman. She took to new challenges quickly. The future would offer her a great test for her resolve, as her problem solving skills would play a much larger part in her life than she ever imagined or experienced up to that point.

Amy, ever the dynamo, bored of the architectural life quickly and wanted more action. She was still quite young and needed to do something she both enjoyed and found challenging. Being of a lawyer background, but not wanting to return to the courtroom defending people, she decided that she would first take a tae-kwon-do class, and then see what, if anything, she could do with the experience. It sounded like such a good idea that Amy became giddy with excitement. She didn't have her parents to call and tell, not that they would care anyway, and she was now without a boyfriend. Amy decided to take herself out to dinner downtown and celebrate her newfound sense of independence.

*

After being interviewed by CW Docking in Seattle, Blake was offered the job. He accepted, and then flew back to Toledo to pack his luggage and bid Mom and Dad adieu. He knew he could handle the job and he wanted that desperately needed fresh beginning. Seattle would be the city in which he would attempt to start anew.

There were a number of things he liked about Seattle including the picturesque downtown, the cool weather, and the fact that they had an American League baseball team. He would be able to see the Tigers a couple of times a year when they traveled in on a road trip. He also knew he'd have to be careful, as this city offered a wonderful nightlife filled with alcohol and drugs, if he so chose to seek out the dangerous substances. He was to the point in his sobriety where he started feeling a bit guilty that he was still smoking cigarettes. He didn't miss the drinking, as his head had swelled with pain each morning after, and the blackouts had gotten to the point of scary. Going to sleep *(passing out)* in the living room, only to open your eyes and be looking directly in the bathroom mirror, razor blade in your hand, was very disturbing. This wasn't mentioning the vomiting, diarrhea and overall unhealthy feelings that aggravated anxiety and panic. Blake was sure he could handle such temptations and stay on the path of the clean and sober. The challenges he would face in the Emerald city would be rewarding and tempting, scary and exhilarating. It would unquestionably change his life forever.

    Blake bid farewell to his tearful mom, filled with pride dad and drove away. He had one stop to make on the way out of the area, Sandy's house. He wanted to make sure he didn't leave without letting her know and saying goodbye. As much as Blake liked her, and in some instances wanted to be close to her, he never spoiled the wholesome friendship relationship they had forged. Sandy had always wanted to take it further, but Blake never bit on the hints. He was about to change that when the anxiety struck him the first time. He took that, at least partly, as a sign to leave Sandy alone. The energy of the universe also spoke to him. He figured there were reasons for everything.

    Luckily, or tragically, whichever way Blake wanted to look at it, Sandy was home. She rushed out of the house and ran to him, jumping in his arms. She was welcoming and happy to see, what she considered, her soul mate. In her mind, they would eventually be together and live a wonderful life with kids, a dog or cat, and a white picket fence. After hugging and squeezing her hero, she noticed the back seat of Blake's car; it was filled with luggage. She felt the euphoria of the moment wash away.

"What's going on Blake? What's with all the suitcases?"

Blake didn't, *couldn't*, answer. This was harder than he imagined. His tongue stuck to the roof of his mouth as he searched for the right way to say goodbye.

"Blake. Tell me what's up. Are you leaving?"

The tears began streaming down Sandy's face, as she knew at that very moment what the luggage meant. Blake continued to struggle for words.

"I uh, I have to, umm, go. You know? Right? I kinda have to leave and start over. You understand. Umm, ahh, I know you do."

"Take me with you. I won't let you go without me, Blake. I'm in love with you. Please don't leave me."

"Sandy, you're not in love with me, you just think you are; that's all. I'll be out of your mind in a few days and you can continue on with a wonderful life full of good things."

"**NO! NO!** I don't want that life. I want a life with you. I love you Blake. Don't leave me here alone to rot in this crappy city."

The tears had turned into a steady flow on Sandy's cheeks. She was broken-hearted, and Blake was feeling her pain as well, but he knew he had to go. He didn't feel the same about her as she did about him and wouldn't tug at her heartstrings any longer. He released from her hug and began walking to his car. Sandy quickly followed. She grabbed Blake by the hips and turned him around. She tried to kiss him passionately, but he turned his head. Sandy's head bowed forward as she laid her chin on her chest.

"I have to go Sandy. I love you, but like a friend, not a husband. I need you to understand so we can move on in the directions and paths that are meant for us."

Sandy couldn't speak; she only wept.

Blake opened the door and seated himself behind the wheel. Sandy stood three feet away, hands over her face and howling with hurt. She had never slept with Blake, but felt a connection with him that she'd never felt about anyone in her life. She was convinced that Blake was her soul mate, her life partner, her future husband. These thoughts were both healthy and damaging. Healthy in that watching someone you feel a deep connection with leaves, or dies teaches you how to let go. It wasn't healthy in that some people would go to any lengths to try to make something work when nothing existed. That was the reason they made movies and wrote books depicting fatal attractions. Sandy would have a great deal of thinking to do in the next couple of months, as her feelings for Blake would never change. She wasn't entirely sure she could simply let Blake go so easily without at least a fight to try to win his heart.

*

Blake headed down the road to a new life. Watching Sandy disappear in the rear view was one of the toughest things he'd ever had to do. Blake cared deeply for her, but he felt the need to release all things past and leave them behind. It wouldn't bode well for his future if he lived in his past. A few tears dripped from Blake's eyes, but he dried them and soldiered forward. He had a three day trip ahead of him and would need all of his energy and focus to get to the new city he would call home. He was excited, nervous and skeptical. All the feelings swirled around in his mind with questions, but no real answers. He didn't know what he was getting into. He'd done a bit of homework when he interviewed for the job and saw that Seattle had a few decent places to live that weren't too terribly costly. He found a rental house not far from his work on Elliot Avenue. His new digs were at 200 Queen Anne North, a humble place that gave him a bedroom, bathroom and kitchen with a small living area. It would cost him a whopping six fifty a month, but the place was one of the cheaper digs. It was the best he could do with all the searches and shopping he'd done. He was to net about a thousand a week, so he would make plenty to pay for the apartment, get groceries, and smoke, if he continued with the nasty habit.

    Fargo, North Dakota was Blake's first stop on his travels, some eight hundred miles from Toledo. It took him a good sixteen hours to get that far and he still had another twelve hundred plus miles to go. If he stuck to the road for sixteen more hours the next day, the third day would leave some four hundred miles to travel. That would be a cakewalk in comparison.

Blake found a Super 8 off the expressway, purchased a room, and crashed hard on the bed. He didn't even bother to pull back the comforter. Even though he needed it immediately, he'd shower in the morning. Everything would stop for six to eight hours, and then Blake's journey west would continue. It would be a journey unlike any he'd ever taken. The end of the line, Seattle, would hold more emotion than Blake had ever been through in his entire life. He wanted change, and he would surely find it.

Shaun Webb

"The Queen she likes 'em red. If she saw white instead; she'd raise a fuss and each of us would quickly lose his head."

Shaun Webb

5

Off with her Head 1

Her hair blew clean and blond through the dry desert air as she perused the view around her. Although the temperature was high, it was much cooler driving 95 MPH in a '09 Lamborghini Convertible. It was a gift from her marvelous boyfriend Jake, and she loved it as much, if not more, than sex. That was saying a lot, since she was horny twenty-three hours a day.

Kathy Joseph would've never lived this kind of life with that dolt Kurt. He was a loser in her eyes that would continue losing. She hadn't missed him, or for that matter, thought much about him since the divorce. Now that she was with a poker playing livewire who seemingly never lost a hand, the thought of life with Kurt would pop into her head from time to time, if only to make her wretch.

Jake was rich from poker championships and shared his winnings with Kathy, as she shared her body with him. The lovemaking was earth shattering as they were meant for each other. Kathy had silicone-enhanced breasts, bleached blond hair and a tan furnished mostly by a bed in the basement of their home. Jake was a bit older than Kathy was, but had two facelifts and a liposuction procedure to thin his waistline. They both looked as phony as three-dollar bills, but were perfect tens in each other's eyes. The life they led was exquisite, but rare for a pair of uneducated people. Kathy had trouble adding two and four, while Jake couldn't read word one from any book, magazine, or newspaper. His special relationship was with the cards. He could read them perfectly while at the same time reading the eyes and mannerisms of the opponents at the poker table. His best night had happened two weeks earlier as he took home over one hundred and fifty G's in an eight-hour marathon. He wiped the table, and his poker foes, clean. Kathy was always able to spend the cash up quickly and Jake never questioned her about it. He averaged about forty to sixty grand weekly and re-supplied the money line with regularity. Kathy was careful to some extent, as she didn't want to see the cash flow disappear. Life was far too comfortable for the pair. They would be brought down to size soon enough.

*

The van teetered and tottered on the road as the soundtrack from Alice in Wonderland blared from the dashboard and door speakers. The sound was quite static strewn, as Kurt had never bothered to put in a decent stereo system. He kept the volume low enough so that he could still understand the words to his music. Kurt had spent the last two months souping up the van for his trip. He'd installed a bed in the back, put some lights above on the dome and built a cabinet on the left side that was always locked. He was driving a box van, so it was extra-long, extra wide and extra high. It gave him plenty of room to make any improvements he saw fit. The locked cabinet area was about ten feet long and came out from the wall of the van two feet toward the inside. It gave him plenty of room to maneuver back and forth as needed as well as giving him a spot for his "collection."

As Kurt drove west to Las Vegas, the scenery of eastern Colorado took him. It was nicer than anything he'd seen in Michigan. Of course Michigan was nice, but this landscape took the cake. He saw mountains and rolling plains; nothing of which existed in his home state..

Kurt arrived at the split that separated I-80 and I-76. He would ride 76 to Denver before stopping for a rest. Everything was going perfectly. After relaxing in Denver for a few hours, he would pick up route 50 through Colorado and into Utah. From there, it would be I-15 south to Vegas, and his *real* work would begin. He turned up the stereo.

When I shave, I lose the time I save...

Kurt was singing along, bobbing his head to the music and enjoying his *trip*. The smile on his face was as wide as his behavior was nasty. He knew what would happen in Las Vegas and he could hardly contain his excitement. It would be a most satisfying undertaking he would perform. Life as he knew it couldn't get much better. He would soon get his revenge on Kathy Joseph.

*

Their house was on a hill and the view was breathtaking. A pool shone with the glistening of the bright, hot sun during the day, while interior lighting made the swimming, *skinny-dipping*, spectacular at night. The wet bar had everything available to not only make your favorite drink, but also become a raging alcoholic if one so chose. The couple's bedroom was located to the side of this area, separated by French doors, and the patio in which they spent most of their time was artificially air-conditioned. It was a pure waste of energy, but Kathy couldn't have cared less. Jake usually joined his woman in the mid to late evening, just in time to pour himself a stiff drink and take a nightly nude dip with her.

Kathy never had to toil. Jake worked, but at playing cards and teaching poker, his two favorite activities. He was nicknamed "paws" due to his talent of hiding the cards within his large hands instead of leaving them on the table, as was the usual style of ninety-five percent of the competition. His fellow players marveled at his skill and adeptness at avoiding mistakes that would be costly for some of the more amateurish players. He had a habit of making the right choices with his strategies time and time again, thus winning repeatedly. He'd been kicked out of many a casino in Vegas because the house thought he must've been cheating to be so good. Jake didn't cheat; he was simply brilliant at manipulating the odds and counting cards in his mind. He would need much more than card skills if he were to buck the largest and most difficult odds he'd soon have to face.

*

Kurt crossed into the city of Las Vegas at about nine in the evening. His timing was perfect, as he could stop and get something to eat before heading down the road to find his ex-wife. He would also have to locate the exact directions so he wouldn't get lost in the desert or make any mistakes. Kurt stopped at a phone booth, ripped the White Pages guide from the flimsy chain that hung it two feet under the receiver, and took it with him to a local diner. He looked under Joseph, but as he expected, found nothing. He decided to look up the name "Jake", but with no last name because he never made the effort to listen to Kathy whenever she spoke of him. Kurt knew he was wealthy and self-centered, so he did the logical thing and looked under "Poker" in the business section. He found the name "Jake's School of Cards" standing alone in two spots. He thought to himself that Jake's cocky attitude would lead him to put his *first* name in the book so nobody would misinterpret exactly who he was, coupled with the fact that he felt the name "Jake" was easily recognizable in the Vegas area. He obviously lived in the more affluent area of Vegas.

After grabbing a bite to eat, Kurt offered his server a twenty spot if she would answer a simple question for him. She looked at the twenty and then looked at him, enamored more with his wispy dark hair, chiseled facial features and stunning green eyes. She nodded for him to ask his question.

"Is this n-name here the s-same Jake that's s-so good at p-poker?"

The server stayed mute until Kurt slid the bill closer to her waiting hand. When she reached for it, he grabbed her by the wrist and gave her a stern warning; "I c-could b-break your arm with a s-simple twist. D-Do you know that?"

"Yes sir, I do. Please let go or I'll scream."

"W-well now, we wouldn't w-want that. If you s-scream, I'll do worse than b-break your arm."

"Okay, mister. What was your question again?"

"J-Jake. Is this the p-poker champion? The m-man listed here? Is t-this his a-address?"

The young server took a closer look. "Yes, it's the poker champion and no, he lives in a different place. This book lists his business location. It'll cost you more than twenty bucks, though, to find out where he lives."

Kurt squeezed a tad harder, putting a great deal of pressure on her wrist. His voice lowered into a sterner, and surprisingly stutter free growl. He kept his lips tightly pursed together and spoke through his gritted teeth.

"Answer the fucking question. I'm getting impatient with you…**MA'AM!**"

Knowing now that she was pushing her luck, she answered quickly, "2500 West Sahara Avenue. It's just off of fifteen north of the city."

Kurt released her wrist and she quickly scooped up the twenty. She had one more question for the man before he left.

"What happened to the stutter? You were stuttering when we started talking and then it disappeared."

"Stutter?" Kurt quizzically asked, "w-w-what s-s-stutter?" He flashed a sarcastic smile toward her.

The server puzzled at Kurt and walked away muttering to herself.

"Damn he's strange, but he's cute as hell."

As he walked out to his van, he was unknowingly singing in a very soft manner; *"I'm late, I'm late, for a very important date, no time to say hello, goodbye. Goodbye Kathy."*

*

It took upwards of five hours to reach Jake on his cell, but Kathy finally succeeded and was relieved.

"Where are you, silly? I want you to come home and spend some time with me."

"Somebody has to win the cash, love. Give me another hour or so and I'll be there. Why don't you slip into one of those sexy little nighties that you like so much? Maybe we can take a skinny dip, when I get home."

"Oh baby. You read my mind. I'll be waiting with open, uhh, legs when you get here."

Kathy hung up happy in here ability to continually turn on the man with the money. She at times thought that she'd lost that "thing" it takes to make men lust over her, but she was always reminded in one way or another. Kathy was big on "the hell with tomorrow, let's live for today." It was the only way she could deal with getting older.

She undressed and stepped into the huge walk-in shower with three heads and benches on each end. A feeling of warmth and security overwhelmed her. Kathy was as happy as she'd ever been in her life and wanted so badly to be with her man at that very moment. She was overcome with a strong sensation of well-being as she rubbed the soapy scrub brush over her body. That action made her warmer and hornier. After skimming over her taut nipples, she lowered the brush down, took a showerhead off its swivel and began to massage her lower regions with the warm pulsing of the water. As she felt she would start giggling in orgasmic delight, she thought she'd heard music playing in the house. She hadn't turned any stereos on, so that would be virtually impossible unless Jake had arrived home earlier than expected. After thinking about that possibility for another moment, she found that it would be impossible for him to get off the phone and arrive home that quickly, unless he was tricking her and was nearly home when she called. Kathy turned the water off and listened closer to the melody playing from what seemed like a distance away.

They're going to lose their heads. For painting the roses red. It serves them right. They planted white, but roses should be red. Oh, they're going to lose their heads...

Where did she recognize that music? She thought about it for a moment, and then it hit her. Alice in Wonderland. Perhaps he'd found this song on a cd to romance her.

"Romance me with an Alice in Wonderland song about cutting off heads?"

She wasn't sure either way, so she dressed and headed toward the music.

When she crossed through the kitchen, she noticed a dozen red roses sitting on the dining room table. Happily, Kathy walked over to smell them and give them a woman's soft touch. She noticed that the petals appeared to be *painted red*. As she rubbed a finger and thumb softly on the flower, her suspicion was confirmed; the roses had indeed been painted red.

"Oh, that's so romantic," She whispered. "It's just like Alice in Wonderland. Jake must want to do a bit of role playing tonight."

She could still hear the music from a distance. She slowly walked through the kitchen and came to the edge of the living room area; still no Jake. Perplexed, Kathy continued to follow the music, which now sounded like it was on a tape loop. It was repeating itself. The same lines she originally heard about *"painting the rose's red"* kept playing.

"But where is it," she asked herself.

After crossing the living area and carefully tiptoeing down the long corridor toward the garage, the music became louder. Now she felt that she was tracking down the sound. A smile crossed her lips as she wondered what her silly boyfriend was thinking. After her initial skepticism, she had convinced herself that it was, in fact, Jake. After all, who would put on such a flamboyant show if not him? Very few people ever visited unannounced and it was late. Kathy continued her trek through the house, now more than ever excited about her boyfriend's follies. As she reached the garage door separating in from out, the music was playing at a mid-level volume. There was no doubt that when she opened the door, she was in for a big surprise. She turned the knob quickly and flung open the door. She didn't find what she'd expected.

*

After Kurt had garnered the information from the stubborn server, he headed to the address to pay a visit to Kathy and her "lucky" boyfriend Jake. Kurt had heard about some of the professional poker player's exploits on TV and in the newspaper, and of course from Kathy herself. Jake was a card playing champion, but Kurt didn't care. The only thing Kurt was concerned with was why he ever chose a bimbo like Kathy. That was one question he'd never be able to answer.

The road was all but clear, save for a few stray cars heading into the city. It was also a very hot night; a dry heat of about 107 with no humidity or breeze. It felt like standing in a furnace. This fact didn't bother or slow Kurt down. He was focused on the task and would take great joy in the carrying out the grisly duties.

Fifteen minutes after he left the diner, he arrived at the gates to Jake and Kathy's home. He didn't have a code, so he tried punching in random numbers. After two minutes, he'd had enough. He backed his van up, aimed for the gate, sped to about thirty miles per hour, and crashed cleanly through the fence. He hopped out of the van to see what damage he'd done. To his surprise, it was minimal. His front grill was moved over an inch or two, while the brown paint took a minor scratch. He looked back at the gate and found it pulverized; it was pushed hard to the side and bent to oblivion.

"They'll n-need a n-new gate." Was Kurt's mellow response.

He continued his trek up the three quarter mile long winding driveway and finally reached the garage. An all-terrain vehicle was parked on the outside and the doors were unlocked. Kurt reached in, pulled the visor down and clicked the garage door button. He went back to the van, opened the side door and took out a few items that were needed for his excursion. Lastly, he placed his top hat on his head and felt transformed. The sanity slipped away, replaced by an urgency to giggle uncontrollably. After walking quietly and unseen into the kitchen area and setting up the first of his props, he went back to the garage. He turned on the portable CD player he carried with him to *"Who's been painting my red roses."* It was an Alice in Wonderland number he found very fascinating and apt for the occasion. He stood in a darkened corner and waited patiently for either Kathy or Jake to come to the door; he gripped his machete as it ominously hung at his side.

He wasn't sure whom it would be coming through the door, "but tough luck to whoever it was," he thought.

Kurt slowly rocked his right hand back and forth to the tune of the music. Surprisingly, it only took two minutes for the door to fling open and expose Kathy Joseph to her estranged husband. Kurt stepped out of the shadows and Kathy's smile quickly turned into a frightened frown. He noticed red paint on her fingers; that made him smile.

"H-hi there K-Kathy. How are y-you?"

"What the fuck are you doing here, asshole?" Kathy responded with more than a hint of anger.

Kurt clicked the CD player off, and then answered.

"Well, I've c-come to collect your h-head."

Kurt pulled up the machete and approached Kathy. She put her hands up in a defensive manner and screamed at Kurt.

"DON'T DO IT. PLEASE. I HAVE MONEY, YOU CAN HAVE MONEY."

"Quiet woman." Kurt angrily insisted.

Kathy quieted. He pointed the machete mere inches from her face.

"For crimes against your ex-husband; me, I, with the Red Queens approval of course, sentence you to death."

Kurt approached Kathy. She looked at him out of the corner of her eye and asked, "W-what happened to your s-stutter? It's gone. You had it a s-second ago. W-what's with that h-hat? Are you c-crazy?"

"There's no need to stutter any longer. You're the one who's stuttering now. The hat, my dear, is because I'm a hatter you see; christened by the Queen herself."

Kurt's stutter did indeed calm as he was getting closer to his goal of collecting Kathy's head. It was as if he forgot about his impairment when getting so angrily excited about his revenge.

"Enough babble," Kurt insisted, "**OFF WITH YOUR HEAD!**"

The machete swung around with a breezy whiff and in a flash, Kathy's head was separated from her body. The cut was so clean that her head flew straight up in the air and her body collapsed under it. When her head came down, it landed on her stomach. For a split second, Kurt could have sworn the eyes were still moving, but dismissed it as over excitement in his vengeance. The blood spouted out of Kathy's body as is natural when the carotid artery is severed, and the head was leaking from underneath. It wasn't a problem for Kurt as he picked up her head, placed it on the tool bench and fired up his blowtorch. He turned it sideways and cauterized the bottom of her neck, thus sealing in everything that was still intact. After doing the same with her torso, he picked up Kathy's head, turned the CD back on, and began dancing to the tune. Kurt twirled and danced, looked into Kathy's dead eyes, and danced some more. He kissed her bloody mouth repeatedly, even sticking his tongue inside. Soon he tired and returned to his van with the lifeless orb. After placing the appendage inside, he returned to the garage to collect the items he owned. He left the painted roses.

A short time later, Jake pulled up in his convertible and quickly jumped out. He had noticed the smashed gate and now a large brown box van in his driveway. Standing on the edge of the garage opening was Kurt, a smile affixed to his face.

"What in the blue blazes is going on at my house?"

Kurt looked at Jake and explained. "Well, I j-just t-took Kathy's h-h-head."

"What? What the hell are you talking about?"

Kurt lifted Kathy's headless torso off the floor by the collar and showed it to the now squeamish Jake."

"That's w-what." He pointed out.

Jake slowly backed up until he bumped into the front of the van; he turned around and saw, in the windshield, Kathy's head sitting on the dashboard looking back at him. Before he could scream or turn back around, Kurt had wrapped an extension cord around his neck and dragged him into the garage. When he was sure Jake was all the way in, he clicked the wall button, thus closing the two of them inside together.

*

After three days of not hearing from Jake, a friend of his made a trip up to the house. He saw that the gate was damaged. Curiosity piqued; he called 911, reported his findings and drove up the drive to the garage. He saw both Jake and Kathy's vehicles uncharacteristically sitting outside in the driveway. He walked over to Jake's vehicle, grabbed the remote and clicked it. When the door swung up, he was shocked and revolted by what he saw. Kathy's headless body hung from the wooden rafters, a rope around each wrist and the letter Q with a slash through it like a No Smoking sign, scrawled on her torso with what looked like red paint. In the corner sat Jake, bound and gagged, but struggling to get his friends attention. Upon walking over and seeing that he was wearing sunglasses, he began to untie his hands. He was again jolted when he saw that every finger was missing from both of his hands. He looked at Jake and pulled the gag from his mouth. He still sounded like he was gagged, though. He asked him to tell him what happened.

"MMMPHHH." Was all Jake could utter.

The friend pulled Jake's sunglasses off his face and to his horror both of his eyes had been gauged out. Jake's friend recoiled. Jake lurched over to where he thought his friend was standing and opened his mouth. His tongue was also missing. Fingers, eyes, tongue; all cut out and cauterized to limit bleeding. They were all the items Jake needed to be a poker champion. Without them, he was useless. He wouldn't be able to identify Kathy's killer either. No fingers to write with and no tongue in which to speak. Kurt had covered his bases well. He also had the first victim in his van; her head anyway. When Jake's friend leaned onto the tool bench from losing his balance due to stress and light-headedness, he saw sitting there a Queen of Hearts playing card and both of Jake's eyeballs looking up at him. The card had writing on it. Upon closer inspection, it was obvious as to what it said; **CRAPS!** The man vomited at his feet.

*

The Vegas police investigated the scene, but found nothing more than the torso, a bloodied and mutilated Jake plus a few smudged fingerprints. The investigators were baffled as to who had committed the crime. They were able to scrape some brown paint off the bent gate, but many vehicles had brown paint. It would be a laborious task to find and go over each and every truck and car in Las Vegas and the surrounding area that matched that color. As they finished processing the scene, inside and out, they failed to notice one important bit of information. Kathy had red paint on her finger and thumb from touching the roses. The investigators at the scene didn't connect that with the roses on the table, which were bypassed at least fifty times during the search and investigation inside the house. Kurt had successfully pulled off his vengeance on Kathy. He re-focused his attention to the next person in line, someone who had done Kyle Beauregard so wrong- Soo-Chin Xing.

*

Las Vegas (newswire) — Kathy Joseph, the woman whose torso was found hanging at a historic Las Vegas mansion, has been laid to rest by her family and millionaire boyfriend as the mystery over her death remains unresolved. Investigators with the Las Vegas Sheriff's Department, who are probing the suspicious death, await more results from Joseph's autopsy.

Sgt. Rod Franklin of the department's homicide unit said, "We're still weeks out" from concluding who might've murdered Joseph. He said they are also looking into any connection to the maiming of her boyfriend allegedly after her murder in the home.

"I've really got an open mind," Franklin said of Joseph's death.

Joseph's sister, Mary Margot, 33, issued a written statement on behalf of the Margot family saying, "Kathy valued her life and lived her life to its fullest. Kathy loved God, her family and life." Margot said she and other members of her family are grief-stricken and don't know what to think about how Joseph died.

Kathy Joseph, 32, who came to Las Vegas a few months ago to live with her boyfriend, poker champion Jake Reynolds, was buried Saturday by her family in Flint, Michigan, where her parents and other family members live. Reynolds and Joseph lived in Vegas and spent most of the last six months in the 12-bedroom mansion, originally built in 1908. Reynolds paid $12.75 million for the home four years ago.

Franklin said police responding to a call early July 13 found Joseph's body in the garage of the mansion. He said Reynolds friend Adam Thomes, 47, reported he found her headless torso hanging by the wrists from a girder with a large red "Q" painted on her blouse with a red slash painted through it. Her feet were tied together, Franklin said. The friend also found Reynolds on the floor with duct tape holding his hands together. His fingers were cut from his hands and his eyes removed from his head. His tongue was also missing.

Frank said investigators are probing "self-mutilation," or the actions and state of mind of Reynolds before Joseph's death, and whether her death may have been related to Reynolds injuries.

"Any time there's a death such as this we're always going to look at self-mutilation," Frank said. "What was going on in his or her life? Jake's incident is something we would look into as well. "To say it's associated ... that's still up to the investigation," Frank said.

Jake Reynolds has not publicly commented beyond two brief written statements, issued jointly with his friend. One disclosed the death of Joseph; a second lamented "the unfortunate attention" news media have given to police records in Vegas about the couple's possible quarrels and any allegations of physical violence toward each other. No arrests were made when police responded to two domestic disturbances in the last six months.

Reynolds and his first wife were divorced in January. She maintains a summer home in Las Vegas near Reynolds Mansion where the twin tragedies took place.

The death, under mysterious circumstances in the wealthy area where violent crime is a rarity, has attracted worldwide attention and speculation.

Reynolds was not in the home when the Joseph body was murdered, according to a statement made through his friend to police.

Frank said Reynolds and other family members have cooperated with investigators.

Shaun Webb

6

Blake Falls Down a Rabbit Hole

The trip to Seattle was more arduous than Blake could've ever imagined. Although he had grasped the idea that anxiety and panic attacks were the mind's way of warning you of danger, realistic or not, he still felt the cold buzzing through his veins as he trekked forward. He had now crossed into Montana and experienced wide-open, lonely roads. He tried to relax, but the inner demon of nervousness kept squeezing. This was no place to have an attack, he thought to himself, but anxiety didn't have a plan, position or even a conscience; the spells hit when they hit and it was up to Blake to try and ward it off with positive thinking and careful breathing.

"In through the nose, out through the mouth. In through the nose, out through the mouth."

Blake was working hard to chase the inner beast away, if only for the time being. He didn't want to take too much of the tranquilizer Xanax, but in cases like the one he was in, he thought it to be the best idea. The doctor had given him a prescription for thirty tablets at .50 mg strength, so it made sense to use it only when necessary. He wanted to get further down the road, thus closing the gap between himself and Seattle before nightfall. He was afraid that the tablet would tire him too much, causing him to stop sooner than he wanted. After mulling and fussing within himself for another half an hour, he did what he thought would help the most and popped a pill. He would have a good twenty minutes or so before the tablet kicked in, so he'd concentrate on the road the best he could so when it did affect him, he'd be ready for the drowsy eyes and sleepiness that came with it. It certainly wasn't impossible to drive while on Xanax, but it made more sense not to do it. The medication was very good at knocking down the symptoms of anxiety, but very poor at keeping one awake.

    Blake drove with a purpose. Twenty minutes went by and the pill began to work. The feelings of fear and isolation he'd had a few minutes ago began to wane. It was a breath of fresh air for the young man. He continued to drive with little to no adverse effects on his ability. Perhaps the medication brought him down to a "normal" state of thinking instead of sleepy because he was so tensed up. Whatever the reason, Blake was glad to be at least temporarily free of the tension. He passed Billings and hoped to make it to Missoula before quitting for the day. The pill would give him a good ten to twelve hours of relief, so he thought he could make it with minimal difficulty. Stopping in Missoula would leave him with a very doable chunk of driving the next day, thus getting him into Seattle with four days to spare before his first day on the new job. He was excited to get to know the city at least some before having to grind ten to twelve hour days six days a week.

Deer Lodge, Montana was as far as Blake made it. The very tiny community was about seventy-five miles East of Missoula. It was okay, as he needed the rest after such a tumultuous day of battling with the inner demons that caused him emotional pain. He checked in, took his key and went straight to the room, not bothering to bring anything in from the car. He'd get what he needed in the morning. It was a quarter short of midnight, so morning would come very quickly. Rest was imperative for Blake if he wanted to complete the trek the next day.

*

Tae-Kwon-Do class was everything Amy could've asked for and more. She loved the workout it gave her, and was especially fond of the contact battles she had with her *all male* class. So far, she had done well enough in the group to be given special attention from her instructor, Claude Ronet. This made the men angry and envious. Amy was all of five foot four and weighed no more than one hundred and ten, but she packed a mean wallop. So far, she had gone up against three of the average talents in the class. On this day, Claude pitted her against Amos Galias, the nastiest of the group. Looking at the six foot eight inch, three hundred plus pound Amos gave Amy a slight twinge of nausea in her stomach. Giving him a good battle would help her achieve a deep amount of confidence.

That the instructor put her against the beast was either a penalty for being a hard-assed, mouthy woman, or a privilege, as all the men that had gone up against Amos were soundly routed; one ending up in the hospital. Amy walked to the center of the mat and met Amos. She had to look up at a steep angle to see his glowing embers called eyes.

"I'm gonna fuck you up bitch." He growled.

Amy gulped hard. She put out a hand for Amos as a good sport gesture. Amos grabbed her arm by the wrist and elbow, lifting Amy straight up. He then dropped her backward on her back and bottom. Amy, instantly winded as the thud to the mat took every ounce of air, struggled to her feet and turned to face the giant.

"That's not nice, Amos." Amy breathlessly scolded with her hands on her knees. "You have to wait until I'm ready and the instructor gives us the green light."

Amos was not amused with Amy's rules or her having so much as opened her mouth. In a nasty grunt, he threw himself to the mat and swept a kick not more than two inches off the floor. He connected with Amy's ankle and she flew backward. Landing on the back of her neck stopped the fall. Amy rolled to the right and moaned with pain as the stinger went down both arms and back up again, settling in her spine just under the cerebellum. The latest move without question aggravated Amy, but amused the men in the class; especially the ones she had already whipped. She quickly jumped back to her feet in a show of courage, shook off the heavy blow and took a fighting stance. She motioned her fingers in a "come hither," daring the giant to attack.

"C'mon you big ugly sack of shit. You don't want to play by the rules, no problem, but don't say you didn't ask for it."

Amos snorted and rushed Amy with his hands straight out, seemingly to grab her by, and wring, what he thought to be her scrawny neck. Amy timed the rush and at the last possible moment dropped to the mat in a front roll. Amos had too much momentum behind him and couldn't lift his feet fast enough. The large man fell hard and with haste. When he hit the mat, it was with his jaw and Adam's apple. The giant was shaken and Amy took full advantage. She rushed over to Amos, who was lying on his stomach, and jumped a solid twelve inches off the floor. When she came down, she aimed her bent knee at his tailbone. With as much thrust as she could muster, she landed on Amos, eliciting a scream from the giant and a gasp from the other men standing around the mat. Even Claude, grimaced.

"Take that you stupid piece of shit," Amy hissed. "How d'ya fuckin' like me now?"

Before Amos could answer, Amy pulled a sap out of her pocket and gave him a shot to the back of the head. Amos shuddered as the ball of solid leather rapped off his skull.

"Does that feel good? Want some more?"

Amy arose, ran to the other side of the mat and turned. The giant Amos was struggling with the bruised tailbone while blood trickled between his fingers and ran down the back of his neck. Amy lunged forward to give the big guy another shot. She would go for the back of the knee this time. Just as she was ready to ascend and drop, Claude grabbed her out of mid-air and locked her in a bear hug.

"Let me go, fucker. We're not done here. I'll kick his sissy ass. Look at him; he's crying like a baby. What's-a-matter, pussy? You need your momma?" Amy was struggling to free herself, kicking screaming and scratching.

"Calm down Amy. Calm down. You win. Shh, calm down for me."

Amy started to slow under Claude's bear hug. At last, she relaxed. He let her go.

"Why'd you stop us? His ass was mine. He fought like a pansy and I dropped him."

"That you did Amy. Very impressive. I've never seen anyone get the best of Amos."

"No? Well you haven't met me yet, have you?" Amy shoved her index finger into Claude's chest. "I don't give in to anyone, especially when they don't fight fair."

Claude nodded to her and smiled. He was most enamored with her sass and feistiness. He knew she was a special student. Amy stood three feet away and gave him back the slightest of grins. Her hair was askew and her opponent was finally getting up. She looked at Amos and readied for further action.

"No, no." Amos said sheepishly. "I don't want any more from you. What the fuck did you hit me with?"

"My fist you cheater. You deserved it."

"Your fist my ass! Just forget it. Truce?"

Amos put his hand out to shake with Amy. She walked over, put her hand into Amos', and handed him the sap she'd hit him with.

"Next time keep one of these in your pocket. They really help if some big lug is trying to kick your ass."

They both started laughing and shook for real. Amy had garnered the respect of the biggest and toughest man in the class. The rest of the guy's cheered and laughed behind them.

"Fraser! Get your ass in my office, pronto!"

Claude signaled to Amy. Her smile was erased and she followed him to his office. She wasn't sure what he wanted, but it would turn out be more exciting than anything she'd experienced in her life thus far.

*

As he passed Spokane, Blake knew his journey would end in a few short hours. It was a lengthy ride, but the job and apartment he had waiting for him would be the cherry on top of his personal sundae. Blake had to give himself credit for making the change in his life. It would be difficult for a mentally proficient person to do, let alone an anxiety and panic sufferer. Despite the buzz of nervousness that insisted on presenting itself throughout the trip, Blake never gave in. The medicine was a helper, but much could be attributed to his ability to concentrate on his breathing and realizing, at least to some extent, that the symptoms were *not true*. Of course, Blake knew that it was much easier to tell a sufferer to "get over it" or to tell yourself that it was a figment of your own vivid imagination, but the fact remained that it was one of the hardest emotions to shake off once it sunk its sharpened claws into your brain.

    Blake decided to stop at a local Spokane diner off the expressway. Despite all else, he was hungry and insisted on filling himself for the home stretch. He settled on a truck stop, hearing they had the best food outside of a greasy spoon. When he left the highway and turned onto the service drive, it was apparent to him that he was in an entirely different part of the country. He had ventured some two thousand miles from his cozy home and it was sinking in. The feeling was positive, as he smiled and gave himself a second pat on the back in congratulations to himself for being less than a coward.

    He enjoyed his meal. He kept to himself despite the truck stop being filled to capacity. He could feel the patron's eyes spying him when he wasn't looking, but dismissed it as curiosity. At one point, he looked to his left and saw a gentle enough looking woman with a child. He smiled and tipped his Tiger cap to the woman, only to be given back a look of contempt along with a nasty sneer. Blake lifted his brows, lowered his eyes and whispered "o-k," as he took his glance in a different direction. Dismissing the encounter, Blake continued to mind his own business. He was feeling shaky because of the mini standoff, but was still able to keep his focus enough to concentrate on the task. He had a lot to do when he finally would arrive in Seattle. Apartment, job, tour the city. That thinking kept him afloat until a situation arose that left Blake shaking in his delicate mental boots.

As he walked back over to the soda fountain to refill his cup, a middle-aged man with a "not-so-friendly" look met him. He had a button up flannel with the arms cut off to expose the man's heavily tattooed biceps. He also wore a dingy Mariners baseball cap and smelled of booze. Blake didn't know what he wanted so he extended a welcoming hand.

"I don't shake hands with home wreckers, boy."

"I have no idea what you're talking about sir."

Blake's response was filled with voice cracks and high pitches. He felt his heart rate increase and the adrenaline flow. It was as if he'd been kicked in the gut.

"You were making eyes at my girl over there. See her there? The man pointed to the woman of which Blake had tipped his hat. "And I hate the fucking Tigers."

"Yes sir, I understand that you hate the Tigers, but you live some two thousand miles from Detroit, and about your girl; I was simply being friendly, not flirty."

"Is that so? Well, she told me you wanted to get in her panties."

The man inched within a hair of his nose and his substantial stomach bumped Blake's arm as the conversation continued. Blake was becoming more nervous. He didn't want a fight, and wasn't crazy about this confrontation. He tried reasoning with the man.

"Look sir, if I've offended, I apologize. All I did was tip my cap. I never spoke with her or gave her the impression that I "wanted her", but I will certainly tell her I'm sorry if that's what you'd like."

The man flashed a sheepish grin, as he now knew he was dealing with a less than tough character. He thought about things for a moment, and then gave Blake his orders.

"I want all the cash you have right now, or we step outside and I kick the ever-loving shit out of you."

"I only have fifty bucks sir. All my cash is gone."

"Don't bullshit me boy. I saw your plate. You're from way east of here. You have money. I'll bet my life on it."

Blake had money hidden in the car. Five grand was in the trunk under the spare tire in a small wooden case. He wasn't about to give that money up. He made a counter offer.

"Alright. I'll give you the fifty and pay for your meal. I think that's fair, don't you?"

"Okay," the man said, "I'll spare your ass. I'll get the bill from dinner."

The man walked over, spoke with the woman for a moment and walked back to Blake. Blake handed him the fifty and took the bill. There was one more thing the man handed Blake; a tampon.

"What the hell is this for?" Blake inquired.

The man howled a hearty laugh and gave Blake a clap on the shoulder. "It's for your pussy, dude. I've never in my life seen such a pussy."

Unhappy, but not willing to risk a fight, Blake smiled and walked toward the counter cash register. He handed the server the bill and a credit card.

"You're paying for his meal too?" The server asked.

"Uh, yeah. We spoke and he's a nice guy. I thought I'd help him and his girlfriend out a bit."

The server, chewing her day old stick of gum, leered at Blake with her head almost lying on her shoulder. "You aren't the first guy that he's done this to. Why do people let him bully like that?"

Blake wasn't interested in a conversation; he wanted to pay the bill and leave. "Here, let's get this evened up so I can move on."

"Suit yourself mister, but I wouldn't do it for that turd."

The bill paid, Blake quickly exited from the restaurant and made a b-line for his vehicle. He fetched a tube of super glue from the glove compartment and walked over to the man's rig. Apparently, he and his girl traveled together. Blake had seen them exit the semi together while he was eating. He walked to the passenger side of the cab, saw that the door was locked, and squirted more than a liberal amount in the lock. He went to the driver side and did the same thing. A squirt was also administered into the lock of the door for the sleeper right behind the cab. Blake went back to his vehicle and drove off, knowing that the bully and his girl were in for an unpleasant surprise when they returned to the rig,

"Now that," Blake reasoned, "was worth a fifty dollar bill and two meals."

Blake merged back onto the freeway and continued his drive to Seattle.

*

"Amy, I have a proposal for you."

Amy had heard it all before. Proposals had been a staple of her life. As a lawyer, she heard plea deal proposals, jail time proposals and prosecutors proposing this and that. When she went into architecture, a job she now began to hate, she heard building proposals, money proposals and contract proposals. If all that wasn't bad enough, she heard construction workers proposing marriage all the time. In the bars, it was proposals to sleep with her by men and women alike. Amy found proposals to be boring and mundane. She hoped this proposal would be different.

"Okay, Mr. Instructor; shoot. What do we have to lose?"

"I need your attention Amy, not a half-hearted glance into the make of the ceiling tiles over your head."

Amy shifted her focus back onto Claude and straightened her frown into a neutral glare.

"What I'm proposing Ms. Fraser, is that you work for me. I have a business that may be of deep interest to you."

"Work for you? I don't even know your..."

"Claude Ronet, the name is Claude Ronet. That's all you get. I don't share any other information. I suggest you keep that to yourself. I don't want anyone who's not invited knowing my business."

Claude Ronet was a former member of the Seattle Police Department, but he wasn't exactly a cop when he was there. Claude was a bounty hunter. He was now looking for a fresh face to join his personal crusade against crime. Having been a Navy Seal, he learned a great deal about defense and espionage.

Toughness and discipline were his middle name. Claude wanted someone like himself to help him out, as he was boring of the "seeking out and finding" part of the job. He wanted to sit back and let others do the dirty work.

He was a tall, handsome mid 50's man. His receding hairline was just a touch off his forehead and he wore a long ponytail down his back. It was wrapped with a series of rubber bands that kept it neat and thin. The tan he wore was dark and made his skin look like leather, but in an attractive way, according to the women. He was very distinguished but with a fierce and competitive edge like Amy, only much more controlled. Claude was also very quiet and revealed nothing about himself to anyone. Whenever he had a job to do, he did it without flash or pompousness. Go in, capture and retreat was his motto. The enemy rarely if ever saw Claude coming.

"Okay, Claude; what is it you want to "offer" me?"

"I worked for the Seattle police department Amy. My job was to track criminals and bring them to justice. I quit the force and now do the hunting only. If you take the job, you'll do the hunting for me. Your role is to take whatever name I give you, track down the perp and bring him or her to the cops. For that, I give you anywhere from a grand up, depending on the danger factor, ease in which you catch the culprit, and other intangibles. It will never be less than a grand, though. I pay well."

Amy was stunned. She had never thought in a million years that she would be considered for such work. She had more questions.

"So I bring in a perp, and you pay me an extraordinary amount of money? Is that right?"

"Yes. Mind you, it will never be easy work. You may have an easier time catching someone who doesn't use their smarts, but you will also run into some individuals who would rather die than be caught."

"What about a gun? What about a license? I can't just jump out there Death Wish style and start whipping some vigilante ass."

"Don't worry about that. It's all covered. You don't even have to go to training school like the one you would if you wanted to be a cop. Your training has been with me, and by the looks of Amos, you've passed."

Amy gave Claude a mild grin and found herself lifting her chin up in victory. She also thought to herself that this would be a good opportunity to make noise in a field she liked. A kind of hit woman in her eyes, but without the death, or so she hoped. After glaring at the dimmed lights in Claude's office for a few seconds, she accepted his proposal.

"I'll take the job, Claude. I want a contract, though. How do I know I can trust you?"

"No contracts and you'll have to trust me if you want the job. Oh, and no talking about our conversation. No sharing what we talked about in this room. If you do, I instantly fire you and send three Amos' to eliminate you from the scene. Get my drift, Amy?"

"What if I want to quit someday?"

"That's no problem. If you quit, we go our separate ways. However, if you as much as whisper to anyone, I'll find out and you'll pay a hefty price. I don't think that'll happen, though. I feel a strong disposition from you and a great sense of responsibility. I would never hire someone I didn't think could pull their weight. You're smart, perceptive and smooth. You also have a natural beauty that will leave men exposed and easier to snare."

Claude put his hand out before Amy. With only a hint of hesitation, she shook. He pulled open a locked drawer and gave Amy a gun, a badge and a five thousand dollar "signing bonus." She took all of these things and headed for the door.

"Amy, before you go out; take some gun lessons. I want you to make sure you can handle that thing perfectly. But if you get called before you have a chance; then, well, you're on your own."

Amy nodded, looked at the gun and glanced back at Claude. "Don't worry about me Claude. I know how to handle myself."

Claude smiled and said one more thing, to which Amy mildly shuttered.

"If you die Amy, that's your problem, not mine."

*

Leaving the restaurant, Blake wondered if he'd done the wrong thing by gluing the man's locks shut. In retrospect, he thought he should've handled it in a more mature way.

"How could I though," he wondered aloud. "I tried to be the better man, but that jerk wasn't going to listen. Oh well."

As much as Blake wanted to let it go, he couldn't. It crept into his minds vision repeatedly until he started to have nauseated feelings in his stomach. Soon the same old feelings that blocked his psychological path were back to their old tricks. It started with the stomach, and then worked its way into his chest; from there it went into his subconscious, where the negative thinking existed.

"I know these feelings. I've felt them before and I'm in control. Breathe in through the nose 2, 3, 4; and out through the mouth 2, 3, 4."

Blake's air was getting thinner and it was tougher to breathe. Despite what his doctors, Mother, Father and friends have said to him in the past, he couldn't let go of the fact that he may be dying. A wave of hot tingling blood started at his feet and washed over him quickly. He tightened his grip on the steering wheel and began praying for his God to free him from the illusion of nervousness and sure death. He thought about pulling off the road, and then changed his mind. He wanted a pill, but didn't take one. Too many thoughts raced and clanged through his mind. It was what Blake felt to be too much information overload for anybody to handle. His heart was racing at one hundred and fifty beats a minute. Not just beats, but thunderous slams against his inner chest wall.

"My heart might stop." He unrealistically reasoned. "What if it does? What if I die today? I'm scared."

Blake began to weep behind the wheel. Other vehicles passed by him and paid no attention. Nobody's focus was on Blake Thomas, but on the road ahead. His anxiety attack meant nothing to others who were consumed and tied up with their own lives and destinations. Soon, through the sheer power of prayer; at least that's what Blake thought; the symptoms began to wane. The breathing was the first bodily function to return. Next, his heart slowed its beats down to a tolerable rate. As fast as the attack had come on, it was leaving. He took a deep cleansing breath and enjoyed the feeling of peace and harmony. The hands that gripped the steering wheel with a piercing death grasp relaxed, and the attack was gone. He saw a rest stop and pulled in for a time-out.

      Blake grabbed of all things a cup of coffee. He knew he'd just been through a panic that rated nine out of ten on his scale, but still bought a caffeinated beverage to wash it down. As he perused the rest stop maps and signs, he found that he was only a couple hundred miles from his destination of Seattle, Washington. It struck him again that he was actually in the Pacific Northwest, some two thousand miles from his old stomping grounds. Suddenly, things were different. A new life, new friends, new everything. He had a lot of work to do when reaching Seattle, which he figured to do before nightfall. He wanted to find his new apartment and at least throw a few things inside to make it feel occupied. He'd then roam around the city, lest anxiety reared its head and put an end to the festivities. Now that he was over the latest attack, he thought clearer and with more sensibility, so he figured he'd probably be fine when the time came. After an hour of collecting himself, Blake felt good enough to continue his adventure.

Back on I-90 near Moses Lake, Blake was keeping to himself when the unthinkable happened.

"We'll roast the blighter's toes. We'll toast the bounder's nose. Just fetch that gate; we'll make it clear that monsters aren't welcome here!"

Shaun Webb

7

Smiling Like a Cheshire Cat

The power that Amy felt when handling her new weapon was addictive, giving her a sense of life feeding euphoria. She was supplied with an IPhone; only Claude knew the number; a placard with her picture and name, and two holsters for her gun; one for her ankle and one for her torso. Depending on the jobs she would be given, the choice of holster was up to her. Claude was adamant that Amy only carry when it was necessary.

That evening, Amy paced back and forth in her apartment, chomping at the bit for her first job. She constantly checked her beeper and fooled with her gun in case the time suddenly came for her to spring into action. She kept remembering the Sean Connery line from the movie "The Untouchables"; "Did you check the gun already? Well then leave it alone." It made her chuckle uncomfortably.

There were no calls or texts on that first evening, so she dissipated her energy by doing some yoga and taking a walk. The exercises were important for two reasons; one was to keep her disciplined and relaxed, while the most important aspect was warding off any mental illness that would attempt to creep back into her psyche. She had gone a very long time with no recurrence of the PTSD that had haunted her back in Flint, and she fully intended on keeping it that way. Her doctor had told her that exercise was important in keeping her mind straight. Amy was confident that she had beaten those demons down and wasn't interested in a recurrence.

One of her problem was loneliness. She wanted to snuggle up with a strong man and even make love if the energy was right. The sex with Hank was good, and she enjoyed a healthy carnal life, but with Hank gone, she was reserved to thinking about her version of the man she wanted. A strong, tough man was good for fantasies, but what she really longed for was a deep thinker with a soft heart. Amy had a soft interior, but on the outside, she could be sarcastic, hard-edged and somewhat degrading. As much as she never meant to present herself in that way, it was who she was. The hard-boiled Amy was healthy for her when it came to tracking down criminal runaways, as she could ignore the "kind and emotional" self in lieu of the tough "catch them and turn them in" ego. She had shown her hard-hitting side when battling with Amos at the Tae class, and she figured that was a part of the reason Claude had selected her as his "go to girl".

Despite all the emotional thinking and her new job, the fact remained that she was alone. Amy was a beautiful young woman with many good characteristics to offer the right man. She relaxed in the fact that when it was meant to be, it would happen. She didn't have any true "best girlfriend" in Seattle, and preferred it that way, especially after being given the responsibility she now owned. Amy didn't get along well with other women because they were more sensitive than most men. When she would kid around with other females, they always took it wrong and responded by freezing up. It made her feel bad as she was usually joking. Every now and then, however, Amy handed out a black eye or a bruised ego to whoever was brave enough to drive her one-step too far. One of her Architectural co-workers, who was pushing Amy hard on her break-up with Hank, ended up wearing a glass of Coca-Cola on her face. She should have considered herself lucky, as Amy's wrath could get quite nasty.

Amy showered, watched the TV for a while and went to bad, confident not only that the nerve-wracking first assignment would soon come, but that love wouldn't be far in the future.

*

Following his last rest stop, the remainder of Blake's trip to Seattle was supposed to be a nice smooth trek with little drama and hopefully no anxiety. That all ended when out of the corner of his eye, he saw the truck whose doors he'd super glued shut a few hours earlier. The driver apparently had to pry the doors open, as there was a large bent area and scratches exactly at lock level on the passenger side. He suddenly knew that his hour-long stop at the rest area was a very bad idea. It had given the trucker a chance to catch up to him west of Moses Lake, Washington. At first glance, the female passenger, whom Blake tipped his cap to during his meal, didn't notice him. He tried to keep his focus to the road directly in front of him while leaning ever so slightly to the right in hopes of being less noticeable. Blake wanted to slow his vehicle down, but he was trapped with a slower car in front of him and a faster car to his rear. The rate of speed in which he traveled kept him directly to the side of the trucker, thus mashing Blake's already frayed nerves into oblivion. Not being able to stand it any longer, he took one more glance up toward the truck. That turned out to be a mistake as looking back down at him with the evilest of eyes was none other than that girl. She recognized him right away, flipped him a bird, and lipped "fuck you" clearly enough that Blake could feel it sear onto the front of his head. He knew he could be in trouble, so he slowed the pace by ten MPH, trying to let the trucker get ahead of him. That strategy only alarmed the driver behind him, causing a blowing of his horn with steady, long streams of honks that felt like they would never end. This warned the trucker to what Blake was trying to accomplish, so he toned down on the throttle until they were again side-by-side. The fear and apprehension that Blake had just successfully fought off was returning, although now it was a reasonable fight or flight situation. In this case, his fear was genuine and warned him of danger, exactly what anxiety in a healthy individual was meant to do.

    Before he could react any further, he saw two more semis in his rear view mirror. He wasn't sure what was happening, but the first semi passed the mean trucker on the left and moved in front of the car that was in front of Blake's vehicle. The second semi moved closer to Blake's rear. It was obvious that he was being cornered. He figured the driver whose locks he'd glued shut had called his friends, and they came rushing to his aid. Blake's car, another vehicle, and three truckers all encompassed in one mass of dangerous metal moving at upward of seventy-five miles per hour. Blake thought, "This isn't good, this isn't good at all," as he gripped his wheel with granite hands.

    He didn't have a lot of time to think before he saw the woman hang partly out of the cab's window and point what appeared to be a rifle with a scoop directly his way. Blake froze with terror. His motor functions felt as if they were betraying him. He had to urinate, defecate and vomit all at once. After he'd gasped at the rifle-wielding woman, he threw the car to the right and on to the shoulder of the freeway, inches from the guardrail. He punched the gas pedal and caught up to the vehicle in front of him. This vehicle had a bumper sticker on the back with five stick figures next to a caption that read, "We're a family for God." This gave Blake confidence that they would call 911 upon his request. He moved closer to the smaller vehicle's passenger side window. When he looked in, he was greeted with not one or two, but *four* middle fingers directed toward him. "Some Christian family," he huffed as he desperately tried to get them to listen. He honked and flayed his arms, but it was of no use. To the family, he looked like some crazy driver who'd had a nip or two more than he should have at some small town bar and grill.

The only vehicle separating Blake from the woman's rifle then disappeared, squeezing by the semi in front of them. Now it was three semis and Blake along the guardrail moving at a solid seventy miles per hour. He was trapped, as the three drivers were now a team of utter terror. Whenever he tried to speed up, hoping to pass the front semi on the shoulder, that driver veered slightly right, threatening to force him over the rail and into a deep ravine. It was the same with the rig to his rear. Blake was surrounded. He couldn't speed up and he couldn't slow down. He couldn't go right, lest he end up ramming the guardrail; risking life and limb, and he couldn't stop. He hoped his death would be quick and that he wouldn't feel much pain. He glanced up and saw that the woman, now only feet from him, aiming the rifle his way. Blake focused his eyes front and center and heard the gun discharge.

*

The call finally came the next night at two thirty in the morning. Amy jumped out of bed with a youthful leap and fumbled the pager as she excitedly tried to see the message face. It was short and simple:
 "Lee Stevens, black male, 25 yrs. old, brown hair, very tall, 197 lbs., 26200 E. Yesler Way, bring to Seattle PD, wear placard, they'll be waiting."

Amy was so excited she almost whizzed in her pants. She found her placard and placed it around her neck. She put on the body holster and wore the gun by her left breast. She was right handed, so it'd be easy to reach in and grab the weapon at a moment's notice. She wore a lightweight raincoat, as it was pouring per usual. Her dark overcoat would help her stay hidden when searching out her prey. Out she went into the night. She jumped in her jeep, set the GPS, and found exactly where her enemy lived. She was on her way.

It was about a twenty-two minute ride from her apartment on First Avenue to the perp's pad. Amy was excited and nervous as she drove from the safety of her home to a seedier part of Seattle. She put on her radio to try to calm her nerves. Out of all the songs that could've been playing, Filter's "Nice Shot man" filled her ears.

Amy was rocking so hard she shook the jeep as she drove. The fire flowing through her veins was intoxicating as she inched closer to the suspect's home. She saw that she was within three minutes of the location so she turned the music down a few notches.

She wasn't sure why, besides jumping bail, he was being pursued. It wasn't a question for Amy to ask or answer; she was given a task and completing it successfully was her focus. Whatever this guy did was his problem. Her problem was capturing, subduing and delivering her prey. She had to take on a sort of "cop's attitude."

Amy had a plan and put it to use. She parked one block short of the location and walked through the pouring rain until she reached the apartment's entrance. She read the address on the buzzer, and figured the name on it either wasn't real, or belonged to an acquaintance of the suspect. No longer caring about the small details, she pushed the button. After thirty seconds, when she was about to push it again, a male voice announced "What da fuck you want? Who is dis?"

"Lee Stevens?" Amy asked.

"I don't know no Stevens. Get da fuck on."

"My name's Amy, I'm with Seattle PD, and I'm here to take Stevens with me. You can come down and go quietly, or you can wait for me to come up."

There was no further correspondence, so Amy discerned exactly what her prey was doing. She quickly circled around the building to the fire escape and waited in the shadows. Just as she had so smartly assumed, someone opened a window on the second floor and ducked out onto the ladder. It was probably Stevens. He climbed down to the last flight and pushed the sliding ladder out, confident in his escape. When he leapt off the ladder onto the pavement, he turned around and met Amy's gun; it was two inches from his face.

"Oh. Bitch got her gun, huh? You best get dat shit outta my face."

Amy snickered and kept her poise.

"Yeah, that's right. This bitch got her gun, and this bitch is taking you in. If you'd like, we can go easy. If not, we'll go hard and you won't like my shitty methods."

Stevens, a six foot eight inch black male, only exhaled a small burst of wind and stood his ground.

"I tell you what bitch; you take dat pretty face home before I fuck it up. After I beat you ass, I'm gonna stick you, but not wit a knife. Get what I mean...BE-ATCH?" Stevens was pointing at the side of Amy's face with his head tilted left. He was making his best attempt to be menacing. "Bitch, what are you, fifteen years-old? You ass need to be in the bed."

Amy calmly pointed the gun at Steven's toes and fired. She hit him right behind the big toe on the boniest part of his foot. Steven's crumpled in a heap before her, and in obviously excruciating pain. He looked up at Amy with a contemptuous glare.

"Bitch, you shot my foot! What da fuck wrong wit you? You a fucked up bitch!"

"Please stop calling me a bitch, Mr. Stevens. Ma'am will do fine, or perhaps you'd like a bullet on the other foot. It's really not a problem."

Amy circled behind the stricken man and pulled a large zip tie out of her pocket. She began to pull his hands behind his back when Stevens showed one more hint of resistance. He tried to grab her arm when she was zipping him, so she pulled out her handy sap and it was lights out for Mr. Stevens.

Now that she had zipped Steven's hands behind him securely, out came the smelling salts; another of Amy's supplies she had stashed in her coat. A few waves around the nose and he was awake enough to rise. Amy led him to her jeep, managed him into the backseat and cuffed his hands to the roll bar separating the front from the back. The trip to the Seattle PD took five minutes. A right on 12th Avenue, then straight up to E. Pine. She arrived, led the large black male inside, stopped at the front desk and made her announcement.

"Lee Stevens, 26200 E. Yesler Avenue. Delivery complete. Do I need to sign anywhere?"

The cops looked at Amy with wonderment. One cop had to open his mouth.

"*You* corralled that punk?"

Amy responded with a tilt of her head and a hint of surprise in her face. She looked over her shoulder.

"Do you see anyone else who brought this man in?" Everyone looked at the cop, who had no answer. She spoke again. "Now, as I was saying, where do I sign?"

The desk cop handed Amy a clipboard that she signed and handed back. A cop came from around the desk to take custody.

"Hey. What happened to his foot? He's bleeding all over my fuckin' floor."

"I did what I had to do, officer. My task is done here."

Amy headed toward the door and exited into the deep, wet Seattle night. Stevens looked at the cop who had him by the arm. The very large and obviously in pain black man had but one comment.

"Don't go fuckin' wit dat one. She a crasy bitch."

The cop led him away.

Upon arriving back at her apartment, Amy undressed and was sliding back into bed when she spotted an envelope with her name on it sitting on her pillow. She opened it and saw twenty crisp one hundred dollar bills inside with a note that read

"Nice work, I knew you had it in you."

No signature was present.

A Killer for the Queen

*

Blake gave himself into the fact that his life would end. The woman was pointing the rifle at him while he drove on the shoulder of I-90, pinned in by two other semis. He pouted and began chanting the Lord's Prayer: *"Our Father, who art in heaven, hallowed be thy name."*

The rifle loudly discharged and Blake saw the bright flash before his eyes. He thought to himself how colorful and painless death was, and relaxed in the fact that he would be free of any further anxiety attacks. He looked for the light, but all he found was a blob of red, green and blue paint on his clothes, face and dashboard.

"What the fuck?" was all he could muster.

It quickly became clear; the woman's rifle was nothing more than a paintball gun and Blake was the recipient of a rather nasty joke. He looked up and saw the woman roaring with laughter. She looked down at Blake and lipped **"DI-RECT HIT"** slowly enough so that he would have no trouble understanding exactly what she was conveying. He wiped the paint from his face and looked at her again; this time she yelled out **"NOW WE'RE EVEN!"** Blake heard her loud and clear.

The trucks in front and behind shifted back into the far lanes and the semi that the woman occupied went ahead of Blake and magically mixed itself into the traffic. Blake was now free of the barrage. A long deep cleansing breath washed over him as he stopped on the shoulder to clean himself up. He fished through the glove box until he found his tranquilizers and took one. He wanted to head off any further panic before it hit. Blake shut his eyes, took more cleansing breaths and waited for traffic to calm so he could safely pull back onto the expressway. Unfortunately, the adventure wasn't completely over yet.

The siren and lights behind him were unmistakable: **WHIRRRR.** Blake looked in his rearview and sure enough, a State trooper had pulled up behind him on the shoulder.

"Oh, that's just fucking great." He lamented. "What now?"

After pulling behind Blake's vehicle and waiting for twenty minutes, the Trooper emerged from his cruiser. It was obvious to Blake that the cop had run his plates to see if any warrants existed. As far as he knew, there were none, but with the way the day had played out thus far, he wouldn't be surprised by anything. He was toweling off his face when the trooper approached.

"What the hell happened here? Why are you covered with paint?" The cop asked.

Blake mulled over his answer and then spoke, "I was paint balled by a broad in a semi. They pinned me in and nailed me. I thought I was going to die."

The Trooper smiled. "Did you get the plate number?"

Blake handed him a slip of tattered paper with the information the Trooper was seeking. After looking up I-90 to the west, and then back to the east, the trooper further quizzed the obviously exhausted Blake.

"What did you do to piss those people off?"
"What do you mean? Who? Piss who off?"

"The trucker. I know who he is and you must've ticked him off to get a reward like your wearing right now."

Blake explained the confrontation at the diner. The only thing he omitted was the fact that he'd glued their doors shut. It was a part of the story Blake thought better to be excluded.

"Well kid," the Trooper said, "I see you have Ohio plates. That's a part of the reason they got you. This happens all the time. Are you alright?"

"Yeah, I think so. Are you going to arrest them?"

"Nah. They're harmless. In fact, I think it's somewhat good that they keep outsiders on their toes. It isn't upright if out-of-towners come here and act as if they own the road. No big deal."

Blake sighed as he listened to the Trooper's story. He asked if he could be on his way.

"Where are you headed?" the Trooper inquired.

"Seattle. I'm moving there. I found a job at the docks and I'm starting new."

The Trooper grinned and asked Blake to hold on a second. He took his license and registration to the cruiser. Another twenty minutes went by and the Trooper returned. He handed Blake his stuff plus a ticket for sitting on the shoulder.

"I'm getting a ticket? I had to wipe the paint off my face. Why are you ticketing me?"

"Well, kid; it's illegal to stand on the shoulder of a busy highway, and you're lucky you didn't cause an accident."

·

Blake looked up and down I-90, and it was virtually empty. Not wanting to push his luck, he simply took the ticket and kept his mouth shut.

"Welcome to the state of Washington, kid. I hope your stay is charmed."

Blake gave the Trooper a half-hearted smile and carefully pulled back onto 90.

*

Three hours later, Blake could see the skyline of Seattle. He thought it to be beautiful. He passed Eastgate, drove over the bridge to Mercer Island, drove over yet another bridge and finally reached the downtown area. Seattle's horizon was spectacular. It reminded him nothing of the industrial nature of Toledo. Seattle seemed cleaner and was definitely much bigger.

The only thing left to do was find his new rental on 10th Avenue and East Boston. He knew it was on the north side of town, not far from his new job at the docks located on Fairview Avenue. The Northwest Seaport was his employer. He found his digs quickly. It was then he decided that a trip through the city would have to wait a few hours.

Exhausted from his long drive, plus being perplexed by his ticket and adventure with the trucker, Blake grabbed only a handful of items good for sleeping. A pillow, blanket and comforter were tossed onto the floor of what was Blake's new bedroom and he collapsed on them in a heap. Within thirty seconds, Blake was asleep, dried paint still on his skin, in his hair, and on his clothes. It was a rest he badly needed as the start of his new life, and new adventures, loomed before him.

Shaun Webb

"When clouds go rolling by, they roll away and leave the sky. Where is the land beyond the eye that people cannot see? Where can it be?"

Shaun Webb

8

Sandy's Wonderland

Iris Arnold was the kind of Mother you would read about in the novel Carrie, or Mommy Dearest. She was a staunch Christian conservative with a cold-blooded and perpetually etched frown drawn on her older than her fifty years face. Her hair was kept in a bun and her cheeks angled down into a tiny chin with seemingly no lips on her upper or lower mouth. Her eyes blazed with anger and her hands were rough from years of hard work. Ed Arnold, who had the good sense to die after only fifteen years of marriage to this woman, was a meek man with a quiet disposition plus a love for alcohol. Iris rolled over him like a tractor, sucking his life away.

Sandy was fourteen when her Father died of an alcohol-induced heart attack. She thought him to be asleep and at ease when she found him in the chair. Luckily, she wasn't emotionally close enough to the man to feel the complete effect of his death. Iris, always a dirty spoon in a clean pot of stew, took advantage of his death to make her daughter's life even more miserable. Sandy's father hadn't shielded his daughter as well as he could have, even though he had tried. Now that he was gone, Iris would do things her way, completely.

She bible belted Sandy to near insanity. It was the Baptist Church twice on Sunday and once on Wednesday night. There were countless hours of prayer sessions at home followed by witnessing from house to house year round.

"It's up to us to witness for our Lord Jesus Christ. We'll get the attention of the world. The end times are coming and Jesus shall return, **HALLELUIA!**"

Sandy dealt with it for a few years until she was old enough to understand that her mother was a religious zealot. She was about twelve or thirteen when that happened. Their relationship of Mom and Daughter turned sour and became more ruler and slave. Sandy did all the housework while Iris read the bible aloud and followed her. No matter what Sandy did, whether it be watching TV (which was rare), using the toilet or even showering, Iris was right there reading aloud from the good book.

"THOU SHALT NOT COVET THY NEIGHBOR!"
"THOU SHALT NOT LIE!"
"THOU SHALT NOT KILL!"

Sandy tired of those antics by the age of sixteen. That was when she met the most handsome boy on the block, Blake Thomas. She fell for him right away. She wrote letters that she never gave him and made red hearts on her notebooks and school backpack in honor of her new love interest. She smiled, sang and thought about him all the time. Of course, she kept it from Mother, in fear she would have a religious freak out; worse than her daily tirades. By the age of fifteen, she was running with Andrea. Andrea hated Sandy's mom and told her so in no uncertain terms. Andrea was the outgoing and rowdy personality that Sandy wished she herself was, but couldn't get a grasp on.

"You shouldn't hang with her." Iris would tell her daughter. "She will lead you straight to Hell and an eternity of fire."

"Relax Mom. We're just kids. It's no big deal."

Iris had a habit of sitting nervously across from her daughter in the living area or at the dining room table and wringing her hands on an old piece of handkerchief while she spoke. The tension in the air was thicker than molasses. Few words were shared between the two, less the religious chanting, with Sandy usually retiring to her bedroom to avoid the angst. Iris would often sit in a chair outside her room and sing out of the book of psalms. She made sure it was loud enough for Sandy to hear. This wore on the nerves of the graduating senior. She was figuring out that her mom was crazed and strange.

The straw that broke the camel's *(Sandy's)* back came on a Sunday morning when they were getting ready for another three and a half hour church marathon. Sandy stood completely naked in her room, dressing for the day. Iris bolted through the door and grabbed Sandy by the arms, forcing her to the bed. Naked and feeling extremely uncomfortable and exposed, Sandy yelled for her mom to get out and leave her be.

"GOD HAS TOLD ME TO CHECK YOUR PHYLEM. IF IT IS BROKEN, WE MUST ASK FORGIVENESS. PRAISE JESUS!"

Iris inserted two fingers into Sandy's vaginal opening and it hurt her terribly. This was the day Sandy lost her natural virginity; by her mother's crazed logic. Of course, Sandy began to bleed as her mom had broken the natural membrane that divided an adolescent from an adult.

"YOU ARE A WHORE AND A LIAR SANDY. WE MUST PRAY FOR YOUR FORGIVNESS." YOU HAVE COMMITTED ONE OF THE DEADLY SINS SANDY. YOU MUST ASK FORGIVENESS AND MEAN IT!

Looking into her mom's eyes was like watching embers in a pit of fire, hot and flaming. Sandy reared up and clocked her mom as hard as she could with her right fist. The blow caused Iris to fall backward into her daughter's closet, and moreover, changed the dynamic between them forever. Sandy stood her ground and her mom backed off.

"I WAS A VIRGIN, MOM! YOU BROKE MY INSIDES. I HATE YOU!"

Calmly, Iris explained herself again.

"I pray for you Sandy. May the Lord Jesus Christ forgive you."

Sandy doubled up her fist again.

"GET OUT OF MY ROOM NOW!"

From that day forward, whenever Iris stepped within five feet of her daughter, Sandy would rear her fist and make her shudder. That was a tough thing for a meek girl to do. With the help of her best friend, it became easier and easier to intimidate her mother.

Andrea Jimenez began hanging out at Sandy's house more often and between them kept Iris at bay. The mental damage, however, had been done. Sandy now had to deal with a friend that drank excessively and had the propensity for drugs and sex, a powerfully dangerous combination. Sandy so loved Andrea that she overlooked most of the improprieties and came to adore her. They were truly the best of friends.

The issue became Sandy's obsession for Blake. She couldn't stop thinking about him no matter what she did. At the age of eighteen, she learned about masturbation. Up to that point, she would tremble when the thought of touching herself entered her mind. After meeting, befriending, and falling for Blake, it became a three-times-a-day habit. She couldn't get enough of the man. Her fantasies always revolved around him, and she would stop if an "impure" thought of someone, or something else entered her mind. She never thought about Blake naked per say, it was always about him making love to her in a dark room only slightly lit with a burning candle. It reached a point where Sandy was so sore from diddling that she sometimes couldn't walk right.

"You need to give that girl a break." Andrea would say with a slight chuckle.

Sandy would redden with blush and embarrassment, but Andrea always calmed her.

"Don't worry about it. Anytime I have a chance, my hands are in my pants. So what? Everyone does it."

The embarrassment always turned to laughter between the two and Sandy continued drifting away from her mom and closer to her friend. Although

Andrea was the free spirit to Sandy's shy nature, the gap closed rapidly. However, had it gotten too close, it would easily have ruined their chemistry.

On more than one occasion, a drunken Andrea tried to put the make on Sandy. It never went past a bit of breast petting because Sandy always put the brakes on. It wasn't that Sandy didn't have some interest. She felt that it was wrong for her to think and feel that way. She didn't consider herself a lesbian, although she found Andrea attractive; but in a friendly, womanly way. Sandy's focus was to save herself, or what was left of herself, for the wonderful Blake. Little did she know that his interest was fleeting. It wasn't until the day trip to Cleveland that Sandy thought they might have sex. Blake's panic attack ruined that day, but not Sandy's hopes. What she didn't know was that Blake changed his mind about her and decided not to ruin their friendship. She didn't know he felt that way, and it was questionable whether she would have listened had he told her. The lack of communication was glaringly obvious.

*

She longed for Blake. She felt that she was "in love" with him. The pain of desire ached in her mind and in her heart. During her wonderful dreams, she had made love to him repeatedly, their coupling only interrupted by the misfortune of an errant alarm clock or a peek of sun through a drawn sash.

Pictures of Blake adorned Sandy's room. She also had a photo album filled with "her" man from his youth through to his late teens and early twenties. She had her favorites, like the time she fell off her bike and

Blake carried her home after tending to her scratched up knees. In addition, there was the funny and wonderful picture of Blake when he'd lost his shorts at the beach and had to make his way to his car with a washcloth serving as a towel. She loved the way his cute muscular butt looked as he dashed in front of close to a hundred roaring beach-goers. These memories would last a lifetime for her. Sandy was in her early twenties, but her love for Blake stretched across time and space. The deep, lovelorn sighs Sandy took were both refreshing and painful. She talked to her best friend about these feelings.

    Andrea had broken up with Greg when Blake had his "spell" on their trip and was now a single woman. Greg called her once or twice, but she refused to speak with him. As far as she was concerned, that book was closed. She was thoroughly disgusted with his selfishness and disregard for other people, especially friends. She decided that taking Sandy under her wing was the best move she could make. Andrea thought that Blake liked Sandy too; but couldn't admit it in fear of ruining the friendship they had established. She also feared that Sandy would find out about the "secret" her and Blake shared, even though they no longer carried on. The two had met up for unattached sex on more than a few occasions. It was purely experimental. Andrea thought it would break her friend's heart beyond repair. She never spoke of it and knew Blake wouldn't either, so she urged Sandy to go with her gut. If Blake was the man she wanted, she had to try one more time before it was too late.

"I think we should pack up and find Blake in Seattle." Andrea urged. "That way you can either win him by showing how far you'd go to look for him, or you could find out for good if it's a no go."

Sandy was excited and skeptical. She knew she had to try, but she could always opt to mail him or drop a line from time to time. She also feared being told "no". That scared her more than anything else did.

"That would be the easy way girl. But if you really want that man as much as you say you do, then Seattle is where you find him and express that love."

"I don't know Andrea. What if he found someone? What if he rejects me on the spot? I love him, but I don't want to drive him away."

"Listen to me Sandy; He's already two thousand miles down the road and if he rejects you, then it's his loss. I don't think he will. If he does, we come back here and move on. I'll help you. I think he loves you, but you'll have to dig for it. The best things in life are the hardest things to achieve. If you let your dream die, then you'll never get another shot at it."

Sandy nodded to Andrea and told her she'd mull it over, but that she needed sleep now. Andrea agreed, peeled off her jeans and hopped in the bed.

"What are you doing, Andrea?" Sandy inquired with a raised eyebrow.

"You said you needed sleep. Well, you're not the only one. C'mon."

Both women laughed and Andrea snuggled in the bed next to Sandy, but stayed far enough away from her so that if Sandy's nosy younger brother, or worse, her mother, plowed through the door, there would be no mistake that the two were simply sleeping.

*

Andrea was a study in contrast. One minute the girl would be the best friend someone could have, but depending on the type of drugs she consumed, that could change fast.

A drunken Father and a Mother who spent more time working and running around at night than spending time with the family raised her. She was essentially on her own from the tender age of twelve. She took up smoking, hung with the "tough" girls and dressed as if she was inviting men to charm her. Midriff exposing shirts, see through tops when wearing no bra and no panties under extremely short skirts. This was the norm for the attention-starved girl. She loved the responsiveness it garnered, so she figured it was worth the effort. Andrea lost her virginity at fourteen and started using heroin at the age of fifteen. She kept some control of the habit, though, so she could function at jobs or school. The practice was closeted, as she worried about the effect it would have on her relationships. Sandy suspected something was going on, as Andrea's eyes were sagging a bit and she wasn't eating well, but could never prove it. Had Andrea not hung with Sandy, Blake and the others, she would've probably been six feet under by the age of seventeen. There were no track marks because she shot through her toes and inner legs.

Another slight problem was that Andrea, a bi-sexual, felt a sexual energy with Sandy. The difficulty being that Sandy was so wound up with Blake, getting her in bed was next to impossible. She did the best she could to entice Sandy, but it was a fruitless endeavor. She always changed clothes in front of Sandy so she could show off naked. When they slept, she often shifted a sheet or blanket to expose Sandy's body. On a few occasions, she acted as if she was sleeping and cupped her breast or lightly kissed an exposed nipple. If Sandy awoke, Andrea played dumb.

"Did you just touch me Andrea?"

The response was a silent one. Andrea pretended to be asleep. Embarrassed that she may have been touching herself in her sleep, Sandy wouldn't bring the subject up the next day.

Andrea, the troubled child, turned into Andrea the troubled young adult, but she had a real friend in Sandy that she counted on. In a truer sense, she was looking for love that she'd missed as a younger woman. The mixing of emotions, or mistaking sex for love, was a thorn that Andrea would have to extract from her psyche by herself.

Despite all of her problems, Andrea was in the process of talking Sandy into an adventure that neither of them would ever forget. The idea had disaster written all over it; but to learn, Andrea figured, one must experience life.

*

Having finished his business in Vegas, Kurt packed up the few things he used at the hotel and headed for Portland, Oregon; the new home of Soo-Chin Xing. Soo-Chin was to be next in the line of perpetrators in the "turning their back on Kyle" vengeance tour. Kathy paid for her sins against Kurt, and his Queen, with her head. It was not only for leaving Kurt high and dry, but also for losing the only son they had to the Flint killer. While Kurt had certainly felt bad about his son's death, he now questioned to himself if the boy was actually his in the first place. To Kurt, it was probably as likely that some town stud inseminated Kathy, as it was that he was responsible.

"That k-kid didn't even l-l-look like m-me." Kurt would mull. "I'll b-bet that fucking Kathy w-was screwing s-someone else. That's exactly w-what happened. **D-DO YOU HEAR ME B-BACK THERE KATHY? WE'RE YOU S-SCREWING SOMEONE ELSE OR W-WHAT?**"

No reply. Besides Kathy's lifeless head, the back of the van was empty except for Kurt's supplies of machetes, knives and rope. He also carried red spray paint and a large vase filled with white roses. All the things he needed for his extravagant displays of terror.

Kurt decided to take back roads from Las Vegas to Portland so he could stay under the radar after the incident in Vegas. US-93 would take him almost all the way up to Twin Falls, Idaho, where he could catch I-84 for the rest of the jaunt to Portland. In about twenty hours or so, he would pull into that city and seek out the Chinese-American. When he found her, it would be curtains. At least that's what Kurt hoped. So far, his plan had gone perfectly. He was obsessed with not only revenge, but also satisfying his bloodthirsty Queen, and wouldn't stop until his tasks were completed.

He put in a Jefferson Airplane CD to relax and loosen him up a bit. The song was "Go Ask Alice" or "White rabbit", whichever the listener preferred. He pulled out a joint and lit it. The weed tasted good and he felt an incredible surge of peace come over him.

The song caused Kurt to start asking questions in his head.

"Was A-Alice using d-drugs? The caterpillar; w-was he smoking p-pot? W-Wa-What about the chess pieces, r-rabbit, and the white knight? What d-do they all have in c-common?"

The questions interested Kurt in a most peculiar way. He wanted to know what the logic was, and why it was written. Although there was no sensible answer for it, just like there's no sensible answer for Abbott and Costello's 'who's on first' routine, he still wanted to know why. It was an obsession gone out of control as the fable was being computed in his brain as a true story. Kurt looked to the rear of his box van again.

"W-WHAT'S YOUR T-TAKE, KATHY?" When she didn't answer, he spoke again. **"I C-CAN'T HEAR YOU D-DEAR. YOU'LL N-NEED TO SPEAK UP!"**

Kurt chuckled and turned his attention back to the highway in front of him. He still had a ton of miles to chew up, so he entertained himself with the questions and logistics of the story while he drove. There was one particular part of the song that Kurt loved; the Red Queen's 'off with her head.' It was the center of his goals; the Red Queen ordering the collection of heads, while the head being chopped off would signify the culmination of Kurt's efforts along with the sacrifice for his wonderful, beautiful Queen.

"Off with their h-heads. Off with their p-p-piece of sh-shit heads. Why have they d-done what they've d-d-done? Why did they t-turn their backs on a k-k-kid that needed help? Why was it all waa-women? Those irrational, a-a-arrogant, self-centered, e-egotistical bitches. I'll g-get them all. I'll take every m-motherfucking head for my Queen."

Kurt clicked his CD to repeat. For ten straight hours, he listened to that same song repeatedly. Each time the song finished, he asked himself the same questions. Each time, he came to the same conclusion; that the women were responsible. Kurt knew he was a sexist pig. He didn't care as long as he could collect the heads that he was seeking.

He reached Nampa, Idaho, just west of Boise, when he decided it was time to stop for the night. The next day he would finish the trek to Portland and find Ms. Xing. The evening wouldn't be as restful as he'd hoped.

*

Early morning came, and Sandy woke up refreshed and ready to track down her man. The life she so longed for waited some two thousand miles down the road. Upon going over the trip details with Andrea, they opted to take a train to Seattle, and then rent a car in their search for Blake. Andrea's car was up on miles and down on reliability, flying would cost the two far too much money, so a train was the only feasible option. They both figured it'd be fun, because neither had taken a real train to anywhere.

Sandy packed up a nap sack full of toiletries plus a bag for her clothes. She was showered, dressed and excited as she woke up her friend. Andrea was slightly taken aback by Sandy's enthusiasm; but figured that when a girl wanted her man, there would be nothing no stopping her. Even if she failed, Andrea figured, it'd be a fun vacation to the part of the country unknown to either of them. She also reasoned that she could easily calm a traumatized Sandy if not everything worked out as planned. Andrea honestly thought Sandy's chances at success to be marginal at best, but a trip west might be good for both of them.

"Come on Andrea; get your ass out of bed."

As Sandy ripped the blankets from her friend, she saw that she was buck-naked.

"Oh my God Andrea. You slept next to me naked again. Oh my God, can you cover up?" She tossed the sheet back onto Andrea's body. "Good grief, I've seen you naked more times than I care to count."

Andrea, completely unfazed by Sandy's rants, rose, stretched and walked to the bathroom uncovered. When she opened the door, Sandy's sixteen year-old brother, brushing his teeth over the sink, went into a gaping smile.

"**WOW!**" Was all he could muster.

"Great." Andrea mused in aggravation. She shut the door, walked over to Sandy, grabbed the blanket and wrapped it around herself. She walked back to the bathroom, opened the door to find Sandy's brother madly typing into his cell phone. She grabbed the phone and tossed it in the toilet.

"**HEY! YOU'RE PAYING FOR THAT.**"

Andrea looked at the boy, doubled up a fist and ordered, "Get out of this bathroom you little fungus before I beat your scrawny ass."

Sandy's brother, eyes wider than when he saw Andrea nude, scattered quickly, yelling, "I'm telling Mom." Andrea yawned, dropped the blanket in full view of Sandy and asked one simple question; "Well, do you have a toothbrush or what?"

Andrea Jimenez was not a morning person, and was touchy in her sleepiness. Sandy made a mental note to remember that at all times.

*

Off with her head II (An unplanned collection)

*

Stopping was the best choice for Kurt. He was exhausted and badly needed a break. He found a motel off the highway and pulled in for the night. Kurt would sleep in his van at a rest stop or the side of the road, but that would draw attention, so he smartly opted for the seclusion of an out-of-the-way lodge that had few customers.

He rang the bell three times before a beer gutted old man and heavyset woman came out from behind a curtain to greet him. They were sloppy and presumably married. Kurt thought them to be husband and wife, as couples who stayed together into old age began to resemble each other.

The man was very nice to Kurt. "What can I do for you sir?"

As Kurt was about to answer, the wife, curlers in her hair and a menopausal mustache gracing her upper lip, piped in. "What kind of stupid ass question is that Henry? For Christ sake, what do you think he needs help with? He needs a room you idiot."

"It's okay m-m-ma'am. I j-just need a r-room for one night. Henry w-was doing fine."

The woman gave Kurt a scowled look and had to ask him, "What's-a-matter, cat got your tongue?"

"ELLIE!" Henry quickly responded, "You don't ask people about that stuff." He then whispered to her, "He has a tiny stutter." Henry looked back at Kurt, "I apologize for my wife's obvious ill-mannered approach."

Kurt smiled at Henry, and then looked daggers at Ellie. "That's alright H-Henry. Sh-she doesn't understand w-what a stutter is about or w-w-why people have them. She n-needs an education."

Kurt slowly and slyly smiled at what he considered an old hag. She obviously had no idea the extent of Kurt's danger. Without thinking a second thought, the woman, who couldn't help but take offense to Kurt, continued with her ignorant comments.

"Who are you to tell me I don't understand how life works, mister?"

"ELLIE!" Henry again scolded. "Stop losing your head!"

Kurt chuckled at that remark and added, "Oh she's l-losing her h-head alright. Thank you f-for your hospitality Henry."

The woman grunted and then waddled back to her area behind the curtain.

Kurt handed Henry fifty dollars and Henry handed back a key. "Number 18, mister, its lower level. Have a good rest."

"C-count on it." Kurt happily responded.

Kurt gathered his backpack and made his way to number 18, stopping at the van along the way to gather one additional piece of luggage; his machete.

As Kurt lay in the bed mulling over his trip to Portland while running a finger along the cold steel of the blade, he decided he needed to make a delivery to the front desk. He glanced out the window and saw that Henry had driven down the road, so the time was right to pay the old bat a visit.

The bell rang at the desk. Ellie came out of her den behind the curtain and saw no one. What she did see were a dozen red roses lying on the desk before her. She was thrilled and excited to get such a beautiful gift from her Henry. Having forgotten about the exchange with Kurt, she picked up the roses to move them to a vase in her room when she saw what looked like red paint puddled on the counter. Inquisitively, she put a finger in the pool and sniffed. She was convinced that it was paint. She rubbed her finger and thumb on one of the petals, and learned that the roses were white with a coat of red paint on them. Aggravated, she cursed about Henry being cheap and unromantic. Then she heard it.

"You go through life and never know the day when fate may bring a situation that may prove to be embarrassing. Your face gets red; you hide your head,

and wish that you could cry. But that's old fashioned. Here's a new thing you should really try."

It sounded to Ellie as if the tune was coming from her room only a few yards away. She felt a twinge of angst creep its way up her arms and stomach as she slowly walked toward the curtain. When she gained enough courage, she flung the drape to the side. She saw a CD player sitting on the nightstand. It was playing the tune "How D'ye Do and Shake Hands" from of all silly things, Alice in Wonderland. Ellie cringed as she gave credit for this prank to Henry. She shook her head and turned back toward the curtain to retrieve the fake roses. What she saw was terrorizing and horrific; for standing with a top hat on his head, a gleam in his eye and a machete in his hand was the man she had waited on only an hour or so ago. He wore black and had smooth dark hair that fell near his eyes. She put her hand to her mouth and shaded to a pale green color. Kurt spoke.

"Don't you know how to greet someone in a respectful manner, woman?"

"Well, I...I... uhh. Who are you?"

"Why I'm the Mad Hatter, dear. I've been given the order by the Red Queen herself."

"What order?" Ellie asked. "And where's that stutter you had earlier?"

Kurt answered her quickly.

"I don't know anything about a stutter, but I do have bad news for you. For the crime of ill manners, it has been decided that you shall be executed. **OFF WITH YOUR HEAD!**"

Kurt swung the machete with the precision of an experienced executioner. Ellie's head severed cleanly and went straight up, spinning in a tight circle, much like a perfect spiral of a football. Before the head could reach the floor, Kurt reached out and grabbed it by the hair. He looked into her dead eyes.

"You weren't on my list dear, but shit happens, doesn't it?"

A blowtorch protruded from Kurt's back pocket. He grabbed it, spun it in his hand like a pistol-toting sheriff, lit it and cauterized the bottom of her neck, quickly stopping the bleeding from her brain. The body lay crumpled next to the bed. He picked up the remains, tied a rope to each wrist and hung the body from the ceiling. Kurt then took a can of red spray paint and formed a large "Q" on her chest. He then put an "X" across the "Q", thus eliminating the Queenliness of his subject.

"Not only weren't you planned dear, you're certainly no Queen."

After completing his tasks, Kurt went to his van, opened the cabinet he'd built inside it and exposed the vats of formaldehyde that were lined along the upper shelf. Six vats sat neatly next to each other with one already containing Kathy Joseph's head. Kurt opened the second vat, placed the head of Ellie in it and then twisted the lid tightly shut. Next, he took a Polaroid picture of Ellie's headless body and hung it on a hook under her head. The last thing he did was to take a Queen of Hearts card, mark an "X" through it and hang it on the bottom hook. Kathy's hook contained a Queen of Hearts with no cross through it, as she had been a planned beheading. He still had several vats above him with two heads left to collect. Soo-Chin Xing would now take vat number three instead of two. Kurt didn't care. Neither did his Queen.

Henry returned from his beer run, which took a good amount of time with the nearest store being twenty miles away. When he pulled up, he noticed that the brown box van was gone.

"Must've gone on a beer run himself. I probably should've asked him if he needed anything. Oh well."

Henry shrugged and entered the office. He heard the TV running loud in their room; commonplace for his half-deaf wife. He yelled for her to turn it down. No response. He yelled again, this time stepping closer. Again, no response. Aggravated, he slung the curtain aside and began to scream his third request when he saw his wife hanging from the ceiling.

"Well Goddamn", he uttered, "That man killed that mouthy bitch."

Henry's look of surprise turned into a tiny crease of a smile, and then a wide grin.

"Well ding fucking dong", he bellowed, "The witch is finally dead."

Henry picked up the phone and called 911. He didn't want to touch anything so he himself wouldn't be suspected. He knew that fellow who had come in earlier did it. He also noticed a bouquet of roses on the floor, apparently smeared with red paint.

"Well, I'll be jiggered. That guy romanced her, and then cut her damn head off."

"911, what's your emergency?"

"Well, there really isn't an emergency anymore because someone already killed my wife."

"Sir? Did you say someone killed your wife?"

"Yeah, someone came in and chopped my wife's head clean off her shoulders. As far as I can tell, he took the head with him too because I don't see it lying around nowhere."

"Are you certain that she's dead?"

Perplexed, Henry told the operator to hold on and put the phone to the side. He walked over to his headless wife and asked one simple question.

"Hey Ellie. Are you dead?"

He picked the phone back up and spoke to a 911 operator who was now sensing the sarcasm.

"Yeah. She's dead. Now can you get someone over here?"

"We'll get an ambulance there right away, sir."

"You don't need an ambulance, you need a hearse."

"Are you okay sir? Do you need an ambulance?"

"Hell no, but if you could send some chip dip that would be great. I forgot it at the store."

"Sir?"

*

NAMPA, Idaho (AP) -- A woman has been found beheaded in a hotel room in Nampa, a senior police official said Friday. The body was accounted for, but the woman's head remains missing.

Shaun Webb

"The woman, in her 70s, was running the motel with her 65-year-old husband in the town of Nampa. The husband discovered her body in the main room belonging to them Friday evening. The dead wife and her now widower husband are from Pennsylvania and moved to Nampa on Aug. 11," the official said.

The police have not detained the woman's husband and he is not a suspect. White roses that had been painted red were found at the scene, Police indicated, although no other details were shared.

"The husband had allegedly left the hotel early this morning to get beer. We have questioned him and he had admitted that he had an altercation with his wife recently, but nothing that would warrant him being considered a suspect," he said.

The body has been sent for autopsy.

"We are waiting for the report, although we have a pretty good idea at cause of death," the official said.

More details to be shared as they become available.

*

Sandy urged Andrea to snap it up so they could hit the road as soon as possible. Being the more relaxed of the two, Andrea sighed and continued with her morning preparations.

"You're already packed and ready to roll, Sandy. What will happen if we can't get a train ticket? What about the price? We haven't even bothered to check on it."

These questions and comments made Sandy worry. Andrea was making good points, even if she was looking into a future nobody could predict. What if, what if, what if.

"What if you're right Andrea? What if it's not meant for me to see Blake again?"

Sandy put her pack on the floor and sat on the edge of the bed with a gloomy, "everything is ruined" look on her face.

"Stop worrying." Andrea ordered as she loaded her toothbrush. "It'll all work out. Don't get yourself all worked up like Blake does. It'll just make you sick."

Sandy turned to Andrea and saw the big friendly smile that made her love her dearly. It was a joy to have her as a friend and even more exciting that she was going with her to the great Northwest.

After another hour of waiting, Andrea was finally ready to hit the road. The two women looked fabulous. They were shapely, well dressed and insatiable when it came to drawing male attention. Andrea wore a pair of comfortable capris, and had a mid-riff baring shirt that exposed her chiseled abs and belly button ring. Sandy was the opposite, wearing a pair of slacks and a loose fitting pullover shirt. She complimented that with a light windbreaker. Sandy still looked very alluring, but carried herself more conservatively than her friend.

The women grabbed their bags and headed for the door when lo and behold, from behind, a loud voice beckoned **"GIRLS! WHERE DO YOU THINK YOU'RE GOING?"**

Sandy rolled her eyes up and Andrea tilted her head sideways and blew out a frustrated gust of air. They turned around and faced Sandy's over-conservative and too disciplined Mother. Iris Arnold looked back at the pair with a high graying bun of hair lying on top of her head. Her face was sunken in, and pale skin surrounded her beady eyes, tiny mouth and long skinny nose.

"Mom," Sandy whined, "what do you want?"

"Where are you two headed? It looks like you plan to leave for a while."

"We're taking a trip Mom. We'll be back in a couple of weeks; if all goes as planned."

Andrea gave Sandy a kick to the shin. She had warned her about sharing anything with her mom.

"OUCH ANDREA, WHAT THE HECK?"

Andrea puckered her lips and shushed Sandy as silently as she could. Sandy's mom wasn't buying it. Not one bit.

"I asked you two where you were going and I expect an answer this instant." She crossed her arms and tapped her elbows with her index fingers. She resembled church lady from Saturday Night Live. Sandy pictured it. "So girls, where are you going? To see, oh I don't know, **SATAN?**"

Sandy chuckled with her vision, which caused Andrea to stifle a taste of the giggles.

"I don't find this funny, girls. Sandy, march into your room right now and unpack. You aren't going anywhere." She then turned her attention to what she thought of as the "evil" Andrea. "Just what do you think you're doing young lady? Corrupting my daughter again, I presume?"

"Mrs. Arnold, no, I'm not 'corrupting' your daughter." Andrea said this while holding up two fingers from each hand in a quotation sign. "We're taking a short trip to re-charge our batteries. You know, taking a break from life."

"Well Andrea, there are no such things as 'breaks in life.'" Mrs. Arnold mocked Andrea with a quotation sign of her own. "Life is hard and you girls aren't prepared at all to gallivant all over Hell's half acre. Sandy, I said go to your room; **NOW!**"

"No Mom. I won't. I'm in my twenties now and I can think for myself thank you very much. I'm, *we're* going to Seattle to find Blake and bring him home with us."

"SEATTLE! BLAKE! HOME! Are you crazy Sandy? Have you lost your mind? I thought I raised you to be more sensible. Blake is nothing but trouble and trying to find him will bring you pain and agony."

"It's a chance I'll have to take Mom. I love him and I know he loves me. He hasn't seen it yet, but he'll come to his senses when we get together."

"LOVE! Now you're in love? I cannot allow it. I won't allow it." Mrs. Arnold was pacing at the front veranda and her stress level was visibly increased. "If this is something you have to do, I can't stop you, but you will not be welcome back into this house."

"Fine Mom…Iris." Andrea gasped and giggled at the same time as Sandy did the unthinkable and called her mom by her first name. "I'm going and that's final. I'll be back in a couple of weeks."

Sandy and Andrea made their way into the street and headed for the bus stop and a trip to the Toledo train station. Iris Arnold made a spectacle of herself in the driveway, causing the neighbors to peek out their windows.

"FINE! FINE! Don't come back. Your stuff will be on the front lawn when you return. I'm not kidding." Ms. Arnold made one last foot-stomping plea. **"Come back right now. This is your last warning!"**

Both of the girls ignored her and picked up the pace to the stop. It was with determination that Sandy put her foot down. All she could think about was that this trek had better work or life would never be the same again. A stance of independence, if you will. Andrea opened her mouth to console her friend, but before she could get one word out, Sandy lifted her hand.

"Not one word Andrea. I don't want to speak right now."

Andrea chuckled as the two reached the Toledo depot. Their train of consequence waited.

"How do you get to Wonderland? Over the hill or underland, or just behind the tree."

Shaun Webb

9

The White Queen

The investigation into the Kathy Joseph beheading in Las Vegas was turned over to the feds. The local municipalities had stalked over the crime scene, but couldn't make heads or tails of it. Enter one Wilma Hurst. She of her beady eyes and grizzly stare, which would make anyone question whether or not speaking to her would be a wise choice. She was a no nonsense woman in a world generally reserved for men. Not married and not willing to share even one facet of her personal life, all the feds that worked under her whispered to each other about her sexual orientation, off work habits, and many other mind-numbing subjects pertaining to her. Some even wondered if a penis was nested under her skirt. Her face was unmistakably squared; her jaw a clenched wad of muscle and tissue, and a small scar lived over her left eye. The scar was another taboo subject with the hardened investigator.

Wilma had been with the FBI for over twenty years. She was a tireless worker with a discipline that was second to none. If anyone were going to find the underlying cause of the beheading involving Kathy Joseph, it would be her.

The Vegas police called the feds for help after they exhausted their resources looking into the murder. Sending out Wilma was not what they expected, as she made clear from day one in her meeting with the Las Vegas police force.

"My name is Wilma Hurst. I will be taking over the investigation of Ms. Joseph's unfortunate death and no one will question me or step one foot out of line. Doing so once will earn you a reprimand and a demotion. Twice and you're fired on the spot. Do not ever think about challenging me. I have a staff of two other agents and we alone will solve this case."

Two very straight-laced men stood to the side of her. They both wore dark glasses, white shirts and black suit coats.

"You men are to be at our beckon call. You will perform your normal duties as you always have and will not get in our way. If we need something, we will call on you. If you need something from us, don't bother asking because we won't listen. Do I make myself abundantly clear?"

No one raised their hand or uttered a single syllable. Wilma looked about the room, meeting eyes with every officer present. The cold stare intimidated the most hardened of the cops.

"Good. Now get to work."

Meeting with the press was a completely different story as Wilma showed tact, caring and had a wonderful way with her words.

"I am saddened by the death of Ms. Joseph and let me assure the public that I will find and apprehend the person or persons responsible for the murder. I want you to know that we will spare no expense in solving this awful case. Please be comforted in my words. I care about people and will do everything in my power to make sure no one else is harmed. You have my solemn vow."

The press ate it up, delivering on a three-column article in the next day's newspaper explaining Wilma's stance. It also helped to quell any public fear that may have existed. The murder was hideous and scary; like something out of a horror movie. The people in Vegas were nervous, but felt an ease with Ms. Hurst's heartfelt press conference. The only thing left for her to do was get to work, something that came very naturally for the toughened Fed.

"Let's get to the crime scene," she told her two sidekicks, "and get this Goddamn thing solved."

*

Nampa, Idaho was in Kurt's rear view mirror as his complete concentration was centered on Portland, Oregon and Soo-Chin Xing. He was upset with himself for the beheading at the hotel, but it was necessary as the woman simply couldn't keep her mouth shut or leave well enough alone. Kurt gained a bit of consolation with the knowledge that he probably did that husband of hers a huge favor by shutting the woman up for good.

"S-some people d-don't know when to shut the hell up." Kurt reasoned to himself. "So I sh-shut them up m-myself."

Still, he couldn't help thinking about how sloppy of a job he'd done. He didn't even bother to vase the roses as he usually does; and should have, in retrospect, disciplined himself enough to ignore the old hag. The details that he failed to follow through on could easily put someone on his tail quickly. He didn't know that the Feds were getting involved down in Vegas, and even if he did, it wouldn't matter, as he knew that he needed to keep a few steps ahead of the heat. He also knew that the scene at Kathy Joseph's house would be a tough one to uncover, but linking her to him wouldn't take a rocket scientist, especially after investigators figured out that he was nowhere to be found in Michigan.

*

Kurt's head was wearily bobbing up and down on the steering wheel as he plugged further toward Portland. He would occasionally run over the sound divots located on the shoulder of the road, waking him to the fact that he was headed for the guardrail. He quickly compensated by getting back into his lane. Becoming aggravated, Kurt stopped at the next rest stop for coffee and a wake up break. It was three a.m. and the area was, for the most part, devoid of any people. He went inside to use the facilities and found yet more trouble. Kurt was in Pendleton, Oregon, still a three and a half hour trip from Portland. He had been on the road for fourteen straight hours, less his one-hour adventure in Nampa. He was not in a mood to be trifled with, but that didn't matter to the gay men hanging out in the men's room. Kurt walked in and made his way to a toilet, shut the divider, and sat down. When he looked next to the toilet paper holder, he saw that a penis had been extended through a hole in the large privacy blocker.

Kurt issued a stern warning. "Please t-take your p-p-penis away before I g-get angry."

Kurt heard snickering from behind the partition next to him. There was more than one person in the stall and he was getting sick to his stomach. He looked again and the penis in question was still making itself known beside him. The person who owned it had developed an erection, which further sickened and angered Kurt.

"I w-will not tell you again. P-please remove your p-penis before I h-hurt you."

"Ya know sir," One of the man in the other stall said. "I heard suckin' a cock helps clear up stutterin'. Why don't ya go ahead and give 'er a try."

Kurt was now livid and that wasn't good for him or the men in the stall next to him. He pulled out his razor sharp pocketknife and softly grabbed ahold of the misplaced member. He was ready to strike when he delayed in his action for a split second. He found the penis a tiny bit pleasurable.

"Go on ahead." Said the man's voice. "Suck it."

Kurt snapped out of his temporary daydream and went back to business. He thought to himself "I'm not g-gay." Kurt was disgusted with himself. The anger seethed even deeper into his psyche.

"Okay." Kurt said kindly, "Maybe you're right. Stand still and we'll give it a try."

"That's more like it. Hey, what happened to your stut....**AHHHHHH?**"

The scream was blood curdling as Kurt cut off the man's unit like a hot knife through melted butter. Kurt stood up and exited the stall. As the man in the other stall screamed with pain and his friend tried covering the significant wound with his shirt, Kurt kicked the door open, breaking one of the three hinges holding it. He grabbed the castrated man by his throat and, while he screamed, stuffed his *dis-membered* penis into his mouth. He then punched him square in the jaw, knocking his head against the tile behind the toilet. Down he crumpled in a heap of blood, pain and finally unconsciousness. The second man put his hands up in a combination of "I didn't do it" and "please don't hurt me" gestures. Kurt ignored his pleas and grabbed him by the back of the head. Like a wrestler on WWE, he sent the man's face downward and smack onto the steel flusher behind the toilet. Blood spurted from the man's left eye as he also crumpled to the floor. Kurt turned to leave the stall, but not before sharing one more non-stuttering comment.

"Don't you realize that *no* means *"NO!"*

Kurt washed his hands, went to the lobby for coffee and then jumped in his van. Now fully awake, he would finish his trip to Portland.

*

Wilma and her two silent, sunglass-wearing cronies studied the scene where Kathy had been murdered. They looked over every nook and cranny of the house, hoping to find at least one or two clues that would help with their investigation. They followed blood splatter trails, looked at pictures of the crime scene, and dusted for prints wherever necessary. Wilma did all the talking while her two, standing at the ready, listened closely. Both of her men stood in the six foot five inch range and were physically solid. If a donnybrook of any kind were to break out here or anywhere else, Wilma covered herself well with these two hulks at her side. It was a nice back up for the serious investigator, even though the woman was quite able to handle herself if placed in a precarious situation.

*

Wilma Hurst was born and raised in a hillbilly town in Arkansas. It was a quiet place to live, but the locals could be extreme rednecks, especially when it came to men having sex with underage girls along with nightly fights at the local pubs. Some locals were not good about paying the taxes they owed, but finding and collaring them was another thing altogether as names were changed or aliases used to avoid detection. It was a small city full of sin, yet many were honest, hardworking citizens who obeyed the law and stayed away from trouble. Flannel shirts and NASCAR racing caps were the clothing of choice enjoyed by the men, while the women opted for knee length cutoff jean shorts with multi-colored blouses knotted at the naval. Simply put, it was the way in that part of Arkansas and would remain so. Toothless mouths, deep southern drawls bordering on another language, and hillbillies ruled the roost. The men drank hard while the women were expected to take care of the kids and the house. Heart attacks in this part of the country were on the high side, mainly due to the excessive amounts of lard used to slick a skillet. Schooling was low on the priority list, as the average citizen had an eighth grade education. Overall, it was a challenging place to rise from and become an FBI Agent. Wilma managed it.

Wilma was at first a victim, and then turned into a hero. She was raped at fourteen by a local thirty-nine year-old man who said in court that he preferred younger girls, aged thirteen to seventeen. He went to jail, but not for very long. The men seemed to have the advantages in this out of the way, third world type of town. It affected Wilma by making her tougher. As she grew older, bar fighting was one of her favorite activities, next to drinking. She had a reputation for drinking moonshine straight from the *jar* and kicking rear-ends twice her size. She could take a punch, deliver one, drink half a fifth of shine, and then wake up the next day to talk about it. She started out as a redneck, but soon changed her habits for a civilized way of living.

By the time she hit twenty years-old, Wilma's partying was outdated. As she searched for her calling, Wilma opened up her own art business, "Beading with the Betties", a class that drew seventy and eighty year-old women whose first priority was keeping their aging, arthritic hands limber. Wilma was a great teacher and appreciated the old Grannies wit and charm. However, she soon bored of the very slow pastime and decided that being in law enforcement would offer her more action and excitement. She didn't miss the drinking, but needed to kick some tail now and then. Before joining the police academy, however, she signed up to do a four year stint in the Army, something that she figured would best dissipate the built up anger and frustration that seethed inside her from the mistreatment she endured in her younger years. She thought the gig with the old women might help mellow her attitude, but it only served to make things more confusing as she heard about the women's abuse in the days of yore.

"Back in ma day," an old lady explained, "ya didn't make no fuss, lest ya get a heavy hand a-comin' down on ya. Ya 'cepted things; men; the way they was, flaws and all. If ya tried to divorce 'em, then ya was an outcast. If ya fussed 'bout it, it always got back to your husband and an ass lickin' was in order. Ya learnt ta keep yer trap shut tight."

The Army was a great test for the young Wilma. She excelled at the physical parts of the training, breezing through boot camp with ease. Her social skills were troubling for her. She said little to anyone and expected nothing in return. Her focus was always on her MP training and her instructors. When authority spoke, she listened. When peers spoke, Wilma usually met them with a cold stare and no comment. One day, it led her to a confrontation with one of the classes' tougher women.

Wilma was six weeks from graduation when her assigned roommate, Deb Walters, approached her.

"I've been in the same room with you for six months and you haven't said word one to me. I want to know a little bit about you, Wilma. What makes you tick?"

Wilma was reading her field safety guide and paid no attention to the rambling woman as she did so. Deb had tried many times to speak with Wilma, and now her patience had worn paper-thin.

"I said something to you bitch! I'm talking to your sorry dyke ass." She stood in front of Wilma and spoke much louder, inches from her face. "**LISTEN TO ME LADY!**"

Still nothing, not even a glance. Deb was fed up and went into her room to retrieve the hunting knife she kept in the top drawer of her chest. She returned and snuck up behind Wilma, placing the sharpened steel against her temple while putting her other arm around her neck.

"Now are you going to listen, you pathetic excuse for a human? Are you going to answer my goddamn questions or not?"

Finally, after tossing her book aside, Wilma spoke. "Take that knife off of my head and let go of me before I... *kill*... you."

She said these words with a calm demeanor reserved for stealth fighters like Navy Seals. She didn't appear rattled. Deb kept the knife where it was, just above her left eye. She became shaky with Wilma's calmness.

"Final warning." Wilma advised. "Take the knife away and let go of me."

"Fuck you dyke. I'm going to find out right now what makes you act as if you're better than everyone else is. Answer my questions or I'll cut you."

Quicker than a deer and more agile than a bald eagle, Wilma reached back, grabbed Deb by the nape of her neck and flipped her over her shoulder, causing her to land with a thud on her tailbone. Wilma seized the woman's wrist and gave it a twist to discourage any thoughts of fighting back. During the lightning fast melee, Deb had managed to cut a six-inch long gash in Wilma's forehead. The bleeding was profuse as she leaned over a crumpled and vulnerable Deb. She took the knife from her hand and made a threat of her own. She put the blade to Deb's throat.

"I'd cut the fucking life out of you now if I so chose, but I spare pathetic little cockroaches like you. You're a stupid cunt sneaking on me like that. I'm not answering any of your questions, so do yourself a favor and save your breath. Get it?"

Deb's eyes were pursed with surprise and fear as Wilma looked down at her. The cut from her forehead was dripping blood into Deb's mouth and nostrils. She tried to move in a counteractive way, but Wilma's wrist grip tightened like a boa constrictor squeezing its prey. Finally, Deb tired and looked up to her dominating counterpart.

"Okay, okay. I'm sorry. I give. Let me up."

Wilma let her up, but twisted Deb's wrist grotesquely as she did. A snap was heard throughout the room and Deb moaned in pain.

"You broke my fucking wrist. What the fuck? Why did you break my wrist?"

No comment came from Wilma. She rose from her seat, threw the knife down hard enough to where it stuck in the floor between Deb's legs; inches from her crotch, and headed to her room. Deb, now thoroughly stunned and shaken, went to the kitchen to find a solid handled utensil to use as a brace for her now limp appendage. When she completed this task, she headed for Wilma's room to apologize and ask for help with her wrist. As she opened the door, she was staggered with more shock and outrage. Wilma was standing before a mirror with a needle and thread, sewing the six inches long wound together herself. Wilma stopped for a moment and slowly turned to meet Deb's eyes. Deb staggered backward a few steps, and in a disgusted awe, shut the door. Wilma turned back and continued her task of closing the wound. When she finished, she came out to the living area and offered a bit of advice to her roommate. Her voice was dark, somber and unshaken. She spoke slowly.

"One word to the doctor about what happened to your wrist and you're a dead woman. I know how to kill, hide and move on. No one would ever find you nor would they know anything except that you up and vanished."

Deb, her mouth slightly ajar, carefully nodded her head in agreement. When Deb returned from the doctor, she found Wilma sitting on the couch, head stitched, looking at her field manual. Deb said nothing. She never spoke another word to her roommate.

Wilma overwhelmingly completed her training. She was the apple of her trainer's eyes. She moved onto the police academy, soundly excelled at her craft and was hired by the FBI as a field agent. She quickly ascended the ladder and eventually stood at the top of her investigative field. She was a major nemesis for criminals nationwide.

A Killer for the Queen

*

Kurt was once again on his way to Portland. He had about two hours left in his trip and was wide-awake from his adventure at the rest stop. He was punishing himself for being sloppy and impulsive. It was something he needed to work on, but when his anger was unleashed, he was like The Hulk; blinded while tearing up everything in his wake. Kurt's focus was on three lovely women. One of his planned executions was done, another was coming soon and then the coup de grace was waiting for him in Seattle.

Nobody except for Kurt could fully reason as to why it was women whose heads he took. It had all started in Flint when Old John Garrison was put to death for crimes Kyle Beauregard had committed. The other stigma that Kurt often wondered about was his love for Alice in Wonderland and why it influenced him so deeply. Kurt thought about these questions often and came to conclusions as to why he was behaving in that way.

The Alice in Wonderland music grew into Kurt's soul. It reminded him of his son, and gave him the incentive to take heads. After all, the Queen did what she had to do when people around her misbehaved and acted the fool. It seemed to do the trick, as the citizens watched their steps with her, not wanting to enrage the Red Queen. Kurt thought in much the same way, except that he had sunk further into the abyss of taking it all too seriously. The madness mixed with the vengeance to form a mental wall of storminess in Kurt's mind. He decided that when it was earned, you'd lose your head. He only planned on three, but would collect as needed. The woman at the hotel in Nampa, brought out the worst in Kurt, and the men at the rest stop had inadvertently messed with a very dangerous, and perhaps closeted gay man. They were lucky not to lose their heads, but the injuries he inflicted were severe all the same. One man's injuries were so severe, he'd die.

Kurt's mind shifted back to the task, reaching Portland and collecting his next head. The two collected so far soaked in the jars of fluid in his homemade cabinet behind the driver's seat. Kurt occasionally spoke to the cabinet, thinking they could hear him. They had ears, eyes, nose, a mouth and a brain, but none of it functioned. As much as he would ask questions or hope for a response, it would never come.

"D-Do you know w-why I did this? Do you l-like getting your heads ch-chopped off? Are you g-going to answer m-me or n-not?"

Question after question slung from Kurt's lips, but the lack of response seemed to frustrate him further. He banged on the steering wheel, hit his elbow on the window and screamed at the top of his lungs in frustration. Thirty seconds later, he'd be humming a tune from his CD, smiling all the while. It seemed that his mental state wasn't keeping up with the physical being, because this was happening more and more often and with increased violence.

Kurt finally, after what seemed to him like forever, pulled into Portland, Oregon. The city was cloudy and damp, with a large dose of humidity floating in the cool air. Kurt had been driving for some thirty straight hours and needed rest badly. He checked into the first motel off the service drive and hit the bed hard. In a few hours, he would awaken and immediately begin his search for the next in the collection.

*

"Those roses on the table. Bring me those, vase and all."

Without question or delay, Wilma's men quickly retrieved the roses and brought them to her. Even though they had been sitting for few days, they still had an unsettling freshness to them that made her wonder. She took a single rose out and sniffed it, surprised that there was no odor. She carefully touched the petals with her latex gloved hand, hoping for something; anything. To her surprise, the petals were as hard as rocks. She questioned to herself if they were even real.

"Bring me the kit from the car." She ordered, wanting the satchel that contained a magnifying glass along with a few other assorted tools.

The crony was out to the car and back within one minute, tool kit in hand. He handed it over and she waved him off. He nodded and continued looking over the scene with his partner. There was not a word from either of them, only clear and unyielding obedience for their leader.

Wilma pinned the rose down on a piece of corkboard and studied it with the spyglass. A moment later, she took out a tool that looked like a nut extractor you see buried with the bowl of chestnuts at Christmas time. She carefully began scrapping at the petal. It took her three scraps to figure out what was before her.

"This is a white rose painted red." She whispered to herself. "This rose is painted. Why? Why paint the rose red?"

Wilma, having been a youngster herself, easily tied the painted rose to Alice in Wonderland. One thought led to another and the clues continued presenting themselves.

"The Queen of Hearts of Alice in Wonderland?" she was now raising her voice. "So the executioner gave the victim red painted roses before doing the deed?"

Wilma placed the bouquet in an evidence bag and zipped it shut. She saved the one rose she was working on as a motivational tool. She called her two men in for a huddle.

"You," she said to the first man, "go to Flint, Michigan and find a man named Kurtis Joseph, the victim's ex-husband. I want to have a word with him."

She looked at her other crony, "you come with me. We're going back to the Vegas PD to do some follow-up work."

No words, only nods, and the three headed off in their respective directions.

As Wilma was making her way to the Vegas police department, the Chief of Police contacted her.

"Wilma, we have another beheading, this time in Nampa, Idaho. Don't ask me why Nampa, but...."

Wilma cut him off mid-sentence. "Thank you, Chief. Stand by for any instructions I may have for you."

She clicked off the radio and turned to her driver. "Nampa, Idaho. On the double."

A U-turn and the pressing of a few buttons on the car's GPS later, the vehicle was on its way.

*

Kurt had no trouble figuring out Soo-Chin's schedule. He already knew that she had moved to Portland to work at the medical examiner's facility and only needed to look up her address at the department of records. Kurt thought to himself how wonderful public information was and found it astounding as to how easy it was to acquire. He walked in, asked for her address, paid the clerk five bucks and had a photocopy of not only her address, but a satellite photo of her home from five hundred feet above.

"It's n-not like that in the m-movies," Kurt concluded. "On TV, they have to a-ask questions and search. Here, you g-get everything you n-need."

Kurt thanked the clerk for her time and insolently thought to himself how she had inadvertently contributed to the future murder of a woman in Portland, Oregon. Whenever she'd hear about it on the news or in the paper, she would have no clue as to her involvement. He chuckled and headed out, now even more confident in his ability to case out the clueless Soo-Chin.

As he waited on the side of the two lane neighborly road, he began thinking again; thinking about his motives and his ideas. He wanted to know what made him tick. He was as curious as anyone else would be about the dreams, nightmares and other horrors that danced in his head. He turned to look in the back of his van and spoke.

"So Kathy, w-what is it exactly that gives me the th-thoughts and fears? What's going on in m-my head? I'm t-talking to you d-dear; could you please s-speak up?"

No answer came from the cabinet. The only thing Kurt heard were the chirping of a few nomadic crickets muddling outside. The chirps were rich, sharp and annoying. Kurt turned back to the front of the van and laid his head back on the seat. He fell into a mild snooze; not quite asleep, but awake enough to think.

"Am I gay? Am I a gay heterosexual? Is there such a thing? Perhaps I'm simply bi-sexual; you know, men and women. Maybe I'm swinging from both sides of the plate. Men, though, are ugly and hairy creatures with a nasty appendage hanging between their legs. Women are fussy, gossipy and flighty. Why can't a woman just give it up as a man does? Why are women so stubborn with their pussies? When I meet a woman, she makes me wait days, months or even years before she undresses in front of me, yet all those other women show their tits as if it doesn't matter. When a guy goes for it, he's usually shut out. Why goddamn it? What makes a female so fucking special? What gives them the right to tell me when I can and can't fuck them?"

Kurt's blood pressure and ire were rising. He was getting angrier by the minute. He went to the back of his van and opened the cabinet, exposing the two heads he'd collected thus far. Their faces were of horror and disbelief. The final expression they ever gave had been etched forever more. Fear, tragedy and the end of life was all combined into one grotesque wad of emotion.

"Kathy. W-Why? Why were you s-so stupid? What d-did I do that made you l-leave? I was obedient, c-caring and quiet. I allowed you to l-live; you wanted too. Our r-romance soured and you only m-made love to me once; one fucking time in the last y-year. You wondered why I w-went in the basement and p-played with myself while I watched porn. It was b-because I loved you and I wouldn't cheat. All you had to d-do was show a little m-more caring and understanding. Some caresses and t-touching would've changed everything, but nooo, you had to g-go cheat with a big shot. You had to g-go find your sugar d-daddy to fill the void between your thighs. It's your f-fault I hold your head in m-my possession. It's your fault you sit in a jar w-with liquid. It didn't have to be that way, d-did it? What about you, you l-lousy stinking b-bitch?"

Kurt turned his attention to the woman whose head he collected in Idaho. She was also of an emotional expression, eyes open and staring blankly at Kurt. They could see no more, but told a tale of woe and misery.

"As f-for you, I did your h-husband a favor. You probably t-treated him like shit too. I'll bet he's sitting at h-home right now thinking about how awesome it is to have your s-sorry ass out of his life. Your smart m-mouth and cavalier attitude b-brought you to an end. It didn't have to be l-like that for you either. You c-could've simply been polite when you m-met me. A handshake, a few k-kind words. No, you couldn't d-do that. You also caused this yourself. You d-deserve to be here."

Kurt moved back to his driver seat, having calmed significantly and laid his head back against the seat again. His mind wandered anew as he searched his thoughts further.

*"He wanted me at that rest stop. He stuck his penis through that hole because he wanted me. When I touched it, I felt a surge go through me. Was it a sexual surge? Did I feel his vibe shoot through me as I caressed his manliness before destroying it? We should've talked first. He should've introduced himself before offering me his love. He also deserved his fate. I took no heads though. Why? Was it because I was enamored with him? I don't know. I wanted him, yet he was a disgusting pig. Am I thinking like a woman now? Am I judging this man the way a woman judges men? I hope not. I don't want to be what I hate the most. I don't want to become a woman. I'm the Hatter, summoned by the Red Queen of Hearts. She decides which heads and when. She's the leader of this parade. **I DON'T KNOW WHAT TO DO.** What do I do? What am I? Am I a man? Am I a woman? Or am I simply a crazed hatter?"*

As Kurt was about to fall victim to his rage, he heard a car door slam. He was snapped out of his trance and looked up the driveway. Soo-Chin was finally home. He looked at her with a combination of anger and compassion, of want and distaste. He knew what he had to do. He waited for her to go inside and then began collecting his tools, top hat, roses, CD player and machete. He also grabbed a can of red spray paint and headed toward her door. He walked up the driveway, staying in the shadows cast by the trees. He was moving in for another kill. Kurt was to collect another head because the Queen insisted. It was then that he stopped cold in his tracks. Soo had other people inside the house. There were three others, probably roommates. Kurt, while frustrated, was also smart. He didn't want to deal with anyone else while collecting Soo's head. He was forced to abort the job and wait until the next day. He hoped to get her alone. He would follow her to her job and wait until the time was right. If he had too, he'd knock her car off the road and do it there. Whatever needed to be done to satisfy the Queen's thirst for blood.

*

Wilma and her crony arrived at the scene in Nampa and walked up to enter through the front door. A police officer blocked their path and asked her to show him ID. Wilma pulled out her FBI credentials and showed the officer, but he inexplicably continued to deny entrance.

"What's your name officer?" Wilma inquired with a sly grin.

"It's on my badge ma'am. Look for yourself."

He tapped his badge with his flashlight while moving his hand toward his gun.

"Oh, Officer Dannon. You're a nice young man. How long have you been a cop?"

"I'm not here to talk to you ma'am. I'm guarding a crime....OUCH!"

Before the officer could speak another word, Wilma ripped the badge from his shirt, scratching him with the needle as she did so. Officer Dannon reached for his gun, but was quickly looking down the barrel of a glock, courtesy of Wilma's henchman. The officer froze in his position and Wilma asked again.

"I said how long have you been a cop?"

"UHH, three years. Why?"

"Why?" Wilma asked, "Because this may be your last night on the force, Dannon. It may even be your last night as a cop. How about if I charge you with impeding a Federal Agent's investigation? How would that look on your record?"

"My Chief told me nobody was to cross the line; **NOBODY!**"

The officer looked at Wilma, and then at the man pointing a gun mere inches from his face. He made a good choice.

"Okay, go on in. I saw your credentials. You're good."

"Why thank you Dannon. Here's your badge back."

The officer reached out and Wilma gave him his badge back, needle down. It poked through his skin on the palm of his hand and sent a shock of pain up the cop's arm.

"Officer Dannon, my partner here is going to hang with you while I go inside. Any trouble and I have no idea what he might do. I would suggest you *not* piss him off."

Dannon nodded and Wilma entered the front door of the motel.

Three Nampa cops were investigating the scene. They, along with Dannon, were probably the only three on duty in the entire town.

"Officers," Wilma spoke for attention while holding up her badge. "This scene now belongs to the FBI. Please vacate the premises. We can take it from here."

A Nampa cop walked up, looked over Wilma's credentials and waved the men out of the room.

"You can have it ma'am. It's disgusting anyway."

Wilma nodded, re-pocketed her badge and waited for the men to leave. A few minutes later, her crony walked in, obviously done guarding Dannon because they all left the scene.

The very first thing Wilma noticed was the bundle of red roses lying on the floor by the bed. She noticed the miniscule amount of blood at the scene, and was at first baffled about why there wasn't as much as a beheading would tend to leave. When you slash the carotid artery, the pressure spatter is continuous for up to thirty seconds. The blood loss is equivalent to a gallon and a half of liquid if bled out. It may not seem like a lot until it's everywhere. Figuring that the heads had both been missing from the scene, the executioner was probably wrapping them up quickly and limiting the blood loss. The bodies themselves only had towels thrown on top of the neck, so that collected most of the drip. Either way, heads were being collected and Wilma didn't like it. As with the last scene, the roses were painted red. She didn't need to scrape them to find out, as red paint lay on the counter beyond the curtain. While further perusing the scene, she suddenly caught a whiff of sulfur in the air. Now she had an idea about the lack of blood. She walked over to the headless corpse and threw back the towel lying on her shoulders. It was then that she found out the killer was cauterizing the wounds.

"The woman found the roses, turned to come back into her room and was met by the murderer. He killed her and then cauterized the wound with fire, probably a blowtorch. That explains the lack of blood."

Wilma was talking to her attentive partner who simply nodded with everything she said. "Was she married? Where's the husband? Find me the husband."

Her crony took to thumbing through some pictures in the room and then left. Within five minutes, he returned with the woman's husband. Wilma smiled at her unemotional friend. She started with her interrogation.

"I have some very important questions for you sir. You don't have to answer and you're not under arrest, but any help you can give us would be most appreciated." The middle-aged, beer-gutted man nodded appropriately before speaking.

"Before you ask me any questions lady, I want you to know that I'm glad that nasty bitch is gone. She gave me nothing but pain and frustration for some thirty years." He took a swig from his beer bottle and continued. "She would've been the death of me, but now I don't have to worry about that, do I?"

"That's really swell, Mr. Uh…what's your name sir?"

"Themeski, Henry Themeski."

"Mr. Themeski, while it's all well and good that you don't give the first fuck about your dead wife, I need a description. Can you describe him for me?"

"No," was Henry's point blank answer.

"What did you say sir? Did you say 'no' to me?"

"That's what I said ma'am. I'm not giving any information about him. He saved my life so he can run free all I care."

Wilma became perplexed and angry at Mr. Themeski's attitude.

"Did you know," Wilma informed him, "that you can be booked for not sharing information and inhibiting an investigation?"

"No ma'am, I didn't know that. Did I say 'no' I wouldn't identify him? Well that's because I have no idea what he looks like. I didn't see him myself. You'd have to speak with my wife and all I have to say is good luck with that."

"Oh I see. Did you know that your wife is the second woman that we know of who's been beheaded? Did you know that Mr. Themeski?"

After rubbing his stubble chin and taking another sip off his brew, he gave Wilma a look of contempt. "Yeah? The second woman huh? Sounds like he's doing everyone a favor by getting rid of the bitchy ones then. I'm sure the first one had it coming to her too."

Wilma clocked Mr. Themeski so hard in the temple that he tumbled from the chair and fell to the floor in a heap. He looked up to Wilma and issued her a stern warning. "That's brutality. I'll sue your stupid ass. Goddamn that hurt."

"Brutality?" Wilma responded. "I didn't see any brutality. Did you?" Her henchman shook his head 'no'.

"Shoe's on the other foot, huh Mr. Themeski?"

"You can beat me until I bleed but I won't tell you one fucking thing...count on that."

Wilma was about to clock him again when her cell phone rang, granting the cowering man a temporary reprieve.

"Hello. Yes. Yes. Okay good. Catch up with us in Nampa. Tomorrow morning."

Wilma clicked her phone shut and looked at Mr. Themeski. "It's your lucky day, fat ass. I know who's doing this and I'm going to find his sorry carcass and fry it."

She nodded to her man and he followed her out the door. She stopped and looked back at the fearful man lying on the floor.

"This guy is channeling the Red Queen, Alice in Wonderland or some other sick shit by leaving painted red roses lying around. I have news for him, Mr. Themeski, I'm the White Fucking Queen and I will catch him."

She signaled her man and they left quickly. As she exited his establishment, Mr. Themeski stood up and looked at the bloodstains around the room.

"I don't know who you were mister, but watch out for that bitch. She says she's the White Queen and I believe her."

Mr. Themeski rubbed the side of his head and left the room, shutting off the light behind him.

Shaun Webb

"Alice in Wonderland, where is the path to Wonderland? Over the hill or here or there? I wonder where."

Shaun Webb

10

Drink me, Eat me

The train chugged down the tracks with determination. It wasn't a fairy tale "I think I can" train; it was a train that not only could, but that would only stop when it reached the depot in Seattle. Inside the train were Sandy and Andrea, polar opposites that went together splendidly. Andrea was definitely the wild child to Sandy's conservative nature. Where Andrea would drink, smoke and partake in anything illegal at a party or a bar, Sandy was along for the ride to be Andrea's friend and watch her closely, insuring that she wouldn't be taken advantage of or have to drive home not only drunk, but also sometimes inebriated to the edge of unconsciousness. Sandy played the bird with the broken wing. Whenever someone was too close to the easily convinced Andrea, Sandy would stir up a commotion worthy of everyone's attention. Spilled drinks; the kind that arced thirty feet and landed at the feet of an innocent bystander, were her first defense, while feigning rape aloud was her old reliable if all else failed. Whatever method she used, she would always get her friend out of a bind. Why? Because that was Sandy. She was loyal to a fault, never missing a beat when it came to defending her rather loose friend's integrity.

    Andrea had tested her friends resolve on many occasions and in a couple of instances nearly lost her. Sandy always forgave and forgot, allowing Andrea to clutch to her bosom and beg solace for her wildness. Sandy wanted to party, but couldn't get up the nerve to weaken herself with drugs or alcohol. Although she'd smoked a joint or two in her life, she was the poster child for designated driving. These strong points probably saved her friend's life in many instances. Andrea appreciated the caring Sandy, even if she seemed a bit annoying at times. There were stretches when Andrea legitimately wanted to get laid, but the broken-winged Sandy usually put the kibosh on it. They did everything together except have sex. It wasn't that Andrea wouldn't; she simply knew Sandy would never go for it. Sandy may have chuckled and called her a weirdo, but she would ultimately take it as a joke and move on. Andrea never wanted Sandy as a full time girlfriend either; it was the fact that an occasional fling would be fun to help blow off some steam and not have to worry about it. It would be "non-guilt" sex. These were the reasons Andrea would undress in Sandy's plain sight. She sometimes, not always, wanted to get her friend excited sexually. The only sexuality Sandy expressed was her love for Blake, which was so over the top that she wouldn't so much as expose too much cleavage lest she be "spoiled" for the man of her dreams. Andrea went along with Sandy to not only appease her and get a vacation, but she hoped deep down that Blake might take Sandy up on her offer of being together. It was a one in a million shot, but life could throw some heavy curveballs occasionally.

As beautiful as Sandy was, Andrea thought that she was probably a real dud in the sack. She felt that she needed to give pointers that Sandy could use if the tiny chance of winning Blake really worked.

"Sandy, have you ever even once, you know, did it? You know, like sex and stuff?"

Sandy looked at her friend with a blushed red face. "Not that it's any of your business smarty pants, but I have made out before."

Astonished, Andrea kept on. "So you let a guy play with your tits? Did you French kiss. Did you touch his pen…?"

"ANDREA! Shhh. People will hear you."

"Sandy, were in our own cabin. The noise this train makes wouldn't let a mouse hear its own cheese! So tell me what you've done."

"Andreaaaa," an embarrassed Sandy groaned, "No. I won't let anyone touch my breasts. That's too far, and no, I won't touch their thing either. I want to save myself for Blake."

"Number one, what if you don't get Blake? Number two, if you get Blake, you'd better be ready to fuck,"

"Huh? Andrea! We'd be making love, not F-U-C-K-ing."

"Fucking Sandy. **FUCKING, FUCKING, FUCKING!** That's what couples do. They **FUCK!**"

Sandy was getting uncomfortable and edgy. She asked Andrea if they could change the subject.

"To what Sandy, hand-fucking-quilting? Macra-fucking-me? How about pottery-fucking-molding or making mud-fucking-pies?"

Sandy's appalled look was slowly replaced by a tiny smile. Andrea looked at this and flipped a quick bird. Soon the tiny smile became a chuckle, which then graduated to the point that they were both laughing so hard they couldn't control themselves.

"I need a drink and a smoke. C'mon Sandy, let's go see what's up on this train."

They soon found themselves in the dining area, which had been transferred into a lounge after eight o'clock. Andrea ordered a scotch and soda double, while Sandy opted for Coca-Cola. It wasn't especially crowded, but even a train to Seattle had leeching lounge lizards skulking about. It made the pair laugh when an open shirted fifty-year-old approached them about joining him in his cabin for a "nightcap". They both cackled so hard they turned the man's face red as he crept away, presumably looking for an opportunity elsewhere. Sandy felt sorry for the goat, but Andrea persuaded her not to worry so much.

"Come on Sandy. Forget about that weirdo and celebrate a little. This is so cool. We're heading on a train to Seattle. What more could we want? Have a drink. It won't kill you.

"Well, okay, but just one. I have to stay sharp."

"Sharp for what? We're in the middle of Wyoming, Idaho, or some fucking where. Who cares?"

One drink led to another led to another and soon both girls were giggling uncontrollably while sneaking cigarettes in the empty passenger box three stations away from the lounge. Even Sandy was taking a few small puffs, only to cough them out quickly as her fresh pink lungs rejected the tar.

The two were getting along perfectly and Andrea took pride in the fact that she'd finally gotten Sandy to loosen up a bit. She thought it was good for her girlfriend to have a sense of independence and throw a bit of caution to the wind every now and then.

"So how ya doin, Sandy?"

"I'm good. I don't even feel sick or anything. This is pretty fun."

"I told you. It's okay to let yourself go here and there. No harm, no foul."

Andrea was looking into Sandy's eyes. The green tint mixed with a light brown was breathtaking. Their faces were inches apart and the talking cooled to a slow whisper.

"Do you think I'm pretty Andrea? Am I attractive? Do you think I can win Blake's heart?"

"Oh yes, Sandy. I think you're the most beautiful person I've ever met. You have such a nice smile, soft hair and beautiful skin."

Andrea ran her hand from Sandy's locks down along her narrow cheekbones and finally across her chin. Sandy straightened up in a defensive, but not overly resistant posture.

"I can smell your aura Sandy. You're gorgeous. Any man would kill to be with a beautiful woman like you. Many women would too. I know I would."

As Andrea drenched Sandy with sweet nothings, she inched closer and closer to her lips. The scent of Sandy's perfume became intoxicating. Andrea could hold back no further. The talking stopped as their soft mouths met. Andrea gently slipped her tongue between Sandy's lips and tasted the alcohol-tinged moisture. Sandy accepted it and the kiss went on for what felt to them like forever. Andrea reached up and cupped Sandy's firm breast in her hand, rubbing ever so gently. She could feel her hardening nipple begging for escape. Andrea attempted to push her hand inside Sandy's top, but was stopped.

Sandy carefully took her friend's hand and moved it away. She then pulled back from the kiss, but it wasn't sudden or with malice. She gave Andrea a hug and whispered in her ear.

"I love you so much Andrea; but as a friend, not a lover. I know you've wanted to kiss me and I'll admit I've been curious, but this is as far as we can go. I don't want to ruin our friendship. It means too much to me."

Andrea, while disappointed, knew Sandy was right. She wasn't interested in ruining their friendship either.

"I like boys, *men*. I want to be with Blake. I want you to know that you're my very best friend and I'm so glad we shared a kiss. I do love you Andrea, but not like *that*."

They clutched each other and started to cry when they heard the door slide open behind them. One of the train's ushers screamed at them.

"Hey! What are you doing in here?"

They quickly made a b-line back to the lounge area before the usher could catch them.

After a couple more drinks and smooth conversation that seemed much more relaxed since their "kissing incident," they both headed back to their cabin for some sleep.

The first night in a train headed to Seattle and a lot happened between the two. It was nothing compared to what awaited.

*

The whistle blew and it was time to go to work. Blake was starting his new job on the dock in Seattle. The view of the city wasn't visible from the shipyard, which was situated on E.Westlake Ave. He would have to drive about two and a half miles south to reach the skyline. "As a matter of fact", he thought, "there isn't much of anything in this area." It was true, as that side of town was close to one hundred percent industrial.

Blake lived just north of his work. He could walk if the mood ever struck him. You took a chance in this town though, as rain came and went out of nowhere. One minute, it was bright and shiny, the next gloom and doom. He had only been in Seattle for a weekend and found that to be about the only negative he could surmise. The city itself was beautiful and the people, so far, were very kind.

Loading the boats was work he had never experienced. It was both physical and mental in that the hard labor made Blake sore and weak, which in turn made him worry about his health. He didn't want to keel over on day one, especially without having met the rest of the crew. He went in at seven and work started right away. A break followed at ten, and then lunch at one. Last break was at four and work ended at six. Ten hours a day, six days a week. Blake hoped he would build up some endurance as he went along. The rain that usually came at some point everyday was a welcome relief as it helped cool him and the crew down, giving everyone a second wind.

After day one was complete, it took all of his strength to get back to the apartment and plop down on his bed. He slept from just after six until his alarm went off at six am. He was filthy but didn't care. He changed his clothes, slapped on some deodorant and was on his way. The second and third days were a bit easier, and by Saturday, he was feeling like he'd done this work all his life. Some days were slow in that less deliveries or pick-ups occurred, and when that happened, the crew simply laid around. There was no other work that they were responsible for, so no one was chastised. Blake was getting to know a couple of the guys and went along with the program, bringing no trouble to himself.

The workweek ended on Saturday and Blake decided to get his dinner downtown. He wanted to taste a bit of the Seattle cuisine and have a look around. The drive downtown was nice and easy. He thought things would be a bit more complicated with all the rivers and canals snaking through the city. It turned out that it wasn't bad at all. A right here, a left there, and voila, the city unfolded before his eyes. It was awesome seeing Seattle in the dark. The lights shone down on the water and back up, giving the illusion of two towns looking back at you. Blake could only imagine how it looked from the air. He went down to see the local sports stadiums, which were right next to each other on the south side of town. After that, he headed back to the busiest part of the city and saw a sign that read: Seattle's Finest Cuisine! That was good enough for him, so he parked and entered, looking forward to filling his starved palate. It was here that Blake met someone who would change his life forever.

*

Amy had just finished her latest capture. She was ten for ten and Claude was both impressed and somewhat astonished. The woman had an edge about her that he had trouble pinning down. Claude was a self-professed master of judging a person's character, but Amy threw him off. She was so kind and gentle one second, but on the turn of a dime, one of the most vicious women he had ever run across. She backed down to no one, had the disposition of an angry rattlesnake and brought her assignments to justice without fail.

Amy arrived at Claude's office and he handed her another envelope filled with cash.

"That should see you through, Amy. Five large plus a bonus for being a perfect ten. Can't beat that huh?"

"A perfect ten, you say. Why do I get the feeling that you are either a real smartass Claude or that you want to get in my pants by using a cheesy pick-up line?"

"I'm very taken by you Amy; but I don't ever fuck the help. You're beautiful, shapely, and mysterious, which are the top reasons I stay business only. Fooling around with a chick like you isn't good for a man's sanity."

"How do you know it's so good for me, Claude? What makes anyone think I'm not the one doing the rejecting here?"

In the blink of an eye, Claude brought out and flung a five-sided, razor sharp death star. It hit the lower wall of the hallway outside the office smoothly and efficiently, whizzing inches from Amy's throat as it passed her. She had felt the breeze of death.

"What the hell Claude?" She stated as she clutched her neck. "You could've sliced my throat wide open."

Claude smiled slyly and responded with a tiny chuckle. "If cutting your throat were what I wanted to do, it would've already been done. My action had nothing to do with you. Now go Amy; have a night out and relax. I'll call you in a few days."

Amy stood up and self-consciously nodded to her trainer and turned to walk out. As she was exiting the room, she looked across the hall and saw where the star had plunged into the wall about three inches above the floor. Hanging from it was a large rat, gored in its midsection and suspended with its feet off the floor. Amy's eyes widened as she stood in awe. She turned back to commend Claude on his skill, but he wasn't to be seen. There were no other exits from that room besides out the one door where Amy was standing. She walked back into the room and gave it the once over, satisfied that Claude, in fact, was gone. In the flash of an eye, he had disappeared right under her nose.

"I'm glad I don't have to hunt *him* down. He'd be a tough nut to crack."

She gathered her things and left, but not without taking one more look at the marksmanship her trainer had exhibited. To her, it was better than amazing. She wanted to be like Claude, whom she thought of as a human weapon. She pulled the star out of the wall and wiped it with a tissue. After glancing one final time into Claude's office, she put it in her bag.

*

Amy went home and showered up, ready to get a bite to eat and down a couple of drinks for fun. The apartment was getting less and less lonely each day since Hank had left. She was beginning to get her emotional feet back under her and that was a good thing for any potential date material she might encounter. She was happy with the work she was doing as she continued socking away money for a rainy day, which was nearly every day in Seattle.

Often Amy would spend her free evenings in the basement of the apartment pounding on a punching bag she hung from one of the rusty ceiling beams. She also rode her stationery bike, which she bolted to the floor and applied screw tight glue to the threads to discourage would be thieves. Her apartment complex and the area around her were safe, so she didn't worry too much about it. Stealing from Amy could be a huge mistake, though, especially if she caught you. As well as she had toned down her temper, Amy could, and would, administer a wallop if provoked. It was much better to leave her alone. As Claude said, 'she had the disposition of a rattlesnake', and he was on the money. As Amy made her way downtown, she kept thinking about Claude's disappearing act at the school. He was right in front of her one minute and gone the next. This made her think about how she would handle it if the same situation arose while she was on a job. What if someone simply evaporated before her and she was a sitting duck? This was the first time the new job gave her goose bumps. She felt them rise from her toes to her head. She had to shake them off; knowing deep down that Claude would somehow protect her from that kind of situation. The smile returned to her face as she pulled into an eatery simply labeled "Seattle's Finest Cuisine!"

*

Blake was finishing his salad and waiting for his main course; a salmon filet sautéed in a rich creamy sauce of some Seattle-esqe sort. This was an angler's town, so fish was often the house specialty. That was okay with the young man, as it helped build muscle. He had even heard that it helped your brain function. Whether that was true or not didn't matter, but the idea of it was somewhat comforting. After thinking about his brain and the result fish may have on it, he felt a peace come over him. He strolled to the jukebox situated between the men and women's restrooms, stuck a quarter in, and choose an uplifting song with a harder beat. It was "Alright" by Kings X.

The song played with a catchy melody and Blake felt on top of his world. The song described living each day to its fullest, and not worrying so much about situations that were out of one's control, and with no anxiety or panic bogging him down, he was actually enjoying his evening. He thought seriously about finishing his dinner and finding a bit of the downtown nightlife to keep him in an upright mood. This is when she walked into the restaurant. He was instantly mesmerized.

"Oh my God," Blake whispered to no one, "she's the most beautiful woman I've ever seen."

His heart palpitated and skipped around in his chest like a butterfly was stuck in his throat. It was as if she walked in slow motion. He swore she had an aura around her of a bright white yellow shade.

"She does, I swear. She has a halo around her."

Amy stepped up to the bar, ordered a drink and then found a vacant table to the side as she waited for a dining area to open. Blake couldn't keep his eyes off her. She was wearing a black top that was cut just low enough to be interesting and had red leather pants to go with it. Her hair was a flawless black, jetting long behind her back and curled above her eyes. Her smile, her teeth, her *ambiance*, all perfect to the stricken Blake. She scanned around the room and their eyes met. He still couldn't look away as she gently licked her lips after taking a sip from her straw. She returned his stare, but her smile dwindled into a semi frown and her eyes flittered into a threatening posture. Blake looked away quickly, not wanting to appear too taken by her. He looked up and down the walls, to his left and his right, and then back her way. She was still greeting his eyes with that cold stare. He decided to turn his chair in the other direction. She had looked him down and defeated his male presence with a simple lowering of her brows. He was trying to console himself when he felt a tap on his shoulder. He turned and was shocked to see that she was standing before him. He didn't know what to do, as he'd never been so smitten in his life. Ten seconds of her was all it took to set Blake straight.

"May I sit?" She inquired with a slight rasp in her voice. "Or should I stand here and look stupid?"

"Please, please, sit. Here. Here's a chair. Please have a seat."

Blake fumbled, shook, and felt a hot flash that was stifling, but finally arranged a seat for her. She let out a rough squeak of a chuckle and sat next to the most intimidated man on the face of the earth. Blake Thomas, lady-killer? Not in this case. At that moment, he was Blake Thomas, choke specialist.

"Are you okay?" Amy inquired. "Get a hold of yourself before you fall completely apart."

This time she smiled that bright vibrant grin that was so inviting. Blake couldn't believe that she had actually sat next to him. She smelled like an angel sent straight from heaven. A hint of cinnamon mixed with the odor of her; light and intoxicating.

"So, what are you drinking, uh…I didn't catch your name."

"Blake. Blake Thomas."

He put his hand out and she met his grip with the softest touch he'd ever experienced. Every sense was new to Blake. Every touch, smell, sight, and noise; it was all in hi-def stereo.

"Amy Fraser." She said.

To Blake it sounded slow and echoing, *"AAMMYY FFRRAASSEERR!"* Is what he heard. Blake shook for a solid ten seconds before Amy lifted one side of her cheek and pulled her hand back. She studied Blake with a squinted eye as he looked at her with an awkward smile.

"So Blake, I asked you what you were drinking."

"Oh, oh yeah. Silly me. I'm daydreaming away here. My goodness, is it hot in here?" He was fanning himself with a napkin.

"You're a funny guy, Blake. Where did you get your sense of humor?"

Blake blushed red and snickered. He was trying his best to get a grip on his emotions, but the hint of anxiety was lurking deep inside. Amy looked him over with another smile and an odd eye while Blake squirmed in his seat. She finally stood up.

"I'm having dinner here. Would you like to sit together?"

"Duh, uh, okay?" Blake again smacked himself with a mental open hand.

Amy took Blake by the hand and led him through the restaurant behind the server who was seating her. Blake tagged along like a smitten kindergartener following his cute teacher. They finally reached the table and sat across from each other.

"Dude," Amy asked, "are you alright? You look a bit peaked."

"Um, I have trouble with nerves sometimes. You know, anxiety, panic. It's not important."

Amy mulled over Blake's comments and did what she knew to help him; she excused herself to the restroom and watched Blake from a distance. She wasn't at all sure what the attraction was for her. He was handsome, dressed okay, and had toughened hands, which meant he was a hard worker. All the things Amy liked in a person. She had men leering at her day after day, but this man was different in some way. She wasn't sure how, but went with the feeling.

Upon returning to the table, she snuck up behind Blake and grabbed his ribcage on both sides just above the love handles.

"GOTCHA!"

Blake dove from the seat to the underside of the table and banged his head on one of the wooden legs.

"Damn!" Blake spit. "Why'd you do that?"

"Does your head hurt?" Amy asked quickly.

"Yes it does. It hurts a lot."

"Good, then your nerves are calmed. You're getting color back into your face. My psychiatric skills at their finest. They'll be no charge today; that's on the house."

Blake's squinted face turned into a grin, which in turn led to a belly laugh.

"Are you crazy, Amy Fraser?"

"Yep! Let's eat and then go have a drink. What do you think? Good idea?"

"Sure. However, I don't drink alcohol. Coke is my limit."

"And I care how? Let's have some fun. I don't care if you drink baby formula from a bottle as long as you're nice."

Blake had to reflect backwards rather quickly. The anxiety had hidden from Amy, and he was thinking clearly again. He had to ask her why she approached him after giving such a sour look at second glance.

"Why? I sensed something *nice* in you. You didn't cower or leave; you simply turned the other cheek. Most men are done after I give them that stare."

Satisfied with Amy's answer, he ordered a slice of pie while she ate her meal. Thirty minutes later, they were on their way to the Seattle nightlife to talk and get to know each other better. Blake was flabbergasted that he'd been blessed to have this woman as company, as he figured a ton of men would want that kind of luck. They had known each other less than an hour and Blake found her to be sarcastic, feminine, hardened, funny and devilish all rolled into one delightfully "easy on the eyes" package.

"I'll drive," Amy insisted, and they sped down the road in her jeep. It would be a most interesting evening for Blake Thomas, as he would learn much about the woman that he found to be mesmerizingly beautiful.

*

Whistles blew, brakes screeched against tracks, metal squealed its high-pitched scream and the two out of town women found themselves in downtown Spokane, Washington. It would be a few more hours before they'd reach Seattle, but many plans and rules would have to be laid out for their excursion, which was getting oh so close to becoming reality. The first thing they needed to do was find a cozy internet café to look up Blake, along with learning a thing or two about the large metropolitan city in which they were to attempt hunting down one single person out of over a million that lived there. They headed to the Rainbow Bar and Grill, which was a mile and a half hike from the Spokane Amtrak Station. They had four hours to kill, so this would be the place to research, get a bite and eat the time up.

    Sandy was so excited to get searching that she failed to check in at the bar first before rushing over to a seemingly unoccupied computer. She sat down and began her search. She typed in "Blake Thomas, Seattle." He hadn't been there but for a short time, so most of the hits that came up were Toledo based. Frustrated, she typed in "Blake," then "Thomas" and a number of other possible queries. She finally lost her temper and typed in "Blake Thomas works and lives in the Fucking Seattle city limits." She was shocked at the hits the search engine gave her. Everything from male and female porn stars named "Thomas" to "Where to find sex in Seattle". Undeterred, she kept it up.

    Andrea had approached the bar and ordered food and drinks for the two when she heard commotion from twenty feet away; right about the spot Sandy had seated herself. She looked over and saw a large and ominous man towering over her friend with an unfriendly look on his face. Andrea told the bartender she'd be right back and went to her assistance. The man standing over a shivering and unsettled Sandy stood all of six foot eight and weighed in at least three fifty. He was as big as a house and probably as solid as one too.

"Sir?" Andrea gently asked. "Is there a problem?"

He didn't bother looking at Andrea. "Was I talking to your funky ass?" was his rude reply.

"Well you don't have to be a dick about it; I'm just trying to see what your problem is with my friend."

"Oh, she's your friend, huh. Two peas in a fucking pod." He hurled out a hearty laugh.

"C'mon Sandy. Let's go eat."

Andrea signaled for Sandy to follow, but the gorilla put his hand on her shoulder and forced her to sit back down. Sandy let out a gush of air when she hit the seat, a sign that the force was extra firm.

"Let her up, you big asshole," Andrea ordered, "what's your problem loser? You know that's assault, right?"

Sandy was trying to signal Andrea to cool it by slashing a finger across her neck. That failing, she gave Andrea an umpire's "safe" sign.

The giant spoke. "My problem is this, bitch; your friend here decided to take my seat while I was pissing and use the internet *I* was working. Now which of you two little whores are going to pay for it?"

Andrea did not like being called anything that was degrading to a woman, so she fired back. Her head was bobbling from left to right as the anger was beginning to seethe inside her.

"We're not your 'whores' or your 'bitches,' so don't talk to us like that. We made a fucking mistake and you're being an *a-one* horse's ass about it. Now how much do we owe you, dickface?"

"I figure a thousand bucks ought to do it. What do you think guys?"

The four men sitting two tables away were watching, but didn't find the proceedings particularly funny. They figured if he wanted to pound some man, then fine- but women? That was different.

"Eat me!" Andrea shouted, "We're not giving you a thousand dollars. I'd rather stick my head in a pile of donkey shit."

Andrea was face to chest with the big man and tried to look as large and nasty as she could. Her intimidation tactics weren't working. The man felt no fear. He grabbed Andrea by her collar and lifted her two feet off the floor. Sandy took this opportunity to squirm off to the bartender and tell him what was happening. The large fellow pulled back his fist, ready to clock Andrea. She closed her eyes and started thinking about the kind of make-up she'd need to cover up the bruises.

"Knock it the fuck off Harold. Jesus H. Christ can't you be nice?"

Harold, apparently the big man's name, put Andrea back down and looked over to the bartender whom had a shotgun two inches from his face.

"Aw, I was just kiddin' with the girls. It's all good. You girls go on now. It's been fun."

"Don't bullshit me Harold. It's the same damn thing every week. Now this is strike two. One more and you're out of here. You big dumb redneck."

Andrea and Sandy were sitting at the bar where Andrea had ordered food. The tender returned and had a talk with the pair.

"Sorry ladies. He's a bully. He wouldn't have hit you, ma'am. He's just a stupid overgrown lout."

"Well," Andrea said, "how much do we owe for the time we used his computer?"

"Don't worry about that. Its pennies. Please remember though, to always check at the bar before you grab a seemingly open spot."

"No problem. Right Sandy?"

Andrea looked at her friend with at first a cold stare, but then lightened up and smiled. Sandy nodded her head and blushed red, embarrassed about her idiocy.

After eating their meal, a computer became free and the two paid the bartender for the privilege of using it. The kind bartender gave them a code and told them to go on free, which delighted the ladies. The big bully had left, so there was nothing holding them back except themselves. This time Andrea sat in the internet driver seat to see if she could make heads or tails out of Blake's possible location. They had a couple of hours to search and would take a cab back to the train station so they wouldn't miss the departure. After an hour, Andrea still couldn't figure anything out. Sandy figured it probably would've been a better idea to be more prepared before they left Toledo.

"We'll have to track him down when we get to Seattle. We've tried everything. He hasn't been there long enough yet to show anything on the computer."

Sandy was a bit down, but knew it was a long shot. She agreed with Andrea and they decided to hightail it back to the Spokane Amtrak station.

They hadn't bothered to check into the inner workings or maps of the city, so they stopped at a gas station on the way back and picked up an atlas. They had about seven or eight more hours before arriving in Seattle, so it was time to get down to business, learn something about the city, and then search for Blake.

*

Paradise City played loudly in Amy's jeep. She had the volume at nine out of ten.

"Is that too loud for you?" Amy asked Blake.

"What? I can't hear you." He replied with both hands around his mouth.

Amy rolled her eyes and turned the radio down a few notches. Blake was relieved, as the song continued to echo in his head. He figured he'd obsess over it with the "automatic" playback system rooted in his brain. Amy wouldn't allow it, though. She talked and talked. She asked questions and didn't wait for answers. Amy hadn't been close to anyone for a spell, so this felt good to her.

"You know Blake; it's hard to keep everything inside all the time. I don't know anyone in this city, so I'm sorry if I carry on." Blake this, Blake that, it went on and on…"I'm sorry, I just gab away."

"No, no. Please. Talk all you'd like. I'm a good listener."

"You want to go see a movie? We can go to Cinerama and see a movie, okay?"

"Yeah ok," Blake said with skeptical enthusiasm. He never knew when or where his nemesis named anxiety would strike, so he was always at the ready. It caused him to stay on edge and think about it far too often.

"What do you want to see? Something scary? How about a comedy? Tell me Blake."

He was going to agree and nod, agree and nod because what he wanted to see was Amy undressed on his bed. He kept catching whiffs of her perfume combined with that natural womanly scent. It was throwing him through a loop. He wanted to kiss her, touch her and ravage her into one quaking orgasm after another. His mind drifted to undressing her slowly, moving the glasses of wine to the nightstand and setting the mood with a dim light and sexy music. The top two buttons on her blouse were undone, and he could catch the tiniest glimpse of her black lacy bra underneath. He wanted to remove it with his teeth. He pictured black panties with that exquisite odor that only a female possesses. In his mind, Amy's would be so much sweeter. After slowly removing her panties and feasting his eyes on the beauty that made Amy so insatiable to him, he would...

"Blake! Blake!" Amy was snapping her fingers in front of his nose. He was quickly brought back to the real world.

"What's wrong with you? Are you daydreaming?"

Blake shook his head to clear the fantasy and answered. "Sorry. Sometimes I float a bit. ADHD, I think. What were you saying?"

"C'mon, we're going to see a movie. We'll have fun."

They entered the front doors on the Cinema and headed straight for the popcorn and other assorted goodies.

"I really shouldn't be eating this garbage," Amy told him, "but it's so good. Don't you think so Blake?"

Blake loved junk food and agreed. He bought some Sno-Caps and a coke, while Amy opted for extra-extra buttered popcorn and water. In they went to see "The Help," which was supposed to be the best movie of the summer.

They sat together and watched the film. Amy had taken a liking to the young out-of-towner and continued to sense his harmlessness. Amy so badly wanted a friend and preferred men to women when it came to chumming around. She wasn't sure why, as men had always seemed to cause her the most pain in her life. Blake seemed different to her and she liked the vibe.

She was concentrating on the movie when Blake made the minor mistake of moving his hand onto hers. She looked down and gently moved it back to his lap. Blake was severely hurt and embarrassed as she did this, causing him to turn a shade of red not visible in the darkened theater.

"I'm sorry." He whispered softly.

"SHHH!" Amy struck back. "This is a great part of the movie. Now hush up and watch."

Taken aback, Blake frowned and crossed his arms. The reaction from Amy was sharp and it speared his ego. Blake was about to get up and walk out when for some strange reason, Amy reached over without turning her head and patted Blake's leg. Still not looking at him, Amy spoke very softly, but loud enough so that Blake could hear her.

"It's okay, Blake. Go slowly. There's no rush, ok? I'm looking for a friend right now. I hope you're alright with that."

Blake was astounded for a moment, and then a smile crossed his lips. He was comforted that Amy was paying attention, something that he was used to all his life. Blake's Mom, girlfriends, and other women; Sandy in particular, always gave him one hundred percent of their undivided attention. This was new to the young, good-looking Midwesterner. Without another thought, Blake turned his attention back to the movie. What he didn't know was that a woman who loved him more than anybody else was approaching from the east. Sandy was on her way.

After the movie ended, Blake found out another new thing about Amy; that she was as tough and smart as she was pretty. As they walked back to her jeep parked near the corner of fourth and Lenore, a man walked up to ask Blake for a smoke.

"Beat it bum, we don't have any smokes," was Amy's matter-of-fact response.

The bum looked at her and disappeared into the shadow.

"Those fucking bums. Watch out for them Blake. They want everything if you have nothing. It's already hard enough taking care of yourself in this town without giving any extra away. Oh, I give to charitable causes, but they're not going to stop at the liquor store and blow it on Mad Dog."

Blake smiled and they continued their trek to her vehicle, which was twenty short feet away.

Suddenly, from his blind side, the same bum ran up and jumped on his back. He was pulling Blake's hair and cursing aloud. As quick as he had jumped, the bum let go. Blake turned and saw that Amy had hopped on the tramp's back and in one second flat, pulled the belt off her pants, wrapped it around his neck and tightened it to the last notch. She jumped off the bum and they both watched him struggle to get the belt loose. Amy snickered as Blake stood with his mouth agape.

"Look Blake, he can't get the belt loose. I figure he only has, oh, a minute and a half more before he passes out."

"You mean passes out and then....*dies?*"

"Yeah, dies. What do you think happens when someone can't breathe for more than a few minutes? They die."

"Amy. Don't let him die."

This encouraged Amy as she saw that Blake had a very soft spot in his soul. She nodded to him and walked over to the bum. She gave him a quick kick to the back of the knee which brought him down. After removing the belt and allowing the sweet air to fill his lungs, she issued the bum a warning that next time, his fate would be worse. She walked back over to Blake, gave him a long look as she put her belt back on and offered to him, "Shall we go?"

Blake was both stunned and captivated by her calm demeanor.

The rest of the night was as much fun as Blake had without using drugs or alcohol. They went dancing and stopped in for a dessert at of all places, The Erotic Bakery on Sunnyside Avenue. Amy laughed as she had a slice of cake with the frosting shaped like a penis that had a bow on it, and Blake ate a cookie that looked like a vulva. It was silly fun. When they finished, Amy took home a cheesecake with a rather bountiful pair of breasts on it.

"I'm definitely a boobie girl," was Amy's sharp-witted response. "Besides, I love cheesecake."

Amy drove Blake back to his vehicle and called it a night. She had to explain a couple of things to him before leaving.

"I really had fun with you and I'd like to get together again, but no romance Blake. I'm not ready and I'm not willing. I've been through a lot in the last year and need time and space to grow."

It was what Blake thought of as the typical "Let's be friends" speech. He was disappointed, as he thought her to be everything he wanted, even though he'd known her for a grand total of four or five hours. To him, she was so stunning. To her, he was very nice looking, but he was a potential *friend*, something she badly needed in her life.

"I understand Amy, but you're so beautiful and you smell so good and you…"

Amy covered Blake's lips with two fingers and gently shushed him. "I understand, and thank you. Now you better get going, okay. I promise we'll do something again soon."

With a sigh and a tiny broken heart, Blake did as Amy asked and jumped out of the jeep. She waved and drove off quickly, still jamming "Paradise City" out of her speakers.

*

"Where is she? Where is she? Where is she?"

Sandy's nerves were about to frazzle and she shook her hands in front of her body while looking up one side of the train and down the other trying to locate Andrea. They were to arrive in Seattle in hours and there was no sign of her anywhere. Since they'd returned from the internet café, Andrea had taken to having a few drinks. That turned into a few more, and soon she disappeared. Sandy lost her in the crowd at the train bar, and tried everything she could think of to find her. Sandy began to worry that she'd fallen off the train in a drunken stupor. She asked some of the fellow passengers in the bar if they'd seen her, but was greeted with shrugged shoulders.

The next best thing for her to do was to run to the engine room and find the engineer. She could ask if they had any idea about Andrea's whereabouts, or if they could make an announcement. Sandy had ringed her cell phone three different times and was routed to voicemail each time. She started to feel an ominous sickness in her gut, as she feared the worst. Sandy was one to shift far one way or the other emotionally. She never found herself staying too comfortable. When it came to loving Blake, though, she was in deeper than a painted ocean turtle. However, this situation, Andrea vanishing without a trace, threw her into a panic.

After reaching the conductor's door, Sandy saw that it had a sign reading:

ENGINEER COMPARTMENT
NO ADMITTANCE

She knocked politely to no avail. Again, she tapped on the door. It was too soft of a knock for anyone to hear, so she balled up a fist and went to give it a hard whack with the outside of her palm by her pinky finger. Then she heard her friend.

"Hee-hee. I wanna another drink. Oh you guys."

It was Andrea without a doubt. She had a voice so strong, even Sandy could hear it outside the door of the noisy engine room. Now that Sandy knew where her friend was, she knocked as hard as she could and kicked the door for good measure. The giggling and small talk came to an abrupt halt. Thirty seconds later, Sandy screamed at the top of her lungs.

"OPEN THE DOOR. ANDREA, IT'S SANDY. OPEN THE DOOR."

Her voice cracked as she yelled. It was Sandy at her angriest, which was still far less than aggressive. She balled up her fist and took in a deep breath when the door swung open and her friend was standing there in the wobbled unbalance of drunkenness.

"Whazz up Shandy? What chu doin here?"

"The question is what you're doing here Andrea."

Sandy looked over her friend's shoulder and saw one of the two conductors button up his trousers. This enraged her. She pulled Andrea out, sat her on the floor and gave her orders with a pointed finger; **"DON'T MOVE!"**

She went back into the engine room and lambasted both men with a piece of her mind.

"How dare you take a drunk, defenseless woman in your area and take advantage of her. I'll report both of you to the rail authorities, whoever that may be." Sandy's finger was waggling as she continued. "And furthermore, I'll see that you both lose your engineer licenses."

Sandy put her hands on her hips and awaited their responses. They looked at each other, looked at her and then broke out in a burst of laughter that upset the young woman.

"Ha," one conductor said, "go fuck yourself. And your friend too."

The other engineer nodded, grabbed his crotch in an act of defiance, and the door slammed in Sandy's face. She stood stunned for a moment, and then turned her attention back to her drunken friend.

"C'mon, let's go to the cabin."

Sandy reached down and helped Andrea up from the dirty floor. She swept the dust off her and helped her make the walk. Andrea opened up on the way. She spoke in an emotional slur that only a drunken person could.

"I luf you, Shandy. Do you luf me?"

"Of course I do. Why do you think I've been looking high and low for you?"

"Oh Shandy, Shandy. Oh How mush I luf....Blachhh."

Andrea vomited down the front of her blouse and onto the floor. Sandy sighed as she sat Andrea down to wipe her chin. The pain she felt for her friend was incredible. She thought to herself how much it must stink to be in her shoes. Sandy thought about their kiss from earlier and their brush with sex. Andrea was lonely and needed more than a friend. She needed a man; or woman if she preferred, to spend her time with and make memories.

    Sandy finally managed to get Andrea back to a reasonable cleanliness and took her to the cabin for a better wash-up. She helped her friend change into different clothes and threw the barfed ones right out the window of the moving train. She had no idea where they were, but figured it wouldn't be important under the circumstances. It was a long and strenuous night for her as she held Andrea's hair back as she vomited at least another dozen times. She would clean her up and get her back into a comfortable position. The moment finally came when sleep found Andrea and she quieted. Sandy curled up as close to her friend as she could and fell asleep with her. She loved Andrea. She gave her a peck on the cheek and closed her eyes, knowing that the big city and a new chapter in both of their lives waited.

Shaun Webb

11

Off with her Head III

The office was quiet on the late, rainy evening in Portland, Oregon. A candle flickered in the far corner while a small, refreshing breeze blew in and softly caressed the back of Soo-Chin Xing's neck.

Working late was nothing new for the workaholic Pathologist from Flint, Michigan who had left her ex-boyfriend Jack Beauregard just in the nick of time. Jack pled guilty to murder and other assorted offenses and was slain in prison. Kyle, Jack's son, turned out to be the infamous Black Jack Killer, and was shot dead by his own father. Soo was set to marry Jack, but his harmful demeanor after being voted into office squashed an opportunity for that to happen. Jack ended up knocking out a couple of her teeth and causing severe jaw injuries with one fateful punch. She didn't miss him and hoped he was rotting in hell. She did miss Kyle, although she was feverishly disappointed that he was the killer everyone thought old man John Garrison to be. The scenarios were strange, spacy and especially stress inducing. Soo had been going to a counselor twice weekly to sort out the feelings and get a grip on her new life in Portland. It hadn't been an easy transition and it was about to get a whole lot tougher.

Kurt had been watching Soo-Chin for a couple of days, as he had to make decisions on where and when he would collect her head. He turned to The Red Queen for wisdom and strength, playing Alice in Wonderland music, listening to recordings of the dialogue and studying pictures from the movie. It was his inspiration and obsession rolled into one dangerous fairy tale of violence. Alice was to kids a cartoon character, a legacy of their childhood dreams and fantasies; but to Kurt, it was a real entity with real actions, mannerisms and evil. Had Alice truly been a living character, she'd find Kurt's treatment of the story dreadful. Of course, Kurt didn't care much for Alice; it was on the Red Queen he always focused.

Following Soo-Chin around Portland was easier than Kurt ever thought it would be. He looked her name up at the public records department, found out when she worked by watching, and stood on the edge of darkness as the Queen of Hearts took over in his mind. The Queen spoke with her trademark English accent.

"Kurt, I am the supreme being. I am your greatest companion and counterpart. You ask 'what would the Queen do?' I would chop her pretty little head off and save it for myself. I would put it in a jar of fluid so that it was always recognizable and easy to identify. I would be a proud Queen. Between us, the heads will fall. I will always steer you in the right

direction and give you the guidance you seek. You are my Hatter Kurt; you won't fail."

Kurt nodded and agreed with what the Queen said. He heard the woman in his mind, but it played out as clearly and concisely as if she were there with him. Kurt listened further as the Queen continued…

"Off with her head, I say. Off with her head. She may not have eaten the tart, she may not have offended me the way she offended you but her head must be collected. She let down your hero, Kyle, when he needed her the most. She let you down with her pompous attitude and her cowardly demeanor. Off with her head, Kurt. **OFF WITH HER HEAD!"**

Kurt decided that he would do his brutal work at Soo's work place. He was originally planning to do the deed right at her house, but that idea was quashed when he followed her home and found she had roommates living with her. He followed her closely the next day to see if the opportunity to strike would present itself. To his delight, she decided to work late. It was the most ominous decision of Soo-Chin's life. Wanting the remnants of Soo-Chin visible to everyone, doing it at her work turned out to be the best bet. Kurt was happy that it presented itself in that way. In her home, she would have the shield of other people and Kurt wasn't interested in collecting another three or four heads to get the one he really wanted. It wasn't economical in his twisted mind. Besides that, he wanted her seen and he wanted to be heard, loud and clear.

"Who's been painting my roses red? Who's been painting my roses red? Who dares to paint the vulgar paint, the royal flowerbed? For painting my roses red, someone will lose his head. They're going to lose their heads, for painting the roses red. It serves them right, they planted white but roses should be red. Oh, they're going to lose their heads..."

Kurt sang along as the tune played over the speakers in his van. Soo was going to lose her head, for painting the roses red. In Kurt's mind, it was tremendously metaphorical. Soo left Kyle; she abandoned him in his time of need. She was selfish and obnoxious. As far as he was concerned, she painted those white roses red!

*

The scenes were gruesome, but Wilma didn't care. She had seen as bad if not worse in her time with the FBI. People run over by trains, fallen from a tall building; squashed like flies under a slapping hand. She had assisted in investigating the World Trade Center site at Ground Zero shortly after the attacks, and saw more carnage and wasted life than she could've ever imagined. It was routine for the strict, well-grounded agent. Her cronies were also unaffected by the scenes they encountered, reacting in robotic-like fashion. They weren't afraid to get their hands dirty. No anxiety, no shock, and no nausea; simply a job to do.

A Killer for the Queen

After studying the scene in Las Vegas, and now Nampa, Idaho, Wilma was guessing that Kurt Joseph might in fact be the responsible party. She had sent one man to Flint, Michigan in search of Mr. Joseph, but he had come up empty. Her and her other man decided that the murder in Idaho was by the same perp. Painted red roses, a beheaded body hanging up with no head to be found at the scene.

"Whoever's doing this," Wilma figured, "is for some strange reason collecting the heads. I don't remember the Queen in the story actually collecting any heads."

She was still thinking Red Queen, Alice in Wonderland, and anything else related to that story. She had bought books and tapes so she could refresh her memories of the very famous tale. One night while watching them, one of her men, who whispered in her ear some very interesting facts about Kurt Joseph, approached her. She nodded and shooed him away when he was finished. The two cronies slept in another room, but always seemed to be dressed in their black suits and white shirts whenever they were present, no matter the time of day.

It seemed that Mr. Joseph was a major player in a trial that took place in Flint involving the death of his child. The man who was convicted and eventually committed suicide in the death chamber was John Garrison, a man who hadn't been involved at all. The true guilty party was Kyle Beauregard, the son of the elected Governor, Jack Beauregard.

As complicated and odd as it all seemed, Wilma wanted an investigation into Kurt's son, Jimmy. She wanted to know what, where and when. She also requested a study into his interests before he died. She lay ten to one odds that Alice in Wonderland was a special friend to the slain child. To Wilma, one and one was beginning to make two. She needed more info, though. So far, she had the ex-wife in Las Vegas and the woman at the hotel. What was the link? Where was he going to strike next? If she could find out these answers, she would have a firmer grip on what may be going on and be better equipped to stop it. She sent both of her men back to Flint, Michigan, this time to not only knock on his door, but also break it in and find out exactly what the answers were. Anything less would warrant disappointment. She wanted her men to break the law to get her the information that she was seeking. Never indecisive, they delighted in doing what their boss asked.

  Wilma Hurst counted on her pair often. She wouldn't tolerate failure and if she had to, would strap them down with suspensions and pay cuts if they screwed up. Thus far, it had never happened. The two were always spot on and compliant, never questioning Wilma's methods, and never failing her. They shared an understanding relationship. She never leaked one bit of information about them and people stopped asking after they saw the results she was getting in apprehending criminals. There was also the fact that she'd give the information seeker a good chewing out for asking about them. Her methods were strict. It was a tough job under a tough boss, but the two never flinched.

  She was also the only person that ever heard either of the two speak. She cared very much for them. They were, after all, the two she could always count on to come up with an answer. It reached the point where they acted on command; like a Pavlov's dog type of training. Wilma rang the bell and the two salivated for action. The pair was rarely given any credit when cases were solved or murders were stopped. That satisfied Wilma, as she took the spotlight.

Nobody but the three of them knew of their tactics in the crime-fighting world, and as far as Wilma was concerned, it would remain that way. She had these men well trained and obliging twenty-four hours a day, seven days a week. She knew that sending them to Flint together would unearth more information and more detail, thus helping her get to the practical details of the problem.

*

The Dark Men

*

They were raised differently than the normal children of the world. Taken straight from birth, they were clustered in a camp with other "special" children who, by statistical measure, were expected to be a step above a "normal" person in intelligence, logic, ability to stay emotionally grounded, and other factors that were seen by the government as conducive to specialized training. The parents of these children were not always above average or even on a par; the statistics used by scientists measured the odds of the *child* being above average. There was no test that the parents took to make a determination. It was a gamble that the child would excel where others would fail.

As the children grew in this camp, they were weeded out and sent to foster homes all over the country. The break-up of parent-child relationships meant nothing to the government, because the doctors were told beforehand to deliver the child, send it straight to a "receiver", or a person waiting to take the boy, and then tell the parents that death occurred shortly after birth. A few parental tears were a small price to pay for a possibly excellent specimen that would work for the FBI. It was boys only who were selected, as the powers that were stayed behind the times when it came to the women's lib movement. The FBI thought these "special" kids needed to be boys because they'd need more endurance, stamina and other physical characteristics that by nature were not as prevalent in a girl.

The camps were excruciatingly difficult, and the boys were separated quickly. The meek were out the minute they showed any weakness. Many factors went into the decision making of the teachers; there would be no crying from the age of five and up, no bed-wetting, no bad or good temper, only the boys who could hide their emotions survived into their teen years. No character flaws were tolerated. In a routine year, over five thousand children would be selected from around the country and if ten survived the training and went on to work for the FBI, it would be considered a success.

The two men who worked for Wilma were twins. They were two excellent specimens that the program, up until then, had ever seen. They took pain, agony, torture, and never flinched. They were comparable to unfeeling robots that were made of metal, or iron, or even steel. No tears ever left their eyes after the age of five. No agitations were present when encountering pain. They had to be the toughest of the tough; the strongest of the strong; and the most fearless of their race.

Their trainers were ruthless. The tedium started at age five when their diapers were thrown away and replaced with a uniform that had sharp tacks sewn into the inside of the fabric. It was as uncomfortable as wearing rose thorns. Daily berating and monotony were the themes for eight years, as the boys ate, showered, did small chores and slept. They rose at four A.M., retired at ten P.M. and didn't know about TV, radio, newspapers or media. The only thing the boy's knew was what they were taught at the compound. The books, pictures and any other information that were fed into the boy's minds were heavily censored. Those activities encompassed each day until they entered their teen years. The twins never wavered.

The training at thirteen consisted of handling weapons, rigorous daily PT, and language skills. The boys learned to speak only when asked a question or if pertinent information needed to be shared. They only ate when they were allowed; never out of hunger pain, but out of need and timing. They were taught four languages; English, Russian, Arabic and Chinese. The Government thought those to be the most pertinent for the day and age, as the countries that spoke these languages were the largest threats to the safety of the United States. Up until the age of eighteen the days and nights were filled with the type of training that would destroy the normal human psyche. The twins never wavered.

Years eighteen through twenty were the most important; as this was the time they were programed to follow a leader unwaveringly. Whatever was asked of them had to be done without question. Their bowel movements, emptying of their bladders and hygiene habits were timed to the second, and never changed unless they were ill. They ate the same food each and every day at the same exact time. When pain was inflicted, their heart rates never went above ninety or below seventy. The only time it went into an exercising rate was when they were in fact exercising. The cold stares and callous, straight edged looks were always visible. Never a smile, never a cringe, never an emotion of any kind. At the age of twenty, they wore dark glasses to hide the *lack* of emotion. This was the time they started wearing the dark suits and were never referred to as anything except "Dark Men."

These boys were never named, so they never had identities besides the numbers they were assigned from a young age. Wilma referred to the twins as cronies or men. She often didn't refer to them in any other way except a wave of the hand. Wilma wasn't a Dark Man because of her gender; otherwise, she probably would have made it through the course. She was rewarded with the twins upon their completion of training because the FBI thought that the three of them together could never be stopped. They were right. Nothing stopped the twins, and Wilma allowed them to do all the dirtiest of the work because that's how they were trained. Death never frightened the two. The thought of dying never entered their collective minds.

A Killer for the Queen

They were like machines, only human. The twins were virtually unstoppable.

*

Soo was working late, as she had to clean up after her final autopsy of the day. The rain was drizzling down in a mist that was adequate to water the lawns, but not quite enough to ruin the evening. Typical Portland weather. Soo didn't care about the weather. Her focus was getting the place cleaned up so she could go out for some much-needed food and then home to relax before starting another day in less than six hours.

It was quiet in the lab and Soo had the radio playing softly. There were no security guards working in the building because they'd never had a break-in. It was a good part of the city with no incidents of merit over the previous three years. Tonight it would change.

Skirting along the side of the building wearing a light trench coat was Kurt. He was looking for the easiest way inside without causing a clamor. He was armed with a blowtorch, a dozen white roses, a can of red spray paint and a small CD player with a disc inside ready to play. On his head sat the top hat that was now *the* trademark of his alter ego. While spying the exterior, Kurt came across an unlocked window. He easily wedged it open and crawled out of the rain. He found himself in an inner office that was nearly pitch black. He could see a shred of light quite a distance down the hallway. He figured that it was where Soo-Chin was working. Kurt decided that the space he was standing in would serve as the "home base" that he would return to after he finished his task. Kurt pulled out the roses and the can of paint. It was time to set his plan in motion.

  Soo was softly whistling when she heard a slight thud from a distance. She walked over to her radio and turned the music down. A peek outside of the window of her lab was in order. She saw nothing. Soo made sure the door was secure, although it didn't have a lock for safety reasons. She slid a rolling desk chair against the door to help her feel a bit more protected and secure. Opting against turning the music back on, Soo sat at her desk on the other side of the room and dealt with the stack of paperwork sitting before her. Page after page, she checked the grammar, structure and legitimacy of the documents. This was important work because the slightest error could result in lawsuits, which were among the problems when dealing with the dead. As she kept her mind on the work, the rolling chair slowly creaked its way back toward her, squeaking and moaning ever so slightly as it moved. The door slipped open, and shut with a whisper. Soo was none the wiser until she looked up less than a minute later. She was surprised and slightly freaked out when she saw that the chair was only ten feet from her desk. She tiptoed over to it and then walked to the door; nothing else seemed amiss.

  "Must've rolled over here because the floor's uneven." Was all she could figure.

  She turned back to see the other side of the room and noticed something sitting on her desk. It was hard to tell what it was because of the distance between her and the object. She felt a spine-chilling tingle in her arms, causing her to break out in gooseflesh. The hair on her neck stood up as she shivered. She was getting a serious case of the creeps. She strolled ever so slowly back toward the desk and it finally came into view: a dozen red roses. Perplexed, Soo turned her head to one side and began to feel better as she figured either someone from staff was playing games or one of the guys she thought was cute and had flirted with for some time had come up to the office and snuck in. She strolled to the desk confidently and bent to sniff the roses. They felt wet to her as she wiped her nose off with her index and middle finger. When she naturally looked at her fingers, she saw that they were red. Her first thought was blood, but that quickly disappeared as experience in pathology destroyed that theory. She sniffed her fingers.

"Paint? Is this red paint?"

From a darker corner of the room, the CD began played its eerie song.

"In the room of silent dreams, I've lost the light of life. Now cold darkness embraces me, I'm blinded by my pain. Awoke in empty halls while shadows were dancing on the walls. I try to grip the morning light, but there's just the gleam of silvery moonlight."

Soo backed away from the music and shuddered with fear as she saw what she thought was a man holding a rather large knife. He was still standing in the shadows, so she couldn't make out his face. As he came forward, she froze in terror. It was Kurt

Joseph. She never forgot a face and this one was deranged and mortifying. It was the face of a killer.

"K-Kurt Joseph? Is th-that you?"

"Soo-Chin Xing. I'm the one that's s-supposed to be stuttering here. What's the m-matter? C-Cat got your tongue?"

"W-why are you here, Kurt? I haven't done anything wrong. Why do y-you have that b-big knife?"

"If you give me a minute, I'll tell you. In the meantime, shut the fuck up."

Soo nodded to the known intruder and sealed her lips shut. She had a plan in her mind though. She was a track runner in school and still ran regularly. She figured to have the edge on him for speed and stamina. She looked down and noticed that the blade was stained with blood and that he was wearing a blowtorch on his hip. Being a Pathologist, she immediately derived a conclusion; cut, then cauterize. It made her sick to her stomach. Kurt pulled a scroll out of his pocket as she stood before him. He unrolled it and made his eerie announcement, without stutter.

"By the power vested in me by the Red Queen of Hearts, you have been found guilty of treason for walking out on Kyle Beauregard in his time of need. The penalty for such treason is death. **OFF WITH YOUR HEAD!**"

Her eyes widened and her heart fluttered as Kurt, standing two feet away, raised the machete. Acting quickly, Soo picked up the glass that was sitting on the desk in front of her. It was acid for dissolving skin from bone. She threw the concoction toward Kurt. Even though he'd ducked, a few droplets landed on his cheek and burned like nothing he'd ever felt. He screeched in pain as Soo swiftly set afoot in the opposite direction. Despite the painful burn, Kurt took after her. She rushed out the door and down the hall, Kurt only three feet behind her. She frantically thought of plans as she was running. Soo grabbed a gurney as she fled past it and swung it into Kurt's path. He was tripped up and temporarily slowed, giving her a few more valuable seconds. She had to get to a room in which she could lock the door from the inside and keep him away. It was her only chance. The room she had in mind? Of course, it was the cooler where the bodies were stored. Soo galloped through a door and down the stairs toward the basement, Kurt in full pursuit.

"OFF WITH YOUR HEAD! OFF WITH YOUR HEAD I SAY!"

Soo finally found the door into the cooler and quickly went through it, locking it behind her just as Kurt had reached it. The relief she felt was astounding, as a ton of bricks fell from her shoulders. She slowly backed away from the door and saw Kurt looking through the small window that was only big enough for his pair of eyes, which darted left, right, and then directly at her. She flipped him the bird and told him she was calling the cops. His eyes disappeared. Soo sat down on the small chair sitting up against the wall and began taking deep breaths as she re-balanced her shaken emotions. The door knocked. Soo stood up quickly but cautiously. Suddenly, in the small window, she saw Kurt's eyes again. He moved over and then flashed a set of keys, he yelled through the door.

"I have the key, and I drank the drink, and I ate the cookie, and now I'm tall enough to use it."

A sinister laugh followed.

"Oh no, the fucking key." Was all Soo could utter.

In her haste, she didn't grab the set of door keys that hung right next to the door as a guard against someone accidently locking themselves inside the chilly room. There was only one way in and one way out; through that one lonely, awful door. The room started shrinking as Soo attempted to re-think her strategy. She only had one chance and took it, hoping to avoid death on this rainy evening.

Kurt turned the key and voila, the door opened. When he entered, there was stone silence. He thought to himself that he could hear a dormouse scurry across the floor. Despite the burns on his face that had seared the skin, Kurt barked out another sinister laugh and smiled a black-toothed grin.

"Come out, come out wherever you are."

Soo, as still as she could be, stayed in her position. She knew she was breathing heavy and tried very hard to calm herself. She counted backwards by threes from one thousand, trying to change her train of thought.

"Come on out Soo-Chin. The Queen has made her decision and I'm here to carry out the execution. If I don't bring her your head, I may lose the trust she's put into me."

"Nine ninety-nine, nine ninety-six, nine ninety-three..." she whispered.

As Soo continued to count backward, everything happened in a flash. The sheet was quickly pulled off and the machete came down with a harshness reserved for slaughtering cattle. Soo's head dis-connected from her body and flew backward, splatting into the wall with great force, leaving a smear of blood behind. Kurt pulled out and lit his blowtorch, cauterizing the gaping wound above Soo's shoulders. When he completed that grisly task, he walked over, picked up her head and cauterized the neck. He looked in her deadened eyes and spoke.

"N-Number one, when the Queen w-wants a head, she g-gets it. Number two, if you're g-going to pretend to be a b-body under a white sh-sheet, don't wear b-black socks."

Looking about the room, each body present had their bare feet exposed and a tags banded to the big toes.

Kurt was proud of the fact that he sealed the wounds so fast, eliminating any large pools of blood and making clean up much easier. He did what he had to do and departed exactly the way he'd come in; through the unlocked window. He settled into his van and put Soo's head into a vat of formaldehyde. He noticed that she had a bit of blood on her nose from the head crashing into the wall. He reached in, pulled the head back out, licked her face clean of the blood, and then put it back in. He screwed the top on tight and put a picture of her headless body on the hook below followed by a red Queen of Hearts.

*

The cronies returned to Wilma with news. They had gone to Flint and brought back a few goodies for their leader. The two dark figures led Wilma out to the car and showed her the black leather suit Kurt had sewn together in his basement. Wilma smiled and insisted on seeing more. Without hesitation, the two pulled out a series of Alice in Wonderland tapes, CD's, movies and toys.

"Who cares about this? This doesn't prove anything. We already know he likes Alice in Wonderland. What Else?" Wilma asked.

The two then pulled out a series of pictures they had taken from the son's bedroom. Where there used to be a whole series of videos and CD's, it was now half-empty. Any and everything that had a picture of the Queen of Hearts was gone. There were all kinds of stuffed toys, but no Queen toys. Kurt had made off with everything that had to do with the Red Queen of Hearts.

The pattern was as obvious to Wilma as it was to her men. She waved them off and studied the goods on her own. She was very close to positive that Kurt was the culprit, but had no murders past Nampa, Idaho.

That would change in mere hours.

*

The forensics and pathology teams arrived at the building around 8:30, which was close to the usual starting time. They liked to get a few slugs of coffee in before beginning what some would find to be extremely boring work. Looking in telescopes wasn't the most exciting job for some; but for these people it was their worlds, not to mention it paid very handsomely.

John Hadley was the man who, every morning, had to count out the bodies to make sure they were all accounted for from the night before. As silly as it may have sounded to some, John would explain the term "necrophilia" and what it encompassed as far as severe mental illness. The people he told usually shuddered with disgust. To John, it was a shrug and not much else.

He walked through the myriad of slabs counting, marking on a clipboard and lifting the sheet to identify the face in the picture. As he was finishing, he noticed that there was a splat of blood on one of the sheets. He looked it over, lifted the linen and didn't notice anything wrong with the cadaver. A scrape against the skin of a dead person usually didn't cause them to bleed, but it did happen from time to time. As he looked around the area, he noticed a sprinkle of blood on the floor a few feet away from the body. He stood in the spot and studied it as another drop of blood came down and hit his nose. He felt it, looked at his fingers and then looked up. The ceiling tile above seemed to be saturated with blood in one corner. He walked over to the janitorial closet, grabbed a stepladder and headed back to the spot in question. Occasionally, the team played some sick jokes on each other. As dis-respectful as it was, you had to be careful or you'd find a finger in your soup or a toe in your tennis shoes. John thought this to be another joke, so he proceeded without caution. A young woman walked into the room as John was manipulating the tile; he looked down at her and laughed.

"Someone getting their sense of humor on again."

The young woman didn't have time to chuckle when the tile gave way and Soo-Chin's body tumbled out with force, knocking John off the ladder and onto the floor. The tile met his tailbone rudely as his look of horror said it all. John saw Soo-Chin, one of his dear friends, hanging out of the ceiling without her head attached to her shoulders. There was a large "Q" painted on her chest with a circle around it and a cross through the circle. "No Queen" is what it appeared to be saying. The young woman screamed and everyone came running. Looks of horror, squeamish cringes and shrieks filled the room. Everyone stood in a state of shock at the site of Soo-Chin Xing hanging dead before them.

*

Wilma had taken the items collected from Kurt's house into the Nampa police station where they had settled after discovering the body at the hotel. One of her cronies walked up with a piece of paper that had writing on it. It was an initial press release that had not yet gone public.

STOP…WOMAN FOUND DEAD IN PORTLAND, OREGON FORENSIC LAB. **STOP**…..SOO-CHIN XING IDENTIFIED AS VICTIM…..**STOP**…..VICTIM BEHEADED…..**STOP**…..HEAD MISSING….**STOP** PRESS RELEASE FORTHCOMING…..**STOP**.

"Get me that fucking case file from the Flint trial."

Wilma's crony was gone and returned within seconds. Wilma snatched the file from him and began speeding through it. Pages were falling on the floor as she searched. She finally found what she was looking for; Soo-Chin Xing had testified against John Garrison at the murder trial in Flint. Wilma shooed her cronies away. She sat down and perused further. It was starting to make sense. First Kathy Joseph, and then Soo-Chin Xing. Wilma immediately figured the victim at the hotel was only by circumstance. She had gotten in Kurt's way somehow. Inundating herself in the paperwork, Wilma began looking at all the players from that trial. Most were dead. Jack Beauregard, Kyle Beauregard, Lyla Helms, Dan Wheeler and Garrison himself. Now Kathy Joseph and Soo-Chin Xing were dead. The only name that was on the list that hadn't been killed was Robert Long, and he lived right near Kurt. Reading further, Wilma saw that the prosecutor was also dead, but by Jack Beauregard's hand.

"That left who?"

That who was Amy Fraser. It appeared to Wilma that Kurt was going after the women who had somehow been involved at the trial. Wilma began running a Sharpie on a map of the United States.

"Flint, Michigan to Las Vegas, Nevada to Nampa, Idaho to Portland, Oregon."

Wilma bet her life that Amy was nearby somewhere. She called one of the men into the room.

"Get a bead on Amy Fraser. I want to know where she lives, where she works, whom she fucks, everything. Move it."

The henchman nodded and fled, seeking to satisfy his boss.

PORTLAND, Oregon (AP)--A Chinese-American woman was decapitated in the county morgue by an unidentified assailant police said Thursday.

Soo-Chin Xing, was killed Wednesday night after staying at work late trying to catch up on paperwork, Portland Police Chief Wendy Flinchman said.

Her attacker is unknown. According to FBI reports she knew the attacker, although no motive for the slaying or any names would be mentioned, Flinchman said.

Police received two 911 calls shortly after 9 a.m. Thursday, Flinchman said, and were on the scene in a little more than five minutes to take reports. It is known that the victim's head is missing.

The FBI is investigating.

Oregon Gov. Tom McClaine offered condolences to the family.

"My thoughts and prayers are with the friends and family of Soo-Chin Xing today--and with the broader Portland community," he said in a statement. "The tragic attack on her this week has no doubt supplied terrible memories for members of the Xing family."

12

Curioser and Curioser

Amy decided she should call Blake and ask if he wanted to go on another "friend" date. Amy figured it had to be a bit tough for him, as he probably hadn't done anything in the city besides work since he'd arrived. She pulled out her cell phone and before she could call out, Claude called in.

"Amy. Go to Denny Park. A female perp has been spotted there. She murdered her husband, so proceed with the utmost caution. I would consider her armed and dangerous. Take her to Seattle PD when you apprehend. I repeat; proceed with caution."

"Okay Claude, but you still sound like you...."

The phone slammed down and Claude was gone. Amy had a job to do, Claude gave her the particulars and then he was out as quick as that day in his office when he "vaporized".

"Well fine then, Claude. I'll get right on it."

Amy was sneering at her phone. She gathered up her goods, hauled it to the jeep and then took off. Being that it was two miles to the park, followed by a few more to the police station, Amy decided to call Blake. She figured this to be easy work and she could still get out for a while.

"Hello, Blake?"

"Hello?"

"Yeah. Hey Blake, what's cookin'?

"Oh, hi Amy. What's going on?"

"Let's get together. I want to do something tonight, and I want you to help me do it."

Blake had been struggling with anxiety and panic throughout the day and tried to turn her down.

"Uh, I don't know Amy. I'm not really feeling all that great today."

"Whatcha mean, Blake? What's wrong?"

"Oh, nothing big, just some nerves. My heart kind of feels funny. It's skipping around in my chest."

"Skipping around in your chest? You mean palpitating?"

"Yeah, I guess. I better stay home."

"Bullshit. You're just bored. You need something to take your mind off it. It's that anxiety you talked about the other day. It'll pass."

The anxiety sufferer, which Blake was, didn't figure that you could actually have a feeling and it *not* be something serious. Amy wasn't as familiar with it as he was, and didn't understand the way he did, but being that she had struggled through PTSD and hallucinations, she could somewhat relate.

"Really Amy. Something might be wrong in my heart. Maybe I should go to the ER."

"When we get busy with something," Amy reasoned, "you'll feel better."

"What if I collapse when we're together?"

Blake was "what ifing" the problem to death. Amy kept up the pressure, insisting that Blake go out with her. She was getting closer to Denny Park, and her phone began acting up.

"So Blake...meet...Denny...few min...we...go."

"What?" Blake asked her to repeat.

"Den...Park...ew...minute..."

"You want me to meet you at Denny Park in a few minutes?"

Blake had misinterpreted Amy's message, which was that she would pick up Blake later, as she had to stop at Denny Park for a few minutes, and then go downtown. The phone on Amy's side finally fizzled into a dropped call. Blake, not being kind to himself or his inner child, shook his head, wondered why *he* was such a pain in the ass and got ready to go to Denny Park. He liked Amy so well; he was convincing himself to meet her despite his "ills."

Amy hung up and continued toward the park, which was about five minutes away. Little did she know that Blake was also headed over to the park to meet her. An unpleasant situation was manifesting and neither of them knew it.

Blake, figuring he'd ride with Amy, took a cab, which whisked him down to the entrance of Denny Park in mere minutes. He paid the driver and lingered around the street for a few minutes before becoming restless and walking down a path that led to the center of the park. He wasn't at all sure where Amy wanted to meet him, so he figured if he kept moving, his chances of running into her brightened. He was quite nervous to begin with, and roaming around the park at night wasn't helping. There were only a few people present, but they were dark and ominous. Blake seated himself on a bench near a light tower. He was alone for a grand total of one minute. Out of the woods walked a woman. She was attractive, but looked as if she'd been in a bit of a tussle. Her hair was blown to one side unnaturally and her make-up was slightly smeared.

"How you doing there, buddy?" She inquired. "Are you looking for someone, or *something*?" as if she was offering him a sexual favor.

Blake ignored her and stared straight forward. He felt tension in his muscles and his heartbeat seemed to start scattering around in his chest again.

"Hey man. I'm over here. What are you looking at?"

The woman was trying to get Blake's attention and he didn't want to give it, so he stood up to leave. She walked over to him. She was six or eight inches shorter than Blake, so she had to look up at him. He finally responded.

"Look lady, I'm waiting for someone. Go find something to do, okay?"

"I have something to do, mister. I've been doing it for ten bucks a pop. Want me to blow you? You're cute so I'll only charge you five."

Blake rolled his eyes up and gave her another warning of sorts.

"Scram lady. I don't need your nasty services. You need to go home and get a life."

The woman gave Blake a cold stare. She went into a sob story.

"Look man, I've got no money and no home. I'm just some helpless woman asking for a donation. If me blowing you isn't an interesting proposition, then why don't you *give* me five or ten bucks."

"Will it make you go away?" Blake asked.

"Maybe." She said. "Or maybe not. How much money do you have in that pocket boy?"

Blake was getting agitated. "Beat it bitch. You're cramping me up. Go blow someone else, okay. Leave me alone."

The unkempt woman walked closer to Blake and brandished a large knife.

"Oh fuck." Was Blake's only coherent thought.

"Hand over your cash, fuckstick, or I'll slice you wide open like I did my husband. Hurry it up."

Blake, not amused at his lack of luck and even less amused that he let Amy talk him out of the house, opened his wallet and handed the woman five hundred cash.

"All of it son. Credit cards too. Gimme all of it."

"NO!" Blake insisted. "I just gave you five hundred. What the fuck?"

The woman put the knife to Blake's throat. He could feel the cold steel touching his skin as he began to sweat.

"I cut my own husband's throat. Do you really think I give half a shit about yours? You have five seconds before I start slicing."

Blake pulled his wallet back out and began slowly filtering through his credit cards when he heard her.

"FREEZE YOU FUCKING BITCH OR I'LL BLOW YOUR FUCKING BRAINS OUT!"

*
I think I can, I think I can...
*

The locomotive finally pulled up to the depot in Seattle. Sandy had been snapping pictures out the window as they approached, taking in all the sights. Andrea was only then arising with an excruciating headache and the smell of vomit on her breath.

"What happened last night? Andrea asked while holding the palm of her hands firmly against her eyes in an effort to keep the light out.

"You're an idiot, that's what happened last night."

"Really Sandy? I didn't ask for your opinion. Just tell me what the hell happened, okay?"

"Well, you were drunk off your ass and wandered into the engineer's area. The two engineers gladly took you into the front of the train to give you a firsthand look at the tracks."

"Ohhhh," Andrea moaned painfully.

Sandy, aggravated and not very happy, continued scolding her friend.

"Ever since we got on this train it's been one thing after the other. You kissed me and I'm sure wanted to go further, you argued about everything I said, and then you blew the engineers. Nice going Andrea. We're supposed to be concentrating on finding Blake and you can't keep your head together; or out of guy's crotches."

"Fuck off Sandy. I'm not the only person here with "issues." You're looking for a guy that walked away from you back in Toledo, and it's all you talk about: Blake, Blake, Blake. Does it always have to be about you Sandy? Why can't it ever be fun? Does there always have to be a stupid drama that goes with it?"

"I saved your ass last night Andrea. Who knows what those guys would've done."

"So you saved my ass last night. Did you forget about the café back in Spokane? That guy was going to cream you and I was the one who ended up against the wall two milli-seconds from having my face re-arranged. I put my ass on the line too."

Andrea faced the bowl of the toilet and wretched. She didn't have much to deposit, as her stomach was all but empty. Strings of saliva hung from her bottom lip, nauseating Sandy. The headache was crunching and the queasiness aggravating. Sandy looked at Andrea struggling and softened considerably.

"I'm sorry Andrea. I get upset sometimes. I'm taking my frustration out on you."

"Fine, I'm sorry too. Now where's a towel; I need a shower."

"We're in Seattle, Andrea. You'll have to wait until we find a hotel. The train is emptying by cabins. We'll get off in about fifteen minutes."

Andrea looked on the bed and saw that Sandy had packed everything. She was glad. Sandy was always on the spot. Andrea did her best to wash up, straighten her hair and brush her teeth. She brushed three times, even though she didn't remember blowing anybody the night before. She had to take Sandy's word for it.

The ticket taker finally reached the girl's cabin. Again, on the spot Sandy had the passes safe and sound. She gave them to the man. He looked at Andrea and couldn't help but comment.

"You better see a doctor young lady. You look pale."

Andrea gave the man a long look, noticed that he had to be just shy of seventy and spit back, "Yeah? You think so? Well mister, I'm sick and hung over, I drink and I smoke, yet I'll still outlive you. Now fuck off; we're leaving."

The man stepped aside and let the girls through. As Sandy walked by him, she shrugged her shoulders and smiled sheepishly.

The two jumped off the train and one minute after starting their trek to the nearest hotel, it started pouring with rain. Sandy was looking for cover, but Andrea stood in the downpour; delighted in its cooling and refreshing affect. Andrea was wearing a tank top, so she rubbed the rainwater on her stubble ridden armpits and appeared as if she were bathing right on the street. People walked by, glanced and then continued on, not wanting to be too close to the strange girl. Andrea didn't care. It freshened her up, so she basked in it. Sandy yelled for her to come along and they continued their walk to the hotel. They found and stopped at the Café Umbria for some much-needed coffee. After drinking their fill, Andrea was starting to come out of the fog. They found a cab outside and told the driver to find a decent hotel downtown. They were taken to the Grand Hyatt on Pike Street. The room was one hundred and eighty dollars a night, but Sandy had brought ten grand with her in cash and travelers checks. Andrea had five hundred bucks. Sandy urged her to hold onto it.

"I brought us here, I'll pay. You use your cash however you'd like."

Andrea kissed her on the side of the head.

After settling in and taking a nap, the girls readied themselves up for a trip downtown in search of Blake Thomas, Sandy's true love. Neither of the girls had any idea where he worked, lived or hung out. They would have to go through town, show his picture and hope that someone recognized him. It was a crapshoot, but they had to try. They started their tour in the downtown area near Madison and fourth. They had no real plan of attack, so they skipped in and out of establishments along the corridor asking, looking and inquiring. They were surprised at how nice the people were in Seattle, less the occasional jerk who wanted twenty bucks for information he didn't have in the first place. After spending a good six hours searching, they called it a night. On the trip back to the hotel, Sandy was blubbering in the backseat about Blake and her chances of finding him. The cabbie overheard her and piped in.

"Aye, you talkin' bout Blake Thomas?"

"Yessir, yessir," Sandy howled with delight. "Do you know where I can find him?"

"Nope. Never 'eard of 'em. **HAR-HAR!**"

The cabbie laughed from the depths of his substantial gut. Andrea, as angry as she can remember being, cuffed the driver in the back of the head.

"ASSHOLE!" She screamed.

The cab quickly pulled to the curb. The girls jumped out and began running.

"AYE! I WANT MA FUCKIN' TOLL! YOU BITCHES! I'LL KICK YOUR FRICKIN' ASSES!"

Although they had no idea where they were, they ran all the same. They finally stopped at a park. The sign above said Denny Park. They were closer than they ever knew.

*

"I SAID GET YOU'RE FUCKING HANDS UP! I"LL SHOOT YOU. LET THAT MAN GO!" Amy was more than pleading with Blake's captor.

"FUCK YOU! THIS HERE'S MY HOSTAGE. BACK OFF OR I'LL CUT HIS GRIMY THROAT!"

The woman dragged her victim toward the light. That's when Amy saw that it was Blake. Her mouth dropped open as her heart rate increased. She now had a more serious problem on her hands.

"BLAKE? What the fuck are you doing here?"

"You told me to meet you. You said that on the phone."

As Amy kept the gun pointed at the woman, she continued the conversation.

"I said I'd pick you up later after I made a stop at Denny Park and then downtown. How'd you get 'meet me here' out of that?"

"Your phone was breaking up. I couldn't hear you well at all. I guess I got it wrong."

"I'd say you did. Now look what happened."

"AYE! BOTH OF YOU SHUT THE FUCK UP. WHAT IS THIS, FAMILY FUCKIN' AFFAIR?"

"SHUTTUP!" Amy screamed.

"YOU SHUTTUP!" The woman screamed back.

Blake heart continued skipping beats and the panic was settling in. The woman sensed it at she held him.

"What's the matter with you? You're getting all weird. Why ain't you breathing right?

She looked at Blake's eyes and he had paled considerably. He felt like he was going to die.

"I SAID WHAT'S WRONG? WHAT THE FU…?"

Blake slid out of the woman's arms and onto the blacktop path. Her attention was swayed just long enough for Amy to clip off a shot, hitting the woman in the left shoulder. The knife dropped as the woman grabbed her wound. She turned to run, but Amy was on her in a split second. She forced the woman to the ground and struggled to get her zip tie on her wrists. In the meantime, Blake was to the left of the two women gasping for air and trying to use his breathing techniques, which were not coming in handy at that moment.

"I said sit still bitch." Amy ordered.

"Screw you. You're not taking me in."

Amy was getting angry and had had enough of the wrestling. She grabbed the woman's wounded shoulder and squeezed. The woman shrieked in obvious agony. Amy finished zipping the ties onto her wrists.

"Oh yeah bitch. You're going in all right. I'm taking your husband killing sorry ass to jail."

*

"What's that noise," Sandy asked her friend. "It sounded like a firecracker."

"It came from over there." Andrea answered. "Let's go see."

The two were no more than fifty yards from Blake.

*

"Are you okay Blake? Blake?"

He finally opened his eyes and saw Amy's soft face looking down at him. She was beautiful and he felt better knowing she was there.

"I think I need mouth-to-mouth Amy. I'm having trouble breathing."

Amy chuckled and ordered Blake to his feet.

"Help me get that nasty bitch back to the jeep. You know you could've gotten killed out here?"

"Sorry. I thought you said to meet you here."

Amy shook her head and the two of them picked up the woman, now silent from the pain in her shoulder, and dragged her to Amy's jeep, which was parked about fifty yards away; the opposite direction from which Andrea and Sandy, were coming.

*

"I think it came from right over there Andrea."

The two stepped slowly so not to cause a commotion. They wanted to look through the brush and see exactly what was happening. All they saw were two people walking away in the dark with somebody in between them dragging their feet.

"Oh my God," Sandy gasped, "did someone just get murdered?"

"I don't know, but shhh. Don't get their attention."

The two waited a few minutes until they knew the people they'd seen from behind were out of site. They lurked up to the spot under the streetlight where they thought the action took place. They saw a pool of blood on the blacktop.

"Ewww!" Was Sandy's eerie response.

"Oh wow," said Andrea. "Let's get out of here. This is no place for either of us."

"Shouldn't we call the police?" Sandy whispered.

"Hell no. We've been in the city all of twenty minutes and we get involved in a possible murder? No way, no how."

Despite Sandy being the ever-vigilant soul, the girls left the scene and went back to the road at the park entrance. They waited for a cab to show up, which it did, and carefully climbed in; ever the more attentive to who was driving.

*

"Wait here Blake. I'll be right back. I need to take this bitch inside the cop shop. Don't do anything, just stay in the jeep."

Blake nodded as Amy strode off with the woman, who was crying and whining about her wounded shoulder. He waited patiently, trying to ward off the continuing anxiety that was causing his heart to flutter in his chest.

"Breath 2...3...4, breath 2...3...4."

The fear was gripping him with its powerful talon. He felt that it was morphing into out and out panic, as his entire body began to flush. His breathing became more difficult and his mind raced with thoughts of death, hospitals, ambulances and worst of all, embarrassment.

"C'mon Blake. Get a grip. Breath 2…3…4, breath 2…3…4."

A tear began to well up in his eye as he felt his chest squeeze uncomfortably. Blake was beginning to think he would die in Amy's jeep. He wondered to himself why he always thought the same thoughts of death and negativity every time he had these spells. What reason was good enough to expect death or hospitalization? After all, it had never happened before. He always worked his way through it. He fished out his bottle of Xanax and carefully began shaking a tablet into the palm of his hand.

"BLAKE!"

Blake jumped so hard he hit his head on the roll cage of the jeep. His pills flew everywhere. Now you see them, now you don't. They cascaded downward and were lost in the darkness. You could hear them piddling onto the blacktop, all but lost. There was no way he could possibly recover fifty pills. He looked over and saw Amy standing there with her hand to her mouth in a failing attempt to stifle her laughter.

"Blake, are you jumpy? What's the matter? All your pills went flying. You should've seen your face.

Not amused, Blake hopped out of the jeep and began gathering up any pills that he could find. He looked at Amy and tried to scold her.

"Look what you've done, Amy. I spilled all my shit everywhere. Jesus H Christ, why do you sneak up on me like that? I'm having a panic attack."

Again, Amy stifled her laughter. She dropped to her knees and helped Blake pick up his wayward medication.

"What is this Blake?" Amy quizzed.

"It's Xanax. It helps with panic and anxiety."

"You don't need these. You need to relax, that's all."

Annoyed, Blake inquired as to Amy's MD skills.

"I know you can kick someone's ass and now I know you can handle a gun without much trouble; but what made you a fucking doctor?"

Amy straightened and gave Blake a very sensual glance.

"Because I know what would make you feel better, and it's *all*-natural."

Blake hadn't looked at her, so he failed to see the seductive look on her face. He clipped his lid shut and finally lifted his head.

"Oh you do huh? Tell me….."

Before another word could be uttered, Amy placed her pouty, soft lips on Blake's mouth. She skillfully slid her tongue into his mouth. Blake reciprocated; he thought to himself how she tasted like candy. Their tongues continued a soft and sensual dance. Their sweet moisture mixed, causing an extremely combustible combination of passion and throbbing inner thighs. Amy released and asked Blake where he lived.

"Uh, uh, 10th and East Boston, why?"

"You drive," Amy insisted.

The excitement mounted in Blake's entire body. The most beautiful woman he had ever seen was coming onto him sexually. He thought it too good to be true, but tried to go with it. They both jumped into the jeep and Blake moved out for the two or three mile trip. He looked to his right to smile at Amy, but she had other ideas. She had lowered her head into Blake's lap and was working the zipper on his pants. Without fanfare, she easily maneuvered him into place and put her mouth on him. Blake was hard-pressed to steady the jeep as Amy continued with her "under the wheel" activity. He managed to steady the vehicle, but wasn't sure for how long he could steady the orgasm that was quickly building inside of him. Without warning and with extreme explosiveness, Blake erupted. Amy swallowed him and rose to meet his eyes.

"There now, is the anxiety all better?"

To his unbelievable surprise, the anxiety, panic and whatever else was bothering him was gone. There wasn't one trace of it.

"I told you it was only boredom, Blake." Amy looked up to the top of the crest where Blake had pulled over. "Is that your house Blake?"

"Um, yeah it is."

"Well aren't you going to invite me in?"

The door wasn't even opened and shut again as the two clutched each other in a wild and passionate display. Books falling, clothes flying and fingers probing. Blake undressed Amy and soaked in her natural beauty. She had erect, dark nipples that were perfect for her breasts and wore a strip of jet-black pubic hair between her thighs. It wasn't too much, just enough to give her a womanly appearance.

 Blake gently guided Amy to his bed and carefully placed her on her back. He spread her wings and returned the favor from the jeep. To Blake, she tasted like the nectar of the Gods. She was sweet and musky at the same time. Blake noticed a tattoo was present just above her pubic hairline. In the tiniest of symbols, it read 名词, which meant "woman" in Chinese. To Blake, she was all of a woman. She was a petite girl, and her gifts were also petite. He still couldn't believe he was with her. He knew this wasn't a girl that simply gave "it" away. He worked his way up her smooth mid drift, past her golden bellybutton ring and toward her breasts. He gently, yet firmly tugged at her nipples with a delicate combination of lips and teeth. Amy's left nipple was pierced with a small hoop, which turned Blake on even further. She allowed him entrance and the two gyrated to each other's rhythm on top of the comforter. Blake was surprised to find that he was fully erect mere minutes after his first explosion in the jeep.

 Blake wasn't a particularly large man, sporting about six and a half inches erect with above average girth, but Amy was so tiny, so petite, that her womanhood wrapped him in a sensual grip. The two carried on for hours. Blake and Amy orgasmed at least three times each. Blake felt that he was in the arms of an angel. Amy was also very happy and pleased. She knew, though, that this was probably not going to be a regular event. She tried to think of the love they had just shared as she cuddled into the softness of his shoulder and drifted to sleep.

As the two slept, a man with a black hat stood outside of their window. He was taking pictures of the couple as they slept naked.

*

Sandy lay in bed and cried. Andrea sat on the chair with a bottle of Jack Daniels and the TV remote control, flipping through the channels and drinking like a fish. It was turning into a problem in Sandy's eyes. Andrea was drinking too much and Blake seemed like he was still a million miles away.

"Why is my best friend drinking so much?" She said to herself. "She's going to kill herself with that stuff."

The other question was also surfacing in her mind. "What is it about Blake? Why do I love him so much? Do I need to destroy myself over him?"

Sandy began thinking of her past and what could be the reason for her obsession, which seemed to be getting worse. She was beginning to feel that something was amiss in her mind.

Sandy was born in Toledo, raised by a drunken Father and an ultra-conservative Mother. She spent most of her time with Mom, wearing skirts that went to her ankles and going to the Baptist church three to five times *per week*. The first ten years of Sandy's life went fine. She tolerated the church and her mom, and all but ignored her dad's drunkenness. Then, when she was fourteen, Dad died. Her mother's reaction was the typical Baptist story.

"He deserved to die," she'd say. "The Lord tolerates no blasphemous drink or smoke. Jeysus has penalized the sinner and sent him to Hell. The Lord is all powerful and has sent the demon to the fiery pits of Hell to burn forever."

Sandy often tired of her mom's sermons and would retire to her room, or out for a walk, or anywhere she could go to avoid having to listen for another second. Never having that Father figure, Sandy ran around with Andrea, Blake and the others. Often, she and Blake would talk. He started to tell her about other ways of life, other things to do. Sandy was born and raised very strictly, so it was tough to teach an old dog new tricks. She listened intently though, loving how he expressed himself and spoke with a confidence not heard with the other boys. Blake was mature past his fourteen or fifteen years of life. She started to seek Blake more and more, as it seemed he was filling a roll that had been missing from her life. Every young girl needed a man to speak to, confide with and follow. Blake was unwittingly that man, even in his teen years.

Andrea was the wild one of the group; always daring this or that for thrills. She was sexually active and drank wine. She also smoked a little dope, but never used the hard drugs like coke or heroin. She was Sandy's alter ego. Andrea would bare her breasts for the boys; hang around some of the troubled guys who were simply looking for a piece of ass, and get into trouble with the police for staying out too late or drinking. Andrea's mom and dad didn't care less, as long as she was out of their hair. Occasionally, her dad would take a strap to her, but when he'd whip her, she'd moan in ecstasy as if she liked it. Needless to say, the whippings stopped. Getting weird with her father put the brakes on just about any situation that Andrea didn't like. Despite her extreme wildness, Sandy looked up to her. She liked the side that couldn't be controlled. Perhaps she wanted that for herself, but had no idea how to attain it, so she'd follow Andrea around and act out *through* her. When Andrea whipped out her breasts, she begged Sandy to do the same, but there was no way Sandy was exposing herself. Sandy would go to parties with Andrea and wait in the other room with strangers while her friend was in the other room having sex, sometimes with two people at once and even with another girl now and then. It disgusted Sandy, but she still had a deep caring for her friend. She'd try to tell Andrea she would regret her decisions, but Andrea only scoffed. Three days later, on cue, there'd be Andrea crying on Sandy's shoulder about having a bad reputation or seeing her name next to the word slut on the bathroom partitions at school. Even Blake and the boys would give Andrea a hard time, despite the fact that Blake was fooling around with her from time to time. She reached the point where she started wearing dark eye makeup and more gothic type of clothing. Sandy wasn't upset. She was there for her friend whenever needed. She'd pulled her out of bad situations, much like on the train, and still be there for whom she considered her very best friend.

  Despite everything else, Sandy would do anything for Blake. She *would* show him her breasts, but he never asked. She *would* do any sexual favor he wanted, but he never asked. She practically threw herself at this man until finally; she thought the night of lovemaking was imminent. Alas, he had that cursed anxiety attack and it put the flame out. She wanted to be Blake's, and she wanted Blake to be hers. It was an abnormal fixation. She was obsessed.

*

After spending two hours crying and thinking, she looked over and saw Andrea slumped over her bottle of booze. She noticed she had wet herself extensively. With the nature of a kind woodland creature, Sandy roused Andrea and guided her to the bathroom. She put her in the tub and gave her a bath. Andrea was coming around and Sandy again had tears rolling down her cheeks. It was a painful reminder of finding her dad dead in his chair. She didn't want to find Andrea the same way someday. She whispered in Andrea's ear.

"I love you so much. Please don't do this anymore. I need you Andrea. You're so young and have so much to look forward to in your life. Please don't let me find you dead someday."

Andrea stirred before vomiting into the bathwater. With a sigh, she removed her from the tub and re-drew a bath. Finished, she slipped Andrea under the blankets and allowed her to sleep off the booze. Sandy cleaned the urine from the chair, and then lay back down, now exhausted from her tasks. She fell into a deep, curious sleep. Something was going wrong in her mind. She wasn't sure what it was, but knew something was amiss.

*

Amy woke up to the sound of her beeper going off. Blake slept soundly, as it was four in the morning and the Xanax he took was keeping him in a slumber. It was Claude, and he wanted to see Amy so he could pay her and have a chat with her. The prized pupil that she was, Amy arose, got dressed and hightailed it to the warehouse in the downtown area where Claude wanted to meet her. On her way, she smiled at the marvelous night she'd had with Blake. He was better sexually than she thought he'd be, but figured his nervous tension added to the experience.

Amy arrived at the warehouse Claude had mentioned on the phone, but didn't see any signs of life at that very early hour. She exited her vehicle and started walking toward the door when someone approached her silently from behind and put her in a headlock. The pressure exerted from the strength in the person's arms put Amy first into a slumber, and then an all-out nap. The oxygen had been temporarily cut from her brain and she couldn't fight it. The man had her in a perfect position for keeping her at bay. She reached behind a couple of times, but it was no use as the grip was solid.

Amy was out cold in downtown Seattle at five A.M., not a good time to be wandering. The biggest question loomed; where was Claude?

13
A Very Important Date

Now that he had taken Soo's head and added it to the rest of his collection, it was time for a celebration, Kurt Joseph style. He slid the CD in the stereo slot on his van's radio and began swaying and dancing with the tune.

> *"A very merry un-birthday to you.*
> *A very merry un-birthday to you.*
> *It's great to drink to someone,*
> *And I guess that you would do,*
> *A very merry un-birthday to you!"*

Kurt rocked and jigged in the van. He had the cabinet open and was singing along with the music. He seemed to be personally recognizing and dedicating the ditty to each of the heads. Kathy, his ex, the woman at the motel, and now Soo-Chin splashed around ungracefully as Kurt continued to dance. Their eyes were blank and gray, their mouths were shaped in the same horrific frown they had given a mille-second before their heads were removed and despite the chemical that kept them from decomposing, their skin was taking on a pale hue. Kurt didn't care. He danced, he capered, he twirled and he pranced, while in reality he was short on rhythm. As happy as he appeared to be, he still had one job that lay before him. He still had one head that needed removing. He needed Amy Fraser's head. The collection of her head would give him the most joy, as Amy herself played such a large role in all of the festivities that led to his actions.

Then suddenly, the CD stopped playing, the magic in the air evaporated, and Kurt was left aimlessly stuttering to himself. The wind removed itself from his sails.

"A v-very ma-ma-merry un-b-birthday t-t-to you."

His eyes grew cold and his smile disappeared into a bitter frown. The depression seeping into him brought him down at an alarming rate. Five minutes ago, Kurt was the happiest man on the earth; now he looked sickly and sad. It was a change no less amazing than a super hero shrinking back into what he really was, a mortal human. As the negative thoughts crept in, Kurt started getting antsy and impatient. He held his eyes shut tightly with his fingers as he tried in vain to search for a thought, any thought, that would relieve him of the awful nosedive back into the depths of a depressive abyss. Kurt began talking to himself. He sat on the floor of the van in front of the cabinets and thought.

"Why would I listen to that ungrateful bitch of a Queen? What's she given me? Nothing. She wants the heads, but doesn't want to pay the piper. I'm her tool; her hands, arms, and machete. Can I sink any lower? Why am I doing these things?"

Kurt looked at the dead faces illuminating with moonlight that snuck in through the van's front windshield. Their expressions remained the same. There was no hate, no judgment, and no dirty looks; only the fear of which Kurt had gifted them before taking the heads. Underneath the bodiless death hung the Queen of Heart's card, the picture on it without emotion. Kurt heard the rain drops begin to tinkle faintly on the roof of his van. It brought him even lower. He was staring straight ahead with his cold, dark eyes. His face now brandishing a burnt scar, courtesy of Soo-Chin. Suicide crossed his mind. He was having a scary moment, and knew deep down wasn't sure about what he was doing. Killing and decapitating wouldn't comfort anyone or bring his precious Jimmy back. He wept silently as he curled into a ball on the floor. His thoughts raced faster as his emotions sunk rapidly.

"Do I deserve to live? Do I deserve to be the one who collects the heads for that bitch? Of course not. She gives me not even a fucking thank you. She simply calls the shots and I carry out her personal war. Why? Because she's a coward; a measly little coward."

Kurt thought he heard something on the outside of the van. He stood up and looked out a peephole that was taken from an apartment door and installed on the back door of the van. He could see a wide swath of the landscape while whoever was outside couldn't look in. After assuring himself that the coast was clear, he turned back to the heads and was ready to rip the Queens off the hook. That's when he saw what he needed to see. His spirits raised dramatically, his eagerness; just a moment ago lost, was regained. Kurt's frown turned into a widening smile. He chuckled with both relief and idiocy. How could he ever say such things? How could he ever doubt his wonderful Red Queen? He looked again to make sure he wasn't hallucinating. Each of the Red Queens on the hooks below the heads were...*smiling*. Kurt knew the smiles were for him. He felt the loyalty re-energizing him.

The manic depression had taken hold of Kurt, rendering him useless one minute, on top of the world the next. He was back on top for the moment. He knew that he needed to head for Seattle and finish the job. Now that the Red Queen had smiled, showing her satisfaction with the job he was doing, he was completely rejuvenated.

He felt he had one more thing to do before locking up the cabinet and heading north. He opened the lids to each chemical filled vat and pulled the heads out. He lined them up on the small bench he had built inside the van. After a thorough washing and wiping, he picked the heads up one at a time; starting with Kathy. He kissed her deeply, inserting his tongue into the appendage's mouth; swirling it around with a sexual excitement that was both disgusting and sickened. After pulling her away from his grip, his mouth dripped blood. He repeated the vile act for the other two heads and put them back in the jars. This time when he looked at them through the greenish fluid they floated in, he saw that they no longer had the terrified looks of death, but the crooked smiles of what he thought to be satisfied kisses.

*

"What's the fucking holdup? Where the fuck are those guys?"

Wilma didn't so much as get the words out of her mouth when her phone rang. The crony she'd sent to Seattle was calling. He was having a hard time communicating with Wilma, as she was too busy chewing him out. He eventually managed to update her as to his situation. After a couple of moments, she spoke clearly.

"Don't do another fucking thing until we get to Seattle, understand? It'll be a couple of days. Monitor the situation and that's it. Nothing more. I didn't ask you to do anything else!"

After an affirmative response, Wilma called her other crony, who hadn't answered the phone for two hours. This time, though, he did.

"Get your ass up here. We need to get on the road. What the fuck have you been doing?"

After a pause, Wilma spoke again.

"Get up here now, we have to go."

Wilma snapped her phone shut and sighed. All she needed was a couple of wayward associates messing up her investigation.

"They're sidetracked." She reasoned. "I'll straighten them out later."

Soon the crony met up with Wilma and they took off for Portland, Oregon to investigate Soo-Chin's death. She had also heard of a very horrific castration case at a rest stop in Pendleton, Oregon and decided it would be worth a look. One of the guys survived, barely, and Wilma needed to speak with him. Perhaps he could shed light on the perpetrator; even though she knew it was Kurt. She thought the men deserved to have their butts kicked for doing what they did in the public restroom, but not castration for one man followed by being choked with his own penis. The other guy lost an eye, but was otherwise physically healthy, even though he would be emotionally scarred for life. Obviously, if Kurt had done this, the two had no idea as to his danger factor. She bet her life it was, in fact, Kurt. A beheading in Nampa followed by another *beheading of sorts* in Pendleton. Those were followed by yet another in Portland. One and one made two to Wilma. She easily saw the connection. Alas, knowing who the perp was wouldn't help if you couldn't stop him.

It was a bit of a backwoods drive for Wilma and her partner, but they finally found the home of the live victim involved with the rest stop murder. The yard was unkempt and the house looked like it hadn't been painted in some twenty years. The shingles were a mess and the shutters on a couple of the windows hung menacingly. The wind was howling and it was getting dark. The entire monstrosity was surrounded with thick, ominous woods. Wilma tried to incorporate a bit of humor.

"Looks like a haunted house, eh? I hope no ghouls get us."

Wilma laughed, but was given a bored look by her crony, who still had his sunglasses on.

"You fucking dark men don't get anything, do you?"

Another blank stare.

Wilma shook her head and they both walked toward the front door. She was being very careful in her steps, while her crony seemed to think that there was no viable threat in sight. He walked with purpose. He rang the doorbell twice and finally they heard creaks and groans as somebody headed for the door. The knob turned with a slight squabble and the door moaned open, allowing the scent of spoiled food and mold to fill the two agent's noses. Wilma cringed as the "lady" of the house showed her face. The Dark man simply looked forward, no expression present. The woman looked like a corpse. She had stringy, unwashed brown hair in a double pigtail. One strand lay on her left shoulder while the other hung curiously off her cheek. She was paper thin with heavily drawn in cheeks and when she slightly smiled, there were two teeth visible, as most of the rest had rotted out. The dress she wore had been repaired a number of times and the color was faded. She was so thin that when she put her hands on her boney hips, you could see the armpit hair hanging down in a tattered, nested mass. She smelled like spoiled meat and in Wilma's estimation, was mere months from death.

"What can I do ya for?" The woman asked.

"We're here to see your, uh, husband, Theodore."

"Well you wait rights here. I'll see if he's a done jerkin' his bacon."

Wilma looked at the crony, but he stared straight forward, unaffected by the gruesome description of the man's activity.

"You know," Wilma said to him, "it wouldn't kill you to smile at least once a year. Good God."

Another blank stare. At that point, Theodore came to the door.

"Theodore Jenkins?"

"Yep. What the fuck do ya want with me?"

Theodore looked rough too, but not as rough as his woman did. He wore a filthy food stained wife beater with a pair of jeans that starched themselves. He stunk like his wife. He also wore a patch over one eye.

"Hello, we're both FBI agents and we were doing a follow-up investigation into the murder of your friend. We were wondering if you could answer some questions for us."

"Well, I reckon. I'll help ya if'in it'll get that creep off the street."

Wilma was perplexed by his southern drawl. She asked him where he was from; when he said the hills of Arkansas, it all made sense to her.

"What can you tell us about the man that killed your friend?"

"He was an average size fella. 'Bout six two or three, weighed bout two bills maybe. What stood 'em out though, was his stutter. He was a stutterin' fool."

"What exactly did he do?"

"He cut ma buddies pecker off and choked 'em with it's what he did. I never saw somethin' so disgustin' in all ma life."

"What about you Ted? What did he do to you?"

Theodore tore the patch off his eye, exposing a dark, infected looking hole that was running with a mixture of pus and tears.

"That's what he done. He slammed my head into the toilet valve. It read *Standard* between my eyes for two days. I was knocked cold. When I woke up, the police was already there. Someone musta' saw the blood or somethin'."

"Could you identify this man if you saw him?" Wilma asked this question with enthusiasm. If Theodore could match the picture she had with the man that beat him up and killed his friend, she'd have at least one murder charge under her belt. She pulled out the picture and showed him.

"Oh yepper. That's him all right. He had a stutter when he first spoke, but it went away when he busted into our stall. Seemed he was mad and that straightened his words up."

"Thank you Theodore. Now do me a favor and hang around here okay? I may need to speak with you again later."

"Do ya reckon ya got a bead on 'em?"

"Don't you worry about that Ted." Wilma smiled. "We'll take care of everything. Oh, and do me and yourself a huge favor."

"What's that?"

"Stay out of the public toilets. If you need to do that kind of crap, go pick up a male hooker or something. That's disgusting."

Theodore replaced the patch over his eye and scratched his rear end while he watched the agents leave. His wife came up behind him and asked about the ruckus. He told her not to worry and the two engaged in a toothless, slobbery kiss. Wilma saw it from the car and became nauseated. She looked at her crony.

Another blank stare.

*

"I'm late; I'm late, f-for a v-very important d-d-date. No time t-to say hello g-g-goodbye I'm l-late I'm late I'm late I'm l-late...When I shave, I l-lose the t-time I save, I n-need to go get Amy's head and p-put in a j-jar I say..."

Kurt made up his own version and loved it. He thought he could be a big recording star. The classes he'd taken to improve his stutter helped a great deal, but he still stuttered. It was frustrating, but he knew he was getting better with it, so he let it slide. He had a three-hour drive to Seattle and wanted it to be carefree and smooth. He stopped at I-5 at the 504 interchange for a couple of slices of pizza at Papa Pete's, and then took off again toward his destination. While at the pizza shop, he was warm and friendly, even though ten feet away from him laid a copy of the Castle Rock, Oregon newspaper with a picture of him right smack on the front page. It was the same picture that the injured man IDed when he was with Wilma and her crony. The night before, she had sent out a wire release to all the newspapers in the US requesting them to print the picture. She made it a point to let the towns between Portland and Seattle know first because she figured him in the area. Despite that, Kurt was met with no resistance as he ate his food, cajoled with the help and smiled the entire time. He said thank you very politely before he left.

Kurt rolled along. He had all his tools in the cabinet with the heads and was now after Amy. He wondered if this would be the last head to be claimed, as the Queen instructed. It didn't matter to him, as any additional heads would be mere child's play. At this point, Kurt actually enjoyed his work. What the Red Queen requested, the Red Queen would get.

Not being the smartest man; *the brightest bulb in the lamp*, Kurt had no idea that the authorities' would follow him until he was corralled; dead or alive. He had a woman pursuing him that was of the highest obsessiveness who wouldn't stop unless she was dead herself. It was quite surprising that Wilma had not called for roadblocks on the route or at least had a check-in station or two on the road, but she was smart enough to know that Kurt could easily change his route and take side streets, back roads, or whatever directions were necessary to make life easier for him.

As Kurt rolled up Route 5, he was entranced with some of the towns and street names on the way. Happy Trails Drive, Paradise Resort and other pleasant places that made him smile. There was no telling when Kurt would slip into another state of depression, so he tried his best to enjoy the lucid time he was given. The Queen was still lurking. She was somewhere close and had no intention of letting up until the tasks were complete. Even then, she could come up with yet more death and dismemberment ideas. Kurt knew it, and he kept smiling. He made his next stop in Napavine, Washington, which was about an hour and a half outside of Seattle. This was where Kurt's resolve would be drastically tested.

He stopped at a place called the Inland Market so he could load up on a few supplies. He wanted food, coffee, matches and a few other miscellaneous items. He grabbed a couple of packs of cigarettes, even though he hadn't smoked in over a year. He also wanted to gas up the van and not have to stop again until he reached Seattle. As he finished filling his vehicle, he noticed a row of newspaper boxes at the front of the market.

"Aw, w-what the hell?"

Kurt decided he'd check on the weather forecasts for the area and see if they had any news about Seattle. When he took his fifty cents to the box, he was struck with his first real taste of being pursued. The papers on all three boxes had his mug plastered on the front. There was a Seattle newspaper, a local newspaper and a Portland Oregonian. All three had the caption **MURDERER?** above his picture. Kurt got a copy of the Seattle Times so he could look over the article and see if they really had the goods on him. As he sat in his van perusing, he heard a loud HONK behind him. Annoyed, Kurt flipped his middle finger out the window in haste. To his dismay, he had flipped off a Washington State Trooper who had pulled in for a fill up of his own. This was not a good situation for Kurt. He cursed his hair trigger temper and saw that the Trooper had put his lights on to "pull him over" even though he was already stopped. Without a second thought, Kurt started his engine and peeled out, spraying rocks and other gravel-ridden debris onto the

Trooper's windshield. The chase was on as the cruiser squealed out behind him, intent on not only pulling him over, but also taking his carcass to jail.
Obviously, the cop didn't have the first idea as to who was driving the van, or what it contained. All he knew was that he'd catch this creep and bust his chops but good.

    Perhaps that wouldn't be such a good idea.

*

    After departing from the creepy man's house, Wilma and her sidekick headed toward Portland to get an up-close look at the Soo-Chin Xing murder and see if in fact it was related to the others. Wilma was already positive that she'd have the same MO on her hands, but nonetheless had to check to make sure before moving further. Little did anyone know that about five and a half hours up the road, Kurt was running from a State Trooper in Washington. Wilma was closing the gap, but ever so slowly.

    The four-hour drive from Pendleton to Portland only took her man about three hours and fifteen minutes to complete. Wilma didn't care as long as she reached her destination in one piece. She ordered her henchman to get them to the Portland morgue so they could have a look at Soo-Chin, or at least what was left of her. Without fanfare or delay, he had her there in fifteen minutes. They went inside to check it out.

    Despite a short haggle with the building receptionist, Wilma and her partner made their way into the coroner's office. The head coroner, who took them inside to see the crime scene, met them.

"Here's where my employee found her, Agent Hurst. She was stuffed into the ceiling and blood had dripped onto the floor. When he went up to investigate, down she came, but without her head."

Wilma had already known that her head was missing; matching that part of the MO, but blood dripping down was a bit sloppy, as Kurt had cauterized the wounds of the previous victims.

"Can we see what's left of her please?"

"Of course. You do know she was my best worker. She was offered the head pathologist job, but refused it. Apparently, she wanted to keep things simple."

Wilma didn't care, but nodded and smiled politely so she wouldn't compromise seeing the body. The henchman followed silently. A door here, a walkway there and they reached the destination. The coroner grabbed a set of keys hanging on the wall and unlocked the door.

"Do those keys always hang there?" Wilma asked.

"Yes. If someone is locked in, then someone can unlock the door and let them out. I know it seems dumb to have the keys right there and lock the door anyway, but it's what the state wants us to do."

"I understand." Wilma muttered, even though she didn't understand the sensibility of such a system.

The three walked over to a series of gurneys that were lined up in alphabetical order.

"The police think it happened there. Luminol was used and they found blood on the wall."

She pointed to the other side of the room. Wilma and her crony walked over and studied the area.

The crony didn't speak, but made hand gestures that told Wilma the murder happened here, and the blood spray went that way. Wilma agreed.

"He whacked her so hard; her head flew off her shoulders and crashed into that wall."

The henchman nodded in the affirmative.

They walked back over to the gurney where Soo lay and removed the sheet. It wasn't as bad as the coroner had made it out to be. A normally healthy woman's body with no head. After further inspection, Wilma concluded that her head had in fact been cauterized, but more sloppily than other times. That allowed for a trickle of blood to drip out and onto the floor. The henchman nodded in agreement. Wilma guessed that Kurt had done it on purpose so the body would be noticed. A slow seep and discovery also gave him time to get well down the road.

"Thanks for your time. We'll be going now."

The coroner wanted more.

"Well? What do you think? Do you know who murdered her?"

"We have a pretty good idea." Wilma explained. "But let us worry about it. You keep running a tight ship. I don't think the killer will be back."

"You don't? Why?"

"Because he already took what he wanted…Soo's head."

The coroner gulped hard and led the two out of the building.

*

Not wanting to give in to his impulsiveness, Kurt abandoned his idea of running. If he kept going, the trooper would surely signal his buddies and the quest would end with either too many cops to handle at once or his own death. By pulling over, he could take care of the situation quickly and move on his way.

Kurt stopped at an abandon building three blocks from where he peeled out at the Market. The trooper wheeled in behind him and broke every *cardinal sin* that a trooper could break. Instead of calling for back-up, *(cardinal sin # 1),* the arrogant cop approached Kurt's van with his gun drawn.

"Step out of the vehicle NOW!" he ordered.

Before exiting the van, Kurt had opened his three-inch long pocketknife and using trickery he had learned when he was a child, held it in the crease of his palm hidden under his long flannel shirt. He saw the fear in the trooper's eyes when he looked at him. His gun was quivering and his voice shaky.

"Put your hands up mister, and turn around. Don't look back or I'll shoot you."

The trooper slowly approached Kurt. The problem here was that he didn't take into consideration the danger factor. After a quick, incomplete pat down *(cardinal sin# 2),* Kurt allowed the trooper to cuff him and take him to the squad car. He placed him in the back seat and went to have a look inside the vehicle. As the trooper attempted to open the back door of the van, Kurt went to work with the precision of a professional safecracker. He used the pocketknife to pick the lock on the cuffs. It took him no more than twenty seconds to free himself. He then went to work on the locked door of the squad car that only opened from the outside.

The trooper, hat sitting tilted forward on his shaved head and strap tightly fastened under his chin, stepped into the van and began mulling around. He noticed the locked cabinet on the left and reached into the driver's area to retrieve the keys from the ignition. He began trying keys until he found the right fit. Not noticing or watching his rear *(cardinal sin # 3)*, he had no idea that Kurt had picked the inside door of the squad car and slowly exited. He left the door ajar so that he wouldn't startle the obviously inexperienced trooper.

After finally finding the right key and opening the cabinet, the site gripped the trooper with nausea and weak knees; before him were pale, dead faces staring back at him with sinister grins. He attempted to reach down for his radio, but instead felt Kurt's hand against his own. In an instant, Kurt plunged his knife into the front of the trooper's throat, just below the Adam's apple. He then jerked the knife hard to the right, severing the trooper's carotid artery from the *inside*. A gargling, choking sound came from him as Kurt applied more pressure to make sure his knife made the fatal cut. He knew he'd found the mark when the trooper spewed blood from his mouth and onto the inside wall of his van. Kurt had intentionally turned the trooper to the right so he'd miss the inside of the cabinet. One minute later, he finally weakened under Kurt's extremely strong grip until he went limp and stopped choking. Knowing the job was complete; he dragged him back to the cruiser and took a few minutes so he could set up the scene for whoever came along to find his handiwork. He wanted to use this trooper as an example of his, and his Red Queen's power.

Kurt dove off with nary a care and found his route to Seattle. He was an hour away from the destination that he hoped would bring the Queen her biggest thrill since the carnage had begun back in Vegas.

*

The radio hissed and cracked as the FBI dispatcher came on to give Wilma the news.

"Wilma, you there? Over"

"Yep. This is Wilma, what's up? Over."

"We got a dead trooper in Napavine, Washington. How far away are you? Over."

"About an hour. Over."

"I'll make sure the scene stays secure Wilma. You have to see for yourself what this sicko did. Over."

"I appreciate that. We're heading there with a load of steam. Over."

"You might want to take a barf bag along with the steam, Wilma. From what I've been told, it's an awful sight. Over"

Wilma hung up her radio and looked at her bespectacled partner.

"I don't give three fucks how fast you go. Get us to that scene NOW!"

The dark man's foot hit the pedal. The car shifted up two gears, and off they went to another scene of despicable horror left by what Wilma considered an obviously deranged man.

*

Kurt headed up highway five, knowing he was a short distance from the destination. His skin tingled with excitement, as he knew Amy wasn't far from him. He could see the lights of the city from a distance. He could also see the Seattle Space Needle, which towered some six hundred feet over the city. He began singing again, this time without a stutter.

"I'm late; I'm late, for a very important date. No time to say hello Amy, I'm late, I'm late, I'm late I'm late...When I wave, I lose the time I save, I'm taking your head Amy and there's nothing you can do ha-ha. I laugh and then I dare to chop, and here's the reason why, I'm taking heads and yours is next, Amy you better hide..."

It went on and on as Kurt drove through the downtown corridor of Seattle. He had finally reached the pinnacle of his task. The removal and collection of that damn Amy Fraser's head. He didn't care how, where or what; he was only concerned with when. When could he take her head? It had to be soon, as he figured the boys in blue couldn't be too far behind. What Kurt didn't know was that Amy was now an experienced bounty hunter. It could be a whole lot tougher than he might've imagined. Not knowing or caring in any way, he was determined, and obsessive determination was a hard nut to crack.

Now that he'd reached the city, Kurt had to be extremely careful to avoid being spotted. He stopped downtown and bought an expensive pair of sunglasses. They were enough to shield his bright green eyes.

He also needed a place to sleep. He would drive up and down the main arteries in town until he reached a satisfactory dwelling to bed down. Kurt settled for the Grand Hyatt on Pike Street, which happened to be where Sandy and Andrea were taking up residence. Being the largest and most inexpensive *decent* place to stay, it was no wonder that any of them had selected it. The only difference was that Kurt went to the second floor, while the girls stayed on the third. It was closer than anyone realized. Such a large city, but also such a small world.

Upon reaching his room, Kurt settled in for a shower. He'd lost some ten pounds since he left Flint, so room service was in order. Despite all the grotesque deaths he had inflicted, he was in the mood for a thick, juicy, rare steak. As he strode around the room in a towel waiting for his meal to arrive, he caught a glimpse of himself in the mirror and he liked what he saw. His black hair had grown to just short of shoulder length and wisped with its thinness. It hung in his eyes slightly and made him think of a movie star look. His abs had tightened into a six-pack. He dropped his towel and discovered that his penis hung some six inches toward his feet in a flaccid state. Out of curiosity, Kurt played around until he was fully erect. He now sported a whopping eight and a half inches with thickness to boot. It seemed that the more killing he did, the more weight he lost, which in essence raised his confidence level from a two out of ten to a solid nine. Kurt smiled in the mirror while flexing his muscles and admiring his own penis. He was delighted and astonished to find that there was no flab at all. He looked repeatedly as he strode in his confidence. Kurt was a good-looking man and he now knew it.

As he continued his strutting, the lights dimmed down and the mirror lit up before him. He was baffled as to the sudden change and thought for a moment that the power had failed.

"KURTIS! Kurtis Joseph?"

Kurt looked around, saw nothing and then looked in the mirror. The Red Queen stood before him, as if in another realm, or dimension. She sized up Kurt's torso and smiled bashfully.

"Oh my Kurtis, what large manliness you have. Would you mind taking your Queen for a ride?"

Without hesitation, Kurt strode toward the mirror. The Queen lowered herself to her knees and began what Kurt thought to be her servicing him with enthusiasm and vigor.

'D-Do you love m-me, Red Queen?" He asked in a breathy tone.

She looked up at him. "Oh how I love thee Kurtis. You've made me so happy. You collect the heads which give me the power to live."

She continued with her work as Kurt writhed and moaned with ecstasy.

"It w-won't be long, good Queen. K-Keep going…Keep going…D-Don't stop."

As Kurt emptied his pent up frustration, the lights came back on and he found himself standing before the mirror, a reflection of himself the only presence. The ejaculate dripped down along his likeness and onto the floor. His hand was lathered up and had remnants of his seed on it. Kurt had masturbated into a mirror. He was taken aback, but happy. That was, until he heard the dinner cart.

The woman pushing the cart had been looking down as she entered his room. The door was ajar, which was a sign in hotel speak that entrance without knocking was permitted. She looked up to call out his name and saw a very handsome man standing before a mirror, penis in hand.

"Humph, sir?" The server said while clearing her throat.

Kurt nodded slowly as the seed continued to drip down the mirror.

"Here's your dinner. Will this be, uh, cash or charge? No. Forget it." She raised her hand up while looking in the other direction. "I'll just put this on your tab. Don't move, sir. I'll take care of it."

It was hard to tell who was more embarrassed, the server or Kurt. He opened his mouth to speak.

"No," said the woman. "Don't say anything. You don't even have to tip me. I'll be going. Don't worry sir, I've seen much worse."

Kurt picked his towel up and began cleaning himself. The woman marked the tab and headed out of the room with haste. She turned at the last minute.

"I don't share what I see, sir. Your business is your business. May I encourage you to lock your door next time? It'll save everyone a lot of embarrassment."

Kurt nodded slowly, "Uh-huh."

The woman was lucky. Kurt would've killed her had she made too much of a fuss, but she was friendly and understanding, which played well with him. Had she decided to make a big deal out of it later, he would add her head to the rest of his collection. He didn't think it would be a problem.

"W-well," Kurt said to himself, "she's p-probably seen it all."

As he walked over to dig into his meal, he heard a voice from behind him.

"Was it as good for you as it was for me, Kurtis?"

Kurt whirled around and saw nothing. What he did notice startled him; all the semen that was on the mirror was now gone and he hadn't yet wiped it away. Kurt smiled a seductive grin. He answered his Red Queen.

"Y-yes, it w-was."

*

The trooper was in the driver seat of his cruiser. His head had been twisted completely backward. The front of his torso faced the windshield, while his head looked directly *behind* him. The FBI dispatcher had said it all on the radio. It was disgusting and brutal. Wilma knew Kurt was the culprit and it made her mouth water. She desperately wanted that man on a spit. She didn't care whether he was dead or alive. Not only was he a sexist pig in her eyes, he was also a complete maniac with no feelings for anybody except himself. What she didn't know was that he did have feelings for another, but not in the way anyone thought.

Looking closer, Wilma saw a tiny red blotch in the corner of the trooper's mouth. At first, she thought it was blood, but upon closer inspection, she saw that it was different.

""Help me here," she told her crony. "There's something in his mouth."

The crony pulled out what looked like a shoehorn, only much smaller, and pried the dead man's mouth open. Wilma reached in with a pair of tweezers and pulled out a Red Queen of Hearts card. Written on it, in Kurt's handwriting, was a message.

"*You'll never catch me. I'm three steps ahead of you, and will always be three steps ahead of you. If you want to die, keep up the chase. I'm warning you; if you find me, you find death. I will collect your head for the good Queen and put it in with my collection. Try me if you might, but you WILL die.*"

Indubitably yours,
The Hatter

The Queen had a smile drawn onto its face. Wilma turned the card over and there was more.

"*I can't explain myself sir, because I'm not myself you see.*"

Wilma seethed at the note. She placed the card in an evidence pouch knowing it wouldn't be needed. She had plans to kill Kurt herself. She could taste the spite on her tongue.

"Let's go!" She ordered. Her crony followed her with anxiousness and an axe to grind.

"We need to get to Seattle and put a stop to this creep. He's a thorn in my side and I've had enough. He's making me look bad."

The dark man chuckled.

"What's so fucking funny?"

He pointed to the card and then whispered in her ear. Rarely did a dark man speak.

"While every rose may have its thorn, also remember that every heart can be broken."

Wilma smiled.

Shaun Webb

"Well, I went along my merry way, and I never stopped to reason, I should have known there'd be a price to pay,

Someday, someday."

Shaun Webb

14
Ocean of Tears

Amy stirred while the man stared into her eyes. She remained in a sort of trance from having the oxygen to her brain temporarily cut off. When she was able to collect some of her thoughts, she alternated between fear and rage.

"Who did this to me? Who knocked me out and bound my wrists? What the fuck is going on here?"

Amy floated in the twilight between sleep and awake.

"You'll be fine Amy. Give it a few more minutes. While you're waiting, though, I'd like to talk with you. Is that okay?"

The voice was recognizable in her sleepy mind. She thought about it for another second or two and figured it out.

"Claude? Is that you? What the hell? Why are you doing this to me?"

A grimace showed on her face. She couldn't believe she was tied up and bound by her boss. There was a hint of relief as she could rest in the fact that it was someone she knew. It still concerned her, as she wanted to know why. Claude enlightened her.

"Amy, have you ever heard of Reiki? Reiki is a Japanese technique for stress reduction and relaxation that also promotes healing. It's administered by "lying on hands" and is based on the idea that an unseen "life force energy" flows through us and is what causes us to be alive. If one's "life force energy" is low, then we are more likely to get sick or feel stress, and if it is high, we are more capable of being happy and healthy. I think you're in need of healing. I worry about you day and night, and now I understand why. Although it hasn't been for very long, the man you're hanging around with; sleeping with; he's troubled."

Claude paced back and forth before a groggy Amy. He had expressions of anger and sadness competing for prominence on his face.

"I really do love you Amy. However, not how you may think. I love you as a father loves his daughter. As I said before, I do not intend to have a sexual affair with you. The thought, in fact, sickens me. My intent is to teach you something that you'll need in the future; the ability to heal yourself. I will teach you and pass it on to you today."

Amy grimaced, but didn't speak. She saw Claude, but it was through dreary, sleepy eyes. Claude continued to speak while she was in the semi-hypnotic state.

"While Reiki is spiritual in nature, it's not a religion. It has no dogma, and there is nothing you must believe in order to learn and use Reiki. In fact, Amy, Reiki is not dependent on belief at all, and will work whether you believe in it or not. Reiki comes from God, but many people find that using it puts them more in touch with the experience of their religion rather than having only an intellectual concept of it."

Claude then began chanting, his hands clasped before him in prayer.

"I open myself to divine love and wisdom. I open myself to divine love and wisdom. I open myself to divine love and wisdom."

He asked Amy to repeat the phrase three times, which she did in her sleepy, dreamy state.

"Just for today, do not anger, do not worry, and be filled with gratitude." Amy listened intently.

Amy felt an energy coursing through her. She felt the spirit; whatever spirit, filling her. Claude continued.

"Devote yourself to your work, be kind to all living creatures, except those attempting to hurt you, every morning and evening, and join your hands in prayer. Pray these words to your heart, and chant these words with your mouth; just for today, I will let go of anger. Just for today, I will let go of worry. Just for today, I will count my many blessings. Just for today, I will do my work honestly. Just for today, I will be kind to every human creature, unless they attempt to harm me."

Claude then untied Amy's wrists and told her to put her hands over her eyes. After thirty seconds, he ordered her to cover her temples, after that it was her throat, heart, sternum, stomach, groin, kidneys and shoulders. When finished, he had her take three deep breaths and brought her out of her trance. Amy came out swinging, verbally. She was now wide-awake. What she thought to be a dream was in fact happening before her.

"Who in the fuck put me here? What the fuck is going on? Who, what?"

"Calm yourself, child. It's me, Claude. If you calm down, I'll explain."

Amy began to settle. She looked around and realized it was in fact Claude standing before her. She shook the last of her cobwebs out and asked him to tell her everything. He did. She wasn't pleased.

Claude pulled out a stack of photos featuring her in various stages of undress and lovemaking with Blake. She wasn't embarrassed, just very, very angry.

"What the fuck is this Claude? Why do you have these? Are you some kind of an old pervert-fuck?"

"I want you to see for yourself that you're losing focus. This man, while very nice, gives off a bad vibe in my soul. I don't quite know what it is, but he's dangerous for you."

"Why can't I be the one who decides that? I'm a big girl now, as you can tell from the perverted pictures."

Claude smiled and rubbed his hand along his unshaven chin. He chuckled quietly.

"Oh, you can make any choice you'd like Amy; but if you choose this man for your mate, our business together suffers. I have great things planned and I must have your full cooperation. I already feel your vibe, and it says you have many doubts."

Amy was astonished. This man seemed to know more about her than she did. After mulling over Claude's words, she asked what he'd have her do.

"I would have you be prepared, Amy. Study the meditation I entranced you with today. Study deep and hard. Your essence is to be severely tested soon."

"Tested by whom? What do you mean?"

"I don't know the answer Amy, but it's coming soon. I can feel it. If you're not prepared, you could *die*."

Silence befell the normally obnoxious Amy. She had nothing to say. She found that she needed to listen. Claude handed her a disk that had the meditation chants on it. Amy had already noticed that she felt refreshed and somewhat relaxed. She took the disk and bent forward in salute to her "master."

"Go forth and do good Amy. Protect yourself and others from the evil that lurks closer than we think. I'm always here to help you child. Be friends with Blake, but let him go; you're not for him and he's not for you."

After he spoke the words, he handed Amy the dirty pictures and bid her goodbye for now. Amy bowed. When she tilted her head up Claude was...*gone*. She looked all around the large room and saw nothing. He had done this in his office and now did it in a more wide-open space. Amy mildly cursed him.

"Stop doing that shit Claude. You don't need to be so dramatic; Christ."

Amy rose, straightened herself up and headed home. As she was traveling on the highway, the realism of dumping Blake hit her. She didn't like the idea, as she wasn't into one-night stands. Unfortunately, she felt compelled to follow Claude's plan. It was a rare site indeed, watching Amy cry.

Sharing the same hotel with a mentally deficient fiend would scare the devil out of anyone, but not if you didn't know. Sandy didn't know and Andrea, drunk off her rocker, couldn't know. There were much more important issues at hand and Kurt wasn't one of them…yet.

Sandy found herself watching Andrea's every move for two straight days, trying to figure out how much she was drinking and if any other drugs were in the picture. When Andrea would go to the bathroom, Sandy would find an excuse to barge in. If Andrea took a shower, Sandy would sit on the toilet and talk to her. Andrea would ask her to leave the bathroom, but Sandy insisted, saying she was "super lonely." Andrea couldn't go for a walk down to the hotel lobby, shower or even have a bowel movement without Sandy tagging along. This caused friction between the two, and threatened to harm their once impenetrable relationship. Finally, after having had enough, Andrea asked questions.

"Sandy, I know you're up to something. What is it?"

"I'm just lonely. I need to be near you."

"But I can't even take a shit without you being two feet away. Are you freaking out on me, or what?"

Sandy continued playing the lonely card. She'd even sleep with Andrea *(sexually)*, if it meant saving her friend from the alcohol and drugs. Sandy was selling, but Andrea wasn't buying.

"I know what you're doing, Sandy. You could act like an adult and come out with it. Stop trying to fool me. If you're a true friend, just tell me what you want to tell me."

Sandy fell for Andrea's trick and broke down.

"Okay, okay. I'm worried about your drinking and I'm concerned that you're using illegal drugs."

"**AHA!**" Andrea barked. "I knew it. If I needed to be watched like a fucking hawk, I would've stayed home with my mother. You're not my mother Sandy, so stop trying to act like you are."

Andrea grabbed her bag and began packing it. Sandy's concern mounted.

"What are you doing? You're not leaving."

"Oh yeah? Watch! I'm taking some time off from you. I'm so pissed right now I could scream. Back off and give me some space."

Andrea finished packing and headed for the elevator. Sandy was in hot pursuit.

"Okay Andrea. I'm sorry. Don't leave. We can work it out." Sandy stood in front of the open elevator with her arms out to each side.

"Step aside, Sandy. Don't make me move you. I will put my hands on you if I have too."

Reluctantly and with major trepidation, Sandy stepped aside. Andrea entered and watched her friend as the doors drew shut. Sandy slumped to the floor and let her tears flow. She was sickly worried about her friend and there was nothing she could do about it. Oh, she could've blocked her way, but it would've only made things worse. It was obvious Andrea was departing and Sandy had to get used to it. The anxiety and fear gripped her and she began obsessing about

Blake in an unnatural sense. She went back to her room, undressed and lay on the bed. She imagined her "man" coming in and ravishing her. Sandy felt as though Blake were present. After ten minutes, she snapped out of her trance and wondered why she lay naked. Sandy was now becoming concerned for her own well-being.

As Andrea made her way down to the lobby, the elevator stopped on the second floor, one floor below her own. In walked a ravishingly handsome man who smelled good, *too good*. His face was finely shaved, showing a hint of dark shadow. He was thin, yet built, and very well dressed in a pair of Khakis and a polo. He had a sort of top hat on his head with a rose in the band. Andrea instantly felt sexual tension, as the man took *hot* to another level. He had thin, wispy dark hair, just beyond his shoulders and, to Andrea's estimation, was packing some major heat in his pants. She couldn't help herself any longer.

"Hi." She whimpered with a broken voice.

"Hello." The man said in return. "H-How are you?"

To Andrea, his voice sounded every bit as good as he looked. She attempted to carry on a further conversation.

"You from around here?" She asked.

"Uh, no. I'm n-not."

Andrea noticed the stutter, but didn't care as his good looks and sweet smell had captured her.

"Oh, that's too bad, because I'm not from around here and could use a tour guide through the city."

'S-Sorry." The man proclaimed, now frowning as if he were being pestered. "I'm in town for a small b-bit of business, and then I'm la-leaving."

The man kept his gaze forward against the tan colored doors. To him, it was taking forever to get to the lobby. He wished this woman would stop talking. Alas, she had more to say.

"I'll come right out with it. You're fucking hot, dude. Is there any chance we could hook up?"

"No." His annoyance was growing.

The elevator doors opened, and the man quickly rushed out. Andrea clumsily gathered her backpack and pursued him out the front door of the hotel.

"Sir, sir, wait a minute."

The man stopped, turned around and took a deep sigh. "Y-Yes, *what*?"

Andrea found this man so undeniably sexy that he could be as rude and obnoxious as he'd like and she wouldn't care.

"What's your name?" She asked.

"That's n-none of your b-business." He hissed.

Andrea figured she needed a new approach.

"Let's start this again. My name is Andrea Jimenez and I'll let you fuck me all night long if you'd like. You can even hit me. I'll tell you what; nothing's off limits. You say it and I'll do it."

Andrea pulled her flask of whiskey out and took a quick drink.

"W-What is that?" The man asked.

"Whiskey. Why? You want some?"

The man's left eye cringed and he offered her a slight smile. He was suddenly interested.

"So you're a c-complete slut AND you d-drink? What a c-combination."

Slightly taken aback, Andrea responded as if the man were joking.

"Oh, I'm not a slut, but I like to drink alright. I'll do anything you want sexually, though. I simply have to eat you up. You are the hottest man I've ever met. I wouldn't act like this with any regular Tom, Dick or Harry."

The man wrote on a slip of paper and handed it to Andrea. She took it. Her hands shook. She was within seconds of an orgasm.

"Your name and room number. Cool. When, uh, Turk?"

"I'll l-let you know." The man said.

Andrea smiled awkwardly, like a sixteen year old who was smitten, and headed back inside the hotel. The man smiled back and headed down the sidewalk.

She hadn't noticed that the pin adorning his shirt was a Red Queen of Hearts.

*

Amy made a b-line back to Blake's house. She needed to have a chat with the man she had made love with mere hours earlier. It was better to let him down now instead of allowing things to get too far off the ground. She arrived at Blake's place and wiped the remainder of the tears out of her eyes. She had thought about what to say and how to say it. As many times as she went over it in her mind, nothing except facing him and coming out with it would do. She felt as if she were on the other side of the relationship, because it was usually the man dumping her. As strong as Amy was mentally and as feisty as she was physically, it was the hardest thing she had to do because she liked Blake a great deal. Sure, she'd only seen him a couple of times, but he was kind and understanding with a vulnerable soft side that seemed to compliment her personality. Better yet, he *seemed* different from other men. Sure, there were hot guys abounding, but Amy wasn't as much into looks as she was personality and charm. No matter, his anxiety and panic problems would definitely slow her down when it came to doing her job while being mentored by Claude.

Blake was still asleep when Amy arrived. She sat on the edge of the bed and gently rubbed his arm until he awoke out of his slumber. A smile came to his face instantly as he saw her beautiful aura before him. He hadn't noticed that she'd been gone. He sat up to kiss her, but she turned her head, prompting Blake to ask questions.

"What's the matter Amy? Are you regretting our fabulous night?"

"No. It was beautiful, Blake. I have to share some unfortunate information though. I don't want you to be angry, but I think you will be despite my hope."

Blake felt his spirit sink. He knew what was coming next, but hoped beyond hope he was wrong. All men seem to own that habit of thinking it's a joke or that the moment was somehow not real. It was no different for Blake. Unfortunately, this moment was as real as it could get.

"I can't be this close with you Blake. I can't share myself like that again. I really need to concentrate on my work and on my future."

"I see." A visibly downtrodden Blake muttered. He pulled his knees up toward his chest and held them with his arms. "I'm not surprised. What could I have ever been thinking?"

"It's really not your fault Blake. I should never have gone that far with you; with anybody." Amy put her hand to her lips in an 'I shouldn't have put it that way' manner. "You know what I mean, don't you?"

"Sure. Wham bam thank you *sir*? Just go. I don't want to talk anymore. I'm tired and need to sleep." Blake turned over and slammed his body down on the mattress.

What he had said couldn't have been farther from the truth, but what more was there to say? He could sit and whine for hours and it wouldn't change a thing, so why linger? Amy bent to give him a kiss on the cheek, but Blake turned away from her.

"Please go." Was all he gave her.

She knew he was upset and figured he had every right to be. He had been shy and timid, but so cute. Amy liked him from the first time she laid eyes on him. She would keep a watch on Blake no matter what; because she wanted to make sure, he was not messed with or hurt.

Upon leaving his house, she shifted back into a non-emotional gear. Claude had told her to take a day to mourn, but that wasn't Amy's style. She rang up her boss and asked for another assignment. Claude refused her and ordered her to bed for some much needed rest. Not for Amy Fraser. She was angry and disappointed and needed to blow off some steam. She stopped at a party store, grabbed a six-pack and two mini-sized bottles of whiskey and went back to Denny Park. She pulled her vehicle off to the curb and cracked open her booze. She didn't want to be bothered, but bothered didn't care.

*

Andrea went screaming back to the hotel room, excited to tell Sandy what was going on. She found her friend sitting in the bed with her jeans on the floor next to her. Andrea didn't bother asking any questions, as she was too excited about her find.

"It's been all of five minutes and you're back?" Sandy announced. "What gives? Why do you play these games?"

"I met this really hunky guy on the elevator. He was interested in having me to his room and said he'd get a hold of me. I can't leave now. We're both searching for love, and I think I found it."

"I see. So the only reason you came back was to use this room as your "staging area" as it were. What's happening to you Andrea? You need to sit down and talk with me, okay? Maybe after that I'll let you stay."

"**FINE!**" Andrea barked, and then calmed. "Whatever. Let's talk. Let's talk until we get it all out. Did you ever think that I don't have anything to talk about?"

"You do though, Andrea. I found a used hypodermic needle that you tried to flush. It almost stuck me in the ass when it came back up in the toilet. Are you a heroin addict, Andrea? Or is that my imagination? Maybe you'd like to forget about that so you can screw the next guy that comes along. You have a drug and alcohol problem, and I'm going to help you fix it."

"I don't have a problem with heroin anymore. I flushed that needle to be done with it. We can go to the hospital right now and you'll see it's not in my system."

"Then why did you have a needle here, Andrea? Do you think I was born yesterday?"

Andrea figured this was not a good time to joke about Sandy's naivety, so she didn't. She answered honestly, using her own style of honesty.

"That needle was from back in Toledo. It was in my purse and I missed it. I'm clean. I cleaned up before we took this trip Sandy. That's why I've been drinking so much."

Sandy sighed, shook her head, and rose from the bed. She put her jeans back on and invited Andrea back.

"Why were you half naked Sandy? Were you jackin' off or something?"

Sandy waved her off and the two sat down for a long chat.

Andrea opened up to Sandy as never before. She told her about the heroin, crack, speed, meth and anything else she'd abused in her day. It appeared that she had weaned herself down to alcohol, but to Sandy, if that was all she was doing it was still a nasty addiction. She forgave her best friend and hugged her tightly. They talked for six more hours before falling asleep. Sandy went on about Blake until Andrea urged her to cool her jets and sleep. To Andrea, it seemed as if Sandy was getting dangerously obsessive about the guy. She promised to broach the subject after her date with the man named "Turk."

The next morning, Sandy expressed being less than thrilled about this new hunk of a man that Andrea had met, and insisted on meeting him herself before turning her friend loose. It was more motherly love from the conservative girl. Sandy insisted that he come to their room first before doing whatever they were going to do. Andrea rolled her eyes, *whatever,* and the two went downstairs for breakfast. It was there that Sandy met the man of whom Andrea was drooling.

Sitting in a far corner reading a newspaper was Kurt. The girls approached him and said hello.

"Hey there," Andrea bashfully whispered.

Kurt moved the paper to the side and Sandy saw what her friend was saying about his good looks. Sandy didn't often express any kind of opinion about anyone else other than Blake, but this man sent a chill up her spine.

"Hi l-ladies. H-How are you?" He greeted in a friendly manner.

Andrea introduced her best friend.

"This is my friend Sandy. She wanted to meet you before we hook up."

"Hook up?" Kurt thought. *"Who said anything about hooking up? I just wanted you to get the fuck away from me. You were so insistent and slutty. Ha! Hook up. I'll take your fucking head and soak it in the same green water as the others. You fucking little slut bag."*

Kurt snapped out of his daydream and saw Sandy extending her hand.

"Hi Turk. I'm Sandy. You seem like a clean cut sort."

Despite his slight stutter, Sandy found him to be nice, and *very* handsome. She shook his hand and murmured. He smelled so good to her. She finished her pleasantries and excused herself for breakfast. She was focused on Blake. Finding him continued to be her top priority.

Andrea sat next to Kurt, not knowing how close she was to a dangerous killer. She noticed the polo shirt he was wearing had a picture of the Red Queen on the upper left chest. His hat sat on the table next to him. Andrea reached out to touch it, but had her hand quickly intercepted by Kurt before she grasped it.

"Please don't touch my hat. Nobody touches my hat."

"Um, okay. Sorry." Andrea shifted gears, failing to pick up on Kurt's lack of a stutter in his last statement. "Alice in Wonderland, huh? You like that story?"

"Y-Yes, I do. It's my f-favorite. The Queen is my preferred c-character. G-Great book. Have you ever r-read it? It's b-by Lewis Carroll."

"No, but I watched the cartoon on TV. It's not my cup of tea. No pun intended."

Kurt shook inside as she mentioned her blasé attitude about the greatest story about the greatest woman that had ever been told. The Red Queen was the epitome of Kurt's being. The anger seethed within him.

"W-Why don't you come up to my r-room today, Andrea? We c-could spend the d-day in, just you and I d-doing whatever we want."

Andrea's body warmed up significantly, as he extended his invitation. She greedily accepted his request.

"What time?"

'S-say elevenish? I need to *sharpen* up before you arrive."

Andrea took Kurt's room number and said goodbye. She grabbed the room key from Sandy and headed upstairs to clean up nice for her adventure, which would last all afternoon and into the evening.

"I've got to get my hair just right."

Indeed she did. Kurt liked the hair done just right.

*

Amy sat in her jeep drinking her booze and smoking cigarettes. All she wanted at that moment was to be left alone to both rue her decision of sleeping with, and then quickly dumping Blake while at the same time missing him. Being as mentally tough as she was helped her a great deal. This was a huge change from only months ago, when she struggled with the demons of Post-Traumatic Stress Disorder. She had come full circle, and Claude was giving her more strength than she originally thought she owned.

Amy continued to take belts off her bottle when a misplaced man approached her vehicle and said hi. He was a strong man with muscles on muscles, but to Amy, he was much less than admirable.

"Steroid junkie," she said aloud.

The man responded the way most people do.

"What did you say?"

"You heard me Brutus. You have a nice muscular body, but your balls have probably shrunk into acorns. Steroids will do that you know."

"Why don't you step out of the fuckin' car?"

He was tugging on his pants in the rear while twitching about as he issued his dare.

"Aw," Amy responded, "I don't feel like fighting right now. Why don't you go find a squirrel? They'd be more interested in your little nuts?"

The man punched the door of her jeep. He put a dent in it. Enraged and bored at the same time, Amy stepped out of the vehicle. She looked over the damage.

"Now look what you've done, you dick. You're paying for that damage."

"I ain't paying for shit, woman. The only person paying today is you. I've decided I'm going to teach you some manners."

Undeterred, Amy didn't ask this time, she simply told him what was about to happen.

"Sir; if I can say something you're not going to believe; I'm going to literally take enough money out of your wallet to pay for that door, and then leave unharmed. You, however, will be crawling around on the ground begging me to stop hurting you. What do you think of that?"

Before another word could slip from Amy's mouth, the hulk took a hard swing geared toward her head. She anticipated and ducked. When he followed through, his head was turned slightly away from her.

That's when she slapped him on the cortex with her sap. A hard leathery slap echoed with the blow. The man reeled to his left and then regained his nearly lost footing.

"What the hell was that? What did you hit me with?"

Amy said nothing. She stood only two feet from the man, hopping on the balls of her toes. He made a second lunge at her. This time the sap connected with his throat and sent the big man to his knees struggling for breath. As he held his hands to his throat, Amy unleashed a torrent of pepper spray straight into his face. Now his breathing was worse as he struggled with his throat and his lungs. Once on his knees, the man fell on his side. Amy grabbed a cloth from her jeep and covered her mouth and nose. She approached the man and put her foot on his throat. He instantly stopped writhing and looked up at the petite woman with a combination of awe and utter disbelief. Amy put pressure on his throat and twenty seconds later, he passed out. She bent down, removed his wallet and took three hundred dollars out. It was what she thought would cover the door damage. The man had a grand, but Amy wasn't interested in stealing from him, only getting her fair share. She dropped the wallet on the man's chest and walked back to her jeep. She figured it'd be best to drive home and finish her morning of mourning in the calm setting of her own abode.

After coming around, the man was approached by a couple of homeless men looking for empty bottles, handouts, and whatever else they could find free.

"What happened to you?" One homeless man asked.

"Um, some big guys attacked me. There had to be four or five of them. I stood my ground for a while, but they were too much for me."

Embarrassed, the humbled man picked up his things and began walking away. His tail was between his legs and his attitude was changed, as he would think twice before ever attacking a helpless petite woman again. Amy was a rare breed indeed, and he felt her nasty wrath of punishment.

*

Off with her head IV

*

Getting herself beautiful was of the upmost importance for Andrea. She shut herself into the bathroom for three hours. Sandy was forced to the lobby to use the bathroom, as Andrea wouldn't let her inside. She washed her hair twice, shaved her armpits, pubic area and legs silky clean. She also sat on the toilet shooting low-grade heroin. Of course, she had lied to her friend. Why would she tell her the truth and risk getting in another donnybrook. Sandy was gullible and Andrea played it to the hilt. She was a wild girl and Sandy couldn't stop that on her best day. She wanted to use heroin, drink booze, smoke weed, and whatever else that made her feel good. Sex? Of course. Sex was the cherry on top of the sundae. Sex was the reward for being hot and attracting men. Nothing beat having an incredible orgasm. To Andrea there was one extra bonus; an incredible orgasm while tripping on whatever drugs she had in her possession. She limited the drinking when she knew she was getting laid, because alcohol had a flattening effect on her, which was to say it dulled the feeling. It also made her tired, which was another bummer.

    She finally finished her primping and dressed in her patented naval exposing shirt along with a pair of tight leather pants. No underwear and no bra though. That would make for much easier access. Sex, acceptance and drugs were Andrea's life, a life that had only lasted twenty-two years thus far. Her birthday was coming in two months, so twenty-three was up in the air considering the dangerous man she was calling upon that evening. She gave Sandy a hug and headed out. Sandy thought her eyes looked a bit bloodshot, but that was probably from being tired and drinking too much. She also noticed that Andrea hadn't been drinking, so that was good. She wanted her to stay sharp just in case the man she was meeting turned out to be a jerk. The problem was that Andrea wasn't sharp, and that could very well cost her dearly. Sandy decided to go out on the town that evening in search of Blake. It was possible she could find him anywhere and at any time. That's why she was in Seattle, after all. Another spell of obsessiveness and despair struck her. She managed to shrug it off and get herself ready for the search.

    Kurt, awaiting Andrea's arrival, was setting up his room so that she'd be even more smitten with him. He had a wonderful red bouquet of roses ready for her and the wine was chilled on ice. Kurt set up a couple of surprises for his guest, which he would keep a secret until the best possible moment. Andrea had no idea what kind of night awaited her. He played his Alice in Wonderland music while preparing for her arrival, but would turn it off until the precise moment that the situation called for it. Kurt had used three of the six formaldehyde jars he had brought with him. His plan was to use three, but the woman at the hotel was unplanned. One was reserved for Amy Fraser, so it left him two extra. Perhaps he'd use one of them for Andrea. It was all up to the Red Queen though. She had to give the order. Kurt assumed she would go ahead with the action he was planning. All independent thinking had disappeared since his Queen had smiled at him. Kurt was ready to do whatever she demanded.

    Andrea arrived some ten minutes early, but that was fine, as he had everything set and ready to go for his visitor.

    Kurt was polite, offering Andrea a drink. He turned on some soft music and sat on the chair across from her so he could stare deep into her eyes. Andrea felt a bit funny, but the feeling soon departed as the heroin did its work of bringing a euphoric feeling inside her mind.

    "So Turk, what do you do for a living?"

    "I'm a h-headhunter, Andrea."

    Taken aback, Andrea did what most people do when they think there ears have deceived them; they repeat the subject of the sentence.

    "A Headhunter?" Andrea predictably asked.

    Kurt was smiling ear to ear and it looked almost sinister. He had Andrea in a nervous tense and decided to toy with her.

"Y-Yes, a headhunter. Are you s-surprised about that? D-Didn't I appear to you to b-be a headhunter?"

Her tongue was tied firmly in her mouth as she thought about how to answer. She decided, despite the euphoric high of heroin, that is was time to leave.

"Okay Turk, it was nice meeting you, but I'd better go now. Maybe another time?"

"Oh. D-Don't go Andrea. Did I alarm you? A h-headhunter finds jobs for p-people out of work. You didn't think I was a r-real headhunter, like in a tribe or something, d-did you?" He chuckled menacingly.

Relieved yet still skeptical, Andrea sat back down. Now that Kurt had loosened her up, she felt better. She asked for another drink.

"Could you make it a double?"

"Of course, b-but you know alcohol severely thins the b-blood, right? It makes a headhunter's j-job that much m-more difficult."

Andrea laughed as she made sense of Kurt's humor. He brought her back a double scotch and she drank greedily.

"Slow down g-girl. You'll get too d-drunk. We have a l-long night ahead of us. D-Don't get ahead of yourself." He stared at her with an uncomfortably straight edged look on his face. Andrea was becoming worried.

"Oh, I'm fine Turk. I can handle my liquor."

In reality, Andrea sensed something strange. She wasn't sure what it was, but this was a different man than the sarcastic joker on the elevator, or the much friendlier version in the breakfast nook. This time he seemed creepy. It was as if he was on the edge of *something*, but what that was she didn't know. His eyes seemed wider, his smile broader and his glare more menacing. She looked up to see him staring at her with his head tilted down and an evil grin across his face. Uncomfortable, Andrea decided to abort the operation, find Sandy and look for Blake with her. She suddenly found herself missing her friend deeply. The tiny voices stated in her head that perhaps Sandy was right in cautioning her about this hook-up. Nerves started swelling in her veins as the buzz of the heroin rushed through her body quicker, the rising heartbeat in her chest assisting in the breakdown and metabolizing of the drug.

"You know Turk. I think I'm going to go. I don't feel my best and I really need to find Sandy. She's out somewhere in the town and I have a bad feeling about her."

Kurt walked over to the portable room wet bar and brought out red roses for Andrea. He handed them to her. It was a half dozen beautiful long stems.

"These are for you. I hope you like them. Compliments of the Red Queen herself."

"Did you say 'Red Queen', Turk?"

"I did. I did say Red Queen. The Red Queen of Hearts Andrea. Remember I'm a big Alice in Wonderland fan. Why aren't you?"

She noticed that his stutter had disappeared.

"Sure Turk. You know you're totally creeping me out? I'm leaving."

"Ah. I didn't mean to creep you out. How about another drink? I'm sure the Hatter wouldn't mind a bit." Kurt disappeared into another room.

Andrea's thoughts started spinning.

"The Red Queen? The fucking Hatter? What have I gotten myself into this time? This guy's an Alice in Wonderland freak. That explains the pin in his tie. This guy has an unhealthy obsession. Oh my God what have I done? I need to get the fuck out of here and fast."

The music came on and the lights dimmed. The song "Paint the roses red" played from the speakers of the jam box he had sitting on the bureau. Andrea looked at her six long stems and brought them close to her nose. That's when she noticed that these roses had, in fact, been white, but painted red. She now went from at first concerned, to scared, and now petrified. She looked around and didn't see Kurt. The lights had dimmed and the room was not quite dark. Her breathing thinned considerably and her heart jacked up the adrenaline another notch. The buzz was gone, replaced by the flight or fight mechanism instilled in every human being. She ran to the door and found it locked. She unlocked and pulled hard, but the door wouldn't budge. She looked up and saw that when she came in and the door shut behind her, Kurt had already installed an automatic deadbolt that clasped shut at the top. It was tight and the door wasn't moving. She ran to the window, threw back the curtain and saw that this wouldn't work either. Kurt had nailed three by five hunks of wood across the frame, leaving no room for exit. She was trapped like a rat and knew it. She noticed something scurry on the floor next to her and looked down; it was a small mouse that had the ability to slide its very adaptable body under the door. She wished she had the same ability.

"**A Dormouse, I'd say!**" Kurt shouted from the other side of the room. "**The Dormouse always gets away!**"

Andrea backed up only five feet, as she encountered the wall. It was a *dead* end. She could faintly see in the dimmed light that Kurt had some items. As he walked a bit closer, but was still ten feet from her, she saw a blowtorch, rope and what looked like a baseball. He was wearing the now dastardly top hat. She screamed loudly, but it was no use as the rooms on either side of Kurt's room were unoccupied. The music continued as he spoke and tossed the round object to Andrea. She caught it and looked; it was a cat's severed head.

"I finally got him," Kurt proudly announced. "The Queen has been looking for that damned cat for years. He isn't smiling now, is he Andrea?"

Andrea dropped the head and looked back up toward Kurt. He was now two feet in front of her and looked at her with that sinister grin.

"Cheshire Cat, you know? The Queen's wanted his head for years. I found him in the alley. He couldn't disappear or changed places before I snuck up and **WHOP!** I took his head."

Faintness surrounded her. She was reeling, but Kurt caught her and brought her to the chair. He sat her down and tied her feet and waist with a rope. He secured her hands on the armrests. A few minutes later, he lightly slapped some water across her face, she awoke. He had emptied her purse and found the other six syringes Andrea had stashed for her future

A Killer for the Queen

fixes. He also found the baggy full of heroin. He poured the powder in a glass, mixed in a bit of water and began heating it with his blowtorch. Soon the mixture bubbled and he carefully filled each syringe with the concoction. He laid the items down next to Andrea and took a seat close to her. She attempted to scream, but he had gagged her, making the sound nothing more than a muffled whimper.

"This ought to give you the buzz of your life," Kurt squealed. "I do hope you enjoy this. Oh but wait. There's one bit of business before the drugs."

Kurt pulled out a scroll and unwound it. The bottom fell to the floor in front of the helpless Andrea. He began reading.

"For being a complete slut, and for using illegal drugs along with abusing alcohol, the Queen has put you on trial and found you **guilty!** The sentence? **OFF WITH YOUR HEAD!**

Andrea's eyes grew to the size of small flying saucers as Kurt pulled out his machete and approached her. He had his blowtorch in his left hand and drew back the machete with his right. It was a clean strike, easily taking Andrea's head. It was one of the best swings he'd ever taken. It felt like a hot knife through melted butter. Andrea's head stayed on her shoulders temporarily, her eyes still wide, and then softly fell in her lap. Before more than a squirt or two of blood had exited through her carotid, he was already blow torching. He had her sealed up in less than ten seconds. He did the same with the head. Very little blood was spilled. He picked up the head by the hair and whispered softly, "The Queen's law is always done." He then stuck his tongue in her deaf ear canal.

*

Sandy returned to the hotel at three a.m., with no success in finding Blake. She was somber but determined. She came in, threw off her shoes and headed straight for the bedroom. It was dark, but with her eyes now adjusted, she could see the lump of her friend in the sheets on the bed. She changed into her PJ's and hopped in next to her. Sandy reached over and placed her hand on Andrea's shoulder.

"I'm sorry I was such a bitch earlier. I love you Andrea. We'll work it all out. She pulled the cover back to give her a kiss on the cheek, but there was no cheek to kiss. Sandy whirled out of bed, ran to the light and clicked it on. She grabbed the sheets and pulled them as hard as she could. To her absolute horror and disgust, there laid her headless friend, heroin needles lining both arms and grotesquely sticking out. Sandy managed a scream, but it was weak and pale. She stumbled to the phone in a drunken-like stupor and called the front desk. After making the call, she sat on the chair and puked on the floor between her feet. Her friend had been murdered, and by that very nice looking man, she presumed. The door knocked and she let the police in, and then went back to the chair to continue her wrenching. She thought to herself, "What's happening?"

Only the Red Queen knew the answer to that riddle.

"Sentence first -- verdict afterwards." - The Red Queen of Hearts

Shaun Webb

15
All in Wonderland

As Wilma and her dark man reached the Seattle city limit, the radio buzzed for Wilma's attention. Another murder had taken place, and once again, it involved the removal of a head. It was at the Grand Hyatt on Pike Street in the downtown area. Wilma ordered her man to drive to the scene quickly. She called her other "dark man" and summoned him to the hotel; she also ordered him to bring her all the news about Amy Fraser that he had gathered. The three met at the Hyatt two hours later.

Wilma bristled at the sight, which was as bad, if not worse, than the rest of the murders. The heroin needles were horrific, but the "Q" spray painted on the girl's torso with a slash drawn through it made perfect sense. None of these women had been the "Queen" of which Kurt was looking. She feared Amy might be the most important of the collections.

Her crony arrived and filled her in as to where Amy had been hanging out and clued her into a man who Amy met every so often for short periods. Wilma asked if he drew a bead on that guy, and the crony didn't give her a definitive answer, only telling her that his name was Blake Thomas and that he slid in and out of the picture. The Dark Man explained to Wilma that he was too busy concentrating on Amy's moves and didn't trouble himself any more than he needed to with the male subject. He found out his name by snapping a picture of him and then feeding it into the specialized computer ID device that was built into the console of the car. Wilma gathered up these pieces of information and sat down with Sandy to see if she knew anything.

"First of all, I'm sorry about your loss, but I really need to ask you some questions."

Sandy, visibly shaken, agreed to the inquiry.

"Do you know anything about the man you mentioned to the police; the man with whom Andrea was hanging around?"

Sandy wiped her tears away and spoke with Wilma at length.

"The man was very handsome. He smelled good and dressed himself perfectly. He had a Queen of Hearts brooch or pin on his tie. He was tall, thin and had wispy black hair. His eyes were mesmerizing and his face angelic. I met him in the lobby downstairs and was very impressed with him. He was polite, kind and soft spoken. He said his name was Turk. Oh, and he had a slight stutter."

As Sandy wiped her eyes, Wilma continued with her questions.

"Did he say anything that you found to be suspicious? Did he give you any clue as to his motives or where he might be going?"

"All I know is that his name was Turk and he seemed super nice. I had no idea he was going to chop

Andrea up and leave her body in our room. Why would he do something so sick and degrading?"

"Because he's sick and degrading Sandy. He's a monster that needs to be stopped. Can I ask you why you're here in Seattle?"

"I came to find Blake Thomas. I love him and want him back. He left Toledo to come here and work. He's the love of my life. I can't find him though. I've checked all over Seattle and there's no sign of him."

"Well, Sandy, my man knows about Blake. I'll have him summoned here to the hotel. Would that be okay?"

Sandy's face brightened. The only thing that could help her feel better now was to see Blake. It would give her solace. She didn't give it much thought as to why her dark man knew of him, as it failed to cross her somewhat fuzzy mind. The dark man, who already knew who he was, simply needed to locate him. It wouldn't be a difficult task.

"Thank you for the time Sandy. I'll get back with you. By the way, I'll arrange another room for you to stay in, okay?"

Sandy smiled and gave Wilma a tight hug. Wilma thought this girl was way out of her element, a bit "out there" in that her eyes seemed distant, and needed to be safe at home with her family. Surely, the murder of her friend played a role. She'd find Blake, get the two together and let them decide how to proceed.

She took her two sidekicks down to the check-in counter to see if they could find out which room Kurt was using. Perhaps they could surprise him, if he were still in the Hotel.

"I need the room of a man named Turk please?"

Wilma flashed her FBI badge and the clerk went to work looking up the name.

"Even if a Turk is listed here ma'am and I have an entry, I can't, by law, tell you or give it to you."

Wilma completely understood what the law was and didn't hold the clerk responsible. She called into the Seattle Police Department and asked for a warrant to confiscate the hotel records. Within fifteen minutes, a warrant signed by a local judge whirred through the fax machine at the desk. The clerk read it, made a copy for Wilma and then handed her the entire read-out of all hotel occupants' check-ins and check-outs from the previous seven days. Wilma thanked the clerk and took the records over to the local coffee shop in the lobby of the hotel. She sat down with one dark man, her other out locating Blake, and dug through the records. It didn't take long to find the entry.

"AHA!" Wilma exclaimed. "Here it is; Turk Josef. Kurt backward and the last name a bit different. He didn't check out, and I'm not surprised. I'll bet ten shillings he's gone though. He was in 312. Let's go see 312."

The room was as clean as a whistle. The housekeepers hadn't yet reached it for cleaning, but it was exquisite. There wasn't a drop of blood or a sign that anything fishy had happened. As Wilma was looking about the room, she noticed above the door the presence of screw holes. She had her crony get a chair and she investigated closer. She saw a small chip of paint that had been knocked out of the door six inches from the top, and she knew that a device had been used to keep the door shut tightly, locked or not. Kurt had installed some kind of door latch that flipped down and locked in place when the door shut, and now Wilma figured that the crime had undoubtedly been committed in this room. She sent her man down for luminal and a blue light. He returned quickly and began spraying the room down. It didn't take long for them to see that the murder itself had taken place in a chair. Surprisingly, there wasn't much blood present, but that was par for the course in this case, as Kurt always sealed the injury with fire before too much fluid could be spread. While it didn't help with Kurt's location, it did mean she was closer to him than she'd ever been. A smile creased Wilma's face as she figured it was only a matter of time until the menace would be bagged. By her hand.

*

Amy packed the last of the few things she owned and headed out the door. She knew it was time for a change of scenery and it would be a good idea considering the type of job she held and the danger that went along with it. She didn't want anyone getting the lowdown on her, so she up and left in a one and a half day span. She'd been at First and Cedar since her and Hank had moved to Seattle, and he had since gone back to Michigan. She decided that living in a place for six months or so at a time would be the best bet. It would have her on the move quite often, and make it tougher to nail her down.

She didn't have much in the way of items to transfer, and frankly didn't care. She was, at her essence, a very simple woman that only needed simple living conditions. She figured a couple of years or so doing the bounty hunter work would set her up financially to quit and go somewhere far away for the rest of her life. Say Hawaii, Puerto Rico or even the Bahamas. It would be a very fair trade; having little now, but doing whatever she liked later. She was moving into a house near 12th and East Pine, due east of where she'd been living. It was less populated on that side of town and would keep her out of the limelight encompassing the downtown area. Amy smartly allowed Claude alone to know her whereabouts.

She thought about Blake often for the first couple of days since their encounter, but it was getting easier for her as time ticked away. Amy had the uncanny ability to harden up and let emotion roll off her shoulders. It was a pleasant experience with Blake and that was that, supposedly.

Amy's cell rang and it was Claude.

"Amy. Are you practicing the Reiki like I taught you?"

"It's only been a couple of days. Give me a little slack; I'm in the middle of a move. I'm trying to stay out of the way."

"Very good idea Amy. Perhaps one day you'll be more like me and learn how to come and go with the wind. Until then, I'm warning you; danger lurks close. Keep your eyes open. The time of your greatest test comes very soon."

"In what way, Claude? What do you know that I don't? Is something going on that you don't want me to know?"

"I know nothing except what I feel in my spirit, Amy. My spirit worries about you while at the same time knowing any enemy that approaches you is in for the fight of their life. That's why the Reiki is so important Amy. It will teach you patience, self-healing, and control. Use it Amy. Use it to your advantage."

"I will Claude. When will this "danger" occur?"

"I don't have the answers; only the feelings."

Amy thanked Claude for the warning, told him where she was living and hung up. She sensed something was lurking around her. She could feel it in her bones. Dangers lie in wait and she hoped it didn't involve Blake. Amy shook off her tepid thoughts and went back to the work of settling into her new home.

She selected an okay neighborhood. She went for a walk to see the sights and learn her escape routes, hiding spots and whatever lessons could be taught by watching, listening and feeling. She lived near a liquor store, a café and a Wine Shoppe. She had never realized how many alcohol outlets there were in Seattle, but figured all the rain and cloudiness lent itself to heavy drinking, and probably suicide, which was up there among the leading causes of death in the town. It was a beautiful city, but a very wet and dreary one. If you were prone to bouts of depression, this was not the place to live.

As she walked, she received the customary whistles and catcalls; something that happened so often she hardly heard it. That was one of the reasons Blake was such a cool guy. He didn't hawk; he ducked. His shyness showed her something she hadn't seen in a long time; vulnerability and a kindness not present in many men. Some men exuded too much confidence, while others went beyond laughable with their smugness. After mulling over the thought of him for a moment longer, she scolded herself. Still, she couldn't get the guy completely out of her mind. The liquor store seemed like a viable option. She didn't drink much, but would tonight. She grabbed herself a bottle of rum, a soda, and went back to her new house for a night of drinking and probably thinking about Blake, at least occasionally. It was okay when healing, even after a single sexual experience.

Before she could pour herself the first drink, Claude paged her to a bond jumper downtown. With an exhale and a shake of her head, she put the alcohol away and went about her business, the business of catching bad guys. A business that would soon test her in the most extreme of ways.

*

The door knocked. It knocked again. After the third rap, Blake managed to crawl out of bed and answer it. It was some man in black sunglasses and a black suit. Blake wasn't interested in opening up, so he asked his visitor what he wanted by yelling through the door. The man in black moved toward the window and flashed his FBI badge. "Oh great." Blake thought. "What did I do this time?"

The uncomfortable feeling that comes with facing any kind of authority, especially FBI, was not fun for Blake. Even though a quick scan of his criminal past could find nothing objectionable, he still stepped cautious. His flight or fight response was tapping on his central nervous system.

"What can I do for you?" He said, again through the door. "I'm not dressed."

The man went back to the window, and this time flashed a picture of Sandy Arnold. Stopped dead in his tracks, Blake felt that horrible wave of anxiety approaching. This time he opened up and let the well-dressed man inside. Blake felt faint and thought he may pass out.

Blake sat down heavily on the comforter spread across his beat up couch and began his deep breathing exercises. The dark man looked at him puzzled.

"Don't worry about me, mister; I'm having a panic spell. You and that picture were the last thing I expected today."

The man handed him the picture of Sandy with the address to the Hyatt on the back; along with the room number. He turned to leave.

"Hey," Blake hissed. "That's it? Don't you have something to say? Is she okay? Is she alive, dead, or what?"

The man gave Blake an A-OK symbol with his index finger and thumb before walking out the door. Blake followed him with more questions.

"How'd you find me? What's your name? What's the story here? You just hand me a picture of one of my friends and split?"

No response. The man slid into the driver seat of the sedan and screeched away with haste. Blake was left standing in the street with his boxer shorts and nothing else covering his body. He looked up to the skies as he walked back toward the apartment.

"Huh, looks like rain...again."

Blake plopped back down on the couch, mulled over the picture of Sandy, and began thinking about what had just happened. It was a shot from outer space. This was absolutely the strangest thing that could've taken place. He wondered why Sandy of all people was in Seattle and what she wanted. It was so odd that it seemed surreal. He felt as if he didn't really exist in the world. It was much like an out of body experience, as if he were detached from reality. He'd heard of that disconnected feeling that sometimes occurred with anxiety, but was now feeling it for the first time. He went into his bedroom, fished out a pair of Xanax pills and popped them with a small glass of water. He sat back on the couch and began reminiscing about what had led to this place in his life.

"Why Sandy and why now? I left that life back in Toledo for something new and fresh. Now I feel like that was a bad choice. Maybe I should have stayed and tried a bit harder to make my life work. Was I too quick in my decision? Did I jump the gun yet again? I wanted to escape the old life of drugs and alcohol that haunted me. I ran away from friends and family because of the feelings I had. That's opposite of what I'd ever learned. Usually people get closer to their families when the chips are down. Not me. I had to be the brave one and start a new life here. What mess did I get myself in?"

Blake soon shifted his thinking and started pondering about what may have contributed to his deep-rooted anxiety.

"They say you're supposed to get out of your comfort zone and start facing what scares you. I haven't died from my problem. What causes it, though? Where in my life did things change? It started while I was using drugs with my friends. Maybe it was the drugs."

Blake's heart began to pound a bit harder and his breathing labored. He felt his heart doing "flips" in his chest. He continued with his thoughts.

"It's nothing. It never is, and never will be anything at all. It's all a figment of my overactive imagination. Could it be I think myself into these situations and feelings? Is there a chance that my thought pattern is wholly to blame? I know I'm tired of it. I'm tired of feeling tired, of feeling sick, of feeling "off". It has to end somewhere. I had a good childhood with good parents and great friends. I've been lucky in life with everything. Perhaps it's attention I'm seeking. Maybe even control. Whatever it is, I'm tired of it."

Amy slipped into his mind. She had spent the night with Blake and left in a hurry. He missed her, and was sorry that it didn't develop further. Still, he wanted to know why she up and left. Blake felt like he was a one-night stand.

"What happened? Why did Amy go so quickly? I know it was too early for sex with each other, but so what. Shit happens in this world, sometimes good and

sometimes bad, but man, I didn't expect that to happen. I'm glad I was given one night with her though. She's beautiful and smart. There's something different about her though, something mysterious. I wonder what it was about her that's so intoxicating."

It was hard for Blake to let her go. He hoped to see her around as friends. He had no idea what the chances of that would be. He hoped all the same.

Sandy finally squeezed into his realm of thinking. She was sitting at the Hyatt in downtown Seattle; presumably waiting for Blake to show up. He wasn't sure how to handle it, so he went over it in his mind.

"Why, Sandy? Why did you come looking for me? I blew you off back in Toledo. I didn't listen to you at all. I always took your hints at a relationship, but I always re-buffed your meek advances. We grew up together in the neighborhood, but I never once thought about "hooking up" with you. What brought you here? What is it that you have to tell me that couldn't be said on a telephone? Why are you here?"

Blake had his eyes closed and thought about all the clutter, all the pain *and* all the happiness. He wanted the positive to outweigh the negative and win the battle in his mind. It was a struggle, but Blake wasn't a quitter. He decided that the first thing he would do is find out about Sandy's agenda and see what would happen next. He put himself together and set out for the Hyatt.

"What's the worst thing that could happen?" He thought to himself. He'd find out.

*

Kurt laughed and toyed with the CD's, dolls, and books he had with him that represented Alice in Wonderland. Of course, he favored the Queen, as she was the glue that kept him together. He paid homage to her every single day.

After taking Andrea's head and adding it to the collection, he cleaned up the hotel room and headed out looking for another spot to hang low. He found the perfect abandoned building on the East side, a few blocks from Denny Park. He was pleased as he could pull his van completely under the structure and take the stairs up to an abandoned loft. It was empty, dirty and stinky, so Kurt spent most of his time at the location in which he parked the van. If ever he became bored, he walked around the loft looking for anything interesting that would occupy his mind. The rest of his time was spent drawing pictures of the Red Queen in various poses. The most disturbing of his drawings, though, was the depiction of the Queen standing in *his place* during the beheadings. It was as if she'd done the work herself through him.

Later in the day, Kurt heard the calling of the Queen. It sounded like it was coming from the loft. He made his way up, following the voice that called him.

"Kurtis, come to me. Come to me now."

When he reached the loft, he found his beautiful Red Queen levitating. She appeared happy and without worry. Kurt asked her why she was here.

"To see you, my love. Approach me, my subject of admiration"

Kurt's eyes opened wide. Her lipstick was in the shape of a heart and her red hair made him melt with longing. He wanted more of her. He moved closer.

"STOP!" the Queen ordered. "You mustn't come any closer. You cannot touch me Kurt, or I'll disappear from view forever."

"B-But what about the c-contact in the hotel, Queen? W-What was that which happened in the m-mirror?"

"That was you Kurt. I watched you with delight as you entertained me. You are my Jester, silly. You're taking care of that which is impossible for me to accomplish."

"I d-don't want to be your J-Jester. I want to be your *lover*. I want to b-be the King!"

"Silence!"

The Queen stopped smiling.

"There is already a King, Kurt. He sits in the dungeon with all the vermin. Would you like to sit with him?"

Kurt was saddened. He turned to walk away. The Queen had disappointed him and he felt hurt and used.

"Ah, Kurtis. Are we having a spell of 'woe is me' today? Don't you know that you are my greatest gift? Would thou like to hear only the good, but never a criticism? Why do you seek pity?"

He turned back around and answered.

"While I m-murder for you, maim for you, and c-carry out your wishes, all I receive in r-return is a small s-smile on a playing card. It makes me w-want to stop helping you in your aim to k-kill."

"Tis you who kills and maims, Kurt, not I. I give you the means in which to put your craft to good use. The heads are in your possession, are they not?"

He thought she made a good point, but not good enough.

"I will k-kill no more, Q-Queen. I will g-go back to Michigan and f-fall on the b-blade myself. I don't n-need you any longer."

"Oh, but Kurtis. I have helped you gain vengeance on the people responsible for both the death of your son and Kyle. I have given you power where weakness existed. You're down to but one, Kurtis: Amy Fraser. When you collect her head, your job is complete. They can all join Kyle in Hell for their punishment."

"But w-what of my p-punishment Queen? W-What happens to me when this is over and I d-die one day? Do I p-perish in the same Hell as the others?"

The Red Queen danced toward Kurt with a smile and a new aura. She was spinning, twirling, cartwheeling and dancing.

"Your reward, my Hatter, is to join me in Wonderland. It will happen immediately after Amy's head is collected. You will be with me in the land of wonder forever and ever. Thou shall be next to my throne at all times."

This revelation brought a smile to Kurt's once sour face. He was happy with that news.

"I w-would love sitting n-next to your throne, Queen. It would b-be an honor."

Kurt bowed before the Queen, convinced of her good will.

"Then you must bring me Amy's head. Tis the most important one Kurtis. Remember, 'sentence first, and then the verdict.' She *is* Alice."

The Red Queen slowly lifted toward the ceiling of the loft, and then vaporized through it. All that was left was a cloudy steam that floated back down onto Kurt's head. It gave him new life once again. He could feel the Queen touching him through the mist. It was warm and soothing. Kurt went back down to the van to open the cabinet and have a dance with the bodiless craniums.

*

She gave the dark men their orders; "Find Kurt Joseph and bring him to me."

Wilma wanted the killing to stop. It was too much already and she didn't feel like finding any other bodies with missing heads.

The men said nothing; they simply did what they were told. They were experts at seek and find, so locating and capturing Kurt would be of no hindrance to them. The two were also experts in the disposal business, but it wasn't the order. It was a find, capture and return Kurt *alive* deal. They figured they'd get a crack at him once Wilma was finished questioning him, and before the press was notified.

They drove around Seattle, trying to look for any clue that would lead them in Kurt's direction.

They went north, stopped at a few bars and stores while showing the picture of Kurt to people inside. Nothing. They tried the sidewalks. Nothing. They went south with the same results, and west gave them no clues. It was when the two went east that the doors began opening. They stopped at a party store not far from where Kurt was holed up in the abandon apartment complex.

"Yeah," said the cashier, "I seen dat guy. He comes in a lot to get beer and smokes. A little food too."

With a nod of their heads, the two went further down the road. They ran across coffee shops, restaurants, and wherever else they thought Kurt might frequent. If they stopped getting positive responses from merchants, then they switched the route slightly. It was a time-consuming and tedious job, but the dark men were bred for it. Their training included extensive hours of sniffing out whereabouts using their own senses. Sight, smell, hearing and following logical avenues were the main components in their search. The two ended up circling up and down Westlake Avenue near Denny Park. They were on Kurt's trail. The more they used the process of elimination, the closer they would get. Finally, after hours of painstaking elimination, they both zeroed in on one of two places; the abandoned apartment complex on the corner of Westlake and Denny, or the unused warehouse two blocks further down Denny. After more careful study, they decided on the abandon apartments, because the warehouse area had too many homeless men and women in the vicinity. They figured Kurt would want to be alone.

The entrance to the facility was boarded shut, but the ramp to the parking area wasn't, so they walked slowly and carefully down the slope and into a garage. That's when they saw a van. A brownish colored box van with the side doors open, but no sign of Kurt Joseph. They approached carefully and quietly, not wanting to stir up any noise in case it was in fact his van and he was within earshot. One crony came from the south side of the van while the other approached from the north. They nodded and made hand signals to each other as they held their pistols tightly.

Following his dance with the dead, Kurt had stopped at Starbucks for coffee and a bite to eat. He was walking back to the parking garage without a care in the world. He was wearing a white tee shirt and blue jeans; both freshly laundered the night before. A dark trench coat and his fancy top hat completed the garb. He also wore a belt consisting of a chain hooked above the fly with a C-bolt. Two twists of the bolt and Kurt would have the belt in his hands and ready for action, if anyone were so foolish as to confront him in a threatening manner. The penalty Kurt doled out for messing with him was usually fatal.

His hair blew gently in the Seattle breeze- a breeze that was present often by being so close to the ocean. Women would walk by and double take at Kurt, his sharp green eyes glimmering brightly in the sun (when it shone), and his hair a perfect length and style. The first glances by the women were always at his face and hair, but lately the top hat took most of the attention, which was exactly what he wanted. The second glances zeroed in on the substantial bulge that Kurt sported in his jeans. Many women say that they're more enamored with a man's hair, face and torso. To Kurt, that was a pack of lies because he saw for himself how women looked at his crotch when he walked by them.

"They say that g-guys just think about T & A." Kurt would muse to himself. "They say w-women don't pay attention to a m-man's package. Liars; they have s-sex on their mind way more often than they l-like to admit."

That line of thinking caused Kurt to start his cycle of woman hating which was a common occurrence. He would get so upset that he sometimes had to take a nap from the energy he'd expel from the thoughts. He hated women and thought they were only good for two things, sex and rearing children. The experiences all started with his Mother's abuse and grew with him into adulthood. Since he'd been away from Kathy, he felt better. He always smiled when he'd think about her head floating in the jar of formaldehyde.

"Those lousy bitches had it coming to them. I'd take Mom's head if she were still here. She had the good sense to die before I could get her. Hell, maybe I'll dig her old ass up and take it anyway. I'll add it to the collection of bitches in the van."

Kurt was two blocks from his hideaway. He continued his sexist thinking.

"I should've let those pieces of shit suffer more. A nicely sliced head is easy and quick, and the only pain they really feel is the fear before the knife cuts.

There's not but a second of consciousness afterward, and that's a warped sense. Once the spine severs, there's no feeling anymore. Maybe I should've water boarded them for a while. Make them think they're drowning. Perhaps even cutting them in certain places, allowing them to linger before I did the deed. I should've let them think about what was coming. Those fucking bitches! I hate them all."

As Kurt walked down the ramp, he heard the tiniest of bumps from inside. He threw aside his Danish, tossed his coffee away and loosened his chain belt. Something was amiss, and Kurt would put it back in line.

*

It was quiet in Wilma's realm. She had sent her men out to get Kurt and bring him back to her, preferably alive. She knew it wouldn't be long because when her men went after something, especially something Wilma wanted, they rarely, if ever, failed. She had sent them out after some of the worst and most dangerous killers in the land and they came back with the goods. Sometimes they were in more than one piece, but the killing would stop. To her, it was worth their effort.

Wilma had a soft spot for her men. On one occasion, she was destined for certain death, but her men came through. Straight out of a Batman and Robin comic book, the villains had her tied up over the water on a fishing yacht. The bad guys took her out to sea, were to stir up the sharks with a blood and guts cocktail, and then drop her directly into the feeding frenzy. The only problem was that the villains didn't check the boat for stowaways. That was their fatal mistake as they themselves ended up on the menu. Her unflinching men saved her life. They were brave and unrelentingly loyal to their boss. There was no need for thanks or pats on the back, as they were simply doing their jobs. They didn't throw the leader of the pack overboard, though; they let him linger on death row for six years before the state gassed him. That was one of the few times Wilma ever saw her pair crack even a sideways grin.

    She put her trust into these men and expected Kurt's arrival any minute. They wouldn't; couldn't fail. On the other hand, could they? Were they as infallible as Wilma thought? Did they have the same resolve with Kurt as they did with the other cold-blooded killers? Time would tell.

*

    Blake took a cab to the Hyatt. He was both nervous and charged up, mixed with repressed anger. He was not pleased that she was in town. He was sure she wanted to hook up with him and he wasn't budging. He thought there was still a chance with Amy.

    "People don't just make love with the power and passion that we did and not stay interested." He reasoned. "Now Sandy thinks we have something. She came all the way to Seattle for me."

As he spoke to himself louder than he originally thought, the cabbie peeked at him through the rear view mirror.

"Can I help you?" Blake sarcastically asked.

"Yeah! You can quit talking to yourself already. It's creeping me out."

"Well don't fucking listen. I'm nervous enough without some stranger like you amping me up even more. What is it with you cabbies? You think the world revolves around your broken down piece of shit car and your sky high fare."

"It feeds my family Mac. You're a weird dude. I'm pulling up to the Hyatt now. It'll be good to get rid of you. You give me the heebee jeebees."

Instead of continuing the argument and lowering himself to the cabbie's level, he gave him the Five-dollar fare and then added another five bucks.

"That's for being nothing more than a complete douchebag!" Blake snapped

"Whatever." The cabbie explained. "I deserved it for having to deal with you."

Dismissing the entire conversation, Blake made his way inside the Hyatt and stepped to the front desk.

"Sandy Arnold's room please. She's expecting me."

Wilma, standing to the side in anticipation of Blake's arrival, walked up and introduced herself.

"Wilma Hurst. I see my agent did the job and gained your attention."

"Yes, he did, but he wouldn't speak. Where is he?"

Blake moved his head left to right around the room, but saw nothing.

"He went on another run. No worries, let's talk."

Blake sat down next to Wilma in the lobby and she came right out with it.

"Your friend Andrea Jimenez; do you know her?"

"Of course, what about her?"

"There's no real good way to put this, but she was murdered last night."

A pale flushed over Blake. His heart rate sped up and nausea inundated him. He had trouble breathing. Wilma recognized the reaction right away and had a cup of water next to her. She'd offer him a drink if he could take one, or she'd throw it on his face if he ended up horizontal and hoarse. He was able to shakily clutch the cup and take a drink.

"Slow down, Blake. You're not a suspect. We know who's committing the crimes. Do you have anxiety problems, Blake?"

He nodded his head in the affirmative and started using his breathing technique. Deep-breath 3, 4…ex-hale 3, 4. He repeated it twice more and started to gain his color back.

"Good Blake. Feel better?"

Blake again nodded yes and Wilma asked if he was ready to see Sandy.

"How did it happen?" Blake asked. "Was it bad?"

"Don't worry about that. We have the killer in our sights. He'll be off the streets today. My men are on him like flies on sticky tape."

"I asked you how it fucking happened." Blake's eyebrows furrowed into a cinched look of contempt.

"Fine. You really want to know? He sliced her head off. It was clean and smooth. She went to his room and that was the last bad decision she ever made."

"Oh. That's bad." Blake paled anew.

"You wanted to know; now you know." Wilma explained, "Let's go see Sandy. She's been looking for you."

She led Blake to the elevator so they could ride up to Sandy's floor.

*

Staying busy catching crooks and thinking about Blake more often than she liked took up all of Amy's time. She still hadn't taken a slug out of her whisky bottle, and now lost the taste for it. Amy was confused and her stomach hurt. It wasn't like her to have stomachaches, but the entire situation was tough on the normally staunch woman. She cursed it and continued with her captures. She was getting meaner too, as the crooks and bail jumpers felt her frustrated wrath. The criminals kept coming in to the police station with more and more injuries. Black eyes, broken arms and legs, and bruised egos had some of the criminals expressing their relief when Amy turned them in. The cops didn't care as long as she brought these people to justice.

"Get me away from that crazy bitch."

"Dat Beatch crasy."

"Where da fuck you find dat nasty little broad."

Lately, Amy would give them a smack in the back of the head on her way out, elaborating on a point that was already well taken. Claude expressed concern, and would call Amy regularly and insist on her practicing the Reiki and meditating "more and more, deeper and deeper."

The stomachaches persisted and she began vomiting. Every morning it was the same thing; vomit, puke and then vomit again. After two or three hours, the nausea would stop, but her stomachache persisted. Amy's concern heightened when she started getting sensitive nipples. Her bras, shirts, and even soft bed sheets hurt her if they so much as came near her breasts. It had only been a couple of weeks since her encounter with Blake, but Amy faced a question in her mind and body; was she pregnant with his baby?

The EPT was a necessity if she was going to put her fears to the test. She made a trip to the drugstore and after finishing her morning puking routine, peed on a stick. She was astonished that with all the technology and gadgets that had been invented through the years, it all came down to urinating on a tongue depressor. She set the test aside and tried to make herself useful. She cleaned every inch of her house and then did it again. She would clean what was already cleaned, sit, stand, sit, turn on the TV, turn it off, clean some more, and do everything she could to avoid looking at the stick. At ten that night, as she was getting ready for bed, she checked it. Positive. She was pregnant with Blake's baby.

"Now that's just fucking great." She despondently expressed, "One time, one night and I get knocked up. Of all the shitty luck."

The next day, Amy bought another kit. It was another positive. Two days later; positive again. One last try; positive. She made a doctor's appointment.

"Yep, Ms. Fraser, you're pregnant alright. Who's the lucky guy?"

Amy was not amused.

"How much for an abortion?"

"We don't do abortions here Ms. Fraser." The nurse told her in a disgusted tone.

"You know there's always adoption."

"If I wanted your opinion, I'd kick you in the ass and wait for it to reach your mouth." Amy rudely told her.

"Hey lady, just because you screwed up doesn't mean you have to be nasty to me. I think our appointment is over.'

"Good! One more look at you would take my morning sickness to new levels."

Amy turned to throw up in the trashcan, but intentionally missed, thus messing up the floor for the unhappy nurse.

"Sorry. Looks like you have a mess to clean. You better get on that." The nasty Amy was present and pulling no punches.

She walked out of the office and into the street, tearing, but not crying. She pulled her phone out of her pocket and called the only person who she could rely on; Claude Ronet.

She went to the Tae Kwon Do studio to meet her mentor. She was surprised that he didn't fire her and tell her to take a hike. That wasn't Claude though. He was her ally and confidant, not a cruel taskmaster.

"What do I do Claude?"

"You keep working. This will take care of itself. You are a strong woman with strong beliefs and opinions. You will not be slowed by this blip on your radar screen."

"Blip?" Amy asked and told with the same stern tone. "This is no fucking blip on a screen Claude. This is a baby in my womb. A life inside a life. You act as if it's no big deal at all."

Claude rose from his chair and walked over to his star pupil. He knelt in front of her and gave more of himself to her.

"You will persevere, Amy. You are strong and undaunted. I have no doubt about your resolve; or your future working for me." Claude stood and continued. "You will work until you're showing. You will then be hidden from public view until the baby comes, after which you will return to work with me and the child shall be raised within. You will be a teaching Mother and I shall be the mentor of a new child birthed from my very best and deadliest student. The child shall be raised in your image, Amy. Now go. I have things to do."

Amy stood and without argument headed out the door. She stopped, thought about turning around but didn't. She knew Claude wouldn't be there.

*

Off With Their Heads

*

The chains from Kurt's belt rattled slightly, but he managed to silence it before anyone could hear. He decided to go up the fire escape and work his way down. It would be easier to take care of any intruders if he could look down at them, however many were present. Kurt gracefully scaled the fire escape, carefully looking inside the half busted windows as he passed each floor. He held his chain belt tightly, ready to strike at any moment, if needed. He finally reached the third floor and decided to enter there. He quietly worked the window open and entered like a ghost in the breeze, nobody hearing even a squeak from him.

He carefully walked the floor until he reached the apartment door, and stealthily opened it. The door groaned and Kurt quickly stopped the movement. The dark men, two floors below him, stopped, listened and then dismissed the noise as a breeze or the creak of an old building. It was the pair's first error. Kurt waited a second, made sure he heard nothing, and opened the door just wide enough so that he could squeeze through. It made no sound this time, to his satisfaction. He snuck out to the rail that was placed along a spiral staircase. He looked down and saw the shadows of two, maybe three people headed upward. He quickly moved back to the shadowed corner of the corridor he was standing in. He did it silently and with extreme care. He was only one man, so it was less likely to cause a sound under his feet. To his amazement, he heard nothing from the people headed up either. Could it be that they were just as skillful at keeping silent? He knew it wasn't the blundering clumsy police, because they always caused a ruckus when entering anywhere.

"Hit men? Why?" He asked himself. "They know nothing about my whereabouts."

Kurt kept silent and waited patiently for the prey to reach him.

*

They heard a slight groan from one of the floors above them. The men instantly looked at each other with the same exact thought, "who's up there?"

They needed no words to communicate efficiently with one another. Nods of the head and hand gestures told them both what they needed to know. They approached the rising stairwell with extreme caution. One Dark Man a step ahead of the other. They walked single file to avoid any possibility of both being shot at the same time. They would shield each other; protecting one from harm so the other could return fire. They were a team that never wavered when it came to concentration and care. They took equal turns in front and didn't fear death. If it came, it came; but these two would be tough outs, as they had survived years of service with nary a scratch. They'd been in much worse situations and came out on the surviving end each time. You couldn't say the same for the enemies, who often came out in more than one piece. They were rarely taken by surprise.

Up the steps they lumbered, slowly and with silence their greatest ally. They neither heard nor saw anything else, but stayed alert and ready every second. One minor letdown could spell doom. The shadows held no answers as they reached the second floor. They had their pistols drawn and eased from left to right and back with alert readiness. Turning the corner, they again saw nothing. It was simply a dark, abandoned floor. They looked at each other and signaled up another flight. This time the other man would lead the two. They stayed two feet apart, making it virtually impossible to kill them both with one bullet as the human body could endure a punishing blow; even from a high-powered rifle.

    They heard nothing else as they carefully creaked up the next flight of stairs. It was getting darker and more ominous with each step. They had ten steps on the left side, a small corridor with room to turn, and another ten steps up to the next floor. They reached the corridor and stopped. Both men had heart rates at seventy. The average person would be up around one hundred and twenty, but these were no ordinary men; they were Dark Men, trained for such encounters. Their breathing stayed consistent and regular, and they didn't sweat. Pure nerves of steel.

    Eerily silent and disturbingly slow, the men headed up the last ten steps to the floor from which they thought they'd heard the sound. Nine steps, eight, seven. Bold and unafraid. The sixth step, fifth and fourth. They had eyes that were steel, souls that were fearless. They finally entered the vestibule and headed inside the ajar apartment door when the lights suddenly went out.

*

A Killer for the Queen

The men were climbing the stairs as Kurt tucked into the shadows. As their footsteps came closer, his heartbeat accelerated. It wasn't uncomfortable, but invigorating. Kurt backed up further and further until he reached the door of the apartment that he'd left open. A great idea entered Kurt's mind. An idea that would possibly help him out of this tight situation. Not worried, but mildly concerned. Kurt backed his way into the vacant room, silent and steady as he did.

The Dark Men started on the last flight of twenty-five steps. They were slow and careful in their ascent. Kurt, figuring he had three minutes before they'd reach the room, jumped out of the window, ran down the escape and retrieved his machete from the van. He scaled back up and stealthily re-entered the room. In all it took two minutes and forty-five seconds. Kurt stationed himself, machete in hand and a bead of sweat dripping from his brow. He could've simply waited by the van for the men to come down, but he wanted to do the dirty work now, while he was psyched and pumped up with adrenaline.

He finally saw the men come around the corner and enter the apartment. Two men with guns, dressed in black, separated by a foot or two, one in front of the other. The time was now. Kurt sprang into action.

*

The pain was virtually non-existent, and there were no shots fired. The swiftness in which Kurt worked was a step ahead of the men. He had balanced himself above the door on the tiny jamb that ran around the rectangle frame. He propped his one hand on the ceiling while the other clawed and squeezed the deadly instrument of death. As soon as the second Dark man entered the room, Kurt dropped quickly behind them. He screamed **"Off with your heads!"** and before they could turn around, both heads spun off of their shoulders. The bodies lurched forward and fell on top of one another. The heads sat quietly off to the right. Both men were taken with one swing. It was magical to Kurt, as he felt the surge of power go through him. It was a rush that couldn't be explained. He felt slightly dizzy, could feel the blood rush to his brain, and he released chemicals that felt better than his best orgasm. It was a strong, pleasant feeling. When he came around, he walked over to the heads and picked them up. Both men had blank, emotionless stares. Kurt searched the bodies and found everything he needed to find. Notes, paperwork and phones. Everything he needed to place Wilma Hurst as the leader of these two dopes. He also saw some notations and locations that included the names: Sandy Arnold, Blake Thomas, and of all people, Amy Fraser.

Now that he had all the new info he needed, there was one extra job to do- kill Wilma Hurst.

*

"Wilma, there's a package for you here at the station. Will you come down and get it?" The Police captained had phoned Wilma in hopes that she'd pick up the package sent to her from the FBI.

"Okay. Give me a few minutes. I've got some wrap up to do here."

"Ten-four, but don't leave this lying around for too long or someone else will get curious and take it. Even here in the station there are crooks."

"I gotcha. I'll be over in thirty minutes tops."

Wilma finished up her report at the Hyatt, made sure that Blake and Sandy were sufficiently settled in, and left for the Seattle PD. They had an office for her and went to every length to make her stay as comfortable as possible. She appreciated it and would tell her superiors.

She drove toward the PD in hopes that her home office in Washington DC had finally sent her the paperwork, history and anything else they had found on Kurt Joseph. She also knew that soon she'd have him in a room and would be carrying on a violent interrogation. She picked up her cell and called one of her men. No answer. She tried the other with no luck.

"Huh, I suppose they have those phones on silence, especially since they're pursuing Kurt. I'll catch them later."

She arrived at the police station and headed straight to her office. The box that was described by the Chief sat on her desk. She picked it up, finding it very heavy, almost as if a bowling ball were inside. She cut the tape off the top and opened the flap. The shock that hit her was legendary. She couldn't believe what she was seeing. She put her hand to her heart and gasped loudly. The Chief ran in after seeing her reaction through the glass.

"Are you alright Wilma? What is it?"

"Oh my God. Take a look." Wilma slid the box across the desk.

The Chief looked inside and smiled brightly.

"Wow, Wilma, the FBI really did you good. Can you believe that?"

The Chief pulled out three thickly sealed envelopes, and a small trophy that resembled a police officer giving a salute.

"They honored you well, Wilma. Agent of the year? That's a big deal. Congratulations."

"Thank you so much." Wilma saw a note taped to the statuette. She opened it and took a look.

Dear Wilma Hurst,

Congrats to you. You were voted best FBI agent for the first time. Although I thought you should have had it twenty years ago, at least it finally happened. Me and a few of the other agents went in together and got you a little gift. It should serve you well during your stay in Seattle. Congrats again Wilma.

Jacob Wheeling, Agent, FBI

Taped to the back of the letter was a Starbucks gift card.

"Wow, fifty bucks. That ought to get me a lot of coffee."

*

A Killer for the Queen

After trying to contact her men a couple more times, Wilma retired for the evening. She had rented a room at the Hyatt, so she went back with all the paperwork that the FBI had sent her. It didn't tell her a lot for being in three large envelopes, but she didn't figure it would. There were divorce papers, pictures and autopsy photos of her dead son. The fact that Soo-Chin Xing had conducted the autopsy was no surprise, and the fact that she was now headless even less. Wilma had her fill and went to sleep; confident she would be interviewing Mr. Joseph the next morning.

*

The sun broke through the window early and Wilma stirred awake. She showered, dressed, stopped at the breakfast nook in the lobby and went out the door to head back to the station. She had that spanking new card, so a coffee would be the first order of business. As she was walking out to the squad car she had been loaned by the PD, she noticed on the far side of the lot sat the vehicle her men had taken the day before in their pursuit of Kurt. Excited, she rushed over. She noticed that it was only the two and no Kurt was in sight. She was disappointed, as her men rarely failed. As she moved closer, a dark feeling began to befall her. The scene didn't look right, as there was no movement from within the vehicle. Wilma thought to herself that there was as serious problem. A pit formed in her stomach as she moved closer. She reached the vehicle, opened the car door, and knew right away that her beloved dark men were dead. She shook one cronies shoulder and not surprisingly, his head wobbled off his torso and landed at her feet. She recoiled, and then raced to the other side of the car. It was the same thing; beheaded. There was a spray of blood across the dashboard. She pounded both of her fists on the roof of the car, causing the second dark man's head to fall to the floorboard and stare blankly back at her. Both men had a Queen of Hearts pinned on their suit jackets. Kurt had come in at night and dropped off the car and her two cronies. He didn't keep their heads though; she wondered why. When she saw the note sticking out of the first dark man's suit coat pocket, she grabbed it and read.

Dear Wilma Hurst,

Although I am indeed a collector of heads, I only collect two kinds; the ones that are on my list, which includes Kathy, Soo-Chin and Amy Fraser, but also the two that got in my way; the woman at the hotel in Nampa, and Andrea. If I take a man's head, the Queen is less than satisfied. She wants only female heads, not those ugly, expressionless male kinds. That's why I've decided, with the Red Queens approval, of course, to add your head to the collection. I happen to have room for two more, you and Amy Fraser.

Enjoy your morning surprise and I'll see you....soon!

The Hatter

Wilma wept next to her lost men, crumpled the note in her hand and screamed but two words:
"MOTHER FUCKER!"

Shaun Webb

16
Which Road Do I take?

"What to do, what to do."

Amy couldn't get that particular thought out of her head no matter how much she tried. It was bad enough thinking about making love with Blake, but now she was carrying his baby. That changed everything. How was she going to tell him about the predicament? Would she tell him? Perhaps it'd be easier to move forward, have the baby and raise him or her in Claude's capable hands. Although Claude had gone over what *would* happen, Amy had the bottom line and could easily trump his wishes. It would probably end their working relationship, and that she didn't want. She was partial to Claude because he had led her in a positive direction and taken her under his wing. How would he feel if she turned her back on him? Amy wasn't very interested in finding out. The ugly word "abortion" crossed her mind.

Amy stepped out the door to get her newspaper, and noticed an envelope next to them with "Amy" written across the front of it. She thought at first it was another payment from Claude, but knew he wouldn't leave cash lying outside for anybody to pick up. She threw the paper on the sofa and took the envelope to the kitchen table to mull it over. She propped it up on the salt and peppershakers and stared it down. She didn't recognize the handwriting and thought for a moment that throwing it in the fireplace would be the best option available.

Amy went about doing what she always did when she became nervous or upset; she cleaned the house from stem to stern. Her focus turned to vacuuming, dusting, washing dishes, laundry and whatever else she could find to kill time. Still, the envelope kept itself propped on the condiments. It didn't disappear or end up being a figment of her imagination. Amy finally sat down hard in at the table and grabbed it. She held it to the light, shook it slightly, and leaned it back up. She went through the house and pulled all the blinds before returning to the table. This time when she picked up the white papered enclosure, she slowly stuck a kitchen knife under the flap.

"There could be anything in this envelope, so why am I so suspicious? What the hell? It could be a card from the paperboy wishing me whatever paperboys wish you. Maybe he wants a tip. I know I would if I spent half of my day delivering newspapers in the pouring rain. It could be a neighbor's welcome. They may have given me an invitation to a party or to dinner. Who knows? Screw it. I'll just open the stupid thing."

Amy slid the knife along the flap until the envelope opened. She turned it over and poured its contents on the table. Her heart skipped a beat when she saw what it contained.

*

"Why did you come here Sandy? What in the hell could you have possibly been thinking?"

Wilma had kept her promise and delivered Blake to Sandy. She stood in his presence, forlorn and aching with hope and love. His first words upon greeting her were not what she had been hoping he would say.

"I miss you and want you Blake. You shouldn't have left. I should've told you how I felt about you. Do you love me Blake? Because I love you. I love you more than anything I've ever loved in my life. I can't go on without you in my life. Please, Blake."

The tears rolled down Sandy's cheeks like a salty river. Blake held her tightly to support and attempt to reassure her. It wasn't in a romantic way, but as friends; a friendship that Sandy was testing severely. Blake couldn't see it turning into romance. He had feelings for Amy, whether anyone liked it or not, and couldn't share the same passion for the innocent Midwest girl he was at that moment trying to ease.

"You should never have come here Sandy. I thought I made my intentions clear when I left Toledo. Did you not get the point then? Were you so lovelorn that you wouldn't listen to my words?"

Blake wanted to scold her for bringing Andrea along and though not causing her death, contributing to it. He couldn't do it. He knew Andrea to be a free spirit who took chances. This time it cost her dearly. Blake simply held Sandy and tried to comfort her. It was all he could do.

He walked Sandy back to her room and lay her down on the bed. He sat in a chair by the hideously fake wooden dresser that the TV sat on and lit up a smoke.

"Oh Blake. I thought you'd quit that nasty habit. We'll need to work on that. You're such a goof. What are we going to do when we get home Blake? Are we going to get married? Have kids? Oh how I want you inside me Blake."

Perplexed and now wondering about her mental capacity, Blake moved past any of the love, marriage and kids subjects she spewed out and responded to the smoking issue.

"I did quit, but the last few days have been a bit of a stressor, so to speak. At least it's not drugs."

"Andrea was using heroin, Blake. I didn't know. I didn't...."

Blake interrupted and gave her a slight earful.

"That's because you're naïve, Sandy. You're a Midwest girl in a place you should never have come. I don't get you guys. Andrea's dead, Sandy. **SHE'S DEAD!**" Blake was standing in the middle of the floor; flailing his arms about in a ruffled fashion. "We're getting your ass on an airplane and sending you home."

The faucets re-opened and Sandy pulled a pillow to her face. She was hurt, confused and acting strangely. She had blankness in her eyes at certain points of their conversation, while being emotionally gripped at other times. It understood in lieu of Andrea's death, but it seemed deeper, more penetrating. She had seen something that was extremely disturbing, and it affected the conservative, timid young woman.

Blake's timing couldn't have been worse. He realized how calloused he had been and sat next to her on the bed. He spoke in a much softer, caring tone.

"Look Sandy, I'm frustrated. I don't know what the hell is going on. One of our friends has been murdered and you're way out of your element. What am I supposed to say? What can I say? I'm rude and insensitive. I'm sorry, okay?"

Sandy's sobbing calmed. She glanced up at her "knight in shining armor" with glassed over eyes and a slight smile. She carefully arose and excused herself to the bathroom. Blake sat on the edge of the bed, monitoring her movement carefully while lighting a smoke. There was something amiss with Sandy, but he couldn't pinpoint it. He flipped on the TV and saw the Andrea Jimenez story on the news. He clicked the TV off again and moved himself back to the chair nearest the ashtray. The bathroom door creaked back open and out walked Sandy. Blake looked up in a synthesis of lust and sorrow. He couldn't believe what he was seeing before his startled eyes. Sandy stood before him completely nude. The razor blade in her hand reflected sharply with the light of the bathroom, causing an image to cast on the walls in quick bursts of flash and movement. Blood ran down Sandy's legs from the cuts she administered above her knees. Blake had to act fast.

*

Kurt was a combination of angry, arrogant and frustrated. He was also very pleased with the information he had found in the pockets of the Dark Men, whom he had eliminated from the picture for good. He had no need for their heads, so he delivered them specifically to the Wilma person he read about in the notes. He saw that they were investigating the beheading of Andrea at the Hyatt and using that building, along with the Seattle PD, as their bases. The information was a gift for Kurt, as he could map out his moves to destroy Amy while at the same time planning the death of the meddling FBI Agent.

Kurt, as sloppy as he could be when angry, still worried about details. That included the incident with the trooper just before he made it to Seattle. He left the Queen of Hearts card in his mouth with a note scrawled on it so there would be no mistake about his determination to complete the grisly mission. That was the pompous, arrogant and furious Kurt. The Kurt who couldn't control his anger, and needed to send the law a warning. He noticed that almost every killer wanted the attention of the press and media. He was somewhat different, as he was sending his message to the people actively pursuing him. He was less Ted Bundy and more Zodiac Killer in his habits. After he finished the Queen's tasks, he would no longer care. His work would be complete and he'd be called by his Queen to join her in the new world of which she occupied. As he continued reasoning, he thought the beheading in Nampa, Idaho was messy, but it needed to be done, as the woman had deeply angered him. The same was true for the men at the rest stop; it was Kurt's anger that caused him to kill. He left the painted red roses at all of his beheadings because it was the will of his Queen. He also knew deep down the murder of his wife and the maiming of her boyfriend would bring attention to him. He guessed that the authorities, Wilma and her Dark Men, had already been to his home in Flint and likely had been tracking him for some time.

All of the discerning by Kurt helped him to keep his focus sharp. The law may have been on his tail, but so far, they had failed to capture him. The Dark Men paid with their lives, as would Wilma, Kurt promised. Try as they may, Kurt was slick. He was like a snake in the grass; he could strike and disappear quickly.

While preparing for his final tasks, Kurt took a moment to open the cabinet and look over the faces of his victims. In order from right to left was Kathy, then the woman from Nampa. After that, he had Soo-Chin, followed by his latest victim, Andrea. He had two jars remaining. The last jar would hold Amy's head. Kurt smile widely. The heads were staying fresh in the fluid, but Kurt was beginning to see some wear and tear around their eyes and mouths. Andrea's head still looked good, as it was his most recent kill. While his mind was focused on the victims, Kurt opened the rear of his van and unlocked a cabinet on the lower right. It contained ten five gallon jugs of formaldehyde. He removed two and pulled all the jars from the shelf. It was time to replace the fluid to freshen the jar's contents.

Kurt opened the first jar containing Kathy's head. The smell that arose was of putrid death. He wore a surgical mask as he did this task. He had an empty bucket that he slowly poured the old fluid into, after which he would refill the jar and replace it on the shelf. Doing this job gave Kurt a sinister grin as he went down the line. Kurt's madness became more pronounced. He finally reached Andrea's jar and was ready to burst out in a laughing, aroused rage. Her head had no odor as of yet and her features were in good shape. The nastiest of moods took over and he did the unthinkable; he placed Andrea's head at hip level on the cabinets table and dropped his pants. He carefully inserted himself into the appendage's mouth. Kurt violently rocked his hips inward and outward with the rhythm of "The Red Queen" song that was playing in his thoughts. It only took Kurt one minute to complete his gruesome mission. He settled backward against the opposite wall of the van. He looked at Andrea's grayish appendage and smiled slyly.

"W-wow! That was v-very good. Your lips, your m-mouth; so inviting; s-soft and so c-cold. What a w-wonderful job you've done."

Andrea blankly looked back at him with wide eyes and her mouth stretched into a circled shape.

"We should d-do that again v-very soon."

Kurt was getting ready to go back to his original task when he heard the Queen's voice summon him.

"KURTIS! COME TO ME KURTIS! YOU MUST COME TO ME NOW!"

Hearing his master, he put Andrea's head back in the vat, filled it with fresh fluid and stumbled sideways out of the van as he was trying to buckle his pants. He landed hard on his side and lay motionless for a few seconds as the pain intruded his body.

"KURTIS! I'M WAITING. COME TO ME NOW! DO NOT MAKE ME WAIT A MINUTE LONGER."

Kurt rose, dusted himself off, and rushed up to the next floor where the angry sounding Queen awaited. He knew why she was irritated and didn't have the first idea on how he would calm her. He had desecrated the head of Andrea and was sure he was going to pay a price. As he moved closer to the entrance of the loft, he saw the fine mist in the air. She was waiting and he was frightened that it was for too long.

"ENTER THE LOFT, KURTIS! ENTER AND BEHOLD MY BEAUTY!"

He did as was he was ordered and threw himself on the floor in homage. She was bright and shimmering with the unmistakable glow of red emitting a steady light from her entire spiritual existence. In her right hand she held a single red rose, while in her left hand was a staff or a prod of some kind. Kurt couldn't quite make it out.

"Approach me, Kurtis. Approach me and kneel before your Queen."

Again, and without hesitation, Kurt, in a crawl, approached and knelt before his Queen. She looked angry and had a slight frown on her face. Kurt was nervous and elated at the same time.

"My most loyal subject Kurtis. I have a problem. Perhaps you can enlighten me as to a solution."

"Oh y-yes, m-my Queen. I w-w-would be d-delighted to help thee."

The stuttering infuriated Kurt and caused the Queen a puzzled look followed by a question.

"Why does thee continue to stutter, my subject? Does your tongue continue to be twisted?"

Kurt tried his best to answer without stuttering and the sweat beaded on his forehead as he did this. His face squinted with the struggle.

"I aaam sssorry o Queen. I knknow nnot of wwhy it hhappens."

After spitting the sentence out in long stretches of consonants and vowels, the Queen asked him to stop.

"Fear not Kurtis. I will help thee find your correct tongue. Close your eyes and bow your head."

The Queen lowered her cane onto Kurt's left shoulder, and then over to his right. Red colored electricity emitted from the staff. It ran up his shoulders and shot through his cheeks. Kurt could feel the heat in his mouth and on his tongue. She uttered a few unintelligible words and brought her cane back to her side. She commanded Kurt to rise. As he stood pathetically before his Queen, she demanded that he speak in rhythms.

"PETER PIPER PICKED A PECK OF PICKLED PEPPERS!" She shouted at him. **"REPEAT IT!"**

"I don't know my Lordess. I may not...."

"KURTIS! YOU WILL SPEAK THE RHYTHMS! DO IT NOW!"

The smoke and mist around the Queen increased. He could see her feet and saw that she was levitating a foot above the floor. Her long royal dress and smoky mist had hid this, but now it was visible. She was as mighty as a warrior was and as sleek as a snake.

"Peter Piper..." Kurt hesitated, assuming the stutter would be prevalent and embarrassing. He was continuing with his sweaty brow and shaking hands.

"Do you not trust me, Kurtis? Do you not trust the Queen of Red whom gives you the power to do anything? I will be dishonored at such an insult."

Not wanting to disappoint his Queen, Kurt rose tall and spewed forth the entire rhyme.

"Peter Piper picked a peck of pickled peppers! Peter Piper picked a peck of pickled peppers! Peter Piper picked a peck of pickled peppers!"

"EXCELLENT! THIS WOULD BE A GRAND DAY!"

Kurt knew he'd pleased the Queen and that pleased him. He forgot that she had sounded angry upon first hearing her. The Queen, however, had not misplaced her anger and now that Kurt had been relieved of his word twisting, the Queen went back to the point.

"I have a problem Kurtis. It is with you."

"Please Queen, please share your concerns. I am here for you, oh beauty in red."

"Open your mouth Kurtis. Open and let me look inside."

Kurt thought that she was going to be livid about the head he had just desecrated, but it didn't appear to be heading in that direction. He opened his mouth as instructed. The Queens red light shone brighter as she was inches from Kurt's face. He could smell the humidity and feel her misty dampness on his skin. She looked for some fifteen seconds and stood straight up again.

"My Kurtis. T'wasn't you whom ate my tarts after all. I was very worried that you may have helped yourself without asking."

"Oh no, good Queen. Never would I take anything that belongs to you without first asking."

"Is that right Kurt? Then do your highness a favor and stop performing sexual deviance with my heads. Those are my heads and you know I will claim them; clean I might add."

Embarrassed, Kurt looked to the floor and felt the heat of anxiety crawl up his leg. He was sure the penalty would be harsh.

"Let it not happen again and I shall never speak of it. Do you understand?"

Kurt nodded his head frantically in a "yes" motion as he felt that his life had been spared.

"Do not fail in your quest for the final heads. First, collect the head of Wilma Hurst. I do not like the wench and she will be a suitable addition. After that task is complete, you shall collect Amy's head and call on me. It will be then that we shall negotiate your trip with me to the other side."

"Yes, M'Queen."

The mist and vapor increased dramatically as the Queen rose toward the ceiling. In a flash of red light and a vortex sucking away the mist, she disappeared, leaving behind no trace of her presence. Relieved, Kurt went back down to the box van and initiated a huge cleanup of the entire area. He cleaned inside until it was spotless, replaced the jars on the cabinet and locked everything up. He wanted it to be perfect in case the Queen returned. He considered himself lucky he didn't lose his head.

*

> "But I don't want to go among mad people," Alice remarked.
> "Oh, you can't help that," said the Cat: "we're all mad here. I'm mad. You're mad."

*

When she opened the envelope and saw the Tarot card depicting a Queen like figure on it with a note from Claude that explained his warning of trouble, she froze. She couldn't figure out why he added the tarot, as the card itself meant nothing to her. The only way she'd find out for sure was to ask her Zen master.

She dialed up Claude, who told her that "yes" he had indeed left the card on her doorstep. He explained why he left it.

"You weren't home, or I would have handed it to you and discussed it then. To be honest, I'm not exactly sure what it means, but I have a strange feeling about it. The Queen is relevant. I wouldn't be surprised if the danger that awaits you doesn't have something to do with it, or *her*. Some kind of strange aura stirs inside my spirit. Soon the answer will come. Soon."

Amy was satisfied with Claude's response and threw the card in the fire. It gave her the creeps and reminded her of the Jack of Spades card back in Flint. She decided it would be a very good idea to work on her self-awareness exercises and try to relieve some of the energy building inside her. Amy felt angry, frustrated and restless.

"I open myself to divine love and wisdom. I open myself to divine love and wisdom. I open myself to divine love and wisdom."

Amy was following Claude's advice and doing a self-healing Reiki meditation to try to soothe her frayed nerves. The only problem was that it wasn't working. Amy couldn't stop thinking about Blake long enough to concentrate. The man was her baby's father and she was debating hard about how she should move forward. The thinking continuously interfered with her meditation. She tried three times before rising form her seat and frisbeeing the CD across the room. It hit the wall and landed harmlessly on the floor.

"STOP IT! LEAVE ME ALONE! I CAN'T KEEP THINKING ABOUT HIM!" She screamed as she put her hands on her head and stomped through the house.

"I've got to get out and walk. That's what I'll do. A nice walk in the crisp air will clear up my brain."

A Killer for the Queen

It was two a.m. when Amy decided to make the excursion around the block a couple of times. It probably wasn't a good idea being it was a bad hour, but she figured it would do her good. Amy's hoped nobody would trifle with her. Most people had no idea how dangerous she could be; they simply saw a five foot two inch woman, who was very nice looking, walking the street at an ungodly hour.

As she made the second trip around the block, a very handsome man strolled up, a cigarette dangling from his mouth, and asked for a light. She looked at his face and thought he was drop dead gorgeous, but despite his good looks, she was unflinching as she strode past a man who was probably out doing the same thing as she; clearing the cobwebs. Ultimately, she didn't feel like talking or stopping. Not to be ignored, the man turned and grabbed her by the arm, insisting that she face him.

"Did you not hear me? I said I needed a fucking light, bitch. Now either light my smoke with some fire or I'll light your ass with this blade." He looked Amy up and down and snapped open a three-inch switch that Amy figured would have trouble cutting through melted butter. "Damn, you're a fine little piece, ain't cha?"

"First and last warning." Amy blandly expounded. "Let go of my arm or you're a dead man."

The man barked out a hearty laugh. He squeezed her arm tighter and brought Amy a few inches closer.

"Don't you tell me what to do you fucking whore. I'm taking you back to my place and we're having some fun. I'll bet you got a nice tight little ass in those pants, huh?"

Amy swung around with her free arm and out from her sleeve she wielded a *ten-inch long* hunting knife that she had positioned in case of an emergency. She lashed forward and the man's ear instantly started bleeding. She had cleanly cut off an inch of his lobe. He dropped his flimsy blade and grabbed his ear. He also released her arm. Amy lunged forward with a front kick that connected in the middle of his chest. He went down backward in a solid clump against the concrete, hitting the back of his head hard on impact. She quickly bestrode his flattened body and leaned close to his face. She grabbed a handful of hair and placed the knife against his rapidly pulsating jugular vein.

"You nasty, nasty man." Amy sneered. "I saw you and thought you were kind of cute. Now I'm not sure whether I should kiss you, cut you again, or just fucking kill you. You are one sorry piece of shit."

"Lady!" The man started, breathless at that point, "I'm sorry. I won't mess with you again. Let me go. I'll disappear."

He held one hand out in a careful defensive posture as his other held the rapidly bleeding wound. The blood ran down his arm.

Amy spoke through clenched teeth.

"Let this be a lesson, tough guy. You never know whom you're going to run into when you start messing with people. Tonight you picked the wrong bitch to screw around with, didn't you?"

"OK! OK! I'll go home. No problem. I'm sorry, ok lady?"

Amy carefully backed off the man and stood up straight. She was still wielding the knife. She looked at his ear from her spot; it was bleeding pretty badly.

"If you didn't drink so much, your ear wouldn't bleed like that. Go home and take care of it."

The man stumbled to his feet, and looking back only once, scurried into the darkness, his lesson learned from one dangerous woman.

"Damn," Amy repeated, "and he was hot."

She shook her head, retracted the knife back up into her sleeve and continued her brain-clearing walk.

Amy arrived back home, picked the CD up and re-inserted it in her player. She assumed the yoga-like position and did a forty-five minute Reiki meditation. She cleared her mind and spirit and felt renewed. Amy owed it to the good-looking jerk she had cut an hour earlier. She didn't enjoy hurting him, she simply did what she had to do and it re-focused her mind.

*

"Put the razor blade down Sandy."

She stood completely nude before him. This was the first time Blake had ever seen Sandy naked. She was bustier than he originally thought, probably due to her wearing loose fitting tops, and had a small tattoo on her hip depicting a moon and stars with the initials B.T. on the moon. This was something he found hard to believe considering her ultra conservative upbringing along with the fact that she was more smitten than he had ever realized. Blake's surprise, however, turned into fear and concern as Sandy held the razor blade far too close to her wrist.

He was genuinely scared at the look in her eye and the confusion that was permeating in her demeanor. He didn't think she was a cutter and was surprised to see the slashes above her knee. It didn't appear that she had any marks on the rest of her body. It may have been the first time she'd ever done such a thing. Nonetheless, his heart began to race and he feared a panic attack on the spot. He tried to breathe deeply and exhale slowly, in hopes of warding off the oncoming freight train of panic.

"Blake, help me. I love you so much. I want you so bad, but you don't want me. The record keeps skipping in my head Blake. It keeps playing the same tune repeatedly: Andrea's death and my love for you. Take me now Blake and fuck me. I want you to fuck me or I'll cut myself. I want you to be my first and my last. I love you so much. I won't mess it up Blake."

The blade was set right against her veins in the wrist and she was smart enough to know that you go 'down the road', and not 'across the street' when it came to inflicting the worst possible suicidal damage.

Blake had to think quickly, and that was becoming increasingly difficult with his panic bubbling to the surface. He felt the blood seemingly rush into his head, causing temporary deafness. That in turn caused him to begin the cycle of rapid heartbeats, difficult breathing and a dizzy, swimming feeling in his vision. Despite his insides vibrating in a violent manner, he did the best he could and asked Sandy why she wanted to hurt herself.

"There are other ways to deal with this Sandy. Hurting yourself won't solve any problems at all."

"But Blake, the record keeps spinning over and over in my mind." She was sobbing. "It keeps playing the same thing. It won't stop Blake."

Speaking with someone who was having obsessive thoughts was very difficult for someone who was having a panic attack. A nude woman stood on one side of the room with a razor blade against her wrist while Blake stood on the other side with a flushed, drawn feeling of impending doom. He had to talk Sandy out of her funk, rush her, thus risking injury for both or watch her slice her wrists to the bone. Talking seemed to be the best bet.

"Okay Sandy. Come to me. Put the blade down and come to me. We'll make love Sandy. Put the blade down and come here."

"Really Blake? She smiled with enthusiasm. "But I've never had sex before. Will you teach me?"

"Sure, sure Sandy. You have to put that stupid blade down and lie on the bed, though. I can't make love to you with a blade in your hand."

Of course, Blake did not intend to make love to Sandy. He was planning to disarm her and get her the help she so desperately needed. Sandy looked Blake over in an obviously lustful way and threw a curveball.

"Take your clothes off first Blake. I want to make sure you're serious and not trying to trick me."

"I wouldn't trick you Sandy. Don't you know me well enough by now?"

"Take off your clothes Blake. Do it now or I slice."

Inhaling a deep breath, and then exhaling a larger one, Blake did as he was told and striped down to his underwear.

"Those too, Blake. I want to see your penis. It'll be the first one I've ever seen in real life, and it'll be yours." Sandy sighed with an air of anticipation.

Another breath, and down came his underwear. Sandy ogled at his manliness and appeared to be impressed. She threw the blade to the side and rushed to Blake. He caught her and held her tightly, not in a passionate way, but in a hold her down way. He wrested her to the bed and continued to hold tight to try to keep her still.

"Blake. This isn't how you make love. You're being too rough with me. You're hurting me."

"We're not making love Sandy. Not now, not ever. Now calm down so I can let go of you."

Sandy only resisted more, causing Blake to have to clock her in the jaw with a hard right hand. It successfully knocked Sandy unconscious. He retrieved her clothes from the bathroom and dressed her, after which he tied her arms to the bedposts. He did it tightly so she couldn't get loose. Blake put his clothes back on and sat in the chair. He lit up another smoke and waited for Sandy to come back around.

*

"I will fucking kill him. I'll slice his throat and leave him the same way he left my men. He's a fucking dead man."

The fire in Wilma's eyes was bright and chilling. The mortician had left with her two cronies; this time the crime *victims*. Never in a million years did she ever think her men would be so much as scratched by the enemy, much less killed. It put a new determination in Wilma's craw. She was going to search out and kill Kurt herself. She was to have vengeance despite being trained to deal with death and obey the law to the tee.

Wilma was also trained to inflict death. She was an assassin in her own right. The people she had killed in her career were too many to count. If it had to be done, then so be it. She didn't like it to be that way, but it was, after all, for her own survival. In Kurt's case, it would be a pleasure to watch him choke on his own blood after inflicting a slash to his cowardly throat. To watch him kneel down, clutch his neck and slowly die would be orgasmic for the skilled FBI Agent.

Her superiors had called and told her to avoid any emotional outbursts. She kept her cool and fooled her boss in every way possible.

"Of course, sir. I would never think of that sir."

Despite doubts, the boss believed her. He could pull her from the case on the spot, but didn't. Wilma would've been apt to resign had that happened. She was going to get Kurt and make it look like it was necessary, even if it wasn't. She would watch her P's and Q's closely, making sure she didn't leave any clues as to her vengeful actions.

Now, at the height of her loss, Wilma glanced around the office looking for a way to vent. She threw the case file against the wall, watching the papers and notes scatter into a disorganized mess. Since that felt so good, she threw everything in the office against the wall. Coffee pot, random files, pens, pencils, pictures, and even the chair she sat on. The Captain, hearing the commotion, looked in through the glass and saw

Wilma losing her mind. He cracked the door open to see if he could calm her. What he saw was scary; her eyes glowing with anger while her hands and body shook with rage. She picked up a glass ashtray and chucked it towards the door. Had the Captain not ducked out, he probably would've had a serious concussion. He shut the door and advised everyone in the office to leave her alone and allow her to vent.

After some ten minutes of office destruction, Wilma opened the door and appeared in the hallway. Nobody dared meet her glance in fear of retribution by an emotional woman. She walked to the Captain's office, cracked the door open and told him she was taking a few hours to cool down. Without hesitation, he okayed the request.

The first place Wilma stopped was at Mario's Clothing Store on 6th Avenue. There she did a bit of shopping, and then headed back to the police department. She went to the locker room in the back of the station to change and came back out to the gasps of the officers who were present. She was wearing a black suit. Black pants, white shirt and black tie with black sunglasses. She looked like a cross between the Men in Black and her very own Dark Men, whom she was channeling. The Captain approached her.

"Are you sure you should continue with this case Wilma. I mean, dressed in black like your men? It looks kind of weird."

"I'm simply channeling them Captain. Call it a kind of dedication. I don't need to be relieved from duty sir. I have all my wits about me."

The Captain shook his head, but didn't say another word. After Wilma exited the building, he went straight to his office and called her superiors. He thought she was losing it and needed assistance. The FBI office agreed. They told the Captain they would contact her immediately and bring her back to DC. At least that was the plan.

On her way out the door, Wilma whispered to herself.

"I'm going to cut him, then kill him, and afterward, I think I'll kiss him."

Shaun Webb

"Only the insane equate pain with success."

Shaun Webb

17
We're All Mad Here

I. Kurt's madness

After leaving his message for Wilma and cleaning out his van, the lineup of jars made the top shelf of the cabinet complete from left to right and back again. There were four heads so far, and two more would complete the task. Following the collection of Amy's head, he would be taken to another dimension or land by the Red Queen to live forever by her side. Some would think Kurt to be crazed and mad. He thought himself to be perfectly normal, without flaw, and carrying out orders given to him by a woman in a red suit that was covered in hearts.

*

Kurt needed to find Wilma. He decided that staking out the police department would be his best bet. After all, it was where she based herself for her investigation. Kurt skulked in the eye of the hurricane; and felt the safest right near the teeth of the law. Who would ever guess him to be sitting outside of a place that wanted him the most? He also thought that Wilma might be a very tough nut to crack, as she was a professional and had tailed him all the way to Seattle. She had to be a good agent to do that, and although she hadn't found him, he knew it was a matter of time. There was more than one reason to take her head, but the fact that she was sniffing so close to him was the prime excuse for doing such a thing.

Disguised in a fake moustache and sunglasses along with driving a car he'd "borrowed" from an adjacent parking lot near his hideout, Kurt was able to keep a fair distance between him and the police station while giving Wilma a long look. He had seen her picture in the Seattle newspapers, as the case was getting more coverage than he'd originally thought, making Kurt more popular than even he could imagine. The fact that he had beheaded four people so far from four different states, and killed a State Trooper and a gay restroom denizen, it should have come as no surprise to him. The case was even featured on an NBC Timeline report starring Lisa Ling, which featured Kurt's growth from a young man to an adult. It also highlighted a possible love of everything involving Alice in Wonderland. An entire two hours was dedicated to Kurt. He was proud of the fact that the authorities couldn't catch him. He watched the entire program at a local bar and didn't bother disguising himself. The people present were either not paying much attention, or were too drunk to watch the program and recognize him. Seattle, Kurt found out, was a drunken town. The rain and gloomy weather cast a pale on the city a high percentage of the time. It was no wonder to him that a large number of people were drinking themselves to death.

Wilma rarely left the police station and the stakeout was getting dull and boring for Kurt. If she didn't leave at least occasionally, he may never have the opportunity to work his evil magic. He couldn't understand how she could be looking for him while not leaving the safety of the station. He observed the parking lot and had seen the Dark Men's car that he had delivered earlier, gifts for Wilma included. He figured that's what she'd be driving. If she weren't, then the joke would be on him, as he was wasting valuable time he could've spent searching for Amy Fraser. The only problem with that was that the Queen, for some odd reason, told him *specifically* that Amy had to be the last head collected. Kurt often tried to figure out why, but it never did him much good, as her reasons were never shared.

Finally, on the third day of his stakeout, Wilma exited the station. To his surprise, she was dressed like her Dark Men. She had on a black suit and dark sunglasses. He wasn't exactly sure why, but figured it to be an homage of sort to her lost men. As Kurt had fully expected, Wilma loaded herself into the car the men had used and drove off. Kurt followed. He had his machete carefully stashed under the seat and was ready on that very day to collect her head and move on to his next victim.

Wilma drove and drove and drove. She went through, around and across Seattle as if she were lost. Kurt was running on a quarter tank of gas and needed her to stop at some point. If he ran out of gas or needed a fill-up, his hopes for that day would be lost. Finally, after four solid hours of driving and Kurt's back screaming out in pain, she stopped at a hunter's shop. It was a Gander Mountain on Ballard Avenue, well north of the city. The store was surrounded with trees and seemed out of the way enough for Kurt to do his business and be able to make a quick escape. Luckily, the store wasn't crowded.

Wilma parked, exited her vehicle and went inside. Kurt took an extra two or three minutes to let her get settled in the store and he followed suit. Upon entering, he was surprised at how enormous the building appeared. It was much like a warehouse with its high ceilings and wide aisles, a fact that made him uncomfortable. Not to be discouraged, he began his search for Wilma. Up and down the aisles he went, looking like a store detective waiting out a shoplifter. He finally spotted his pray near of all places, the knife section. There were large knives, short knives, machete like knives and any other knife for hunting that existed. Wilma was perusing about twenty feet away. Kurt inched closer and closer, lining up his pray in his own personal crosshairs. He approached Wilma from behind and prepared to remove the machete from his jacket when surprise hit him like a runaway freight train.

2. Sandy's madness

The murder of Andrea sent Sandy spiraling into a deep depression, offset by the new hope of Blake's arriving at her hotel room.

Blake tried reasoning with Sandy to help her see what was happening. His concern for her elevated and he wanted her to get back to Toledo so she could find the help she needed. He wasn't sure what her problem was, but he knew she wasn't acting normal or rational.

"We really need to get you some help, Sandy. You cut yourself, and were going to kill yourself. You've made me feel concern for whatever's going on in your life. I know you're shocked by Andrea's death, but I think it goes deeper than that."

"I promise to never do it again Blake. I just want you so badly. I'll do anything to have you for my very own. Why doesn't it seem like you feel that vibe? I'm throwing myself at you and it's like you don't care."

Her words worried Blake, as he had fallen for another. He decided that he would call Amy and they would meet as three. Perhaps she could offer some insight as to how to handle Sandy before sending her back home. In Blake's mind, she would need extensive counseling in Seattle before she'd be fit enough to go anywhere. He saw Sandy to sleep and flipped open his phone, dialing up his one night lover.

"Hi Amy. It's Blake. Can we talk?"

Amy, on the other end, had been wondering whether to tell Blake about the baby, and now convinced herself that she would, in fact, be fair with him and share the news.

"Yes Blake. We do need to talk anyway. Where and when?"

"Um, I figure the Pike Street Market. Say ten a.m. tomorrow. I have to tell you one thing though; I'll be bringing a friend."

Blake explained everything from A to Z, and Amy, the kind soul that she is, thought it a good idea to gain a bit of perspective by meeting this Sandy woman herself. Amy figured if nothing else, she could lead them in the right direction for help.

The next day arrived, and Blake readied Sandy for the trip over to the market.

"You're going to meet a friend of mine Sandy. Her name is Amy Fraser. I really think you'll like her."

Sandy reluctantly agreed, put herself together as best she could, and off they went to deal with more than even Blake could anticipate.

Amy had already garnered seats at the market, as she was fast and prudent; two things she obsessed about more often than was necessary. It was her obsession, though, and she dealt with it the best way she knew how to, by being early for everything. Blake arrived ten minutes later than their scheduled meeting with an obviously shaken Sandy. Amy ignored the tardiness in light of the situation.

"Amy, Sandy. Sandy, Amy."

Blake started out with the prerequisite introductions before the three would partake in a very deep and sensitive conversation. Blake led off by telling Amy about the incident at the hotel.

"I heard about that." Amy sadly responded. "I'm so sorry about your friend."

Sandy had ordered a cup of coffee and was nursing it with shaking hands. Amy noticed that and put her hands on top of hers. Sandy at first shuddered, and then accepted the friendly gesture with a weak and meaningless smile. Sandy didn't meet eyes with Amy, nor would she throughout the meeting. After two minutes, Sandy politely pulled her hands free and clutched her warm coffee cup.

A Killer for the Queen

"This FBI Agent, Wilma Hurst, is heading the investigation. She said the man's name, but it escapes me."

Blake scratched his head, thinking as hard as possible. Sandy piped in, looking into her coffee and seeing what she felt was a pathetic reflection of herself vibrating like a tiny Tsunami with the trembling of her hand.

"Kurt Joseph. That's his name. Kurt."

Amy winged up out of her seat with a spring that had been reserved for a fourteen-year-old cheerleader.

"Oh my God! Did you say Kurt Joseph? As in Kurtis Joseph?"

Both Blake and Sandy nodded affirmatively. Amy was shaken and paced at her side of the table. Blake's concern mounted while Sandy sat quietly, continuing to look into her cup.

"He's from Michigan; my hometown. The Black Jack Killer murdered his son. I defended John Garrison; the old man they pinned the murder on. It turned out to be the Governor's son who had committed the crime."

Blake interjected. "Oh. You were a lawyer? I didn't know that."

"There's a lot you don't know about me Blake." Sandy's eyebrow's perked with Amy's words. Blake continued.

"Well, it seems that Mr. Joseph has been quite busy. There have been four beheadings. One in Las Vegas; his wife. One in Nampa, Idaho and one in Portland. Those and Andrea; Sandy's friend, who was the latest victim. Wilma says he's fantasizing some

Alice in Wonderland shit when he's doing it; leaving a Queen of Hearts and painted red roses at the scene. Oh, did I mention the murdered trooper in Southern Washington? The pervert at the rest stop? The two Agents that worked for Wilma Hurst? They're all dead."

Amy had her attention fixated on Blake and Sandy became nervous. When two people liked each other, or in many cases loved each other, there seemed to be an aura, or look, that was given, even if the "lookers" didn't mean it. Sandy saw the look. She glanced at Blake, and then at Amy. She saw what she thought was love, lust, or something very similar. She kept her thought to herself for that moment.

"Blake." Amy explained. "In Flint, Michigan it was the Black Jack killer; now Kurt's leaving Queens of Heart's at the scenes? He's copycatting. **Shit!** That was Claude's warning. **Holy Shit!**"

"Who's Claude?" Blake asked.

"Oh. Umm, nobody important. Does this agent think Kurt's in Seattle?"

"Yep. She also said she knew who the killer was after, but wouldn't tell me. Is it you Amy? Is this guy after you?"

Amy nodded her head ever so slow and put her hands on Blake's hands. That move further infuriated Sandy, but she continued to keep her peace.

"I have something very important to tell you Blake, and I want you to stay calm when I say it, okay?"

"He is after you, isn't he?" Blake guessed.

"Yes, I would say he is after me, but that's not what I was going to tell you. Please, just listen for a moment."

Blake sat back in his chair; ears wide open, while Sandy's heart rate increased significantly. Woman's intuition said something to Sandy, and it wasn't pleasant. Amy took a deep breath and continued.

"I wasn't going to say anything, but I can't hide this from you. Blake, I'm pregnant with your child."

Sandy had heard enough. Her temper exploded as she leapt from the chair and threw her coffee at Amy. She was beyond furious and spat out her feelings.

"So you've been fucking my man huh? You've been taking advantage of my goddamn boyfriend! You insignificant fucking bitch! I'll fucking kill you!"

Blake immediately rose from his chair and grabbed Sandy. She was on her way over the table and that would spell doom for the young girl from Toledo, as Amy would destroy her in seconds flat.

"What the fuck Blake. Have you been fucking this one too?" Amy inquired.

"No!" Blake shouted. "I told you she's ill. She thinks we've been boyfriend-girlfriend since the seventh grade. She needs help. I explained it all on the phone. Remember?"

"Well," Amy interrupted, "you'd better get her some help before she gets hurt."

Sandy continued to struggle with Blake. The entire Pike Street market had gone silent listening to the drama within the group. After another minute of trying to pull away from Blake's grip, she calmed herself, raised both of her arms and serenely told Blake to release her. She gathered her purse and jacket off the back of the chair.

"Don't worry about me Blake. I know when I'm not welcomed. I'll get home myself thank you very much. Amy, it was nice to meet you and I'm sorry I flew off the handle."

She reached out to shake Amy's hand, but Amy kept her hand against her side. Blake was bewildered and anxious. He had just been told he would be a father while at the same time watching a woman's dream go straight down the proverbial drain. As much as it hurt him, he watched Sandy walk away. He wanted to say one last thing to her before she left.

As she crossed the street, he yelled for her.
"SANDY! WAIT! I DIDN'T MEAN FOR IT TO END UP THIS WAY!"

Blake felt guilty and overwhelmed about the situation and hoped against hope that a word or two would soothe it over. He began slipping into a state of panic. Sandy stopped and turned to give Blake one last chance to say he loved her. She stared into his eyes from some twenty feet away, knowing he was struggling. That's when it happened. The worst possible situation became even grimmer. Amy stood by the table in utter disbelief. Blake slipped into a deeper and more serious panic attack.

3. Blake's madness

Every time Blake thought he may be gaining ground on his mental issues, something else would crop up to send him backward. This time it was finding out that Sandy and Andrea had followed him cross-country. When it rained, Blake thought, it poured.

Drugs, anxiety, panic, depression, frustration and finally a new scene. That summed up Blake Thomas concisely. Never one to express his feelings in an overstated fashion, he wasn't too talkative and he was even less of a listener. If something went amiss, Blake's first thought was to change the situation to the best of *his* ability, even if that meant compromising someone else's feelings. Thinking of others was a tough chore because life was completely out of his control, especially with the anxiety and panic attacks. Drugs were his self-medication when he was younger, and freak-outs as an adult were his ultimate penalty for the abuse. The anxiety led to depression, the depression led to frustration and the circle started again with drugs and alcohol. By tearing up the tent stakes and moving to a completely new situation, Blake thought he could interrupt the circle and beat the crosses that were his to bear. It caused more problems, but in a different and even more intense context. It was a gutsy move by the young man, as the real possibility existed that the change could actually make the problem worse. He would learn that it wasn't a change of scenery, but a change in mindset that would be the best medicine for his troubled awareness. You could run, but could you hide?

A big part of Blake's problems consisted of self-loathing, a lack of confidence, and constant berating of his ego. He beat himself up over every situation since he was young and stored more than one "inner child" within his psyche. There was the angry child, the scared child, and the confused child. Where Blake needed to be the adult and Father to his "children", he instead allowed the demons to have free reign over his life. It was a myriad of complications for the young man. Therapy was badly needed if he were to come to grips with the mental difficulties.

Combining with the complications were his relationship with Amy; still very up in the air, his unfortunate meeting with Sandy and a murdered Andrea; someone he grew up with and cared about deeply. Instead of deflecting the blame, he took it upon himself to feel responsible for every misfortune that took place.

So many thoughts ran through his head and seemed to have no escape. They circled him like a small tornado; destroying everything in their wake. The demons of life knew Blake to be vulnerable and took advantage at every turn. At times, Blake put his hands on his temples and screamed for death to take him out of his misery. It wouldn't happen, as the mental breakdowns liked it much better if he suffered hell in his life but stopped short of killing him. On more than one occasion, he put a knife or razor to his temple, wrist and throat; but never had the courage to take the final step. His father owned a gun, a gun that Blake placed under his chin countless times, but never pulled the trigger. Even a slipknot over the girder in his basement called for him, but to no avail as the demons preferred him alive, tormenting and destroying him mentally.

If Blake were to escape his misery, he'd be forced to be the adult to the children; something he wasn't sure he could do. He hoped to forge a love story with Amy, but that too appeared to be waning with each passing second. Blake chose to forge on and see what his future would hold. He'd done it for twenty-some years, so he figured why not one more. What was the absolute worst thing that could happen? He'd find out very soon, while the demons laughed at him in his mind.

*

4. Amy's madness

Why or how it ever came to a tragic meeting at the market was as much a mystery for Amy as anything she'd ever experienced. She felt like she was in the middle of everything strange, twisted and unfortunate, leaving her wondering if she herself was a jinx to other people. It wasn't true, but Amy still took some of the heat in her own mind. All she wanted to do was tell Blake that she was pregnant with his child, but instead had to hear about Kurt Joseph's exploits, Blake's smitten friend, and then witness first-hand the madness that was encircling her world.

Tae-Kwon Do was an activity that she loved. Exercise, self-defense and discipline were the lessons being taught by her instructor, Claude Ronet. She wasn't worried a lot about standing up for herself, but she needed more discipline in her life. She would end up getting far more involved than she had ever expected. Claude had taken a liking to the feisty, dark haired woman and knew that she was the free spirit he wanted and needed.

Claude was a taskmaster. Being a former cop was okay, but he wanted more excitement while keeping bad guys where they belonged- in jail. The only trouble was that Claude didn't want to hit the streets; he wanted to teach.

He had taken a five-year hiatus in the Far East where he learned much about the workings of Zen and meditation. He returned a qualified hypnotist and a helper of people. He learned patience, self-defense and Reiki; what he considered the most powerful form of hypno-therapy. The teachers considered him a natural, as he took to each form beautifully. They considered Claude a gift and held him closely under their wing. When he did return, it was with a shaved head and a powerful arsenal of knowledge. Amy was the lucky one who he would take under his wing and teach.

Claude needed a Bounty Hunter. That was one of the reasons he put the class together, to find the toughest of the tough. It didn't take him long to figure out that Amy was a rare woman indeed. She took no guff from anybody and stood up for herself even with the tiny frame she owned. She was much like a ten-ounce mother bird defending her eggs against a twenty-pound raccoon. You might get the eggs, but you're going to come out of it injured; and perhaps severely. She may come out of it dead, but not without both inflicting damage and standing up for that which she owned. Once an idea was cemented into her mind, everybody would be wise to stand aside and let her through. If you didn't, she'd run roughshod over whoever resisted her.

Claude intentionally pitted Amy against the largest and seemingly meanest man in class. He took the big guy aside and told him to hold nothing back.

"Destroy that little bitch!" Claude ordered.

That was enough for the giant, who went in to maim. It was he, however, who ended up on the short end as Amy pummeled him with every trick she could think up. She had a sap stashed in her sock and fingernails that were sharp enough to cut a crocodile's skin. It was the giant who was close to heading to the hospital before Claude intervened and grabbed Amy mid-air, thus sparing the giant's destruction. It was at that moment that Claude knew Amy had some serious anger coursing through her veins. It was the kind of controlled madness that he was hoping she owned.

Amy and Claude drew closer as he assigned her to the task of bringing dangerous criminals off the street. Amy spared no expense in her methods, which were legendary among the police officers. Amy brought people in shot, beaten and bloodied. She delivered, signed paperwork and never spoke. Certain cops would ask questions regarding her methods, but were given a look of discontent before being ignored.

Amy loved the job, the money, and Claude; but in a Dad-Daughter way. At first, she thought he may be trying to get her into bed, but she soon learned he meant well and wouldn't think of destroying their bond with something as petty as sexual intercourse. Amy appreciated that and did whatever she was told to do, no questions.

Claude began showing himself at odd times- the warehouse being one example. He was teaching her how to find inner peace and to meditate for strength and discipline. He started with Reiki, and then passed her meditation CD's here and there to try to help. Amy eventually reached a Zen-like state of consciousness. She wondered if he were magic, as he could disappear on a dime. Claude would simply tell her that nothing was quite as it seemed. Well, to Amy, Claude was more than a friend and a teacher; he was a mystical person with a special talent for the unexplained.

    Amy now knew what Claude meant when he said the danger factor was rising. That factor was Kurt Joseph and he was unrelenting. She would do everything in her power to prepare herself for what was to come. Claude would see her through as best he could without getting closely involved. He felt that Amy, and Amy alone, had to handle the situation. Claude would help her in many other valuable, but *behind the scenes*, ways.

*

    As Sandy turned her gaze to Blake so she could hear his words, she saw that the panic attack was seizing him. She knew the signs, as she had seen them many times before. Stricken and wanting to help, she rushed into the street, heedless of oncoming traffic. The buses effect against her tiny body sent her flying some fifty feet; not up high on an arc, but more straightforward. She slammed sideways into an old-fashioned light made of solid steel. It had no give and Sandy was slung around the pole and further beyond it by the force of the impact.

"Blake, Blake for God sake come on! We have to help her."

Blake only heard muffles. The sound around him had seized into a flurry of illusions. He dropped to his knees and grabbed his forehead with his cold hands as Amy continued screaming. She ran over to Blake and slapped him hard on the head.

"Get with it man! Come on!"

She grabbed him and somehow he rose to his feet while the sound began re-entering his ears. The people, who had been moving in slow motion, were now picking up speed. Amy held his arm as he floated toward the fallen Sandy. Amy pushed people out of the way.

"Give her room, give her room! Let her breath!"

The crowd separated and the two found themselves next to the injured Sandy, on either side of her head. The injuries appeared fatal. Sandy was lying on her back, but her hipbones were pointing toward the ground. Her pelvis was so badly broken that the split down the middle of her pubic bone was a foot wide, thus causing a "backward" appearance. Her head was bleeding badly, the red fluid of life spreading onto the pavement behind her, and her leg was broken in a number places. It was but a mangled mess of what used to be her limb. It was apparent to Amy that the impact with the steel pole did the most damage. She figured Sandy would die within moments, as the young woman struggled for breath under the rattling sound of death in her lungs. Blake knelt down as Sandy tried to talk. Blake put his ear next to her bloodied mouth as she struggled for the air to push out the words.

"I Love you." Was all she could muster before her eyes went fixed and dilated. Sandy died in Blake's arms. He began to cry as the tears streamed down his cheeks and landed as puddles on Sandy's face. Amy came around and rubbed Blake's back for comfort. He immediately blamed himself.

"I should have paid more attention. I should have been there for her. She was just a young woman."

Amy hugged Blake around his waist and shoulders, pushing her face into his sweaty brown hair. The ambulance arrived and Amy gently coaxed Blake to his feet. The medics looked at Amy and Blake and then covered Sandy's face with a white sheet.

"There is a place. Like no place on Earth. A land full of wonder, mystery and danger! Some say to survive it: You need to be as mad as a hatter."

Shaun Webb

1.8
Off With Her Head V
Wilma's Madness

It wasn't that Wilma was crazy. In fact, it wasn't that she was anywhere close to crazy in an insane sense. She was crazy in a very angry sense. Wilma vowed revenge and by God, she promised herself she'd do anything to get it. If it meant that both she and Kurt die together, then so be it. Anything that involved Kurt's destruction would satisfy her need for blood after the loss of her two men.

Wilma put on the white shirt, blazer and glasses as she channeled the aura and spirit of her lost partners. She was being whispered about as "losing her marbles" in the police station, but that couldn't have been further from the truth. Her bosses called her to make sure she still had the edge that made her one of the most successful agents that ever graced the FBI's hallowed halls, and after talking with her for a short time, were convinced of her sanity. They had thought about pulling her from the case but that wouldn't have stopped Wilma from doing what she was determined to do, kill Kurt Joseph and end the senseless and revolting bloodshed.

Staying put in the police station for a couple of days helped her gain some perspective while allowing her to study the case files, newspaper clippings and habits of her new "prey". She had no idea that outside, some seventy-five feet away, Kurt was waiting for her to depart the premises. The two were very smart, and between them had a mastermind's brain. Wilma was adept at catching the crook, while Kurt was an expert in the extermination process. Together, they may have made a hell of a team. Wilma the thinker and Kurt the killer. Crime would've never been the same had these two been on the case. To outthink one? Rare. To outthink both? Impossible.

After some two or three days of studying the case and calming herself, Wilma decided it was time to venture out and find the implements necessary to carry out her plan. To Kurt's relief, she finally exited the building and extinguished his boredom along with the aches and pains of staking out a target. He followed her all over the city until she eventually came to rest at a Gander Mountain store in north Seattle. This is where Kurt decided he would collect her head. He thought that an in-store collection would be new and exciting, so with his machete hidden inside his trench coat, he followed the beleaguered FBI Agent inside.

*

"Put your head in my hands and repeat after me."

Amy was relaxed under Claude's hypnotic force. She gave herself to his presence and did as she was told, even though she knew that she had full control of the situation. Her head rested in Claude's right hand as he used his left hand to tap various points on her back and scalp.

"I am a strong woman who will not succumb to the inner beasts of my past."

Amy repeated as she was instructed to do. Claude continued.

"I am Amy Fraser, adult. I am confident of myself and confident that I cannot be stricken. I have peace with my inner child."

Claude was instilling in Amy the skills she needed to stay sharp and avoid any relapses of the mental illnesses, which had wreaked havoc on her while she was living in Flint. Since working with Claude, she had gotten stronger and stronger, mentally and physically, with every passing day. He was the father figure that her biological father had never been. Claude was strong and reassuring in his mannerisms and tones. Amy's dad was a weak, drunken shell of a former self. Before he died, he had taken to raping the young woman often and with no provocation. Rape doesn't need a reason, but Amy looked at it as her fault and had failed to shield her inner child who was seeking help, happiness and most of all, protection. She was learning to comfort that child and give her the positive Mother-child relationship she deserved. Claude taught Amy to rub her pinky finger and thumb together whenever she felt unnerved. By doing that, she was able to summon the strength to protect herself mentally in hostile situations. He taught her these things under hypnosis, and it worked without question for the fiery Amy. She was one of the approximately sixty percent of the population who could truly be hypnotized.

As soon as he finished with his work, Claude brought Amy back and the two sat and talked for hours about the present and the future.

"He's after me, Claude. It's Kurt Joseph. His son was murdered in Flint and I assume he's somehow taking revenge for the death. I tried to defend the man they falsely accused, but he didn't stand a chance. The jury, citizens, and everyone else involved wanted him on a spit. I wasn't going to change *that* in any way. When the public gets a thought in their collective minds, and the media feeds it with frenzied reporting, it's virtually impossible to alter."

"I know all about it Amy. I watched from afar. The day of reckoning is coming very soon and you must be prepared. This is a very dangerous man with a mission. You've told me about the Queen of Hearts which seems to be his calling card. That comes from insanity Amy. I've no doubt he's met this Queen in visions and is taking his orders from her."

Amy listened intently as the two had green tea. Amy felt tense, but in a constructive way. No anxieties or fears; only strength coursing through her veins.

"He will be after you soon dear. Are you prepared to face him? Are you ready to deal with the devil himself?"

"I've dealt with worse Claude. I can handle him."

"Don't underestimate his mental capacity. He is as smart as he is insane. You are to be the last of his collections, after which he can rest. All of his collections have been female."

"He killed those agents too, Claude. Chopped their heads clean off; so I don't think it's only a female deal."

Claude smiled at Amy and then laughed sheepishly. Amy looked back with a combination of wonderment and hostility.

"Why do you laugh at me Claude? You know that makes me so damn mad."

"You have to open your ears Amy. He has collected only female heads. *Collected.* Did he collect those agent's heads? No he didn't. Listen closer to me and keep your mind focused."

After taking a deep breath and agreeing with Claude, she began to scold herself.

"No scolding; only learning. Listen and keep your eyes at attention. He's coming soon. Please be ready or he will complete his collection."

Amy said nothing. She bowed her head to Claude, who again took her in his hand and said the words that placed her in a new trance. Within seconds, Claude ordered her to wake. When she lifted her head, he was gone. He had again vanished into thin air. She looked at the table and noticed the two cups of green tea sitting on the side, along with three death stars he had left behind. She scooped them up and hid them. That was all the evidence she needed to know he had really been there with her and it wasn't a dream.

"You know Claude?" She announced to an empty room. "I hate it when you do that."

There was no voice or clue in return except maybe for the slightest of breezes that cascaded pleasingly through her home.

Amy continued her meditation and concentration exercises. The mind was powerful and she needed hers to be on alert at all times. Without that, she feared, she would be dead meat. Amy enjoyed having her head and wanted to keep it. Kurt had different ideas and would go to any length to satisfy his Queen.

*

Inside the Gander Mountain, Kurt snuck up behind Wilma, machete at the ready. It was finally time to collect another head and leave himself one short of the goal in which he set out to achieve. Wilma, of course, had other plans and Kurt wasn't privy to them. When Kurt lifted his weapon of execution, Wilma whirled around quicker than a striking cobra. She threw the hunting knife swiftly, hitting him in the left shoulder. Unfortunately, the six-inch long blade missed the mark of Kurt's heart. The pain was astounding to Kurt as he grabbed the knife by the handle and attempted to pull it out. By the rising intensity in his breathing, he was quite sure that she had penetrated his lung. He knew she'd missed his heart, but it pained him like nothing ever had in his life. Kurt was driven back by the force of Wilma's throw and leaned into the shelf on his right. Items fell at his feet as he struggled to regain his footing. The blade, sunken five of the six inches into his chest, was acting as a tourniquet, keeping the bleeding limited, which was good for him as it assisted in keeping him from passing out. Not to be outdone, Kurt looked up with a nasty sneer, but Wilma had disappeared from his vision. People around him were running out of the store in droves and he knew he'd better find and kill Wilma quick or his days as a head collector would be over in a flash. As Kurt made his way up the aisle, he saw a security guard radioing out, presumably to a police officer. Kurt approached and swung his machete across the man's back. With no more than a small whimper and a gurgle, the security guard fell to his knees, and then to his face. He was lucky as death arrived quickly and claimed him.

  Kurt continued through a now nearly barren store and listened closely for any noise that would give away Wilma's location. In the blink of an eye, a dart stuck Kurt in the side of the neck. He wobbled, cursed and then ripped the dart out in anger.

  "I'LL FUCKING KILL YOU!"

  Another dart came and another sting; this one in his hip. Then it was his arm, his leg and his hip again. Kurt dove for cover behind a checkout counter and pulled the hindrances from his body. He was thinking as hard as he could about what he would do to stop this nonsense and escape the store before being caught. He figured he could get Wilma later. In the far distance, he heard sirens. He probably had no more than five minutes to make his escape. When he was ready to make a dash for it, a young security guard came running down the aisle from Kurt's left to his right. When the guard reached the counter, Kurt stuck his foot out and tripped him up. The guard slid face first for five feet before coming to a halt. When he rolled over, Kurt stood before him; blood dripping slightly from his hands and a rather large hunting knife sticking from his chest.

Kurt had been wise enough to wear a bulletproof vest, but that only covered his vital organs. The knife hit him high in the shoulder, just nicking his lung. Had the knife hit him in the heart, it would have bounced off. Painful; yes, fatal; no. He also figured Wilma would be carrying heat. Wherever the showdown were to take place, Kurt had thought ahead.

He picked up the frightened security guard, and he held him against his body as a shield. He placed his machete at the man's throat and called out to Wilma.

"Don't make a move or he dies. I'll drain the blood from his neck and it'll be your fault. I know who you are and I also know why you've come for me. I'm leaving the store, but this isn't over by any means. You'll pay for the pain you've inflicted upon the Queen."

Kurt slowly moved up the aisle. He was at least one hundred yards from the exit and had to be extremely careful in protecting himself and shielding Wilma using the urine soaked guard as his deflection. As Kurt walked, he kept the machete firmly against the guard's throat, wondering if Wilma would be stupid enough to cost him his life.

*

"You couldn't handle a relationship with me right now. You have unfinished business in your mind that needs to be dealt with. Being around me would only make it worse for you."

After Sandy's death, Amy and Blake had parted for a few hours- Blake to answer questions at the Seattle PD, and Amy to meet Claude for a calming hypnosis session. After Claude fled; in his usually dramatic way; Amy called Blake and the two met at the diner where they'd first met.

"I'm no good for you Blake. You're cute and lovable and really hot, but I can't put you through the torment of trying to deal with my life and a baby."

"Why don't I get a say Amy? Why is this all your decision? I had a part in the creation of that child and should be able to decide for myself if I can be a good father, or boyfriend, or even husband."

"I'll let you see your child anytime you want to, but I can't take any chances with either of your lives. I won't subject you to my violent lifestyle."

"Oh I see. You won't subject me to *your* violent lifestyle, but you'll be raising a baby in the middle of your personal war zone. That sounds safe to me."

The sarcasm was dripping off his angry tongue in large doses.

"The baby will be raised in a controlled environment with Claude. It'll be best for the child. No danger will ever come to him or her, I promise."

Amy placed her hand on Blake's unshaven cheek and tears began slowly caressing her fingers. It broke Amy's heart as she used her thumb to dry them and put her arms around his neck. She whispered in his ear that all would be okay and she would never hurt him in any way.

"I honestly love you Blake, but it's simply not going to work between us. The stress would kill you."

Blake looked up into Amy's soft eyes and reluctantly nodded his approval. Amy smiled and gave him a soft peck on his lips. They both felt the energy slipping into their inner thighs. As Blake held on tighter and firmer, Amy was able to strengthen and pull herself from him.

"No Blake. It can never happen again. I know it was a wonderful experience for both of us, but going back would complicate things to a complete mess. Please work with me on this; please?" Amy was struggling to resist his tight grip.

Blake pulled back from the softness that was the woman of his dreams. Although he'd only had one opportunity to make love with her, he decided to cherish it instead of rue the experience. He thought to himself "it's better to have loved and lost than to have never loved at all". He hadn't lost her though; he had only lost that one part of the relationship. They would hang together, share baby time and try their best to be happy for the sake of the coming child.

It was at this point that they decided to spend the day together rummaging through the city and even going to Safeco Field to catch a ball game. Blake's beloved Tigers were in town playing the Mariners. It would relieve some stress and give them both a chance to relax and enjoy the day. They'd need it, as the clock ticked unremittingly.

*

"Don't worry kid", Kurt promised. "If the cop minds her P's and Q's, you get out alive."

The guard was soaked in urine from his waist down and had taken a ghastly white tone in his skin. Kurt continued down the aisle with him; machete against his carotid artery.

Wilma had climbed up on top of the shelving unit and laid down flat on her stomach so she couldn't be spotted. She was about twenty-five feet ahead of Kurt and the guard. She had her pistol drawn and figured to wait until they were right under her to fire a bullet into Kurt's brain, thus ending the madness. She had to use her exceptional hearing, as to lean out too soon would clue Kurt in to her position and probably cost the guard his life. She wanted to do everything in her power to avoid such a mess. Patience was her key as Kurt slunk ever so slowly down the aisle.

Kurt had no idea of Wilma's whereabouts, but figured she was close. The guard managed to look down and saw that Kurt had a blowtorch hanging from his waist along with a red rose in the lower leg pocket of his pants. They were like carpenter pants, but made of some faux leather material. They didn't squeak as Kurt walked, helping his cause immensely. Kurt continued down the aisle. He had another fifteen feet to cover and he'd be close to the front door. Little did he know that Wilma lingered only ten feet in front of them.

She listened intently as Kurt shuffled down the aisle. Another five feet and he'd be in range. She needed to wait until the precise moment when he was directly under her to fire off the shot. She held her gun firmly and steadily in her sweaty hand, a cold nerve keeping her calm. Kurt and the guard were about two feet away.

The steel blade was pressed to the guard's neck as the two inched forward. Another few feet and he'd be home free, but a foot and a half further and two feet above him lay Wilma, ready to roll and fire.

Wilma knew the time was now. She turned and pointed the gun down toward Kurt and the guard. She had to take an extra second to make sure she cleared the kid before she would fire.

That's all Kurt needed. When Wilma rolled to the edge and aimed, Kurt caught her reflection in the blade of his machete. With the stealth of a mountain lion, he swung his blade sideways and made a connection. Wilma's gun fired, but in a wayward direction. Her detached head fell to the floor with a splot.

Wilma's body clung to the shelf above Kurt and the now passed out guard. Kurt flung him to the side and walked over to pick up the appendage. He retrieved the blowtorch from his belt and a click fired it up. He quickly and efficiently sealed the neck wound and scampered toward the door. There was no time for elaborate positioning of Wilma's body, which drained a large pool of blood in the aisle behind him. He held the head by the hair and raced out toward the vehicle. Pedestrians lined the sidewalk and were horrified upon seeing Kurt holding his victim's open-eyed head. The bravest of the brave stepped aside and let Kurt, wielding his machete, pass untouched. He jumped in his van and fled quickly. He was headed toward the abandoned apartment complex. He made it out of the store with a minute to spare as the police rolled up. A few of the onlookers pointed the way in which Kurt had fled, but a minute was long enough for him to find a deep and abandon alley way en route. He backed the van in and waited, sitting behind his steering wheel with Wilma's head staring coldly toward him from the passenger seat.

*

Amy and Blake enjoyed the shopping, strolling and now the ballgame. While Amy wasn't much of a sports fan, the Tigers made Blake feel closer to home. He found himself longing for his native Toledo and wanting to take a trip back, perhaps permanently. He needed to call his parents to make sure they were doing all right and were healthy. What brought Blake down during these thoughts was the fact that there were to be funerals for Andrea and Sandy back home and he wouldn't be there. He fully expected his mom to call him and was surprised she hadn't yet. He told Amy about these thoughts and she pulled her cell out and handed it to him. She continued to munch on her nacho.

"Call them, Blake."

"But we're at a ballgame. Why would I call from here?"

"You worry too much. Call them and take that pressure off yourself. Quit thinking so damn much."

She was right. He dialed up the phone from his seat in left field and his mom answered. It was great to hear her voice. She thought the exact same thing about her son as news of the deaths traveled east.

"Sandy's mother took it hard Blake. She found out about three hours after it happened. Did Sandy walk into traffic? What's the story? We heard she was hit by a bus."

"Mom, what do you mean Sandy's mom 'took' it hard? Didn't you mean she's *taking* it hard?"

"No, I mean she took it hard. They found her in the shower this morning. She hung herself with a belt."

Blake was saddened, but not surprised; given how Sandy's mom reacted to everything in such a "fly off the handle" sort of way. He asked if the news of Andrea had also reached Toledo.

"Yes", his mom said. "Although a lot of people aren't really surprised. You have to tell me what the hell's going on over there. Who is Amy Fraser?"

Blake's mom saw the caller ID on her phone, and she wanted to know if they were going out together. He wouldn't dare tell her he'd gotten her pregnant.

"I'll explain everything later. I promise. Amy is a friend of mine who let me use her phone. What's up with Dad? How is he?"

Amy sat next to Blake and soaked him in. She thought he was handsome and well kempt. His personality was pleasant and his demeanor soft. It was his mental hiccups that kept her from taking the next step. She trusted Claude and he was the one person who always came through for her. Claude would allow the relationship, but Amy would have to sacrifice what she loved to do. She wasn't ready for that kind of a change. She loved being Claude's "hunter". Blake finally finished his call.

"Yes Mom, I'm fine. It was just unfortunate, that's all. Yes, I'll call more often. Yes, I'll write too."

He hung up and handed the phone back to Amy. She was looking him over fondly.

"I wish it could work for us Blake, but I'm sorry. I will always protect you though."

Her feelings for Blake existed whether she wanted them or not.

Blake smiled back at the lovely woman and forced his attention back to the game; a game his beloved Tigers would go on to win.

There were so many things going on that Blake thought at some points he'd simply go crazy. Everything was happening so fast. Sandy was dead, Andrea was dead and they'd both find out soon that the FBI Agent was dead. Amy was pregnant but didn't want him, and she was in danger from the same man that was killing all these women. It was enough for Blake to beg his Doctor to up his dose on Xanax, which he did. Now Blake was taking a 150 MG Effexor twice a day and .50 MG of Xanax four times a day. It was enough to put down a medium sized horse, but Blake still felt the tension. His anxiety had not alleviated since he'd come to Seattle; it actually increased. Whose wouldn't with the type of stress he was dealing with on a daily basis? He noticed Amy had been calm and collected through all of these incidents and wondered why. He asked.

"Reiki." Amy answered. "It softens everything that's stressful. Call it self-healing."

"Will you show it to me?" Blake asked with enthusiasm. He was always looking for a way to feel better.

"Sure. Let's go to my house after the game and I'll show it to you."

Blake loved it. The self-hypnosis was especially relaxing and slowed down his stress-filled life, if only for a few minutes. Amy cut him a copy of the CD and Blake took it home. He began using it regularly as he tried to ward off the demons that haunted his mind. He had no idea of what was to come.

*

After all the heat had passed, Kurt headed back to his abandoned building with extreme caution. While he waited a few hours for everything to calm down, he placed Wilma's head in a jar of formaldehyde and put it on the shelf next to the others. He also placed a Queen of Hearts on the hook under it. He would've added the picture of her torso, but he had no time to waste at the store. No picture of her torso and no 'Q' written on it with a cross through it. It was still a collected head, though, and was a splendid addition to his assortment. He slid in one of his CD's and sang on his way back to his base.

"Hmm! How doth the little crocodile improve his shining tail, and pour the waters of the Nile, on every golden scale? How cheer... how cheer... how cheerfully he seems to grin, how neatly spreads his claws and welcomes little fishes in, with gently smiling jaw."

The song was perfect as it cheered Kurt up and gave him a renewed sense of purpose.

"I'm the crocodile. I'm the one that welcomes these people in. After that- **PFFFTTT! OFF WITH THEIR HEADS!**"

Now that Kurt had finished his post decapitation party and returned to his hideout, his beloved Queen of Hearts gave him a special visit. She sang to him from the floor above. Kurt dropped what he was doing and headed straight upstairs. He found his Queen, this time sitting on a throne with a dead pig serving as a footrest.

"Approach your Queen Kurtis. Bow at my feet and tell me how much you love me."

Kurt quickly approached and bowed; he attempted to kiss her feet but was rejected.

"Don't touch my feet, sir. You may worship me without the touch of your ordinary mortal skin. One touch of your earthly oils and I'll disappear forever. You may touch when you join me on the next level.

"Wonderland, right my Queen?"

"If it makes you happy, then yes, Wonderland."

"Oh my beautiful Queen, have I satisfied your thirst."

"You still have one more to go Kurtis. You must catch and behead the one they call 'Amy'. She will be your biggest challenge, as she is the *Alice* of this earthly *Wonderland*. She won't go easily. You must be wise and strong. I have an idea that may work."

"I'm listening oh majestic Red Queen."

Kurt found himself ogling over her. On that day, she was wearing a tight red corset with a well-fitted bustier. Her ample breasts bulged from the top while at the same time keeping their perfect form. Her red leather pants were so tight they looked painted on. He became excited as the blood rushed to his groin. She wore blood red lipstick, black eyeliner and her skin was a milky white tone. She was as beautiful as any creature he'd ever seen.

"Take the battle to higher ground Kurtis. Take the battle to a place Amy, *or Alice* fears. To do this you must select a spot and draw her in, or better yet, allow her to lead you to the battleground. Can you do this Kurtis? Do you have the will for battle in thee?"

"I will Queen. I will not fail you. I shall bring her head to you."

"You must hurry, as the laws of this land are closing in on you. A second wasted will cause your quest to be abandoned. They will catch you and skin you. They will drag your carcass through the streets of the village. You must hurry."

"Will my Queen reward me? Will thou take me to your Wonderland?"

The Queen gave him a one better. She rose from her chair and kicked the dead pig out of the way. It evaporated into mist. She stepped down so that she was a foot from Kurt, and warned him not to touch her. As she slowly danced around him, he was inundated with the scent of rosewood and honey. Soon the Queen was inches from Kurt. His gaze was transfixed upon her gothic beauty. She was perfect to him. She of her ample breasts, silky red hair and tattoos on her upper chest, arms and torso depicting nature. The art included trees, wooded areas, mushrooms, flowers and many other majestic scenes. He could smell the sweetness of her. She backed away and spoke.

"For Alice's head, I give you this."

She waved her arms over her body.

"Think about it Kurtis; for her head you spend eternity with me. I will lavish you with everything of which every man dreams. You will be my King and will be allowed to do with me as you wish. Anything Kurt; *any-thing.*"

She said it so slowly and seductively. He could feel the heat running through him. He looked at his Queen, who wore her charmed smile.

The evaporation began. The Queen began to erode before his eyes. His look went from a smile of surprise to sad and melancholy. She melted. Her face, her eyes, her body; all disintegrating into dust on the floor. The throne she sat on started to steam, and then it lit with a large fire. Kurt could feel the heat from the flames kiss his cheek as it burned. In a flash, the chair was also ash on the floor. As suddenly as the evaporation began, it ended. The dusty ashes gathered themselves and swirled in front of him in a circular motion, and then disappeared. As much as Kurt knew she'd be back to get him, he was extremely distraught about her leaving. She was as beautiful and sexy as she had ever been. Now she added the gothic look, which drove him mad. As he walked away from her and back to his van, he heard a slight whisper in his ear; *"any-thing."*

He looked up to the ceiling with a determined look on his face.

"I will not fail you my Queen. Amy; *Alice's* head will be yours."

Kurt went back to the van and opened his shirt to extract the knife. He gave it a mighty tug and screamed into a cloth he had stuffed in his mouth to keep the noise down. He treated the wound, dressed it and then lay down for a well-earned sleep. The next day, the time would be nigh. The ultimate battle would ensue.

SEATTLE (AP) — Seattle government authorities say a man has beheaded a woman in a Gander Mountain Store just within the Seattle city limits.

Security guards did not detain the suspect, believed to be the headhunter who has murdered in the same fashion from Las Vegas to Seattle, after he ran out of the store with the head in his hands, shocking onlookers

A witness told newswoman Rhonda Dalling that he saw the man with a bloodstained woman's head in his hand after coming out of the store.

A government spokesperson said the suspect is believed to have entered the store, and then brandished a machete that he used to assault and behead the woman whose identity hasn't been released.

An on duty security guard was also murdered, a machete wound was found across his back.

The official spoke on condition of anonymity in keeping with department regulations.

19
Alice (Amy) in Wonderland

What could Amy do but wait. She had no idea where Kurt was, but she knew he was in the city. When and where would he strike? Would he try to catch Amy off guard? Was he brazen enough to confront her face to face? All of these questions roamed around in her head and she didn't have an answer for any of them. All she could do was stay sharp and keep her eyes, especially those in the back of her head, wide open. She called Claude and asked what he was going to do to help.

"There is nothing I can do Amy. He isn't after me. This is something you have to take care of yourself. I hope you're ready for the biggest challenge of your life."

It frustrated her because she wanted him there to help. The problem was he didn't know any more than she did about where Kurt would pop up. She had to have a heightened sense of awareness at all times with no letting up.

Logging onto the internet opened Amy's mind to the situation before her. As she had already known, Kurt was wanted for murder *by* decapitation in Las Vegas, Idaho, Portland and now Seattle. He had also murdered three law enforcement officials along with Wilma Hurst, an FBI Agent and her "Dark Men," not to mention the pervert in the restroom. The news on the TV explained the beheading at the Gander Mountain store. She heard the grisly details of Kurt running down the sidewalk holding her head by the hair. People who witnessed the horror would be mentally warped by the incident for a long time to come; especially those who witnessed it up close. The bloodletting and murder needed to stop. The public was beginning to get angry with the city police. It was explained to the masses that they were trying as hard as anyone else to stop the madness. It was very difficult to stop what you couldn't see. So far, Kurt had been smart enough to elude capture. The question was simple for Amy; would she be able to bring the menace down?

Lots of Reiki, self-hypnosis and meditation were her saving grace for the time being. She felt as if she would be ready whenever the hour came. It would be very soon.

*

Kurt was watching Amy closely. He spied around her home, but from a safe distance, and he watched Amy come and go three times during the day. Why didn't he already pounce and finish the job? Because his Queen told him to take her on higher ground. He wasn't sure what that meant exactly, but he figured mountains. Kurt bided his time. He hoped it would only be a matter of hours or less before Amy would lead him to the showdown. It was all up to the one the Queen referred to as *Alice*.

He had stolen yet another car from the street corner near the apartment building and driven to where Amy lived. To find where she had moved, he employed the same technique he had used to find Soo-Chin; he walked smack into the public records department downtown and asked for it. Knowing she'd relocated made it necessary to re-track her. He paid a twenty dollar fee, and voila! It was his address to keep. Public records came in handy when planning murder. He chuckled at how easy it was to track someone down anywhere in the world, and at any time.

As he waited in his "new" car for Amy to make her move, he began thinking like the Red Queen and referring to her as Alice. He pictured her with a white shirt and a blue bib top. A blue skirt also entered his mind. The only problem was Amy's jet-black hair. He hated that hair. Every time he saw it, he cringed. He promised to dye it blond after he collected her head.

Kurt also had with him pictures of all the kills. Everyone was in order on his dashboard from left to right. He even had a picture of the final jar that would contain Amy's head. The line-up of pictures helped him with motivation; not that he needed much with his hot and sexy Queen promising him Kingship and the permission to do *any-thing* he wanted to her. He struggled mightily to keep his libido at ease. It was tough, as she *was* the perfect gothic creature he'd always wanted. The tiny heart tattooed onto her cheekbone just under her eye was especially sexy. Kurt squirmed and scooted in the car as the blood rushed to his groin, causing him to develop a hard penis. The thoughts ravaged his mind so deeply that he finally had to relieve himself immediately. That task accomplished and the tension somewhat alleviated, he returned to concentrating on the one that carried his ticket to the Queen's special land and a place on the throne next to her.

As Kurt continued to wait, a knock sounded on his driver side window. Were the plans about to be severely compromised?

*

Amy lazed around the house, watching TV and surfing the net; all while being spied upon by a raving maniac who thought he had instructions from an imagined Red Queen to chop her head off. Of course, had she known of his presence, the showdown would've taken place on the spot. She didn't, so it remained a waiting game.

Whenever Amy sensed strangeness around her, concentrating on something else was her escape. She felt more in control when she could loosen up. It wasn't obsessive behavior, but it was more soothing. The house was her abode and she felt safer in it, as she knew every angle and hiding spot in case a lunatic, home breaker or common thief tried to cross the line that was her front door or window. Now, she was carrying an underlying feeling of doom or something wrong flowing through her veins. She checked out her windows at least ten times per hour to make sure nothing fishy was going on outside. She couldn't see anything except a stray dog or cat occasionally, or a person walking by with no threat being placed on her safety.

After driving herself crazy for another hour, she called Blake and asked him if he'd like to do something downtown. She also *wanted* to see him.

"Are you okay Amy? You sound like you're worried. Is everything all right over there? Has there been any sign of that creep?"

"I'm fine, but you're right, it's the fact that some nut case is on my tail. I don't know why he hasn't been caught, but until he is, I have to keep my consciousness alert and ready."

Blake went silent on the other end of the line.

"Blake? Are you there? Hello, Blake?"

The phone stayed silent enough for Amy to walk over to her kitchen window and take a glance outside. There was nothing happening that she could see, and she called out his name once again.

"BLAKE!"

"Yeah, yeah Amy, I'm here."

"Well what the hell? You scared the shit out of me. What are you doing?"

"I dropped the phone. I was getting a little panicky when you reminded me of that creep."

"Come over and pick me up Blake. I want to go downtown. It's too quiet here. Is it okay if I spend the night at your place?"

"Sure it is," Blake said excitedly. "But you come get me, okay?"

"Blake. I'll come get you and I'll spend the night; but we can't...*you know*? Okay?"

"I understand Amy. I suppose snuggling is completely out of the question?"

"Forget it Blake." Amy seethed. "I'll go myself."

She was getting frustrated and wanted him to stop with the insinuations. She was about to hang up when his voice spoke up anew.

"I was just kidding Amy. It's all good. Let's go have some fun, maybe get a bite to eat and then back to my house. We'll stop and get a movie or two to watch."

That pleased Amy and calmed her. She agreed, hung up and headed to the shower. As much as she refused to admit it, she missed Blake terribly.

*

The man tapped on the window and Kurt looked up. He had his pictures sprawled across the dashboard, but quickly grabbed them and put them in his coat pocket. The tap on his window brought him out of his latest Red Queen fantasy. He rolled down the window and saw that it was Seattle's finest; two cops; standing next to the car.

"You want to step out of the vehicle sir?"

"No officer, I really wouldn't." Kurt said with a grin.

"I'm not asking you, I'm telling you. Step out of the vehicle or we'll remove you."

"I was joking officer; sorry."

The officer offered no smile. He apparently didn't get the joke. Kurt did as he was told and stepped out. He placed his top hat on his head, proud of its presence. He stood next to the door with one officer facing him and another standing toward the rear of the vehicle with a Taser gun ready and aimed.

"What's with the Taser gun? I've done nothing wrong."

"Shut the fuck up. Give me your license and registration, NOW!"

"It's in the glove box. You should have asked me before you had me get out…..*Copper*."

Before Kurt could chuckle, the cop slapped the hat off his head. Kurt's head barely moved and his smile disappeared. He watched his hat roll in the dirt. The anger worming inside gripped Kurt's being. The cop was to pay for his disrespect.

"That's officer to you fuckstick."

The cop ducked into the car as the other one kept the Taser aimed directly at Kurt's midsection. There was a small building separating them from Amy's house. The only thing visible was Amy's driveway and the jeep parked in it. That was all Kurt needed to keep an eye on. The officer fished out the information from the glove box and stood up. He was about five foot six with what Kurt thought to be a bully's attitude.

"This isn't your car, is it uh….Mrs. Clement?" He was reading the registration. "Did you steal this car boy?"

Kurt stood silent. He looked straight ahead with not a flinch in his eye.

"I'm talking to you boy. You're going to jail tonight you piece of shit."

Both officers laughed. The first cop started to get greedy.

"What did you stick in your coat pocket when you saw me? Pull it out."

Kurt again stood firm and glassy eyed. He wasn't talking or meeting the officer's gaze. The next fifteen seconds would determine two fates.

The bully cop grabbed Kurt's wrists and lowered them to his side as he went for the inner pocket in Kurt's coat. With his left hand, Kurt quickly pointed toward the Taser wielding Policeman. A four-inch stiletto flew from Kurt's sleeve and nailed the cop directly in the forehead just above his eyebrow. With a look of terror, the cop stood in frozen silence, urinated out of the pant leg of his uniform and then folded down as if a five thousand pound weight had been placed on the top of his head. The other officer looked at Kurt and went for his gun. It was way too late as out of his right hand sleeve came a longer knife. It was sharp and gleamed under the moonlit sky. Before a scream could be uttered, Kurt smiled a toothy grin that would be the cop's last memory, and stuck the knife in the officer's neck below his ear in a calm stroke; it exited under his other ear. He grabbed the officer by his hair so the blood would spurt out on the street, not on his clothing. He ripped the knife back out, bringing blood and innards with it.

"You stupid fucks," Kurt fumed. "Why must you always show up when I don't need you?"

Kurt popped the trunk, threw the two police officers inside as one bloody heap and slammed the door shut. He walked back to the police cruiser, turned off the lights and then pulled it ten feet to the right so that it was hidden in the shadow of the building. He went back to his stolen car, sat in the driver seat and placed the pictures from his pocket back onto the dashboard. He looked out and saw that Amy's jeep was still in the driveway. He quipped at the entire episode as if it were nothing to him.

"Mrs. Clement, whoever you are" Kurt mused, "thank you for the use of your vehicle. The next time you open your trunk though, you're in for a big surprise."

*

Finally, after what seemed like two lifetimes, Amy exited her home and started the jeep. Kurt was flooded with excitement as he could finally leave the messy scene and go for the more exciting stuff; namely collecting Amy's head.

He wondered to himself what it was like to die. He smiled when he realized that Amy didn't have much time left. He couldn't imagine in a thousand thoughts what it would actually be like knowing you were about to be murdered. Would it be scary? What would your mind do? Perhaps if you knew you were about to have your head cut off it would be worse. Kurt made it a point that he would remind Amy a few seconds before the swing of his machete. He wanted to study her reaction, the look in her eyes and her face. He wanted her to have an especially terrorized expression. She would be his crème de la crème of decapitation.

Amy headed through town quickly. Kurt followed as close as he could without being detected. He followed as she passed Dawson Plumbing, The Seattle Trading Post and The Seattle Academy on

Madison. They crossed 12th and Denny with Kurt in hot pursuit. Amy was doing about forty-five in a thirty-five, but Kurt kept the speed up even though he intentionally trailed her by at least fifteen car lengths. He knew it would get tougher for him as they neared the city, so he would have to close the gap soon.

As they reached 15th and Prospect, Kurt closed the gap to about six car lengths. It was nightfall and Amy had the top closed on her jeep. She had no idea that Kurt was tailing her. As they continued north, Amy veered to the left onto E. Boston Avenue. She slowed to a crawl and approached a home. As Kurt wondered what she was doing, she pulled into a driveway. He hung back and killed the lights. It was another waiting game.

*

Amy left for Blake's house. She turned on the radio to some easy listening music and sat back comfortably for the two and a half mile drive. She still had that funny feeling teasing at her mind. She wasn't exactly sure what it was, but it caused her to pay closer attention to her surroundings. It was getting dusky outside, which was making her nervous, so she put in her Reiki CD to calm her nerves. She breathed normally and paid close attention to the road. Soon her nerves began to mellow. Amy was pleasantly surprised how well the CD helped her cope and calm down.

She reached Blake's house in half the time it usually took, as her wandering mind caused her to press harder on the accelerator. She had no idea she was doing fifteen to twenty MPH over the speed limit, and she was fortunate not to be pulled over. When she exited the vehicle and started up Blake's driveway, she had trouble remembering the drive from her place. A very common occurrence when one's senses were working overdrive. She looked back down the road to try to regain her bearings. The only thing she saw was a car pulling off the road and shutting its lights off along with an ordinary couple walking down the sidewalk. It was as commonplace and normal as it had ever been. The feeling of peculiarity still clung to her soul.

"Well my gosh Amy, you got here fast young lady."

Blake greeted her at the door and she clutched him with a hug that was as tight as he had ever felt. He sensed fear, but also desperation. He hugged back and led her inside.

"Amy, what's wrong honey?" Blake took her face in his hands. Tears ran down his fingers and along his wrist. Amy was doing something not many people saw. She was crying very hard. Blake was a special person and Amy trusted him.

"I don't want to die Blake. I don't want to be dead. I have a, *your*, baby in me and I want to be a mom and have a full life."

"You? Die? No chance doll. You're much too tenacious and amped up. You're not going to die."

Amy pulled from Blake and stepped backward. He could see her eyes change with her mood. She bared her teeth and continued.

"Someone wants to chop my fucking head off Blake. Someone wants to do the worst thing that could be done. I like my head and would like to keep it on my shoulders thank you very much."

Blake attempted to grab Amy and pulled her back into his chest. She wasn't ready and slapped his hands away.

"I always have to be the one to take care of shit. Catch this crook, catch that crook. Kick his ass, whip her ass. Can somebody fucking protect me for once? Is there any chance that someone would watch Amy's back so she can relax?"

This time when Blake grabbed her arms, she allowed it. He pulled her in close and she cried as hard as she could, releasing strain and tension with every thrust of tears. He walked her into the living area and sat her down gently on the sofa. He sat next to her and gently rocked her in his arms. Amy was still bawling and Blake could feel her moisture through his clothing.

"I'll take care of you Amy. I'll protect you."

Amy pulled away from Blake and looked into his eyes. He saw her swollen, reddened cheeks and her cute nose. She couldn't, *wouldn't* help herself any longer. She pulled Blake in and kissed him furiously. They exchanged the warm feeling of tongues dancing together beyond wet lips. The two looked in each other's souls and nothing more needed to be said. Blake removed his shirt and helped Amy out of hers. They took to the bedroom and Blake finished undressing his goddess. She returned the favor. She touched him as Blake's head snapped backward in pure ecstasy.

The next hour consisted of being together with love in their hearts. They tickled and teased each other, then went back to making love. They did this repeatedly, melting into each other as the passion took them. They never stopped looking into each other's eyes. Amy, while sitting on top of her man looked down and took his hands. She placed them on her breasts and spoke, "Friends with benefits, Blake. That's all. Friends with benefits."

Blake said in return. "Okay Amy. I must say I love you and I've loved you since the first day I saw you, but I understand Amy."

"I'll never hurt you Blake. I promise. I want you to help me raise our child. I want us to be *close* friends."

"But what about Claude? Won't he be angry?"

"He doesn't need all the details. I need to be near you. I know we can make this work to both of our advantages without upsetting the apple cart."

Blake smiled before the two met lips and continued their deep lush kisses. Soon, after both were spent, they decided it was time to go do something together on the town.

"Let's go to the tower Amy. I've never been there."

"Okay. I've never been there either. We'll play Sleepless in Seattle, only tonight I'll be sleeping with you."

She kissed the end of his nose and gave it a slight lick out of playfulness. Blake smiled as he hadn't smiled in years. He was with the girl he wanted and despite Amy's insistence on the 'friends with benefits' slogan; it looked like his dreams were coming true.

There was still one enormous problem hovering over their heads.

"C'mon, c'mon. FUCK!" Kurt banged hard on the steering wheel.

He was losing patience and getting very bored in the car. He also had two dead cops in the trunk and probably an APB out on him. He needed to get this job finished and present the Queen with her final gift. Time was wasting and Kurt was agitated. Not a good combination.

He began slamming his balled fists against the dashboard and having a fit. Kurt had no idea how to control his rage, so hurting and destroying were the outlets that he used for relief. Two minutes after he began his temper tantrum, he was loudly ordered to stop.

"Cease the heated fit of rage!"

Kurt looked in his rear view mirror and she was there. The Red Queen sat behind him in the car. Kurt immediately stopped and turned around slowly. He was within inches of his beloved Queen. She had her beautiful red hair pulled back off her forehead and wore the same tight red jumpsuit she had before. Kurt was frozen with lust.

"Why do you have such fits Kurtis? Those fits are reserved for the ones who will lose their heads. The temper isn't necessary."

"Yes my Queen. I'm frustrated because it's taking so long for Amy to leave that house. I want her head so badly I can taste it."

"Patience Kurt. They had to make love one last time before her end. Give them that much. She will be yours soon."

With that comment, the Queen pointed toward the house as Amy and Blake headed to the jeep.

"There I told you Kurtis! They're leaving now. Follow them."

Kurt started up the vehicle and followed them north. The Queen spoke again.

"You'll have two to kill now Kurtis. One won't go without the other."

"That's fine. Killing doesn't bother me in the least."

The jeep containing Amy and Blake headed north until it turned left on Roanoke Avenue. Kurt followed. Three blocks later, they took another left on Westlake. Now they were headed south toward the city. Kurt stayed back about five car lengths. Blake was driving and Amy sat toward the middle, staying close to him. They continued along the harbor, Kurt keeping the gap close. It was easier this time as Blake drove slower. Soon the harbor was behind them and they headed straight for the heart of the city. The Queen was still riding behind Kurt. He could feel the chill of her mist on the back of his neck, causing shivers to shoot down his spine.

Finally, they turned left on Broad Street and headed straight for the tower that was just ahead.

"Could it be?" Kurt asked himself.

It was. The two pulled into a parking lot next to the Seattle Space Needle. The Queen spoke.

"I told you t'would be on high ground Kurtis. You shall do the deed in that tall needle. You shall take her head on the top of that structure."

Kurt turned to ask a question, but his Queen was gone. He looked in the rear view, turned around yet again and wasn't mistaken. She had disappeared. He turned his attention back to the front. He would park close; wait for them to ride the elevator up, and then follow them about fifteen or so minutes later. That would give them time to settle while separating him a bit from their possible gaze. He noticed there wasn't much of a line. That made him happy as the less people present the better.

Kurt cackled a growling laugh. He loaded his machete in his trench coat, re-armed his sleeves with deadly stilettos and made his way toward the elevator. The time had come. The time had finally come, and Kurt was about to spring into action to complete his collection derived of evil. He flattened his top hat and hid it inside his coat.

"Beware the Jabberwocky, my lass! The jaws that bite, the claws that catch! Beware the Jubjub bird, and shun the frumious Bandersnatch!"

Shaun Webb

20
Off With Her Head V

Built for the World's Fair in 1962, the Seattle Space Needle was a huge part of the city, and cultural icon of Seattle. The tower stood some 600 feet from bottom to the tip of the flag, while the observation level held a great view at 500 feet. It wasn't the tallest structure by far in the United States, but was one of the most intriguing. You could see a number of Seattle landmarks, plus the mountain ranges that surrounded the city. Mt. Rainier, The Cascade Mountain Range, Alki Point, Puget Sound, The Olympic Mountain Range, plus a breathtaking view of Downtown Seattle.

Blake could see the ballparks where the professional teams played and he could even see his own home north of the city if he concentrated hard enough. It was getting quite dark, so spotting his house was more hope than reality. Amy was astounded at the lights of the city and the incredible view. It helped make her feel a bit more peaceful and serene, as it was much quieter from 500 feet.

The two booked a table at the revolving restaurant that circled the city regularly. For the first time in a long time, Blake felt calm and anxiety free. Perhaps it was the fact that he was spending time with the girl he really wanted. He felt terrible for Sandy and Andrea, especially Sandy because she wouldn't take no for an answer. She went so far out of her element that trouble was almost assured. Despite that, he admired her for going after what she really wanted, even if it was an obsession with him that caused her to do it. Andrea had a Satan's pact with drugs, and wasn't surprised by her demise. As he looked over the city contemplating these thoughts, Amy interrupted him with her concerns.

"What'cha thinking about?"

"Oh, just how happy I am to be with a wonderful and beautiful woman such as you. You really make me happy and we have so much to learn about each other. I know what you do for a living and I really don't worry much about it because you seem like you handle yourself just fine."

Amy kissed him, and then turned him toward the light of the city so she could get some photos. Blake happily obliged with daffiness and a silly smile.

"Give me a nice smile Blake. I want to see your dimples. They're gorgeous."

Blake obliged.

The two were thoroughly enjoying their night out. It was a great escape.

The adventure would continue for a while longer, and become more intense than they could've ever anticipated.

*

Loaded up with everything he thought he needed, Kurt headed for the elevator for his trip to the top of the needle. He was both thrilled and somewhat nervous about the task at hand. Kurt wasn't worried about the murder; he was more concerned with the fact that he could be spotted and recognized. He stuffed his hair under a Mariners cap and he wore jeans and a tee with his trench. He also wore light-lensed sunglasses to throw off his look. He wanted to make a quick entrance, quicker exit and head to the land that the Queen had promised.

Surprisingly, Kurt wasn't frisked when he entered the building. No metal detectors were present and no security guards except for the one flirting with the girl at the souvenir shop counter. It was easy as he walked up to the cashier and purchased a ticket.

"Enjoy your trip to the top!" The cashier tried to say enthusiastically; but obvious boredom permeated in her voice.

After lingering around the souvenir shop and giving the place a good casing out, Kurt decided to enter the elevator. There were no more than ten people in the visitor's area and he hadn't seen the elevator move in the five or so minutes he had been there. He figured the top was also lacking a crowd; perfect for his plan to take shape.

As the elevator rose and the woman spoke into the microphone; telling him how wonderful Seattle was and explaining the towers meaning and intricacies, Kurt looked to his right and saw his beautiful Queen standing next to him. She had her arms folded down at her waist and looked out the window of the elevator with a smile.

"This is nothing like where we'll be tonight Kurtis. Nothing at all. This place is stinky, smoggy and full of corruption. It's hideous really."

"I agree Oh Lordess. I can't wait to be gone from this toxic pit of Hell."

The elevator operator turned to Kurt.

"Can I help you sir? Did you ask a question?"

"No, no, sorry. I was clearing my throat."

The eighteen year-old college student who was probably trying to save money for school turned back and continued her spiel. Kurt glanced back to his right and saw that his lovely Queen still stood next to him.

"I'm sorry Kurtis. No one can see or hear me, so it's probably wise to simply listen and not speak. I'll be watching. When the job is done, we will collect all the heads and leave this rubbish can of a world. Is thou with me?"

Kurt nodded. The elevator slowed to a crawl and the lights of the city temporarily disappeared. A moment later, he was stepping out of the box and into the lobby of the tower.

"Enjoy your stay at the top!"

Kurt nodded without a smile and walked away from the elevator. The tower was nearly empty. He saw only a handful of people and was growing more and more confident as he prepared for action.

He took his shades off, but pulled up a hood on the back of his coat. It wasn't that he was chilly; he simply wanted to be private and mysterious in his action. Nine out of ten people he saw in the streets had hoods, so he felt like he was in line with the trend. Blending in was of key importance to the skill set of a head collector.

A Killer for the Queen

*

Blake's hand held beeper began to flash, notifying him that their table in the revolving restaurant was ready. The two, hand in hand, headed for the deck where the eatery was located. The Needle had multiple decks, so it could get a bit confusing when trying to make your way around. No worries this time, as they found it without much trouble.

As they stood at the entrance, Blake noticed to his right, about fifty feet away, a man standing in a hooded coat. It appeared that he was wearing sunglasses and looking their way. Upon Blake noticing, the figure quickly went in the other direction until he was out of site around the circular shaped deck. Blake shook his head, dismissed the figure and the two headed for their table.

"What's wrong Blake?" Amy asked her visibly confused man.

"Oh nothing. Sometimes I get a bit jumpy you know. It's nothing really."

Amy had a good sense about her and read Blake like an old book. She was suspicious.

"Did you see something that disturbed you Blake? You have to tell me because I don't like mysteries."

"Really Amy it's no biggie." Blake lied. "I think I saw someone I knew; but it's been a hectic couple of days; I could be reading into nothing."

Amy reluctantly agreed and the two placed their orders with the waiter. Non-alcoholic Wine was on the docket as Amy wanted to celebrate her pregnancy with the man who helped her get that way. Blake smiled and kissed her. There wasn't enough time in the day to get the kisses in with his "friend". He would've preferred a constant lip lock, as she was as beautiful as any creature he'd ever laid eyes on.

"You are so beautiful and sweet. I'm so glad you changed your mind about us."

Amy responded with the smile Blake loved; her dimples flashing and her teeth as white as ivory piano keys

"It took a lot of thought Blake. I figured being friends and getting frisky occasionally would be all right. I know what you're thinking. Claude will be fine with it when he realizes we're not *really* boyfriend-girlfriend".

Blake excused himself to the restroom as Amy sat with her glass of wine and peered out at the lights of the city. She thought about the fact that she would be making Seattle her permanent home, and Claude would get used to the idea of Blake as her "friend". He had made it abundantly clear that she would stay on for the duration. It was okay with her, as Blake had made it a point to deal with her work.

The waiter, who had brought their meals, snapped Amy out of her trance. She wondered with a curious look why it was taking Blake so long to return.

"How long does it take to go to the bathroom?" She murmured to herself. "He's been gone fifteen minutes."

She decided she would give it another five minutes before checking on him. She returned her gaze out to the city and the minutes passed quickly. After another fifteen minutes, thirty total, she went to check. She knocked lightly on the restroom door, hoping not to disturb any bladder shy patrons. After getting no response, she knocked harder and called out his name. The third try saw Amy opening the door and calling out Blake's name again. When there was still no answer, she barged in. The restroom was empty and echoed her calls for Blake. There was a red rose sitting on the sink. She walked over and picked it up. The rose had been white, but was painted red. Her heart sank. She rushed back out of the restroom and heard the shrieking of a woman in the restaurant, but coming from the other side that was out of her sight. Sensing the worst, Amy dashed over as fast as she could to see what was going on. It was more than even she expected; it was the wickedest, scariest and most upsetting scene she'd ever had to witness.

*

Kurt, still with his hood up, watched Blake excuse himself from the table. This was his chance. He had Amy right where he wanted her. He approached slowly, trying not to alarm anyone or give himself away. He slunk in and came up behind the waiter as he was delivering the food to Amy's table. Safely assured that he was hidden from site, Kurt lunged toward the wall separating him from Amy. He was so close it caused a bead of sweat to drip down his forehead and into his eye. He gripped the machete inside his coat and waited. When the coast was clear and Amy was peering out toward the city, he dashed for the restroom he'd seen Blake enter. Kurt calmly walked inside and saw Blake washing his hands at the sink. He took his top hat out of his coat, flipped it open and placed it on his head. Blake, quietly relieving himself at a urinal, looked up and saw the reflection in the mirror. Kurt was standing ready with his machete out and resting against his shoulder. He had a red rose in his hand, but the red was oozing down onto his fingers, revealing a white rose underneath. Blake knew he was in big trouble. He saw that the blood had dried on the blade and knew at that moment he was face to face with the killer; the taker of heads. The ice water rushed through Blake's arteries with the help of a rapidly beating heart. He could feel the pressure in his head and became fuzzy. Kurt looked at him with a smile and put a finger up to his mouth. "Shhh."

What choice did Blake have other than shushing? He could either do what Kurt said or possibly be stabbed on the spot.

"Turn your back to me." Kurt ordered. "Don't make a move or a sound or I will kill you slowly. I'll grind my weapon into your bones and twist. I've heard that it lingers and hurts very much."

Blake turned around as he was told and Kurt approached him. After dropping the rose on the sink, he told Blake to act natural and to stay two steps in front of him. They were leaving the eatery. Blake walked out of the restroom in an orderly fashion. He stayed about two feet ahead of Kurt as he walked to the opposite side of the restaurant away from where Amy sat. Nobody seemed to notice as the two left the eatery and continued up the next set of stairs leading to the observation area. Instead of stopping there, Kurt had Blake continue on to a door that read **EMPLOYEES**

A Killer for the Queen

ONLY and went through it. Once inside, Kurt picked up a harness and a steel cable. He placed the harness over his head and onto his torso; he then tightened the straps that came with it. Blake was growing more anxious by the moment. It was easy for him to add one and one, and this math equation was not revealing an answer he'd like.

Once harnessed and having steel cable, Kurt led Blake to another door. This one read **WARNING: NOT AN EXIT.** Under it read another **TRAINED EMPLOYEES ONLY.** Blake's stomach tightened as he pushed the door open and the breeze of downtown Seattle hit him squarely in the face.

*

"And as in uffish thought she stood, the Jabberwocky, with eyes of flame, came wiffling through the tulgey wood, and burbled as it came!"

*

What could she do besides look in front of her with pure fear and isolation? Amy felt the walls caving in on her in a sudden rush of steel, brick and mortar. As she approached the scene of the shrieking woman, she looked beyond the table in which she was sitting and knew the time had come. Blake stood *outside* the window, some five hundred feet above the streets of Seattle. Next to him, a menacing figure clad in a trench coat and top hat that he appeared to have pinned in his hair to keep it from blowing away in the strong wind. He had a large knife to Blake's throat and looked at Amy with a smirk. He looked as if he had a cable connected to a safety jacket on his person while Blake stood with no protection. One wrong move and it would be curtains for the young man.

Kurt smiled a wider grin and raised his free hand. He signaled Amy with his index finger in a "come hither" motion. Undoubtedly, the police had been called, but that didn't matter to Kurt, as after he collected Amy's head. His Queen would sweep him away from all of the madness.

All of the restaurant patrons stood gaping as they stared outside. One was overheard mentioning how he looked like the "Mad Hatter." Amy asked the waiter where the exit to the exterior was located.

"But you can't go out there miss. That's off limits to the public."

"Do they look like they care?" She spit back at the waiter as she pointed out the window.

After a sigh, the waiter obliged her.

"Up the stairs and to the right, but I didn't tell you that."

Amy nodded and ran as fast as her feet would carry her. She went up the stairs, saw the marked door and went through it. Kurt had broken the lock to allow the access.

"No goddamn alarm on the door?" Amy sneered.

After entering the first door, she saw the second one immediately and opened it. The scent of the city

A Killer for the Queen

breathed on her without mercy. She saw the traffic down below. The quiet serene setting she had enjoyed inside was the exact opposite on the towers steel roofing. She looked left, and then right; there were no safety harnesses available. She took a deep breath and exited the door. She walked out, staying very close to the handrail that hugged the towers outside observation level. The level Blake and Kurt were now on appeared to be just above the restaurant on the thin steel circular girder that sat between the observation deck and a series of slats that also separated the observation level from the circular girder itself. It was a fascinating and complicated architectural marvel.

Amy's task was to make her way around the orb until she could draw a bead on the killer and Blake. She had her eight-inch blade attached to her inner calf, so she was armed. She was wearing tear away running pants with a pair of spandex shorts underneath, so she could easily gain access when the time came. It was cold and windy, and Amy was shivering; not necessarily from the chilly wind, but from the fact that her man was inches away from death at the hands of a crazed maniac and she couldn't imagine the horrible anxiety going through his system. She wasn't terribly afraid of heights, but this was a bit more than climbing a ladder to the second deck of her house. She was *free standing* some five hundred feet above a pavement that would have no give if someone fell from this level. It was an emotionless and stark reality that the world wasn't taking names or notes; it was simply swallowing people up in its unbiased vortex of life and death.

Shaun Webb

*

As Kurt led Blake to the cold windy chill of the outer tower, Blake swore he would pass out, roll down the uneven surface and fall to his death five hundred feet below. This wasn't the way he planned to die. He had to keep his wits, though, if he had any realistic dream of escaping this obviously impervious problem. Kurt demanded that Blake walk to the outside of the area closest to the restaurant. It was impossible to stand window level, so the best they could do was stand and gain the attention of the patrons inside. It was workable for the tied off Kurt, but for Blake, it was extremely dangerous. The two managed to get to a point where the patrons could see them and before Kurt knew it, Amy was standing on the other side of the glass. He signaled her to come out and she looked at Kurt with daggers in her eyes. It was the most ominous glare permeated on Kurt since his spree started. He was shaken, although he'd never admit it.

Kurt tipped the brim of his top hat as his thin flowing hair by his ears blew in the wind. Blake, in the meantime, was carefully keeping his balance and trying to incorporate thoughts in his mind that would give him more confidence. It was of no use though, as the strength of the panic entombed him, and rightfully so. In this case, fear was his friend; giving him the tools he needed for survival.

A few moments later, the two saw Amy making her way around the tower. Kurt stood with Blake on a three-foot wide flat metal surface away from, but at the same level, as the observation deck. The metal slats made for wind reduction were about six feet between the surface they stood on and the one Amy had her feet on. Amy was straddling the screen that kept the people from jumping off the tower in what would be a successful suicide attempt. She had about a three inch width of metal to balance on as she circled.

Continuing around, she was watching the two men out of the corner of her eye. Another five feet and she'd be within shouting distance. It was so windy that voices had to be raised from even a few feet away. When Amy finally reached the same area as the two, she turned around to face the problem while keeping her fingers in the screen behind her. She saw Kurt with black eyeliner and that damn top hat. He was pale, gaunt, and his eyes sunken. He was a much different man than the one she remembered in Flint.

"LET HIM GO KURT! I'LL GIVE YOU WHATEVER YOU WANT, JUST LET HIM GO!"

Kurt answered, a smile permeating his madness.

"YOUR HEAD AMY! I WANT YOUR HEAD! NO NEGOTIATIONs AND NO TRICKS!"

Blake, with as much courage as he could muster, chimed in with a cracking voice.

"NO AMY! DO NOT DO IT! PROTECT THE BABY!"

Kurt found this nugget to be most interesting. He grabbed Blake by the back of his neck and pulled the bloodied machete closer to his throbbing carotid artery.

"YOU MADE A BABY WITH HER?" He looked to Amy. **"I THOUGHT YOU HAD MUCH BETTER TASTE IN MEN DEAR!"**

"FUCK YOU KURT JOSEPH! I KNOW WHO YOU ARE AND WHY YOU'RE HERE! I"LL TRADE MY HEAD FOR BLAKE'S SAFETY!"

Amy hoped beyond hope that her strategy would work. She thought Kurt might take the bait and she could have Blake safe and be in a position with her hidden stiletto ready to spring.

"DEAL!" Kurt exclaimed. "I'LL TRADE THIS PIECE OF SHIT FOR YOU PRETTY LITTLE HEAD! STEP CLOSER AND KEEP YOUR ARMS OUT!"

Amy was scared beyond fear. She had to balance herself carefully on the beam leading across the slats and nearer to Kurt and Blake.

"STOP!" Kurt ordered. "STAY RIGHT THERE! I'M RE-THINKING MY POSITION!"

"YOU CAN'T DO THAT KURT! WE HAD A DEAL!"

"I DON'T TRUST YOU AMY! HOW DO I KNOW YOU AREN'T ARMED? TAKE OFF YOUR SHIRT. *NOW*!"

Amy looked at Kurt as if he was crazy. She asked him if she could roll her sleeves up instead.

"TAKE THE FUCKING THING OFF!" He said with a grizzle in his throat.

Kurt was angered and cut Blake across his cheek with the machete. Blake reached up and saw the blood on his hand. It made him queasy. Amy quickly stripped her shirt off and let it fly in the wind. She was wearing a sports bra underneath, so she wasn't nude.

"WHY'D YOU CUT HIM? YOU DON'T NEED TO HURT HIM!"

Blake was becoming more and more unstable with the blood dripping from his cheek and the sheer weight of the situation. He began to wobble. Kurt grabbed him tighter around the chest, but Blake was turning pale and losing his grip with consciousness. Amy begged again for Kurt to let him go.

"FOR GOD SAKE KURT, HE'S GOING TO PASS OUT!"

"YES HE IS AMY! HERE YOU TAKE CARE OF HIM."

Kurt pushed Blake hard and he fell between the metal walkway and the slats. Blake had enough wherewithal to catch one of the slats. Amy lunged forward to catch Blake and lost her balance; she too falling between the slats. Both Amy and Blake were a foot from each other, hanging on for dear life. Nothing left to stand on except the concrete down below. Blake had hooked his arm at the elbow, while Amy hung on with both hands. She managed to pull her light body upward and grab the slat by her elbows and hands. Her breasts were tightly pressed up against the metal. It was a dire situation for the two. Kurt easily held the upper hand in this confrontation. He walked over and knelt before them.

"WELL, WELL, WELL! IT LOOKS AS IF YOU HAVE A REAL FUCKING PROBLEM HERE! WHAT TO DO, WHAT TO DO! TEA FOR TWO?"

Kurt made his way closer with the confidence that wearing a harness that had a thin steel cable hooked to a guide wire that circled the structure could give someone. Even if Kurt fell, it would only be fifteen feet and he would stop. None of it mattered though. Kurt looked up and saw his beautiful Red Queen standing on the very top of the tower by the air beacon. She was beautiful towering over the pathetic world. Kurt's gaze distracted him from Amy and Blake.

"**Blake! Blake! Can you hear me?**"

Blake opened his eyes and nodded. He was woozy, but coherent enough to know that hanging on was the best idea.

"**Good. I have an eight-inch knife in my pants. It's on my calf. Get it for me quickly.**"

Amy figured him the stronger of the two when it came to this task. He already had one arm free and was inches from her leg. He reached down and separated the Velcro that held the pants together on her leg. The knife was instantly visible. He reached for it. She had it lightly taped to her leg for easy access. Blake ripped the knife from her. The movement and the noise brought Kurt's attention back to them. He walked over and grabbed a handful of Amy's hair. He wrapped it around his hand three times and pulled up. Amy was still gripping the slat, but Kurt had plenty of room to swing his machete and let her body fall. He would have her head securely in hand afterward.

"**GOODBYE AMY! THE RED QUEEN IS WAITING RIGHT UP THERE!**" He pointed up to the top of the tower, but nothing was visible. "**OFF WITH YOUR HEAD!**"

Blake turned toward Kurt quickly and threw the knife he had just gotten from Amy. It hit him in the upper right arm, causing him to drop the machete and clutch in pain. As Blake clung to the beam as best he could, the expected happened. Kurt fired back with a wrist stiletto, hitting Blake in the left side of his throat. Amy screamed for her friend. He was badly injured.

"BLAKE! BLAKE DON"T LET GO! YOU HANG ON MISTER! YOU FUCKING HANG ON!"

Blake reached out with his good hand and touched Amy's shoulder. He whispered the best he could with the limited air and severe injury to his throat.

"I CAN'T HANG ON ANY LONGER! I CAN'T! I-I LOVE YOU AMY." He spoke between raspy words and blood coming from his mouth. "Take good care of our child. We'll see each other... again."

Blake released his grip on the slat and fell toward the earth. Amy didn't look down; she simply screamed.

"NOOOO! NO BLAKE! COME BACK!"

There was a small thud some seconds later and Blake was gone. No more anxiety, no more panic and no more pain. The tears welled up in Amy's now incensed eyes.

Kurt was recovering from his deep bicep wound enough to start reaching for his machete. He too was badly hurt as Blake made a direct hit to a main artery running up his arm. He was bleeding profusely and weakening quickly. Amy's attention was back toward Kurt and she was furious. She reached into her sports bra and pulled out a death star, courtesy of Claude. The first throw hit Kurt in the hand, causing him to drop his machete. She had one more in her bra and flung it; this one connecting with Kurt's forehead. He fell onto his back and struggled to shake the piece of metal loose. As he did this, Amy managed to climb back up on the slat and pull herself onto the metal platform. She collapsed on her back ten feet from where Kurt lay. Both of the warriors were exhausted, but Amy found a deep second wind. Her adrenaline pumped as the anger surged through her body in floods.

*

Amy stood up, fists clenched, as Kurt budged himself into a sitting position with his legs sticking straight out in front of him. As Amy watched, Kurt continued his struggle until he was to his knees. He then looked up to the top of the tower and starting yelling. The mist of blood running down his face was blowing out with every word he spoke.

"OH MY QUEEN! TAKE ME HOME WITH YOU! I SHALL COLLECT HER HEAD NOW! I WILL NOT DISAPPOINT YOU!"

Amy looked up to where Kurt was looking and again saw nothing. When she looked back down, she saw that Kurt was attempting to rise to his feet. She pulled out two more metal death stars, one from each hip. The first one flung straight into the small of Kurt's back. It was a direct hit to the vertebra, knocking out Kurt's function of his legs. The last star was a twisting throw by Amy. It lodged just under Kurt's cerebrum, again a direct vertebral hit. Kurt lost the use of his hands and arms. Amy walked over and picked up the machete. He followed her with his eyes.

"This yours, Kurt?"

A Killer for the Queen

Kurt's body was unresponsive, though his brain and mouth worked.

"You're not going to do anything Amy! You don't have the guts and your job is to seek right! I'm going with my Queen to Wonderland tonight and there's nothing you can do to stop it from happening!"

Amy again looked up to the top of the tower. She stepped closer to Kurt and grabbed him by his now sweaty thin black hair just under the top hat. She pulled back on his head and looked in his eyes.

"You're not going anywhere except Hell Kurt! You have no Queen helping you now! Where is she? Not here! By the way, I'm keeping the hat as a souvenir."

Kurt looked at her with resentment and frustration.

Amy thrust back with the machete and hit Kurt dead center in his throat. His head came off much easier than she anticipated. Kurt had kept his tools sharp. After the beheading, she kicked Kurt's body forward. It lurched slowly off the side of the tower and halted sharply some twenty feet later. The photos he had in his pocket became dislodged and floated slowly to the ground, cascading and separating during their slow flight down. Amy removed the hat and lifted Kurt's head high. She looked up to the top of the tower.

"HEY QUEENIE, WHO'S GOT THE FUCKIN' HEAD? HUH? I SAID WHO'S GOT THE MOTHERFUCKIN' HEAD? ANSWER ME YOU BITCH!"

Amy began her walk back to the door, head in hand, top hat in her waistband and didn't bother holding the cable next to the observation deck to get there. As she reached the door, the police were arriving. She looked at the first two cops who stood bewildered as they spied the head in Amy's hand. She dropped it at their feet.

"Where's a fuckin' cop when you need one?"

*

"And hast thou slain the Jabberwocky? Come to my arms, my beamish one! O frabjous day! Callooh! Callay!" She chortled in her fun."

*

Amy exited the elevator and was approached by the police. She put a hand up and walked past them. They didn't attempt to stop her. The entire base of the tower was surrounded with yellow tape. She looked up and saw the EMS and firefighters trying to pull Kurt's headless body back up onto the platform for collection. She walked past reporters and other bystanders and grabbed a blanket off the ambulance tailgate. After wrapping her torso in the warm comfort, she walked over to a garden that was planted outside the tower grounds and plucked a single rose. Blake lay under a white sheet as Amy approached. She said nothing to the morticians surrounding the scene as she approached and knelt before her fallen hero. Amy pulled the top of the sheet down to have one more look at his face. She thought he looked peaceful despite the ordeal he had just been through with her. She gently caressed his forehead with the back of her hand and gave him a soft kiss on the cheek.

"You're my hero Blake. If it wasn't for you, baby and I would be dead. You gave of yourself when you didn't think you could. I love you and I'll never forget you. This rose is for you; and it's real."

Amy placed the rose on Blake's chest and covered him up. She stood and thanked the men at the scene. When she turned around, she saw Claude. He stood tall and proud. He opened his arms for Amy. She rushed over and he clutched her close, taking her into his body as if she were his very own daughter.

"Although it cost lives Amy, it would have cost many more had he not been stopped. Blake is at peace and will live in eternity with the freedom from the afflictions gifted to him on this earth. You are both heroes in my book."

Amy unleashed with a torrent of tears as Claude held her close. He knew she was very special and somebody he would always covet and appreciate. Amy was his to mold and he had done a superb job. He bred a hero and knew that the work had only just begun. Many adventures and dangers awaited the two as they would embark together on a long and successful career. There was also the issue of the baby inside of Amy. Claude would see to everything and make sure all would be okay and work out. He looked down at Amy and gently pushed on her chin so their eyes could meet.

"I promise you Amy I will take care of you and your child. You are in the best hands and I will never forsake you. I swear."

They walked slowly to Claude's car. He had already explained everything to the police and would take care of all the other details when Amy was ready. He placed her in the passenger seat and went around to the driver side.

They disappeared into the night.

The Hatter was finally dead.

Epilogue

Shaun Webb

Death

Traveling to Toledo with Claude was one of the best decisions Amy had ever made. It gave her a chance to meet Blake's parents and some of his friends who still had a connection with the family.

It was a sad day as Blake was laid to rest in the graveyard next to plots that his mom and dad had picked out five years prior. They expected to be long gone before it was time for their son to join them, but sometimes the world had a way of making decisions that would go unexplained as long as man existed and beyond.

"Why Blake and why now? He's just a young man." Blake's mom said inconsolably. "He was only trying to do well."

The same went for Andrea and Sandy. Too soon; too young. What nobody knew was that they were probably happy to be out of the ill begotten world. No more anxiety, no more drug addiction and no more weakness. At least that was what Amy thought. Claude agreed. He likened it to a release of pent up energy that needed to escape.

"It's a mystery to us exactly what happens when the energy exits the body, but one thing I believe is in the power of the free soul. No more pain, no more suffering and no more being a slave. The world is complex and strange. The world is also soulless. No one should expect anything from it, for if they do, the suffering will be immense."

"What if they aren't happy Claude?" Amy had to ask. "What if the new world or universe they accompany now is even worse?"

"Take a hard and long look around Amy. Think back to just a week ago when a crazed man wanted to chop your head off. **CHOP YOUR HEAD OFF!** Look at the people he did claim; and he's only one man. What of all the other awful people sharing rental here on this earth with us? What will happen when they lose their collective minds and go on a rampage because of insanity, drugs, or whatever else may trigger the evil? I think anywhere is better than here."

*

After the service, Amy and Claude took a trip to Blake's house in Toledo where his parents were conducting the wake. It was there that Amy thought to be a good a time to sit with Blake's parents and break the news of the pregnancy. She would probably never return to Toledo after this visit and didn't want to mention it on the phone.

"I have what I think to be good news for the both of you." Amy explained to Blake's parents. "I'm pregnant with your son's child."

After an initial fifteen second silence, Blake's mom hugged Amy tightly. Dad sat where he was, but a smile adorned his face.

"Our son's memory will live on, and an imprint is being left. I couldn't be prouder of that Amy." He proudly stated.

Amy was pleased with the reaction. She was worried it could bring out the worst in Blake's parents, but instead brought out the light on a sad day. Mrs. Thomas gathered everyone in the room to make the announcement of the impending arrival of a grandbaby. The applause and hugs were all Amy needed to feel that she was, in fact, a part of the family.

Shaun Webb

Life

"You have to push Amy." The doctor begged. "I can't do this alone. You have to help me."

Claude was Amy's partner in the birth of the baby. Amy was a sweating mess as her labor had reached eight hours strong. Amy was a tough young woman, but this was a severe test. The pain that encompassed her pelvic area was electric. The stretching, pulling and cramping felt like it would never end. She panted, breathed, panted and continued breathing. Claude had insisted on a drug free natural birth, and although Amy had agreed, she was seriously second-guessing her decision.

"Give me some fucking morphine, or whatever the hell you have to make this pain stop." Amy insisted. **"This hurts like hell. Oh my God."**

"No drugs Amy." Claude intervened. "This child must be born pure and with no artificial influence."

"Why don't we switch spots Claude? **OWWWW!** Why don't you lay here and shit a watermelon? Let's see how you like it. **OHHH!"**

"Let me help you Amy."

Claude placed his hands on Amy's lower abdomen, very close to where the birth canal would be. He began to chant words to himself that sounded like someone speaking in tongues. It was unintelligible and gibberish to the pained woman. Soon, however, the pain began to lessen. Amy felt a hint of relief as the squeezing of her lower region softened, the stretching of her pelvic bones let up, and her muscles started the journey back to their natural positions. The doctor asked Amy to give another push.

"Okay Amy, one more time. Give it all you've got!"

The baby came out quickly and the wash of exhaustion quickly engulfed her with the shakes and a huge headache.

"It's a girl!" The doctor announced.

Feeling so much better, Amy made an announcement that consisted of one single word; a name. "Nevaeh."

Claude smiled his approval.

"Heaven spelled backward. Nice touch Amy."

Too tired to react, Amy wisped a slight smile.

The nurses, who a few moments earlier had taken the crying baby to a table to clear out the mouth and nose, swaddled the newborn and brought her back to an extremely tired Mother. They placed the girl on her chest.

"Well hello Navaeh. I'm already in love with you."

As quickly as she uttered those words, she fell asleep. Claude rubbed her head with a cool cloth and picked up the newcomer to have a closer look. His gentleness surprised the nurses.

"You shall be a legend Neveah. You are of your mother's strength. I will help lead you through a journey which you will find fascinating."

The baby opened her eyes. One eye was brown and the other blue. Although it was too early to tell, it did appear as if she'd be a very special child. Blake had blue eyes while Amy's were brown. The child took one of each.

"A very special child from a very special couple."

Claude placed the baby back on Amy's chest. Neveah looked back at Claude from her swaddled blanket and smiled.

Outside the room, two frustrated Government officials walked away. They rued that Amy had birthed a female.

Shaun Webb

The Top hat

It sat on Amy's mantel in her home. The warped top hat served as a reminder of how precious life is, and how dangerous some villains can be.

Shaun Webb

Author's Note

In March of 2011, my dad, Rocky, had called me after finishing the first book in my Amy Fraser series, Black Jacks (Volume One), and said four words that I'll never forget;

"You're one sick f**k."

I didn't get offended because I was very proud of the work and yes, I wanted to shock, scare, tantalize and freak out my readers. If I did that, then I figured I'd written the book correctly. Rocky wasn't the only reader who was shaken, upset or spooked by my work. I had to explain numerous times to numerous people that it wasn't real life. It was a story I made up in my mind that I thought would be entertaining for whoever read it. For the record, I do not practice witchcraft, Wicca, or devil worship, and I certainly don't go around town with a machete looking to chop people's heads off and then save the appendage!

I wanted to continue the four book series with the Queen of Hearts playing card as a natural progression from the Jack of Spades that existed in the first book. When my wife, a teacher, came home one day and told me she was doing the Alice in

Wonderland story for the school play, it hit me right between the eyes. At that point, it all made sense.

Later, I was riding with Rocky to a book show in Michigan when I noticed how many tools and shelving units he had in the back of his work van. It started me thinking again; and before I knew it, I had the idea for the second book in the four book Black Jack series. Oh, I had general thoughts on what the work would encompass, but that day gave me the full skeleton for the story. I was excited and I explained the premise to him.

"What if some crazed lunatic built a cabinet in his van and went around taking people's heads in a vengeful fit of rage? He would collect the heads, take a picture of the torso and hang it under the head along with a Queen of Hearts playing card. What if he was being ordered to do it by the Red Queen of Hearts from Alice in Wonderland? What if he fancied himself The Mad Hatter?"

His answer to my premise?

"You're one sick f**k!

I knew then that it would work.

A Killer for the Queen

Made in the USA
Charleston, SC
05 November 2013